COUP d'ÉTAT

Ben Coes is the author of critically acclaimed *Power Down*. He is a former White House speechwriter, and was a fellow at the JFK School of Government at Harvard. He is currently a partner in a private equity company in Boston and lives in Wellesley, Massachusetts.

Also by Ben Coes

Power Down
The Last Refuge

COUP d'ÉTAT

BEN COES

PAN BOOKS

First published in the USA 2011 by St. Martin's Press
175 Fifth Avenue, New York, N.Y. 10010.

This edition published 2012 by Pan Books
an imprint of Pan Macmillan
20 New Wharf Road, London N1 9RR
Associated companies throughout the world
www.panmacmillan.com

ISBN 978-1-4472-0879-2

5 7 9 8 6 4

A CIP catalogue record for this book is available from
the British Library.

Printed and bound by CPI Group (UK) Ltd, Croydon CR0 4YY

For Charlie.
You make me proud every day.

ACKNOWLEDGMENTS

I would like to thank the following people for their invaluable help:

At the Aaron Priest Agency: Aaron Priest, Nicole Kenealy James, Frances Jalet-Miller, Lisa Erbach Vance, Lucy Childs Baker, Arleen Priest, and John Richmond. At ICM, Nick Harris. Thanks to all of you, especially Nicole, for your hard work, patience, and friendship.

Thank you to all the wonderful folks at St. Martin's Press: Sally Richardson, Matthew Shear, George Witte, Matthew Baldacci, John Murphy, Jeanne Marie Hudson, Nancy Trypuc, Anne Marie Tallberg, Judy Sisko, Kathleen Conn, Ann Day, Loren Jaggers, Stephanie Davis, and everyone I haven't mentioned but who work hard every day on my behalf. A special thanks to Keith Kahla, my editor at St. Martin's Press, for brilliant editing and a wonderful sense of humor. Heartfelt appreciation to everyone at Macmillan Audio, including Mary Beth Roche, Laura Wilson, Robert Allen, Brant Janeway, and Stephanie Hargadon. Thanks to Peter Hermann for his terrific narration.

Stephen Coonts, Vince Flynn, and David Morrell, three great American authors whose kindness to me is so very much appreciated. Edward Luttwak, author of the nonfiction book *Coup d'État*, the source for many ideas and the epigraph by Gabriel Naudé.

Mitt and Ann Romney, two people whose humility, kindness, and selflessness inspire me and many, many others, thank you.

Marc Gillinov and the amazing doctors, nurses, and staff of the Cleveland Clinic.

To my best friend, my little sister, Nellie Coes Edwards, sorry for eating the Twinkie. For their support, friendship, and patience, my business partners Carson Biederman and Bob Crowley. Special thanks to David and Mercedes Dullum, Chuck and Lisa Farber, Gary Foster, Melinda Maguire Harnett, Lee Van Alen Manigault, Teddy Marks, Patrick Mastan, Alex and Kelly Mijailovic, Darren Moore, Mike Murphy, Brian Shortsleeve, Ed Stackler, and Jim Windhorst.

Lifetime achievement award to Brian and Linda Bowman, who have done so much for me, the best parents-in-law any guy could ever hope for, especially a gun-toting, honky-tonk, whiskey-drinkin' card shark like me.

To my wonderful children: Esmé, the future first female president of the United States and currently the most brilliant and beautiful princess known to Upland Road; Oscar, the actual gun-toting one, a soccer and hockey genius whose eyelashes already have the girls swooning; Teddy, whose piano playing, killer looks, sense of humor, and bravery amaze me, the one who, if you haven't met him yet, I encourage you to be nice to, because someday we will *all* be working for him; and Charlie, who this book is dedicated to, my handsome, cool, brilliant, all-sport athlete and inventor, whose kind heart and gentle soul provide nothing but warmth to everyone around him. Thank you all for your love and support, it's what I live for and it's why I write.

To my wife, Shannon, my wonderful Irish beauty, who keeps me humble (or tries to, anyway), while at the same time making me feel like a king, thank you, sweetheart.

The thunderbolt falls before the noise of it is heard in the skies, prayers are said before the bell is rung for them; he receives the blow that thinks he himself is giving it, he suffers who never expected it, and he dies that looked upon himself to be the most secure; all is done in the night and obscurity, amongst storms and confusion.

—GABRIEL NAUDÉ

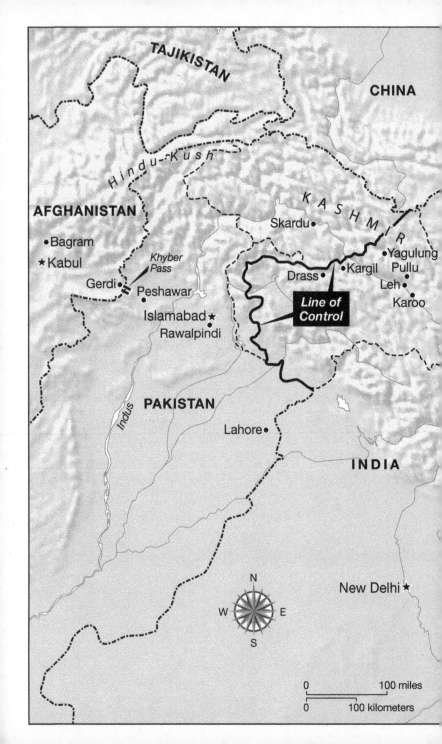

COUP
d'ÉTAT

Prologue

ONE YEAR AGO

With every plane descending from the sky at Karachi's Jinnah International Airport, the enormous crowd gathered behind the high barbed-wire fence at the airport's perimeter became fanatical, screaming and shouting at the top of their lungs.

CNN estimated the crowd to be more than 800,000; Al Jazeera, which had several reporters and cameramen on the scene, estimated the crowd to be at least 1.5 million.

They had begun gathering at the airport the night before, after the polls closed. Already, more than a hundred Pakistanis had died from the heat and more than a dozen had been trampled to death.

Each arriving plane led to a frenzied, almost panicked roar from the crowd. It didn't matter where the plane was arriving from; every thobe-clad man and burqa-clad woman gathered in the scorching afternoon sun knew that sooner or later one of the planes would be the one. Every few minutes, as a PIA, Air Arabia, Etihad, Iran Air, or another airline's jet began its descent, the crowd began screaming and waving small makeshift white flags with a black dot in the middle.

In the distant azure, a white jumbo jet appeared.

Inside the chartered Airbus A321, the rows of seats were mostly empty. The first six rows had exactly one person per row, all Pakistani, all male. They were part of a security detail and wore military uniforms. In the overhead compartments, automatic weapons were stored. As the plane descended, each man moved to the window at the end of the row and tried to get a glimpse of the crowd they knew would be waiting.

A few rows behind the security detail, more men were dispersed. They were all campaign staff members. There were a dozen men, mostly in suits, a few in ties. Some of them chatted quietly, while others typed on laptops. Several pored over newspapers.

More than twenty-five rows back, separated by row after row of empty seats, two men sat quietly across the aisle from each other in the last row. Both men were dressed in bishts. The man on the left, Atta El-Khayab, had on a dark blue bisht with white piping. His beard was flecked with gray. His eyes darted about nervously, belied somewhat by the infectious smile on his wrinkled, kindly face. The other man, in the aisle seat of the right-hand row, wore a plain white bisht. On the chest was a black circle the size of a tennis ball; similar to the flags being waved by the waiting Pakistanis on the ground below. This man also had a beard, though his was completely white. He was taller than his companion, his dark skin deeply creased and covered in hideous black moles. His blind eyes were covered by large black-lens glasses. He did not smile. This man was Omar El-Khayab.

"We're going to land soon," said Atta. He reached his hand across the aisle and patted the back of El-Khayab's hand. "I'm told there will be a crowd."

El-Khayab took his right hand and moved it on top of his brother's hand, gently patting it. But he said nothing.

"It's been a long flight, Omar," said Atta.

"Tell me, Atta, will you miss Paris?" asked El-Khayab quietly. El-Khayab reached up and removed his glasses. Beneath, the sight was grotesque. The eyeballs were balls of murky green and rolled around in the sockets like fish eyes. The skin around both sockets was badly

2

scarred despite the more than sixty years since the accident, the fire, that had destroyed Omar El-Khayab's vision forever.

"Yes, I will," said Atta, looking away from his brother's face and trying to smile. "I'll miss the food. But I'm happy to go, Imam."

"I'm glad to hear it."

"Will you miss Paris, Omar?"

"No." He reached his hand up and stroked his white beard. "The French are a vile filth. But I will miss the madrasa. I will miss the boys. I will miss the moment."

"The moment?"

"There is a moment when it happens," said El-Khayab. "When the education of a young boy truly begins."

"What do you mean?"

"There is a moment when a boy accepts jihad for the first time. When Allah turns a young boy's blood into an angry fever. I cannot see it in their eyes, of course, but I've learned to recognize it in their voices. Once it happens, there is nothing that can bring them back. It's unstoppable. That moment, for me, is like nirvana. That is what I will miss the most."

The plane arced left as the rumble of the landing gear being lowered could be heard.

"But instead of a few hundred boys, brother, you now have a nation of more than two hundred million," said Atta. "You have been elected *president* of Pakistan!"

A smile creased El-Khayab's lips. He nodded his head up and down while stroking his beard.

"Yes," said El-Khayab calmly. "Allah works in wondrous ways, does he not?"

I

HARDWICK'S CAFÉ AND BISTRO
JAMISON CENTRE
MACQUARIE, AUSTRALIA

Josiah Glynn walked briskly through the air-conditioned suburban mall, calmly surveying the shops, restaurants, and people. Jamison Centre was a dump. Out-of-the-way, tired, lousy, lower-middle-class shops; half-empty, badly lit restaurants. The only people he saw ambling about the musty-smelling, windowless mall were blue hairs, too old to remember what good food tasted like.

That was the point though. *Out of the way.*

Glynn felt a patch of cold sweat beneath his armpits, but less than he had anticipated. Certainly less than he had envisioned when he got dressed that morning. Despite his precautions, or perhaps because of them, he was nervous. He breathed deeply. He was fifteen minutes late, but that was intentional.

"These fuckers can wait," he whispered to himself as he ambled casually past a shoe store. Glynn knew it was false bravado, but he needed the bravado, the confidence, to get him through the next ten minutes.

The drive to Jamison Centre from the Customs and Border Protection Service had taken three hours. If he'd driven straight there, it should have taken fifteen minutes. But Glynn had taken a slow, circuitous, out-of-the-way route through the far-flung suburbs of Canberra. A random route. The entire drive, he'd kept one eye glued to the rearview mirror, looking for anyone who might be following him. As far as he could tell, no one was.

Glynn's job was to oversee quality assurance for Australia's Customs and Border Protection Service's e-commerce site, where Australian citizens could apply online for passport renewals. Glynn tested the servers and databases, running various checks on the site to get rid of bugs, broken links, algorhythmic anomalies, and other malfunctioning lines of code. Because he spent all of his working hours in the bowels of the Customs' databases and IT infrastructure, Glynn also had access to any and all information about people coming into or out of Australia.

As he strode toward the bench directly in front of Hardwick's Café, he heard the faint ding-dong of his iPhone telling him he had a text message.

P4 not logged out. where are you jg? MM

Glynn's supervisor, Megan McGillicuddy, looking for him. He tapped her a quick text:

Forgot. pls sign off for me. CU in am. sorry!

God, how he despised Megan. If all went according to plan, in approximately ten minutes he would never have to speak to the bloated, cantankerous sow ever again.

He stepped to the empty bench and sat down. He scanned the crowd at Hardwick's. He saw only senior citizens and a single woman with stringy red hair, stuffing a burger into her mouth.

Then, standing in the checkout line of a pharmacy across the way, he noticed someone staring at him. A white-haired man. Or was it blond? They made eye contact. The man paid and exited the small storefront. In his left hand, he carried a large paper shopping bag. He walked casually across the mall and sat down on the bench.

6

"Mr. Glynn," the man said. "I'm Youssef."

Up close, Glynn saw that he had a mop of bottle-dyed blond hair and olive-toned skin.

"You don't look Arab," said Glynn. "Well, I suppose your skin does."

"Shut the *fuck* up. It doesn't matter what I look like. You'll never see me again. Do you have the information?"

"Yes, but can we talk? Why do you need the information?"

Youssef looked at Glynn, incredulous that he would be asking questions. His casual, laid-back manner turned venomous.

"Stop asking questions," he said slowly and menacingly. "To your left, past my shoulder: do you see the two men sitting at the Thai restaurant?"

"Yes."

"The one with the red baseball hat has a silenced handgun aimed at your skull right at this very moment. Can you see it?"

Glynn looked over. He caught the sight of a silencer, aimed at his head.

"So tell me the information," continued Youssef, a threat in his soft voice. "I am more than happy to pay you, Mr. Glynn. I don't care about the money. But if you ask me any more questions, or if you ever speak of this transaction, you will die a quick and bloody death. I can't guarantee that it will be painful but if I could, I'd make it really fucking painful. It's up to you whether you die right here, right fucking now, or live to spend some of that beautiful money sitting in the bag at my fucking feet."

Glynn gasped.

"Sorry," Glynn muttered, his eyes darting about. "I'm very sorry."

"Calm down and relay the information. When you have done so, I will stand up and walk away. I will leave behind this bag. Inside, there is a million gorgeous dollars with Josiah Glynn's name written all over it."

"Dewey Andreas entered Australia February twelfth, almost exactly one year ago," said Glynn.

"Port of entry?" demanded Youssef.

"Melbourne. That's in Victoria, in the south, on the coast."

"I know where the fuck it is, jackhole. Purpose of visit?"

"He listed tourist. But he didn't fill in the return-by date."

"The return-by date?"

"He didn't say when he was leaving Australia," explained Glynn. "And we have no record of him leaving."

"Is that all you have? That's worthless dogshit."

"There's more," Glynn whispered conspiratorially. "After three months, he filed a work permit at the Cairns Customs office."

"Where's Cairns?"

"It's in the northern part of Queensland. Way up on the coast."

"Is that it?"

"There's something else. He was required to list his job on the form. He's working at a station."

" 'Station'?"

"Ranch. He works on a ranch."

"What's the name of the ranch?"

"He didn't write it down. He's not required to."

Glynn felt his heart pounding like a snare drum, the palms of his hands sweating.

Youssef stood up, stared hatefully down at Glynn, and then, as if by magic, his face transformed itself into a warm smile that nearly made Glynn forget about it all.

"Not bad, Mr. Glynn. I feel as if my money has been well spent today. Remember my warning." He nodded at the Thai restaurant. Then he held his index finger up against his temple, pretending it was a gun.

"Yes, of course."

"Good luck to you," said Youssef. He turned and walked away from the bench.

Glynn eyed the green and red paper shopping bag sitting on the linoleum floor next to him. He reached for the bag, opened it up, and stared down at the bricks of cash stacked inside.

"You too."

But Youssef was already gone.

8

2

The stallion kicked up clouds of dust as he galloped along the dry country path. Deravelle's muscles rippled across his broad haunches, the line between shoulder blade and hip straight despite the weight now on his back; a worn leather saddle, on top of that a large man, who leaned forward on the horse's sinewy incline. After more than an hour at a gallop, the rider eased up and pulled back on the horse's reins. Deravelle slowed. The rider let the big horse catch his breath at a slow trot. Soon, the horse's rapid, heavy exhale was the only sound that could be heard across the plain.

The rider paused and looked around. Low hills covered in grass, stub wheat, and cypress. Empty vistas of blue sky. Untouched ranch land in every direction. A barbed-wire fence running north in a rickety line as far as he could see.

The afternoon sun blazed down dry but viciously hot. The man's shirt was off and a day's worth of dirt was layered on top of a rich brown tan. Thick muscles covered the man's chest, torso, back, and arms. On his right bicep, a small tattoo was hard to see beneath the dark tan; a lightning bolt no bigger than a dime, cut in black ink. But what stood out the most was a jagged scar on the man's left shoulder. It ran in a crimson ribbon down the shoulder blade and stuck out like a sore thumb. Most of the other ranch hands suspected it was a knife wound but no one knew for sure.

The terrain was empty and lifeless for as far as the eye could see. A few large, bulbous clouds sat lazily to the west, just seeming to rest off to the side of the light blue sky. It was almost silent, with only the occasional exhale from Deravelle, or a light whistle from time to time as a slow wind brushed across the dirt veneer of the plain.

Sembler was the largest cattle ranch—or "station" as they were referred to in Australia—in Queensland. More than 18,000 head. Out here, however, in the northwest quadrant of the 12,675-acre ranch, the rider couldn't see a single head. On hot days like today, the cattle stayed south, near King River, at the southern edge of Joe Sembler's property.

Dewey glanced down at the last post of the day. It was almost seven o'clock. He sat up in the saddle, lifted his hat, and ran his hand back through his hair. It had grown long now, having not been cut in the year since he'd arrived in Australia. He reached down and took a beer from the saddlebag. Cooler than one might've supposed, the thick leather insulating the bottle from the scorching heat. He guzzled it down without removing the bottle from his lips. He put the empty back in the saddlebag.

When Dewey first arrived at Sembler Station, the temperature would sometimes reach a hundred and ten degrees. Some days he thought he wasn't going to survive the heat. But he did. Then fall and winter came and the weather became idyllic in Cooktown, temperatures in the sixties, cool nights. In winter, green and yellow grass carpeted the land for as far as you could see.

When Dewey's second summer rolled around, he once again feared he wouldn't survive the heat. But now, as he felt the power of the tropical sun on his back, felt the first warmth of the beer, as he appreciated the utter solitude of a place where he didn't have to see another human being for hours on end, he realized he was starting to like the Australian summers.

Dewey reached into the saddlebag, took out a second beer, and took a sip. For the first time in a long time, he let thoughts of the past come into his head. He glanced down at his scar. After more than a year, he was used to it by now. It was part of him. When the other ranchers asked about the scar, Dewey didn't answer. What would they think if he told them the truth? That he got it from a Kevlar-tipped 7.62mm slug from a Kalashnikov, fired by a terrorist sent to Cali to terminate him? How, in a shabby motel bathroom, he'd cut back the skin with a Gerber combat knife, then reached into the wound with his own fingers and pulled the bullet out? How he'd sutured the cut with a needle and thread from a traveling salesman's sewing kit, then turned, Colt .45 caliber handgun cocked to fire, as a terrorist kicked the door in, machine gun in hand?

Who would believe that this quiet American with the long hair and the jagged scar had been, at one time, a soldier? That he'd been First Special Forces Operational Detachment—Delta. That he loved the feeling that came next that day in that Cali motel room, the feeling he got as he fired his .45 and blew the back of the terrorist's skull across the motel room wall.

He remembered the look of fear on the terrorist's face as he kicked the door open only to find Dewey standing in front of him, weapon in hand, aimed at his skull. It was a look of pure terror. It was a look of realization—realization that there would be no way for him to sweep the UZI across the air in time.

Dewey could have gunned him down that very second, but he waited one extra moment to let him experience the awful knowledge that he had lost and was about to die.

Those were the memories that formed like crystals in Dewey's mind, which opened a flood of emotion. These were the memories he ran to Australia to erase. It was hard to believe it had been a whole year. His life was monotony now. Riding the line. Sleeping, eating, drinking, riding the line. But he needed monotony to remove the memory of being hunted.

Slowly, Dewey closed his eyes, let the silence wash over him, the smell of soil and horse, the sounds of nothing. He thought about Maine. Summers in Castine, working on his father's farm. There, it had been his job to walk down row after monotonous row of tomato stalks, a pair of clippers in his hand, cutting off any brown or yellow leafing. So many rows, so many hours of endless walking those summers. Then it had been the thought of the ocean that always got him through. That at the end of the day, he would race his brother Jack from the farm, down Wadsworth Cove Road for a mile and a half, through town to the dock, where they would jump into the cold water and wash off a day's worth of sweat before heading home for supper.

He took a few more sips from the beer, reached forward, and rubbed the soft, wet neck of the black stallion.

"There we go, Deravelle. Almost time."

Deravelle turned his head to the left. Dewey followed the stallion's sight line.

In the distance, across the barbed-wire fence, the land spread out flat. He watched the land as far as he could see, but saw nothing. He tucked the empty beer bottle back in the saddlebag and prepared to head back to the stables. He looked back one last time and in the far-off distance, he saw movement. He waited and watched. A cloud of dust was the first thing he could see for sure, followed, a few minutes later, by the outline of a horse galloping toward him.

Deravelle perked up, lightly kicking the ground, but Dewey calmed him with a strong pat on the shoulder. The horse was running at a full gallop across the plain and, as it came closer, Dewey saw it was a mostly white horse; judging from its slender size a mare, with speckles of black and an empty saddle across her back.

He climbed down and stepped through the barbed-wire fence. He walked toward the rapidly approaching horse. He held his hands up, waving them, so the horse wouldn't run into the barbed-wire fence.

"Whoa there!" Dewey yelled as the horse approached.

She approached directly toward him, stopping just feet in front of him. She was a muscular horse, a jumper with a white face and black spots across her coat. She stepped trustingly toward Dewey. He raised his hands at the horse then took the reins, which were dangling from the horse's neck, securing her.

"Hey, pretty girl. It's all right. Calm down."

He let the horse smell his hand then ran his right hand along the under part of the horse's neck. It was warm and sopping with sweat.

"You're a beauty. Now what are you doing way the hell out here?"

He inspected the saddle. It was slightly worn, with a single, scuffed brass "H" affixed to the front. Beneath the back edge, *HERMÈS—PARIS* was branded into the leather.

Deravelle stood at the fence. Behind him, the sky was turning gray as nightfall approached.

The horse likely belonged to someone at the neighboring station, Chasvur. Perhaps she'd run away or else taken off during a ride, and someone, somewhere was walking around without a horse.

He patted the pretty horse. It wasn't a ranch hand's ride, that was clear. The saddle alone told you that. So did the horse; she was expensive-looking. None of the typical scars, scuff marks, scratches, or wear and tear from working. This was a leisure horse; a woman's horse.

Dewey took a pair of wire cutters from his belt and cut the wire near the post, then wrapped the loose wire around the post. Dewey pulled the mare through the cut in the fence line, over the low wire. Holding the mare's reins, he climbed back on top of Deravelle.

Dewey glanced at his watch: 7:35 P.M. To the east, the sky was turning into a purplish shade of black. Night was coming. If someone had fallen off the mare, or had been left behind on a ride, there wouldn't be enough time to ride back to Sembler and notify Chasvur. Whoever was out there would have to spend the night in the outdoors.

For Dewey, a night out in the middle of the Queensland nowhere wouldn't be a big deal. For someone else, it might. Especially a woman, or, God forbid, a girl. Besides, what if she was hurt? What if the mare had pulled up and the rider had been thrown off the saddle?

Behind him, a low grumble vibrated somewhere in the sky; distant thunder. Turning his head, Dewey realized that what he had thought was the night sky was much more than that. A black shroud of storm clouds intermingled with the coming night.

He smiled, and casually shook his head back and forth.

"This could get interesting." He looked at Deravelle, then the other horse, as if they could understand him. Dewey found his shirt in the saddlebag and pulled it over his head.

He gently kicked Deravelle's side and the horse stepped across the low wire, followed by the mare. Soon, they were trotting toward the west, tracking the path of crushed wild grass left earlier by the mare, illuminated by the last remaining light of the setting sun, trying to find whoever was out there before the black storm clouds opened up around them.

When the first drop of rain fell from the sky onto Dewey's left arm, he smiled the way only a former Delta—or an adventurous farmboy from Castine, Maine—could.

"You two don't mind getting a little wet, do you?"

3

The white Maybach Landaulet sped along the sun-beaten tarmac at Tehran's Khomeini Airport, breezing behind a long line of parked commercial airliners.

In one respect, the sight of the luxury car was incongruous. A gleaming white million-dollar limousine in a place where the only other vehicles were catering trucks, airport operations vehicles, fuel trucks, baggage dollies, military vehicles, and the occasional police car. Yet there it was, moving along untouched, airport security having already received the orders that the limousine was not to be stopped or disturbed during the three days it was in Tehran.

The back compartment of the Maybach was open to the sky. As-wan Fortuna's shoulder-length black and gray hair was tousled by the wind. Despite his seventy-five years of age, Fortuna seemed young. With chiseled features, he looked like an aging movie star, and his expensive clothing and dark Tom Ford sunglasses would be more appropriate in Cannes than Tehran. Seated next to him was a stunning beauty in a sleeveless baby blue sundress. Candela was only twenty-three years old and she looked like a model. Her jet-black hair framed a pair of expensive Prada sunglasses that were wrapped perfectly across her light brown skin.

The limo pulled into a long, private hangar across from the main terminal, separated by a half mile of tarmac, and stopped in front of a shining silver Gulfstream G500. Aswan and Candela climbed out of the Maybach and ascended the Gulfstream's stairs.

Inside, the plane looked like a low-ceilinged suite at the Four Seasons; big white leather captain's chairs, a large plasma screen on the back wall, a pair of long, red leather sofas, custom-built into the contours of the jet. In the back was a small mahogany doorway, behind it a well-appointed kitchen, then a stateroom with its own bathroom, including a shower.

"Hello, ladies and gentlemen."

The words were spoken by a man sitting peacefully on one of the red leather sofas, dressed in a gray suit, mustached, a block of black hair cut like a bowl on his oversized head. He was overweight and his body pushed against the suit's material, which was too small by at least two sizes. Khalid el-Jaqonda did not look like he belonged on the $75 million airplane.

"Aswan," said el-Jaqonda, rising and stepping toward him with his hand outstretched.

"Thank you for coming," said Fortuna, shaking el-Jaqonda's hand.

"Of course," said el-Jaqonda, laughing heartily. "When you say jump, Aswan, I say, 'How high?'"

"I know the summit isn't over," said Fortuna, "but I need to talk to you about something before we return to Broumana."

"Miss Candela," said el-Jaqonda, "I trust you enjoyed your visit?"

Candela smiled. "If I never come back to Tehran, it will be too soon."

"Give us a minute, will you?" Fortuna said to Candela.

"Of course," she said. She opened the dark mahogany door at the back of the private jet, then disappeared.

Fortuna sat down on the leather sofa across from el-Jaqonda.

"Sit down, Khalid. Would you like something to drink?"

"No, thank you."

"When will you return to Islamabad?"

"Tomorrow. President Iqbar is hosting a dinner tonight at Sa'dabad Palace for the entire Pakistani delegation."

"Of the two leaders, I found President El-Khayab to be far sharper and more articulate than President Iqbar," said Fortuna. "You were right to encourage El-Khayab's candidacy."

"He would not be president of Pakistan without your financial support," said el-Jaqonda.

"I hope it was money well spent."

"You *hope*? What do you mean?"

"That is what I want to talk to you about."

"Were you not impressed by the meetings with the two leaders, Aswan? I worked very hard to set these up."

"I found the president of Iran to be an idiot," said Fortuna. "Always joking around. Does he not realize the historic opportunity that lies before us? For the first time, we have Islamists at the helm of two of the largest nations in the Middle East. One has oil, the other nuclear weapons. There should be nothing that stops us now. Yet both of them are doing nothing."

"Nothing?"

"Iqbar is content to crack jokes," said Fortuna. "At dinner last night he told joke after joke, none of them funny."

"I know President Iqbar," said el-Jaqonda. "I assure you he's as serious about spreading Islam as Omar El-Khayab."

"So what?" said Fortuna. "El-Khayab seems happy to do nothing. Since his election there has been nothing but talk. If there's one lesson from the past two decades, it's that Islam is borne on a river of jihad. Violence is a necessary means to the end. Yet not once in the two days of meetings did I hear any discussion of activities intended to destroy Israel and America. What about India, Khalid? Your hated neighbors, the Hindu? Not once did Omar El-Khayab or Mahmoud Iqbar, or any of their ministers, mention the importance of eliminating our enemies. *What was it all for?*"

"Iran and Pakistan pledged funding to send Lashkar-e-Taiba into India."

"Blowing up some buildings in New Delhi?" asked Fortuna

derisively. "Is that all we aspire to? We have two elected presidents of major countries! And yet all we aspire to is blowing up some buildings and maybe some trains in Mumbai? I feel as if I've wasted my money."

"It wasn't a waste, Aswan."

"Why did I spend twenty-five million dollars helping elect Omar El-Khayab if all he's going to do is sit there, living peacefully, not making waves? It's time to attack, Khalid! It's time to use some of the weapons we've earned the right to use!"

"All in good time," said el-Jaqonda. "El-Khayab has only been president for a year. Besides, despite the precautions of the Iranian security people, we have to assume we were being listened to. We have to be careful what we say, even perhaps here." El-Jaqonda glanced around the cabin of the jet.

"Not here," said Fortuna, shaking his head. "State of the art. We can't be heard inside this cabin."

"Yes, of course."

"I'm getting old, Khalid," said Fortuna, reclining on the sofa. "Last week, I turned seventy-five. I've given a son's life to jihad. The Fortuna family has invested literally hundreds of millions of dollars toward the downfall of the United States and the West. Why am I the only one who seems impatient to take this battle to the next level?"

"And what would you have us do?" asked el-Jaqonda.

"*Fight!*" yelled Fortuna, slapping his fist on the arm of the sofa. "Drop one of the hundred-plus nuclear weapons in Pakistan's arsenal on someone—on Israel or India—or at the very least give one to someone who *is* willing to make use of it."

"I'm sorry you're disappointed," said el-Jaqonda. "It takes time. Trust me when I tell you that President El-Khayab is as committed as you are to the destruction of our enemies. Just this morning, Pakistan agreed to sell Tehran five thousand centrifuges."

"Centrifuges, so what. Why not simply give Iran a dozen or two devices?"

"Omar El-Khayab is not a terrorist, and if that's what you thought you were getting, you were mistaken. What he is, Aswan, is an Islamist willing to use violence to spread the word of Allah. That's different than being a terrorist. I believe it's a hundred times more powerful. He has the people of Pakistan behind him. He's not some sort of maniac sending suicide bombers into pizza parlors in Jerusalem. El-Khayab is the real deal. I've heard him preach. I've never seen someone able to stir such emotion in people."

"But is he a fighter?" asked Fortuna.

"El-Khayab believes in the Ummah. That someday the world will be divided between China and Islam, and that Islam will eventually triumph under a caliphate. Give us time. It's a chess game. The opportunity will come."

"You must create the opportunity," said Fortuna. "You and Osama Khan must create the opportunity. Then, you must convince El-Khayab."

El-Jaqonda smiled, then stood up.

"You have given me this opportunity," said el-Jaqonda. "You pressured Khan to make me his deputy and I will not forget it. I will not disappoint you, Aswan. I thought that including you in the summit meetings would make you happy."

Fortuna abandoned his anger, and a smile appeared on his face. He stood up.

"I *am* happy." He reached both of his hands out and took el-Jaqonda's hands into his own. "To be included was an honor, Khalid. I know it would not have happened had it not been for you."

Fortuna hugged el-Jaqonda.

"You're a good friend," said Fortuna.

"Thank you, but it was my pleasure to have you as my guest. Perhaps next time we can do it in a place more to Miss Candela's appetite, yes?"

Fortuna smiled.

"To think that we have gone from secret meetings in basements," said Fortuna, "to summits in presidential palaces is an amazing thing. I'm just . . . impatient, Khalid. That's all. I don't want to be a witness to Islam's victory. I want to be a part of it."

"You're already a part of it. Be patient. The opportunity we've all been waiting for is just around the corner."

4

YAGULUNG
LADAKH DISTRICT
INDIA-CONTROLLED KASHMIR TERRITORY
FOURTEEN MILES FROM THE LINE OF CONTROL

An old man sat quietly on the ground. His brown face was deeply creased by nearly a century of wind and sun. They had left its markings on him, and he almost appeared as part of the land, so still this morning. To his right, a brown dog lay sleeping. The old man's right hand rested atop the skinny dog's back. The pair was seated against a low windowless hut made of mortar and stone, similar to the other small huts that sat sporadically on the grassy incline.

It was just after lunchtime in the small village of Yagulung. Men and women were in the fields below the village, working in the walnut groves or taking care of the two-hundred-head herd of yak. Those women not in the fields were in their mountainside homes at this hour, some with young children, cleaning up after lunch.

The old man's eyes appeared shut, so thin were the dark slits and so craggy the tan wrinkles surrounding the lids, but they weren't. He'd long ago lost his interest in sleep. He looked now, as he always did at this hour, at the deserted dirt road that meandered through the small mountain village. Soon, he knew, she would come.

Yagulung had been carved onto the side of the small mountain in the Ladakh Range called Kyrzoh nearly a thousand years ago. It was not that unusual or exceptional a village, just another collection of families, generations upon generations now, farmers mostly, Buddhists all, who grew walnuts, wheat, and stub corn in pebbly flatland their ancestors had been able to carve in stepped shelves on the side of the mountain, just below a smattering of small huts that sat close by one another in the rocky, windswept recesses above.

If there was something special about Yagulung, it was the village's location. For if its inhabitants were peaceful, farmers lost in time, their location was at the center of one of the most sensitive political territories on earth, a place where two wars had been fought in the past half-century. Yagulung was one of the northernmost villages in a part of Kashmir Territory controlled by India. It sat fourteen miles from the Line of Control that separated India from its bitter enemy Pakistan. The Line of Control, or LOC, as it was commonly referred to by everyone on both sides of the border, was a random line on a map, drawn by a British cartologist in 1947 when Britain decolonized and Pakistan and India were formally separated, the beautiful Jammu and Kashmir region split in two between the countries.

If the Line of Control ran just north of this small village, not a man or woman in Yagulung knew its exact location. The occasional visit by Indian soldiers was usually noted with taciturn indifference by the villagers of Yagulung. After so many years of watching different governments and warlords come through, it was almost as if a people becomes immunized. Learns to not care which color the uniforms are, or which language is spoken by the visitors. They would always be there in the small village; the others would come and go as they please.

At a quarter past two in the afternoon, the old man sat and watched the door to the village's only establishment, a small café and market known as Satrin-ele. As usual around this time, the door opened. Through the door walked a young woman, a village girl who worked at the café. The old man didn't move. He sat still and watched as the young woman opened the wooden door and stepped out into the sunshine. Her long black hair lay halfway down her back, braided neatly in two thick strands. Her face was lighter than most of the villagers. She was the most unusual, beautiful woman he'd ever seen. In all his years, for all of the young, innocent beauty he had seen walk through the village, never had he seen such a stunning individual as this one. As she shut the door behind her, she glanced over at the old man.

"Hello," she said to him, smiling.

He tried to move, but could not. He was so old now, the lifting of his hand was such an effort. Still, if she could see, if she could understand, what her small gesture did to him every day, how it made his old heart tingle. Her kindness so gentle, the power of such a small gesture to a decrepit man in his dying days.

A noise startled the old man. The sound of talking came from the other direction, down the dirt road, to the west. He heard loud words, then laughter. Strangers. He turned his head and looked down the road, down the brown gravel to the west. Two faces appeared. *Soldiers.*

The soldiers were young. On their heads were helmets. He recognized the soft imprint of their Urdu. *Pakistan.* They laughed as they walked up the street. In front of each soldier, aimed up the road, were large rifles. The old man had seen different governments come and go, but there was one thing he did know: the Pakistani soldiers were not supposed to be here.

"Miss," one of the men yelled out as he walked. "Are you closed for the day?"

The young woman, who had just shut the door to the café, looked at the approaching soldiers.

"I'm sorry," she said quietly. Her eyes stayed focused on the ground. "We're shut for the day, officers."

"Just a sandwich," one of the soldiers said. He took a step toward the woman. He towered over her. "One sandwich."

"I'm sorry."

"Do you disobey us, little bitch?"

She stood in silence, a look of fear on her pretty face.

22

The old man recognized the colors of the Pakistani Army, dark green khaki, red piping. He felt his chest tightening. He knew he was powerless to do anything. Yet, he felt the words arise from somewhere in the back of his throat.

"Leave her alone," he said, a faint bark that made the soldiers heads turn. "Closed!"

"Shut up, old man," one of the soldiers laughed. He turned to the woman. "We are hungry. One sandwich from the whore, then we will be gone."

The brown dog awoke at the words from the soldier. He was a thin mutt, curly tail, brindle coat thick from six winters outdoors in the foothills of the Ladakh Range. The dog stood and began barking. He moved toward the soldiers, his small white teeth forming a vicious smile. The dog barked and ran toward the Pakistani soldiers, who were across the street.

The taller soldier turned. He pulled the trigger on his rifle. A thunder crack echoed in the thin air as a bullet tore into the dog's small head, quieting the mutt, killing him instantly. Blood spurted along the ecru wall of the hut. The woman let out a small cry, a gasp really, at the violence. The old man glanced slowly around him, his heart tightening in fear.

Yagulung's dirt road was deserted except for the two soldiers, the girl, and the old man. The young beauty looked at the old man, then at the soldiers, glancing at the nozzle of the Kalashnikov rifle that was aimed at her head.

She nodded in resignation. What she was about to do was against the law, she knew. Yet fear had gripped her bones.

"I'll be back with two meals," she said, her soft voice trembling.

The soldiers did not answer.

She walked to the café. She unlatched the door, then went inside.

The old man watched as the two soldiers looked at each other. One of the men whispered something. Then they both smiled. They moved to follow her inside the doorway to the café.

The old man felt fire in his veins. He lifted his right hand, raising it to the small wooden post next to where he sat. He slowly lifted himself up, feeling pain down his left side, in his feet. Such pain, the debilitation of the arthritis, the visiting doctor had told him so many years ago, that would gradually make it so that he could not walk.

But he did walk, slowly now, step by pained step, the bolts of discomfort tearing up through his legs and back.

He walked down the gravel road, in a southerly direction, toward the walnut groves. He tripped and fell at the turn that went down the stone walkway to the water hole. He stopped his skull from striking the ground with his old hands. Blood appeared on both hands, where the skin scraped off like tissue paper, but he raised himself up. He saw the topping green of the leaves. The rainbow headdress of one of the woman of the village. But she was so far away. Looking down, he saw that his feet now bled from the soles, so long had it been since he had moved more than a few feet in one day.

But he kept moving. He walked more than two hundred feet down the rough, rock-strewn path. At the bend near the first grove of walnuts, he saw a young teenage boy. He waved at him.

"You're bleeding!" the boy said, running to him. "Your nose is bleeding. So is your mouth. What happened?"

"Get them," the old man whispered, pointing toward the fields with his blood-covered hand.

The boy ran down the line of tall, green stalks. His high-pitched voice, screaming now, wailed across the valley. Soon, the old man could see someone approaching, Aquil-eh, his great-great-nephew, then others behind.

"No!" screamed Aquil-eh as he sprinted up the stalk line. "What is it? Who has done this to you?"

Aquil-eh made it to the old man, then grabbed him, lifting him in his arms and laying him on the ground.

The old man shook his head.

"Leave me," the old man whispered. "Arra. She's in trouble."

By now nearly a dozen farmers stood behind Aquil-eh. A large man with a beard and mustache stepped forward, his eyes bulging. His name was Tok. At the words from the old man, he pushed the others aside and sprinted in a crazed dash up the path toward the village.

The fields emptied as the farmers poured into the pathway. One of the men rang a small iron bell at the beginning of the steppe. At this hour, that would bring the others, the yak herders as well, knowing that the bell meant that something was wrong.

Tok ran up the crooked gravel path, his arms flailing at his sides. Soon he rounded the steppe shift and was on the village road. The others, now more than two dozen, followed, running in a frenzy. Dust was thrown up by the tumult of footsteps.

Across from the small café, the men ran past the dead dog, lying now in a pool of its own blood. Tok reached the door to the café, followed by the throng.

Everyone in the small village of Yagulung knew Arra. Many were related to her. Tok, the large man who now grabbed the latch to the wooden door, was her father.

He pulled the door open. To the left, a young Pakistani soldier, helmet on the table in front of him, calmly ate a plate of corn mash. On the ground, the other soldier was on top of Arra, raping her.

Tok reached the marauder, slamming a hard fist down atop his head. He knocked the soldier off of his daughter, knocked him down to the dirt floor, then set upon him. Tok, despite being a peasant farmer, was a brick shithouse of a man, his arms strong from decades of hard labor in the fields. He set on the soldier and began to hit him furiously, pounding away at his head from above.

Arra covered herself, running into the back room.

The other Pakistani soldier barked out at the gathering horde of villagers, but it was no use. Another man, carrying a large rock, stood above the soldier and raised the rock above his head.

"*Stop!*" the other Pakistani soldier yelled again. He fired the Kalashnikov. The rifle cracked. A slug tore through the man's chest as he held the rock, knocking him off his feet and backwards. Blood splattered in a red gob across the wall of the café. The villager careened into a small wooden table near the iron stove, dead instantly, blood everywhere.

But if the shot was intended to still the farmers now crowded into the small café, it did just the opposite. Another peasant, who had also armed himself with a rock, hurled it at the Kalashnikov-wielding soldier. The stone struck him in the head, at the top of his right cheekbone, hard enough to knock him backwards. Two other farmers leapt at the soldier and wrestled him to the ground. They were soon pounding viciously at the soldier.

Within minutes, the faces of the Pakistani soldiers would not have been recognizable by even their own mothers. The villagers unleashed themselves upon the soldiers in a fury, hitting and kicking their corpses long after they were dead.

Eventually, from the back room, the young woman, Arra, appeared. Tears covered her cheeks as she stepped into the ruined room. Blood was everywhere. The villagers swarmed like locusts. Men she'd grown up with, her father, brothers, uncles, friends; they hovered over the soldiers they'd just killed, their hands covered in blood.

"*Stop!*" she implored. She looked at her father, who knelt on the ground over one of the dead soldiers. His fists were coated in blood.

The room fell silent. Finally, from the back of the small café, a voice interrupted the silence.

"Pakistan will wonder where their patrol has disappeared to," an elderly man said. "They will come for their soldiers."

"We must go to Indian Northern Command," another villager said. "Before it's too late."

5

OVAL OFFICE
THE WHITE HOUSE
WASHINGTON, D.C.

The two seven-foot-long chesterfield sofas had been custom-made in England. They were identical leather sofas that faced each other and were each big enough to accommodate three people comfortably. The light tan sofas were manufactured by a company called George Smith and cost $65,000 apiece, an expense covered by a fund set up three administrations ago to pay for renovations and various projects around the White House. President Allaire's wife, Reagan, had selected them herself. She did not live to see the finished product, but as with everything she did, there was understated perfection and beauty to them.

This morning, and every morning at 7:15 A.M., each sofa had three individuals on them, members of the president's national security team, here for the daily briefing of security flash points around the world. The briefing was run by Jessica Tanzer, the national security advisor. Also present were Bill Winter, the director of the FBI; Harry Black, the secretary of defense; John Nova, secretary of Homeland Security; Hector Calibrisi, director of the CIA; Piper Redgrave, director of the National Security Agency; and Jeffrey Elm, director of National Intelligence.

In the opening at the end of the sofas, a pair of light blue Federal wing chairs held two more individuals, Retired Admiral Tim Lindsay, the U.S. secretary of state, and President Rob Allaire, who on this morning seemed temporarily distracted by the snow that fell in thick white flakes outside the glass-paned French doors that led to the Rose Garden, just outside the Oval Office. The president stared at the endless panes of glass as the snow drifted down, his thoughts temporarily leaving the room as he looked into the distance. Everyone knew the president had stopped paying attention. Everyone knew why too. All eight attendees of the briefing understood that when a man loses his wife to cancer, at such a young age, it's going to tear you away, even from a discussion as critical as this.

As usual these past few weeks, it was the youngest member of the president's national security directorate, the only person in the room who had never been married, Jessica Tanzer, who brought the president back around.

"Mr. President," said Jessica. "We're almost done here. I'd like to discuss Canada, Pakistan, and Iran. These are the only open points left."

President Allaire turned from the window. A smile was on his face. Not the kind of smile that a man has when he is happy. Rather, it was the smile of someone who is among friends, when he knows that they know something is wrong, when he knows they know, furthermore, that he needs their help, support, friendship, and they give it to him, in this case by remaining silent as he drifts away from arguably the most important meeting anywhere on earth, taking a moment to think about his dead wife.

"Yes, Jess," said the president, returning. "Canada. Let's get to Canada, eh. What have those crazy bastards done now?"

The room erupted in laughter as the president leaned forward to pick up his coffee cup.

"Keep it brief," said Jessica, looking at John Nova, the secretary of Homeland Security. "We need to spend some time on Islamabad this morning."

"Will do," said Nova. "This is a quick update. As everyone knows, we completed the border protocol last week. Intercountry penetration tests; random, urban-rural, scenario-based. The Canadians failed virtually everything. They managed to flag some altered passports in Montreal, Ottawa, Edmonton, but that was it. Frankly, if Hezbollah and Al-Qaeda didn't hate the cold so much we'd be in serious trouble. Anyway, we're dealing with that."

"How?" asked the president. "We've spent how much money on this? It's unacceptable."

"Last night, just after midnight, we picked up a minivan carrying two Kenyans in Newport, Vermont," continued Nova. "They had clear passports but one of them popped the TSDB. He turned out to be ex-Gitmo. The other's unknown."

"We pushed out a cross-border alert," said Bill Winter, the director of the FBI.

"Is it an operation?" asked the president. "What are we doing about it?"

"We need to do some work, Mr. President," said Winter. "The Canadians reluctantly agreed to raise the border threat to red."

"Why was he at Guantánamo?" asked Lindsay.

"He was on a cell list of one of the tertiaries in the Dahab, Egypt, bombings in '06," said Calibrisi. "Nothing proven, just a phone number. Your predecessor freed him, Mr. President."

"That was nice of him," said President Allaire. "What'd we find in the minivan? Explosives?"

"The car was clean," said Nova.

"Which means what?" asked Lindsay, the secretary of state.

"It could mean anything," said Nova. "It's too early to know."

"Where is he now?" asked Jessica.

"We flew him to Amman," said Calibrisi, the director of the CIA. "We conducted a pharma package aboard the C-130, but he stayed silent. Obviously, we need to find out if there's an imminent threat here."

"Is he talking?" asked President Allaire.

"Not yet," said Calibrisi. "Jordanian intelligence is working the prisoner. I'll report back if they surface anything material."

"Let's go to Pakistan," said Jessica.

Jessica nodded to Calibrisi, the CIA chief, who was seated across from her.

"The summit in Tehran ended three hours ago," said Calibrisi. "This was the first meeting between Pakistan's new president, Omar El-Khayab, and Mahmoud Iqbar, Iran's president."

"What came out of it, other than the usual rhetoric?" asked the president.

"Iqbar and El-Khayab signed a treaty," said Elm. "They're calling it the 'Mutual Cooperation and Permanent Friendship Document.' It's an economic and military alliance between Pakistan and Iran, technology sharing, planned war games, et cetera."

"We expected this, right, Jeff?" asked President Allaire.

"Yes. In fact we'd already seen a draft of the 'treaty,' if you want to call it that, thanks to NSA. But there is a material alteration between that draft and what came out. For the first time, Pakistan has agreed to assist the Iranians in the development of their nuclear program."

"This isn't a surprise," said President Allaire.

"We've worked very hard to prevent this from occurring," said Secretary of State Lindsay. "The significance lies in the public statement. They're flouting the Russians. The Pakistanis and Iranians are asserting themselves. It is a new and emboldened stance. We have no way of knowing where a unified, radicalized Middle East could go, especially with nuclear weapons and the knowledge and infrastructure to supply chain warheads."

"The Iranians now have enough yellowcake to manufacture thirty to forty weapons," said Calibrisi.

"Where's Musharraf when we need him?" remarked the president, shaking his head.

"What are we picking up?" asked Jessica, looking at Piper Redgrave, the NSA chief.

"We picked up one significant thread involving India, a conversation at a restaurant on the third evening of the summit," said Redgrave. "Two high-level Pakistan security officials. We'll need to brief New Delhi as soon as possible. Lashkar-e-Taiba has two large kill cells, one in New Delhi and the other in Mumbai. There was significant discussion among the Pakistanis about targets, infrastructure and people. It's clear they're planning a strike using Lashkar-e-Taiba."

"I'll call Indra Singh after the meeting," said Jessica.

"There's something else," said Calibrisi. "Aswan Fortuna was seen at the conference, inside Tehran. We confirmed that one of his Gulfstreams was at the airport. They parked it in a hangar but one of the Reapers we had overhead snapped a photo of it before they got it under cover."

Jessica leaned forward in her seat. "Obviously, it couldn't have been coincidental."

"Definitely not," said Calibrisi. "Fortuna was apparently involved in several meetings between El-Khayab and Mahmoud Iqbar, the president of Iran. He's close to El-Khayab. As we all know, he helped to organize and fund the radical cleric's run for the Pakistani presidency. He spent at least twenty-five million dollars to get him elected last year. He believes El-Khayab is the Second Coming of Ayatollah Khomeini."

"How old is Aswan Fortuna?" asked President Allaire. "I mean, not to sound too blunt here, but shouldn't he be dying one of these days?"

"He's seventy-five years old," said Calibrisi. "And if we had any luck, he'd be dead already, sir. It would be a crying shame if this guy died from old age."

"How much of his son's fortune is still floating around?" asked Lindsay.

"When we killed Alexander Fortuna, we were able to freeze more than twenty billion dollars that he had scattered about in various accounts," said Jessica. "Switzerland, Abu Dhabi, England, even the U.S. But he had at least ten billion more than that. Most, if not all, is controlled by Aswan now."

"Why would we not have taken the opportunity to, well, to reduce his presence?" asked Lindsay.

"You mean to kill him?" asked Calibrisi. "There's a presidential directive allowing us to target and remove Fortuna as well as his son, Nebuchar. We're allowed to say that, Mr. Secretary."

"You had him pinpointed in Tehran?" asked Lindsay.

"We took the photos by drone," said Calibrisi. "This has been the debate. Kill Aswan Fortuna and what happens next? I would happily order one of my kill teams to take him out or have one of my Reapers turn him into an ink stain. But we had all better be prepared for the consequences."

"We have significant tracking measures in place," said Jessica, looking at Lindsay, then the president. "We know where most of his money is, where it's going. If we kill Aswan Fortuna there is no way of knowing what will happen next. It will be chaos. Look at what bin Laden did with two hundred million. Aswan Fortuna has somewhere between eight billion and twelve billion dollars."

"That's fine, Jess," said the president. "But we can't just sit back and watch him spend it. That's tantamount to not knowing about it."

"Jessica's right, Mr. President," said Calibrisi, looking at Jessica. "If we take out Fortuna right now it will be chaos, especially when you look at Yemen, Iraq, and Afghanistan. He is a cheap fuck, excuse my language. He's sprinkling the insurgents and various jihadist splinters with a few million here, a few million there. If he's gone, we could be talking about fighting against an enemy, in both Iraq and Afghanistan, with as much money in the theater as the U.S. And remember, these nut jobs don't need cotton sheets and flush toilets like we do. They can go a lot farther on a buck. Right now, we're better off with an avaricious Aswan Fortuna alive than with ten billion on the street. His largest investment to date was in El-Khayab's election."

"We now have a radical Islamist as the democratically elected president of the sixth most populous country in the world," said President Allaire. "A country with a nuclear weapons arsenal. A strong ally of China. Next to a country they've vowed to destroy, India, which, by the way, is a U.S. ally and a key piece of our regional strategy to thwart radical jihad. If Fortuna had been killed a year ago, El-Khayab wouldn't be president of Pakistan."

"It would've been hard to kill Aswan Fortuna a year ago, Mr. President," said Calibrisi. "Just to remind everyone, he went dark following his son's death. We would've had to invade Lebanon to find the guy. Even now it wouldn't be a straightforward operation. He moves around the hills above Beirut on a nightly basis. He has a series of tunnels and safe houses spread over a couple hundred square miles. He's guarded by a small battalion of Al-Muqawama. We would have to just saturate those hills with bombs. The toll in civilian casualties would be tremendous."

"But it sounds like we could've killed him in the past twenty-four hours," said John Nova, the secretary of Homeland Security. "Is that right?"

"Yes, John," said Jessica. "But El-Khayab would still be president of Pakistan. Iqbar would still be president of Iran. It wouldn't change a thing."

"The point is," said the president sharply, looking at Jessica, "there was no discussion. No debate. I should have been told we had the guy in the crosshairs. We could've still determined not to take him out."

"So that's how we want to conduct strategy against the terrorists?" asked Jessica, not backing down an inch, looking first at John Nova, then the president. "Seat of the pants? 'Hey, Mr. President, I've got Aswan Fortuna on radar. Should I kill him?' Is that what you want?" Jessica paused, held the floor, looked around the Oval Office. "We have a policy. That policy is established. The policy is: leave Fortuna alive. Listen to him. Watch him. Track him. Avoid the potentially greater danger of his substantial resources being dispersed across the jihad infrastructure. We can change the policy. We can change it right here, right now. But we shouldn't change the policy just because we suddenly have the guy in the crosshairs."

The room was silent. The president, slightly chastened, looked at Jessica sternly. Then, a slight grin came across his face.

"You're right, Jess," said President Allaire. "As usual. We do have a policy. It's the correct policy, for now. But I would like to review it. I want to know where Fortuna's money is. If we can identify the location of enough of it, isolate it, build contingency around what happens if he's gone, does it make sense to reassess the policy and remove him?"

"The timing for a review makes sense," said Jessica.

"For the first time in nearly a year we are tracking him in real time," said Calibrisi. "Thanks to the sighting in Tehran, we now have redundancy between the air and ground. We should be able to keep him under tight surveillance."

The president nodded. "Anything else?" he asked, looking at Jessica.

"Nothing urgent," she answered.

"Okay, that's a wrap," said Allaire. He stood up. "See you at noon."

The daily briefing broke up, and everyone except the president left the Oval Office.

In the hallway outside the Oval Office, Jessica felt a tap on her shoulder. She turned. Hector Calibrisi, the CIA director, looked at her. He nodded, indicating he needed to speak with her. When the rest of the national security directorate passed by, she stepped forward and stood in front of Calibrisi.

"I need to talk," said Calibrisi. "I have some information I think you need to hear. It won't take long."

"Let's go to my office," said Jessica.

Calibrisi followed Jessica down the low-ceiling hallway to her office suite in the West Wing. Jessica's corner office had large windows that looked out onto West Executive Avenue and the Old Executive Office Building. Snow fell in wind-driven gusts against the windows.

"What is it?" Jessica asked as she stepped around her desk and sat down. "Sit down."

Calibrisi remained standing. "It's about Dewey."

Jessica leaned back in her chair. She smiled at Calibrisi. She looked down at her desk. Then her eye drifted to the mint-green-colored wall behind Calibrisi's head. A framed photo hung of her standing next to Dewey as the president hung the Medal of Freedom around his neck. She hadn't seen him or talked to him in more than a year. In the days and weeks following Dewey's killing of Alexander For-

34

tuna, she had tried to convince him to join her at the White House, or the CIA. But he didn't want any of it.

Jessica, about to take a sip from her coffee cup, paused. "Yeah, what about him?" she asked as she took a sip. "He's gone. I don't know where he is."

"We both know he's in Australia, Jess. I'm not a fucking idiot. Someone on Aswan Fortuna's security team in Tehran said more than he should have to an informant we have inside VEVAK. Fortuna has men in Australia. They're looking for Dewey and they're getting closer. I thought you'd want to know. What you do with it is up to you."

Jessica was silent for a moment. "When you say men . . ."

"Kill teams. Highly trained operatives. Al-Muqawama, the paramilitary wing of Hezbollah. They're scouring the earth for Dewey. Fortuna wants revenge for the death of his son, Alexander. We know he's posted a bounty of a hundred million dollars, but that's old news. This is new. I read Echelon scans going back a month. The information from the Iranian informant corroborates an unexplained incident a week ago. Australian Federal Police arrested two Arabs in a car driving outside of Melbourne on the seventeenth. They were weaponed up and they had a bunch of biograph on Dewey; photos, news clips. They literally had four million dollars in cash in the trunk of the car they were driving."

"Where are they now?"

"It was a shit show: one of the men popped a cyanide pill before they could even get the cuffs on. They got some information out of the other one but when they gave him a bathroom break he garroted himself with an electrical wire he tore out of the wall."

"My God," Jessica gasped.

"They don't know where he is yet," said Calibrisi. "They spent some money in Sydney buying what turned out to be false information. They know he's in Australia and they have a lot of money. It's only a matter of time before they find him."

"How many are there?"

"AFP doesn't know. That was one team. There could be others. There probably *are* others. By the way, I didn't let AFP know Dewey was even in-country. If Fortuna's offering suitcases full of cash for information, I didn't want to run the risk of inadvertently helping them."

Calibrisi noted the look of concern on Jessica's face.

"I haven't spoken with him in over a year, Hector," she said.

"Well, maybe it's time you did."

"Yeah, sure. If I called and told Dewey that Fortuna had men looking for him he'd laugh. It would make him happy."

Calibrisi showed no facial expression. Like the gentleman he was, he didn't wait around to try and read her emotions.

"I just wanted you to know, Jess. That's all." Calibrisi turned and moved toward the door. He paused and looked at the photograph on the wall, of Dewey, Jessica, and President Allaire.

"Do you know where he is?" she asked as his hand touched the doorknob.

"He's working on a ranch in Queensland."

"Do you know which one?"

"You do remember what I do for a living, right?" Calibrisi asked, grinning. "You want a phone number?"

"Sure."

"You got it. I'll shoot it over to you."

"Thank you, Hector."

When Calibrisi left, Jessica stood up and walked to the door, shut it, then stood for a moment and leaned against the door. She shut her eyes and stood still. Then she walked back to her desk. She sat down and stared at the phone. She leaned down and opened the middle drawer of her desk. She pulled a small frame from the desk. It was a sterling silver frame. Inside the frame was a photograph of her and Dewey, his arm around her shoulders. They were both smiling. It had been taken outside the Carlyle Hotel in New York City just before he left. Jessica stared at the photograph. She wondered what Dewey looked like now. Was his hair long? Did he have a beard? Was he happy? Did he, well, did he love someone, someone else, that is?

Jessica stared for a moment longer, then shut her eyes. She fought to keep the emotion from taking over her thoughts. Sometimes she wished she had never met Dewey, because at times like this, for no reason, he would enter her thoughts and just not leave them, sometimes for days. How many times had she been set up on dates, the beautiful, single national security advisor; dates with diplomats and corporate heavyweights, congressmen, and even a recently divorced senator. Each date, every chauffeured limousine, every starlit evening as she sat miserably across from one of them at a restaurant, or next to them at the Kennedy Center, every time, all she could think about was him. *Why?* she asked herself. But she knew the answer.

Jessica felt her eyes becoming moist. She bit down on her lip. She wiped her eyes with her hands. She returned the frame to her desk drawer. Shutting her eyes, she steeled herself away from her feelings. She leaned forward and pressed the green button on her phone console.

"Yes, Jessica," the voice of her assistant said over the speakerphone.

"Get me Indra Singh, India's minister of defense. He's at his beach house in Goa. Tell him it's urgent."

6

CHASVUR STATION
COOKTOWN

By midnight, the rains had thoroughly drenched Dewey, Deravelle, and the runaway mare. Dewey had lost all sense of where he was, with the stars hidden behind lightning-crossed clouds.

The rain had begun more than four hours before and, except for one brief ten-minute stretch, had not let up. He'd put on his long wax raincoat, but was, nevertheless, soaked from head to toe. The water poured down off the brim of his cowboy hat in an unremitting deluge. The one saving grace was the warm temperature, which remained in the eighties. A little cooler and he would have had to pull up somewhere beneath a rock outcrop and build a fire.

He had led Deravelle and the mare straight north to the long granite butte during the last light of dusk. As the first torrential rains began to pour down from the sky, Dewey moved around the butte to a wide-open valley to the north. There he'd searched in the square mile west of the canyon for any signs of life by moving in parallel lines, east to west, then back again, using the lightning strikes to illuminate the area in front of him. The rain had erased any vestiges of the mare's tracks into the canyon and the ground was a wet, shapeless mess of wild grass and mud, rivulets of dirt forming into small streams.

The one fact Dewey recalled about Chasvur was that it was north of Sembler. It was a well-known station, an estate really, a gentleman's ranch, beautiful stone with white pillars and a stunning green lawn that swept down to the ocean a few dozen miles above Cooktown. Dewey had seen photographs of it in Cooktown—framed and hanging at different restaurants and bars, showing off it and the other landmarks of Queensland. In the early hours, Dewey had focused his search toward the north. But after a time, he came up against the ineluctable fact that Mother Nature had outgunned him. Without the stars, he didn't know which direction was actually north.

By midnight, he found himself capable of focusing on three things and three things only: calming Deravelle and the mare every time the lightning crossed the sky and sent panic through the horses; searching the two-foot arc visible in front of him; and, in the moments just after a lightning strike, doing a quick scan of the terrain, searching for something, for someone, for anything that might be out there.

In retrospect, perhaps he should have gone back to Sembler Station, called over to Chasvur and let them handle the whole affair. By the time the people at Chasvur realized their horse and rider had gone missing, it would have been too late to do anything. Maybe an earlier call from Dewey would have let them get a decent-sized search party out before all visibility was lost. Then again, maybe the fact that Dewey hadn't encountered a search party meant the horse was alone and the rider was safe. That's at least what he hoped for.

The odd thing was, the more overwhelming the odds of finding someone, the more convinced Dewey became that someone was out there.

He thought back to his training, first Ranger school, then the year and a half he spent training to be Delta. Survival, they taught you, was about perseverance, calm, and self-reliance. Outsiders always thought that being Delta had to do with what you were capable of doing with a weapon and a team. It was the opposite: being Delta was about what you did when you had nothing.

If you think you have nothing, then you do, and that's when you're defeated.

Day one at Fort Bragg: Dewey and twenty-nine other young, carefully selected GIs were assembled in a windowless conference room.

"Welcome to Delta," a man in plainclothes he never saw again said. "Put everything you have in your locker and be at the tarmac in five minutes."

An hour flight in the back of a Hercules to south Florida, dropped into the Everglades, separated from the others by miles of gator and snake-filled swamp, armed with a knife and nothing else.

Twelve of the thirty recruits in Dewey's class had to be rescued. One got bit by a cottonmouth snake. Another broke his femur trying to get away from an alligator. One of his classmates drowned. Of the ten who made it through, four more dropped out the day they got back to Fort Bragg.

Dewey spent the week in the crotch of an eucalyptus tree, staring at alligators. During the day, he speared the occasional fish with a harpoon he'd carved out of a branch. By day four, he was so hungry and tired that he would eat sunfish, mullets, and shiners raw. At night, he'd tie his wrist to a branch with one of his shoelaces and try to sleep; the lace acted like an alarm clock, waking him up if he started to fall off the tree branch into the dark, alligator-infested water below.

Then, as now, it wasn't about stratagem. It was about buying time and hunkering down.

A huge lightning strike exploded in the sky, turning the black air into white light. To the left of him, he saw the edge of a giant slab of gray, black, and white rock.

Was it the north side of the butte that he'd passed so many hours ago?

He pushed Deravelle forward as blackness returned.

The lightning exploded again. He looked at the ground. For a moment, he saw the same empty plot of land, the lifeless plain of mud dotted with small green shrubs as far as the light allowed him to see. Then, it all changed. As if in a dream, a small, white ghostlike apparition arose in a hillock just a few feet in front of Dewey and the horses. What he saw caused him to jerk backwards in his saddle. There in front of him, less than ten feet away, was a body lying on the muddy ground.

Dewey climbed down from the saddle. He stepped toward the body, then got down on his hands and knees. He crawled, sweeping his hands along the ground as the rain poured down on top of his back. He felt the heel of a boot, then a small, thin leg beneath wet denim, bare skin above the waist, a thin T-shirt, then the back of a head. It was a young girl, long hair, facedown in the mud. Dewey turned her over and brushed the mud from her face. She was cold to the touch.

"Atta girl."

She had to be dead, yet despite that he spoke again.

"It's gonna be okay."

Lightning hit again, a distant strike. In the light he saw the face of the young girl. She had a long, pretty nose. A deep gash cut across her forehead, down to bone.

He felt her neck for a pulse. There was nothing there. He moved his ear to her chest; then he heard it: the faint rhythm of a heartbeat.

He unzipped his coat, reached down, picked up the girl, and pulled her against his chest. For several minutes, Dewey remained on his knees, clutching the cold body against his chest, trying to warm her.

He had to think. She needed help. She needed the kind of help Dewey couldn't provide out here. She needed a hospital and a surgeon. Yet Dewey didn't even know where he was or what direction was home. He knew he needed to go east, to the coast. But if he guessed wrong and went west, any chance of saving her would be lost.

The rain fell in horizontal sheets. He glanced at his watch. One A.M. He was more than five hours away from the first light of day.

He held the child's damaged head against his heart, her wispy torso pressed against his big chest, trying to warm the young girl's body, trying to think.

For the next twenty minutes, Dewey cradled the young girl in his arms, covering her in the folds of the wax coat. She now had a faint pulse and was breathing, but she was in deep shock. Her body felt lifeless and cold.

The rain continued to pour down. With each lightning strike, Dewey searched for a landmark in the distance, but saw nothing to guide him. In every direction, the quick snapshot the lightning allowed was shrub-covered flatland and the tall butte looming over them.

He knew staying there wasn't an option, not if the little girl was going to survive.

"Think, goddamn it, think," he whispered to himself.

The lightning struck again. This time Dewey looked behind him, searching for something, anything, to help guide him. Instead of looking at the valley this time, Dewey found himself studying the tall stone butte. He stared at it as the lightning faded. He realized what he needed to do to save the girl.

Dewey climbed back on top of Deravelle, holding the girl tightly against his chest with his left hand. He pressed his boots into Deravelle's side. They moved forward until, a few minutes later, in the ambient light, Deravelle stopped just inches from the edge of the butte. Looking up, Dewey saw a wall of craggy rock in the dim light.

He climbed down from the stallion. Holding the girl against his chest, he knelt down and searched along the base of the butte for a place to put the girl. He found an overhang, big enough to keep water from falling onto her. He took off his coat, wrapped her inside it, then placed her on the ground. It was raining more heavily than it had all night.

A furious smash of lightning tore across the sky and Dewey's eyes shot up. He surveyed the side of the rock; gray and black, craggy, reaching up into the black sky. Then darkness came again, followed by a low, loud thunderclap a few miles away.

Dewey placed his right hand out in front of him and felt the rock face. He found a short seam in the granite a couple of feet above his head. He put the fingers from both hands into the seam, and with his right boot felt for a hard edge. He found one waist-high, a couple of feet to the right. He stepped onto the edge while he lifted himself up with his fingers. He stood on the small edge, all his weight on his right foot, holding the seam of rock with both hands. He removed his left hand and searched for a higher crack in the rock to grab on to. He found one a foot and a half directly above the first seam. Then he felt with his left boot for another hard edge. He found a small cut-in and put his left toe on it. He took another step up the rock face as water poured down. Standing for a moment on his left foot, holding himself aloft with his left hand, he searched with his right hand. He found a sharp piece of rock jutting out like a dull knife. He tested the rock to make sure it would hold. He lifted himself up the rock face yet again.

He didn't think about the butte. He didn't think about how tall it was, how much farther he had to climb, how long it would take to climb, or how he would get back down. He didn't even think about the little girl, dying a slow death inside his Filson wax coat. He thought only about the next step, the next hard edge, the next foot and a half up the rock face.

Methodically, Dewey ascended the jagged wall of rock. His arms and legs burned. His fingers became raw. But he ignored the pain and moved up the rock face, knowing that one slip and he would fall to his death, knowing that a little girl's life depended on him.

Foot by foot, he moved higher until he could hear, somewhere above him, a different noise; it was the pattern of rain splashing on rock. The lightning struck and he looked down. He was at least a hundred and fifty feet up the cliff face. He had a surprising moment then, not of fear, but rather pride at the accomplishment.

He glimpsed Deravelle and the mare, the small dark bundle, then it went dark. At some point, as he went to reach and lift himself higher, the rock wasn't there. He found only empty air. He'd reached the top of the butte. Dewey pulled himself up. He crawled several feet, then collapsed on the ground. Every inch of his arms and legs burned. He was breathing as fast as if he'd just gone for a ten-mile run. After a minute, he sat up. Other than the flat area within a foot of where he sat, Dewey couldn't see a thing. But he waited. The first minute turned into a second minute, then a third, then a fifth, until eventually he lost track of time, waiting.

"Come on," he whispered into the driving rain.

Finally, the lightning struck. In the brief seconds he had, Dewey searched the horizon in every direction. In the distance, he saw a landmark: the coast. He made out the bulbous outline of treetops and a cluster of lights. That was all. But it was enough. It had to be enough. He memorized the location and charted the direction from the butte in his mind.

The light faded and a thunderclap detonated somewhere to the west. Dewey crawled back toward the edge of the butte, feeling his way with raw fingertips through the darkness.

7

YAGULUNG

By sunset, the villagers of Yagulung had cleared the bodies from the café.

The dead villager, a man named Artun, was carried to his small wood home, where his wife prepared him for burial.

A debate had ensued as to what to do with the corpses of the soldiers. Should they be buried? Cremated? Should they carry the bodies to the far side of the mountain and throw them into a crevice? But calmer heads prevailed. It was decided they would hand the dead soldiers over to the Pakistani Army. But they would not do anything until the Northern Command arrived.

The entire village, about one hundred people in all, was gathered in the dirt road in front of the café. A sense of shock, and fear, reverberated through the denizens of the small village.

As the bodies were being cleaned, Aquil-eh saddled up the village's only horse to ride south toward Pullu.

One of the village elders came to Aquil-eh.

"Where will you go, son?" the old man asked.

"South. Along the Shyok. In Pullu there is an army camp. There will be soldiers."

"Hunder is closer."

"From Hunder I will have to ride again. In Pullu there will be soldiers."

"Perhaps in Hunder they will have a radio and you can call the camp," said another villager.

"Perhaps," said Aquil-eh. "That would be nice."

The old man reached into his pocket.

"Here," he said. He handed Aquil-eh a large leather swatch of material with black markings on it. "This is the chart of the stars. And there," he said, pointing to the leather strip of material, "is Khardung. Pullu is just south of Khardung. You will be traveling at night. You must be careful here, and here. This is where the mountains have the great invisible crevices. You must go around them. I have traveled to Khardung. When I was younger."

"Thank you, Father," said Aquil-eh.

Aquil-eh smiled calmly. But he knew it was a race against time now. He had more than sixty miles to travel. It was a clear night, and he would be able to move beneath the stars. Still, it would be slow going. He felt perspiration start to bead on his forehead but tried not to show his nervousness. The entire village stared at him in silence as he prepared to move out.

He smiled one last time as he glanced at the hushed gathering of villagers. He pressed his boots into the side of the horse and sent the small mare galloping down the gravel path. He had to reach Pullu, and soon. He had to reach the camp before the Pakistanis found their dead.

By 8:00 P.M., twenty-nine miles to the north, at the Pakistani Army Base at Skardu, the topic of the missing patrol had consumed the regional ranking officers of Pakistan's Northern Light Infantry Regiment, or NLI as it was referred to. The soldiers out on patrol had not responded to repeated efforts to reach them on handheld radios, nor had they attempted to report back in. They had left on patrol more than seven hours before, a regular north-south patrol along the Line of Control that separated the Northern Territories of Pakistan from India-controlled Ladakh and Kashmir.

The ranking officer at Skardu was named Mushal. He was a brigadier in the Pakistan Army, forty-seven years old, a Baltee who grew up in Khaplu. He had worked along the Line of Control for more than two decades. Mushal knew that even the smallest incidents along the LOC needed to be dealt with, that tensions were so high between Pakistan and India that small accidents could quickly spiral out of control.

Three separate wars had been fought between Pakistan and India since the British decolonized and left the region in 1947. The most recent full-scale war occurred in 1971, but there had been countless deadly skirmishes along the Line of Control. Kashmir Territory sat at the northern reaches of India and was surrounded by Pakistan, India, and China. All of it should have been Pakistan's by heritage, by culture, and by religion. At least that was the way Pakistan saw it. But the British left the decision of which country to affiliate with to the ruler of what was then called Jammu and Kashmir, and despite the fact that Kashmir was predominantly Muslim, he chose to throw his allegiance to India. Ever since then, tensions had repeatedly flared over the region.

Only now, unlike the wars of 1947, 1965, and 1971, both India and Pakistan possessed nuclear weapons.

At 8:15 P.M., Brigadier Mushal dispatched seven separate patrols from Skardu Base. Each patrol had two soldiers, either in a jeep or on motorcycle, each armed with high-powered Kalashnikov semiautomatic rifles. There were about twenty villages within a fifty-square-mile radius, including Yagulung and a few others that were in India-controlled Kashmir. Mushal told the search patrols to move across the LOC if necessary to search the villages, but to do so quietly, quickly, and to not get caught. He doubted the missing patrol had ventured over the LOC, but he had to know for sure and so he allowed the patrols to go.

In the meantime, one of Mushal's lieutenants contacted NLI general command in Gilgit, to the southwest, notifying NLI's top leadership of the missing soldiers. This action, in turn, established a "Black Flag," so called because it involved the LOC. An alert was sent electronically across the army's chain of command. It was the twenty-third such Black Flag this year. Typically, there were at least a hundred Black Flags annually, most of which amounted to nothing. Still, at 8:44 P.M., the Black Flag went out electronically, reaching the fax machines, desks, cell phones, computer screens, and PDAs of more than eight hundred senior ranking officers in the Pakistani Army.

By 11:00 P.M., Aquil-eh had been riding more than five hours. The night was clear. There was a sharp half-moon, and the stars seemed like candles in the sky above him, so close to the ground.

He paced the small horse along the banks of the Shyok River. The sound of the water rushing by guided him.

He had traveled this far south once before in his life. When he was six or seven, he had traveled to a town called Diskit to see a doctor. But this was the first time he'd seen the peaks and valleys of the Ladakh Range at night, under the stark, beautiful illumination of the stars. He never forgot how amazing Ladakh and Kashmir were, but sometimes, like tonight, its beauty astonished him. The moon cast unusually strong light down from above. It framed the mountains at each side of the plateau. He felt as if he were riding on the moon.

Aquil-eh sometimes wondered what the world was like outside of Kashmir. But tonight he focused solely on his duty to his family and town, and his fear. He felt a constant, gnawing sense of fear as he pushed the horse along at a good pace; a chemical uneasiness at the realization that everything in his world had just changed, forever. He couldn't forget the terrible incidents of the day. He hadn't seen Arra being assaulted, but he had watched Tok destroy the man's skull and had stood less than a foot from Artun when he was shot through the chest.

At a small pond he stopped to let the horse drink. With a match he examined the leather map. He was more than two-thirds of the way to Khardung, if the old man's etchings were drawn to scale and accurate. Twenty more miles. The army camp at Pullu would be a short trip from there. In a mile or two, if the map was correct, he would pass

Hunder, another small village. He remembered the words of the old man; he would stop in Hunder and ask if they had a radio.

The two Pakistani soldiers parked the jeep and walked, one in front of the other, up the steep path to the village. On their helmets, Petzl headlamps cast a bluish glow for twenty feet in front of them. They each carried their Kalashnikovs aimed in front of them as they marched, safeties off. They were more than ten miles across the LOC; they'd done it before—it was part of what they were trained to do—but even so, both soldiers knew they could be shot on sight if they were discovered by the Indian Army.

"There," said one of the soldiers, turning to the man behind him. He nodded at the path. "Yagulung. We're nearly there."

The soldier in back took a radio from his belt and depressed the sidebar.

"This is field unit two," he said. "We're at Yagulung. We'll report back."

The soldiers each pulled a set of ATN night vision goggles from their combat backpacks. They pulled the goggles down over their helmets and flipped the switches on. The goggles gave each soldier a clear view up the gravel road toward the small village. The outlines of the low-flung homes, clinging to the mountainside, were illuminated for the soldiers in apocalyptic orange.

"Let's move," said the first soldier. "I want to be back by sunrise."

Aquil-eh trotted the small horse into the village of Hunder at half past two in the morning. Hunder sat at a higher elevation than Yagulung and he felt the thinner mountain air in his lungs. He had pushed the mare hard, and she was exhausted.

Hunder, a town of nearly one hundred inhabitants, was a collection of wood frame and stone huts arrayed at differing elevations around small steppe plots. In the middle of the village was a small square with a restaurant and a general store. The town was shut down for the night, but remained illuminated by a pair of kerosene lanterns on iron poles in the middle of the small dirt square.

At the first house, Aquil-eh stopped and dismounted. He approached the door and knocked hard on the wooden frame.

"Hello," he said loudly as he knocked. "We need your help." He knocked on the door for more than a minute, saw a light go on through a tiny crack at the eave line of the roof.

The large door opened. A teenager stood inside the door, darkly tanned, with long black hair, shirtless. He rubbed his eyes as he opened the door.

"I've ridden from Yagulung," said Aquil-eh. "The Pakistani Army killed one of our men. The Pakistani Army is coming. They will be there soon."

"Let me get Father," the teenager said.

Within five minutes, a small group had gathered in the middle of the square. More arrived with each passing minute after the teenager's father rang the town bell. Aquil-eh retold the story of the violence at Yagulung to the small group of men. He was interrupted only by a small, stooped elderly woman who brought him a mug of scalding hot chai.

"We have a radio," said one of the men, the owner of the general store. "We can call the Indian base at Pullu. Northern Command is there."

He ran to the store and opened the door. Inside, he found the dust-covered satellite radio in a drawer near the back of the room. The man flipped the switch, then adjusted the dial.

"Pullu," he barked as he depressed the sidebar to the handset. "This is Mar Ah'glon in the village of Hunder. Do you hear me? Pullu, do you hear me?"

After several tries, a scratchy response finally came back.

"Roger, Hunder," the voice said, "this is Northern Command. What is it?"

"Yagulung," the shopkeeper said, speaking loudly into the handset. "Near the Line of Control."

"What about Yagulung?" said the voice.

"The Pakistani Army has been there. They've killed a man, a farmer. There are two dead Pakistani soldiers. The Pakistani Army will be coming for their dead."

In Yagulung, the two Pakistani soldiers walked up the gravel path toward the small town square, mortar and wood shacks were visible through the night vision goggles. They walked side by side now, Kalashnikovs at the ready.

The soldiers walked cautiously into the square. A light was visible; a small kerosene fire that burned in a low steel can near one of the huts. Next to the flames, a man sat, head against the wall. He was barefoot, with white hair, a farmer. He had a small wool blanket across his shoulders. The soldiers moved in silence toward the man, until they stood just above him. One soldier glanced at his watch. It was 3:08 A.M. The soldier kicked a small stone at the man, which struck him in the hand sharply, awakening him abruptly.

The villager looked up, startled. He saw the two Pakistani soldiers, their eyes masked behind bulky black goggles. The nozzles of two Kalashnikovs stared menacingly down at him, less than two feet away from his head.

"Where are our soldiers?" asked the soldier whose rifle was closest to the villager's head. "Our soldiers, old man. Where are they?"

"It was an accident," said the Yagulung farmer. "We've been waiting for you. We're only farmers and herders. We are sorry. It was an accident."

The Pakistani soldiers glanced at each other. The one doing the talking took a step back. "Are you saying they're here?" he demanded.

"Yes," said the farmer, his voice inflecting in nervous fear as he stared at the rifle. "We want to return them to you for a proper burial. They raped a woman and killed a man. We don't want any trouble, Officers."

The other soldier took several steps away from the scene, picked up the handset at his waist and clicked the sidebar three times.

"This is field unit two," he said. "We're in Yagulung. We found the patrol. Both soldiers are apparently dead."

"Copy unit two," a voice returned. "What happened?"

"We're finding out right now. I'll report back. Over."

"Where are the bodies?" asked the soldier holding the rifle.

The villager stood up. He pointed across the dirt square. In front of another building, two simple wooden coffins were lying next to each other on the ground.

Other villagers soon began to appear, awakened by the harsh voices of the Pakistani soldiers. The small square filled with other men, as well as a few women and children. The villager who had been waiting next to the kerosene fire was joined by more than a dozen of his family and friends.

One of the soldiers walked toward the coffins. The other kept the Kalashnikov speared toward the growing throng. He took a step back, rifle aimed at the growing crowd.

The soldier flipped on his headlamp, then lifted the wood from one of the coffins. Reaching inside, he pulled back the cloth muslin material that had been draped over the dead soldier's face.

Beneath, the badly disfigured face of the dead man was unrecognizable. The soldier let out a small gasp. He was momentarily stunned. Unseen by all he closed his eyes and tried to gather himself. He didn't bother opening the second box. Instead, he turned. He looked back at the gathered group of peasants. They stood quietly, waiting. Raising his Kalashnikov, the soldier stepped forward. He aimed the weapon at the group of peasants as he moved slowly across the gravel square.

"Animals!" he barked.

The soldier began firing. A woman screamed as the first slug struck her thigh. The soldier held the trigger back and did not let up, cutting slugs in a horizontal line across the gathered villagers, slaughtering men, women, and children in a tide of bullets and blood.

At the small Indian Army base in North Pullu, the radio dispatcher awakened the base's ranking officer, Lieutenant Benazem Banday,

52

who immediately contacted the larger army base to the south in Leh, part of the Northern Command's XIV Corps. There, Colonel Faris Durvan, the watch commander, dispatched two Mi-25 helicopters, multipurpose choppers designed for flexible missions, including high-altitude combat and reconnaissance.

The choppers lifted off the tarmac in Leh at 4:17 A.M. Each chopper was loaded with four soldiers in addition to two pilots. Each chopper was heavily armed: 9K114 Shturm antitank missiles on the outer and wingtip pylons, PKT machine guns, and Yak-B Gatling guns. The trip to Yagulung would take just over an hour.

After the Mi-25s were airborne, Colonel Durvan radioed Northern Command headquarters in Udhampur, to the south. In turn, Udhampur sent out a "Green Dot" security flash to the Indian Army's leadership notifying them of the incident in Yagulung. It was not an unusual occurrence to have incidents flare-up in Kashmir, including in the remote Ladakh Region, and in other areas along the Line of Control with Pakistan. A majority of the incidents resulted in little activity, not even bloodshed. But often there was bloodshed, which both sides, though neither would admit it, had a strategic interest in containing. Ever since the last war, Pakistan and India had tensely coexisted, nearly going to war in 1999 once again due to tensions in Kashmir. It was in neither country's interest to see a conflict spark in the region.

But if there was one factor that had altered the tense relations more recently, strained the already antagonistic chemistry even further than before, it was Omar El-Khayab, the newly elected president of Pakistan. The radical cleric's election the year before had fundamentally altered the Indian Armed Forces' level of paranoia about their neighbors to the west.

The choppers moved in the dark night across the rooftop of the Ladakh Range, up the thin, winding strip of valley along the Shyok River, toward Yagulung. As the lead Mi-25 rounded the last mountain ridge above Yagulung, the pilot flipped a switch in the dashboard, which in turn caused a red siren light in the rear compartment, where the soldiers were, to pulse on.

The pilot tapped the headset microphone.

"Wing One, this is Wing Five. We're within two minutes of Yagulung."

"Over Wing Five. I'm right behind you."

Soldiers in both choppers adjusted their helmets, checked communication links, and readied their weapons.

The sky at half past five in the morning was gray as dawn approached, the terrain shadowy. Still, even in pitch-black, the next sight to come into view would have been visible to anyone. The pilot in the lead chopper leaned back in his seat, momentarily startled. As they rounded the final ridge just above Yagulung, all eyes were transfixed by the sight of bright flames and billowing smoke raging on the ground below. Violent bursts of orange and red threw themselves into the sky. An out-of-control fireball burned on the landmass where Yagulung once was.

As the chopper approached, it bore down toward the flames and smoke. The lead chopper went to the left, away from the billowing clouds of smoke. The pilot moved the Mi-25 closer. The outline of flaming huts, more than a dozen small square wood and mortar shacks, their skeletons aflame, the fires recently set.

"Northern Command Leh, this is Wing Five," the pilot barked into his mouthpiece as he angled toward the inferno.

"Go Wing Five," came the voice of Colonel Durvan, watch commander at the Indian base in Leh.

"We're at Yagulung. The entire village is on fire. It's completely destroyed."

"Destroyed?" asked Durvan over the radio.

"Everything is gone."

"Gone, Wing Five? Describe the scene."

On the ground, in the midst of the flaming buildings, the bodies of villagers could be seen. On one side of the small square at the center of the village, a stack of bodies was alight in a smoldering hill of flames.

"There are bodies everywhere," said the chopper pilot as he swung down and to the right of the fire to get a better view. "They were piled up, then set on fire. It looks like a massacre."

The heat from the flames caused a warning beacon to ring out within the lead chopper. The young Indian pilot abruptly pulled up. The chopper lifted away from the heat. Then, with an abruptness that caused the young pilot to scream, the steel of the nose cone at the front of the chopper was struck by a violent gust of wind shear created by the intense heat of the inferno below. The powerful air current had the velocity of a hurricane. It blasted against the ten-ton chopper and knocked it sideways. The chopper jerked left and skyward, flipping nearly vertical for a split second. In the blink of an eye the chopper ripped across more than 1,500 feet of vertical air zone. It spun through the air toward the second chopper, whose pilot yanked back on the cyclic and the collective in an effort to avert the collision that was now inevitable.

The first chopper's whipping steel rotor blades caught the tail boom of the second chopper midway down. The blades ripped through the steel of the second chopper like scissors through paper. Both Mi-25s were torn instantly from the air in a helix of flames and metal that shot the two machines toward the ground below. The carnage fell in a swatch of plain just beneath Yagulung, spreading burnt flesh and twisted metal across a quarter mile of walnut groves, which quickly sparked into flames fueled by gasoline from the destroyed attack choppers.

Colonel Durvan, who was monitoring the radar screen over the soldier of a young officer, stared at a suddenly empty radar screen.

"Wing One," the officer barked. "I've lost COMM link. Are you there, Wing One?"

Silence.

"*Wing One, Wing Five*," the young officer repeated, insistent now. "I need some response. Are you there?"

Behind the young dispatcher, Colonel Durvan stood, eyes affixed to the screen in front of the young officer.

"What happened, Lieutenant?" asked Durvan.

"I've lost COMM link, sir," the dispatcher said. "I was just talking to them."

"Get Shelby One in the air," said Durvan. "Now."

Within four minutes of Durvan's order, a MiG-29 attack jet, one of half a dozen positioned at Leh, was airborne. The jet took off as the morning sunlight was cropping at the eastern horizon. The jet lifted off from Leh and was soon scorching through the sky at Mach Two, more than 1,200 miles per hour. Within sixteen minutes, the MiG was in sight line of Yagulung. The first sight he saw was a pirouette of smoke in a wavy black line reaching like a tendril into the sky.

Dawn had come. The early morning light made visibility nearly perfect. The pilot eased off, taking the jet in an arc down toward the base of the mountain, toward the smoke and flames. The pilot was soon flying in a southerly zag between the burning village, and a quarter mile swatch of brush fires. The pilot took several runs over the burning walnut groves. He could see the rotor from one of the choppers, confirming the loss of one of the Indian Mi-25s.

"Leh dispatch, this is Shelby One," said the pilot of the MiG-29. "I'm near Yagulung right now. I'm confirming the downed choppers. You've got debris spread over a quarter mile below the village. It's a bloody mess."

"Roger, Shelby One," said Colonel Durvan. "Return to the base until I have orders."

The pilot turned the attack jet to the north. In the distance, he could see dotted caps of white snow atop the northern peaks of the Ladakh Range running into Baltistan. Somewhere out there along the sharp, beautiful range, he knew, sat the Line of Control.

"Do you want me to do a quick visual check between Yagulung and the LOC?" the pilot asked his commanding officer.

"Affirmative," said Colonel Durvan. "Look for PAF troops. But be careful."

The Indian pilot pushed the nose of the MiG-29 in a course just above the rocky terrain, amping up the jet's powerful Klimov RD-33 turbofan engines. In less than six seconds, the MiG-29 was moving at more than 1,300 miles per hour above the peaks. Seeing nothing, the young pilot continued on past where he knew the Line of Control ran below, infiltrating Pakistani airspace. After a few minutes, the pilot could see the Pakistani military base at Skardu, a line of buildings and vehicles, the frames of several choppers and airplanes strewn about a central nexus of buildings.

"I'm near Skardu," said the pilot. "I don't see much activity."

"Get back here, Shelby One," said Colonel Durvan. "I didn't give you permission to go over the LOC."

As the MiG-29 approached Skardu, the pilot eased up, then began an arc north, into the clouds. A high-pitched beeping from the antimissile radar alarm sounded. He glanced left, where he saw black smoke behind a rapidly approaching surface-to-air missile. The alarm grew louder as the impending SAM honed in.

"*SAM!*" screamed the pilot into his headset. "*They fired at me.*"

"Stay calm and get the hell out of there!" came the deep voice of Colonel Durvan.

The warning beacon went steady, indicating the missile had locked in on the jet. The pilot waited a second longer. Then, with both hands, with all of his strength, he jammed the stick forward and slightly right. The MiG-29 lurched sharply right and down at nearly 1,350 miles per hour. The pilot could not see behind him, and he stayed focused on keeping his flight line steady. The whistling noise of the approaching missile blended in his head with the screaming monotone of the missile alarm, the roar of the jet engine, and the sound of Colonel Durvan demanding to know what was going on. *I'm still alive*, he suddenly realized.

The pilot swerved the stick farther right, the torque nearly causing him to vomit as he continued a nearly impossible evasion technique that sent the jet barreling toward the ground and the green and brown canyons surrounding the winding black lace of the Indus River. The whistling of the missile petered out. The SAM, he knew, had passed him by, its path now randomized as the missile headed northeast, where it would ultimately land several miles into the Ladakh Range.

The antimissile alarm stopped, its silence indicating the failure of the Pakistani SAM to strike the Indian jet.

The pilot let out a holler as he leveled the jet out a few hundred feet above the ground. He pushed the throttle forward and was soon moving again at nearly Mach Two back toward Leh.

"Shelby!" barked the voice of Colonel Durvan. "Shelby, are you there?'

"I evaded it," said the pilot finally into his headset. "I evaded it. I'll be back at base in a few minutes."

"No, you won't," said Colonel Durvan. "You'll take a southwest pass near Kargil and be joined by Shelby Two and Three. This is a live engagement. Pakistan threw the first stone. From Udhampur, I have my orders: you're going back in."

The young pilot's heart leapt as he heard the words. He steered the MiG-29 on a western path toward Kargil. In his headset he heard the words.

"Shelby One, this is Shelby Two. We'll be with you momentarily."

"Roger Shelby Two," said the pilot.

"This is Shelby Three. I have the lead. Follow me in."

In less than a minute, the two Indian pilots behind Shelby One ripped past him and he pressed to catch up. Within a few seconds, the three MiG-29s were flying in a triangle formation to the north, past the right side of Mount Rungo and over Suru Valley. Past the valley, they arced right and climbed toward the clouds.

"You're to empty everything you have on the NLI base at Skardu," ordered Colonel Durvan. "Avoid the city, eliminate the base. Then get back here."

Each MiG-29 was armed with six AA-10 Alamo missiles, which the pilots prepared to fire at Skardu Base.

The jets flew across the Line of Control and into Pakistan airspace, skimming mountain peaks covered in snow. The lead MiG-29 broke toward the ground, followed at each wing by the two other MiGs, now pushing Mach 2.25, moving at nearly 1,400 miles per hour toward the Northern Light Infantry Regiment base at Skardu. The ridge line before Skardu was soon upon them. At their present ferocious speed, they would be at Skardu in less than a minute.

Puffs of smoke arose in the hazy sightline above Skardu as the

Pakistanis launched SAMs in the direction of the approaching attack jets.

"Let 'em rip," barked the lead pilot.

The air surrounding the jets erupted in gray smoke as the pilots launched their Alamo missiles. In a matter of seconds, all eighteen surface-to-ground missiles had been fired at the base. The pilots, upon firing, swerved in three separate, well-rehearsed directions, aiming into the clouds, then dispersing, quickly foiling the efforts of the Pakistani SAMs to remove them from the sky.

At Skardu, a loud siren pierced the early morning air as soldiers ran for cover. In the sky to the south, the sight of the eighteen approaching missiles looked like an approaching flock of geese; a gathering storm, a swarm of fiery, smoke-trailed death. In a matter of seconds the Alamos descended toward their targets. The sound was high-pitched, loud, indescribable; a medley of sonic thrust with the sputtering engines of the turbofan engines.

One by one the missiles struck Skardu Base, its buildings, the ground, the airstrip. Each missile had the power to create a crater a hundred feet wide. The main command center was incinerated as an explosion hit the ground in front of it. A series of missile strikes across the small base destroyed five other buildings, the long airstrip, and the access road connecting the base to the small city of Skardu a mile up the road.

Skardu, Pakistan's northernmost military facility, watch point for the Line of Control, in a brief, violent minute, was gone.

8

As the first light of dawn approached, as if by instinct, Omar El-Khayab sat up. It could not have been the light, for El-Khayab had been blind since the age of three. It was something else that stirred El-Khayab each morning, just as the light was beginning to peek through. Since the time he was a boy, he would awaken with the dawn, the first person in the house to get up.

Now, at the age of sixty-four, on this day, as on every other day, the ritual continued. El-Khayab sat up on top of the simple ash strand mat he brought with him from Paris to Aiwan-e-Sadr when he was elected president of Pakistan a little more than a year ago. He sat up and took a deep breath. Out loud, he said a prayer. Then, a minute later, El-Khayab picked up a small bell and rang it. After a few moments, the door to the small bedroom opened up.

"Good morning, Omar," said the voice in a soft whisper. "How are you today?"

"Stop calling me that," said El-Khayab. "I'm your brother but I'm also the president of Pakistan. I've said this so many times I'm beginning to get angry."

El-Khayab reached up and rubbed the scarred flesh around his eyes. Reaching beside the bed, he took a small wooden walking stick and used it to raise himself up.

"I'm sorry," said Atta, who grabbed El-Khayab's free arm and helped him up. "I seem to forget in the mornings. I see you and it reminds me of—"

"I don't care what it reminds you of," muttered El-Khayab. "Do I ask for much, Atta? I don't think so."

El-Khayab coughed as Atta led him across the small bedroom, a room that had previously served as a walk-in closet for former presidents, but El-Khayab insisted be made into his bedroom, so discomfited was he by the luxury, space, and sheer opulence of Pakistan's presidential residence; opulence he couldn't see but which he'd made Atta describe to him in minute detail upon moving in.

Atta led his brother to the bathroom, helped him clean his face and body, brush his teeth, comb and trim his beard, then get dressed in a clean, simple white bisht, its only decorative flair being a small strip of azure piping along the collar.

"They're waiting for you in the cabinet room," said Atta as they moved from the bathroom to the sitting room, the largest room within the president's personal chambers in the palace. "The entire cabinet is there. General Karreff, other military chiefs. Everyone."

El-Khayab scowled as he entered the sitting room. Though blind, he moved confidently across the large tan carpet. He knew the room well by now. Near the window that looked out on Constitution Avenue, El-Khayab found the simple wooden chair and sat down.

"They can wait a few minutes while the president has a cup of tea."

"Yes, they can wait, Mr. President."

Atta moved across the room and placed a small white cup down on the table in front of El-Khayab. He poured from a steaming teapot into the cup. "Be careful, it's very hot."

"What is the noise?" El-Khayab asked, suddenly aware of a low steady chant coming from outside.

"The crowds," said Atta excitedly. "They began gathering last night after the attack on Skardu. There are more than fifty thousand people in the square right now. The police have shut down part of Constitution Avenue."

"*Fifty thousand?*" asked El-Khayab. "This is good. They are angry. Perhaps we should empty the schools and the offices. The anger of the Pakistani people will guide us in the days and weeks ahead. As Allah foretold to me, my first test would come when a year had passed. Now, a year has passed and I am to be tested by the Hindus."

El-Khayab sipped from his teacup, listening to the low din of the crowds gathered outside. Every few moments, a hint of organized chorus, a chant, would reverberate.

"*Death to India! Death to India! Death to India!*"

A smile creased El-Khayab's mouth. "Listen," he said in a voice barely above a whisper. "What does it remind you of, Atta?"

"I don't know."

"Fridays. At dusk. It's like the reverie."

Atta took a seat on the sofa across from El-Khayab.

"Yes, I see. You're right."

"And I'm the one to answer their prayer."

"But you want peace, brother," whispered Atta, leaning forward. "Do you not remember? It was you they elected because they were tired of the military guiding Pakistan, tired of being led around like dogs by the Americans."

"I was not elected to keep peace," said El-Khayab, urgency in his voice, "nor to make war. I was elected to lead this country. What has happened, what is happening, is not of our choosing. What is of our choosing, of my choosing, is what to do next, how to respond."

El-Khayab sat back, clutching the small cup in his hands.

"But surely a response must entail calming the situation down," said Atta. "It does nobody any good to see destruction and death."

"Unless it's the death of the infidel," said El-Khayab.

He stood and walked to the window that overlooked Constitution Avenue.

"The hardest lesson I had to teach my students at the madrasa was about the need for violent jihad," said El-Khayab, staring at the window, despite his blindness. "That the violence was somehow necessary in order to create a world *without* violence. That Islam, the most beautiful and peaceful of religions, demanded that the blood of the infidel be spilled across the earth in order to wash away the filth of the past. The reason it was hard for me to teach this lesson was because I was hidden away, behind the stones and the ivy, the bricks and the windows and doors, within the comforting walls and sounds of the madrasa. It was the boys who had to go out in the world and sacrifice themselves. They were the ones who had to spill the blood on behalf of Allah."

"Ah, yes."

"Now, it's my turn. I am the one to fight the next battle of Islam. It is my turn to step out from the protective walls and at long last thrust the spear with my own hands." El-Khayab paused and took a sip from his teacup. "It's all happening, just as Allah foretold."

El-Khayab turned back to his brother. He smiled at him.

"You must listen to him," said Atta, "but you must also listen to the men who you have appointed to your cabinet. Your generals and ministers."

"Thank you for your counsel, brother," said El-Khayab. "As usual, you suffer my insults and help to calm me. You always help to give me a compass when I most need it. Today, I woke up not knowing what to do. What does a cleric have to say about war strategy, yes? As always, it is he who provides the answers. It is my time to wage jihad on his behalf."

"But that was not my counsel, Omar—"

"Be quiet now, Atta," said El-Khayab. "Let us listen to the chant for a few more minutes."

Ten minutes later, three floors below, El-Khayab walked quietly into the cabinet room. It was 6:38 A.M. El-Khayab's war cabinet, a collection of ministers, military, and intelligence officials, arose as he entered.

"Good morning, everyone," El-Khayab said as he walked in. "Please sit down. Is General Karreff here?"

63

"I'm here, Mr. President," said Karreff, the chief of army staff of the Pakistan Army, the highest-ranking military officer in the country.

"And what do we hear from the war front, General?" asked El-Khayab. He walked to the end of the large conference table and found his seat at the end of the table.

"The situation is rapidly devolving," said Karreff. "For both sides. The Line of Control from Kargil all the way to the Siachen Glacier is effectively in the hands of India. They've moved more than eighty thousand troops south of Skardu. The Indian Army is advancing by the hour toward Khaplu. They are raining down missiles at our troops to the west. The conflict began less than twenty-four hours ago but already we have nearly ten thousand casualties."

"*Ten thousand dead Pakistani soldiers?*" asked El-Khayab incredulously. A look of rage streaked across his wrinkled brow. "My God."

"It's hell on earth, excuse me, sir," continued Karreff. "Both sides are ramping up on an unprecedented scale. The LOC from the Indus River to the Shyok is running with blood."

"And what are we doing about it, General Karreff?" asked El-Khayab.

"We have designed a two-prong counterattack," said Karreff. "In Skardu and Ladakh, we have several brigades of North Light Infantry. They are supported by heavy air bombardment.

"Second, to the east of the principal battle theater, NLI has thrust into the Mushkoh Valley," said Karreff. "I can report that we have control of land from Mushkoh to Kargil, between the LOC and the India National Highway. Field Marshal Bolin is using a similar attack framework as the 1999 invasion."

"So we are, in effect, swapping territory?" asked El-Khayab.

"You could certainly look at it that way," said Karreff. "The Mushkoh is an easier war for us to wage, sir. Easier to get troops in, less inhospitable terrain, though it is still certainly quite challenging. But unless India can re-induct troops away from Skardu, they will be forced to fight two wars. In Skardu, we will rely primarily on air support—bombing runs from Chaklala."

"What of civilians?" asked Rami Mavilius, El-Khayab's chief of staff.

"Potentially, there will be heavy losses in Skardu and Khaplu if the war continues," said Karreff. "However, I do not believe India will eradicate civilian population simply for the sake of it. In the meantime, by thrusting south, we intend to provide you with effective options, Mr. President. At the very least, we would in theory be able to negotiate the reestablishment of the LOC back to where it was by possessing a highly important corridor to New Delhi. But we also could end up with the areas around Drass and Mushkoh. If the going remains good, Field Marshal Bolin will continue west along the India highway toward Srinagar. Of course the ultimate prize would be Srinagar."

"Where is Bolin now?" asked Mavilius.

"Bolin and the war command are in Drass."

"Why has it begun so violently?" asked Darius Mohan, Pakistan's foreign minister. "Why was there not a more gradual buildup? I don't think either side wanted to reach this point so soon. It's like an argument that immediately goes to fists. There's no control, no sense of proportion."

"You're right, Darius," said Karreff. "The problem is, the Skardu theater is in a uniquely bad geography for war. It is so remote, so difficult to get to and support troop sets. Right now, it is essential that both sides establish secure supply chain right-of-way to the front. Without relatively safe transportation routes in, whatever is at the front will soon be killed off. Ammunition, men, food, fuel; if the lines are at risk you might as well retreat because whatever is in front of the line will soon perish. The Ladakh Range in and around the LOC is treacherous. There are severely restricted means of creating those supply chains. India and Pakistan are now feverishly trying to build, maintain and protect their own supply chains in these early hours while at the same time trying to decimate the approaching enemy. The result is high-volume, high-velocity death count and heavy destruction. We've fired more missiles in the past twenty-four hours than in the entire 1971 conflict."

"How many troops have we sent to the front?" asked El-Khayab.

"More than two hundred thousand Pakistani soldiers are either in the battle theater in and around Skardu or are in the Drass and Mushkoh valleys," said Karreff. "PAF is lighting up the advancing enemy lines from Chaklala. But the Indians have nearly completed a rough artery line up the western shores of the Shyok River, near Yagulung, where the original conflict arose. They're shuttling soldiers in by transport chopper. Our successes thus far have come from aerial bombardment. Field Marshal Bolin believes we have already killed between six thousand and ten thousand Indian soldiers. But already PAF has lost more than a dozen planes. The bottom line is, both sides are being physically pummeled."

"Darius, has there been any outreach from New Delhi?" asked Deputy Minister of Defense Khalid el-Jaqonda. "Russia, Switzerland, the French, America?"

"Nothing from New Delhi," said Mohan. "Not a word. The Swiss have contacted me four times, the Americans half a dozen, as have the others you mention. Everyone is looking for words and apologies. But they are on a hunting expedition. They have nothing from New Delhi, not even a willingness to listen as of yet. There is no guarantee that if we were to reach out in some way the other side would even be willing to open their ears."

"You also have an extremely volatile situation within India," said el-Jaqonda. "President Ghandra is not in a strong political position. The incidents at Yagulung are on the front page of every newspaper in India, including those awful photos of the burning piles of bodies in the village square. It's a front-page story in every newspaper in the free world. Ghandra cannot merely accept apologies or it will be his political future that is alight atop the funeral pyre."

"I received a call from the Chinese ambassador," said Mohan, Pakistan's foreign minister. "It's worth mentioning. I don't know exactly how to interpret this."

"Yes," said El-Khayab. "Let the cat out of the bag, Darius. What did he say?"

"The Chinese are moving troops to Aksai Chin and along the

Karakoram Pass," said Mohan. "The Chinese have shut down the N-35. Ambassador Sun-Jong explains that China is ready and willing to protect its own interests as well as those of its ally by treaty."

"That being Pakistan, of course," said el-Jaqonda.

"Yes, yes," said Mohan. "He reaffirmed China's support for us. He also emphasized the importance of India not moving the Line of Control one inch beyond where it is today, or I suppose, where it was yesterday."

"So why are you concerned?" asked El-Khayab.

"I am concerned any time the largest country in the world moves more than half a million men to my border," said Mohan. "I am doubly concerned when they begin to refer to our military alliance with them."

"I apologize for being so slow today," said El-Khayab. "But why is that? The Chinese are standing behind us. Is that not something we want? Is that not why we signed the pact in the first place?"

"Of course, President El-Khayab," said Mohan. He looked around the large conference room table. "But make no mistake, as I was speaking with Ambassador Sun-Jong, the exact same conversation was taking place between India's foreign minister and the American secretary of state. There are not just two countries involved here, but four. All have a strategic interest in not losing this battle."

"And all," added el-Jaqonda, "have nuclear weapons."

El-Khayab cleared his throat, and the room grew silent for a moment.

"I see," he said.

El-Khayab stood up from his chair, then walked slowly around the outside of the large table. The assembled cabinet members, staff, and military officials all watched as the tall, bisht-clad, blind cleric ambled slowly behind the long conference table. El-Khayab came to the huge window that looked out on the large square in front of the presidential residence.

"Death to India! Death to India! Death to India!"

El-Khayab stood in silence, his dark black glasses aimed at the windows. The sound of the crowd could be heard through the thick bulletproof glass. He allowed the chant to enter the room, inhabit the space, its anger fueling a sense of urgency, energy, and resolve.

"Mr. President," interrupted el-Jaqonda. "The ambassador—"

"Silence," said El-Khayab, moving his finger to his lips. El-Jaqonda stopped talking and looked around. The room was silent again. The angry incantation continued. It seemed to grow louder, as if the crowd somehow became aware that El-Khayab was watching them from the window.

"Death to India! Death to India! Death to India!"

El-Khayab's cabinet members exchanged nervous glances, then all eyes turned back and focused on the blind cleric. Tall, stooped, fragile in appearance, El-Khayab reached his left hand out and pressed it against the window. The angry throng outside the window grew louder, it was unmistakable now. As they'd all witnessed so many times before, the energy, the panic, the fever of the crowd, blood in its pitch, entered the room, the air, and the man. El-Khayab seemed to capture it and become it. El-Khayab's frailty seemed to melt away. His body tremored slightly and the effect was as if an electric current had pulsed from the jihadists outside the palace through the glass and up the blind cleric's outstretched arm.

El-Khayab reached up and pulled the thick black glasses from his eyes then turned from the window to the large table and his war council. El-Khayab's hideously scarred eyes were like pools of inhuman green glass surrounded by pink and red charred flesh. But then those grotesque, dead eyes seemed to come alive with momentary fury, shimmering with untold emotion. He looked around the table at his war cabinet now as if he could see and more than a few at the table shivered under the otherworldly stare of a man who they all knew was as blind as a bat. El-Khayab turned back to the window once again, and they all remembered how such a quiet man had corralled the anger and hatred of so many to become the country's most powerful and feared human being.

After several moments, El-Khayab replaced his glasses and turned from the window. He walked along the back edge of the row of seats occupied by his cabinet. He stopped halfway down the line, and moved to the back of one chair, where General Persom Karreff, the head of the Pakistani Army, sat in stunned silence.

El-Khayab placed his right hand on Karreff's shoulder, patting the olive khaki gently.

"This is not over," said El-Khayab, his voice barely audible above a whisper yet trembling in emotion that mesmerized his gathered ministers. "It is not close to being over. It hasn't even begun." His voice began to rise, like a preacher's, the hissing, fiery words spewing forth like electricity through a fearful, awe-stricken room. "This war *has not started!* We cannot reach out and we cannot back down!"

El-Khayab stepped beside Karreff's chair, to the table, then slammed his fist violently, striking the table with all his might.

"What our soldiers did at Yagulung was shameful, but it was a personal act by criminals. The destruction of Skardu was an act of war sanctioned by a government. The government of our enemy! Whatever is necessary, whatever troops, whatever weapons, move them now to the war theater. One hundred thousand, two hundred thousand, half a million, a million soldiers. Whatever is necessary! The treasury is open. Give Field Marshal Bolin all that he needs. We must fight as if we believe there is no option other than the complete obliteration of India. Anything less will lead to our defeat. We cannot let them," said El-Khayab, pointing to the crowd outside the window, "believe that we are willing to compromise or accept anything less than complete and total victory over the Hindu enemy!"

El-Khayab, the blind former cleric and now leader of the sixth most populous nation on earth, was done talking. He turned toward the door and, feeling his way along the backs of the chairs, marched out of the cabinet room.

9

W hy Australia?" Jessica had asked that morning in the hotel suite when he told her he was leaving.

"I've never been," Dewey had said.

Dewey smiled to himself as the memory came into his head. He had to smile; he couldn't imagine a more ironic memory; the thought of Jessica, naked on soft pima cotton sheets, the sounds and lights of Manhattan thirty-three stories below, contrasted with the present—sharp rock face, relentless rain, darkness—the shitstorm he was now knee-deep in.

He had little to guide him down the rock face. On the way up, his fingers provided the direction, feeling for rock to grasp. On the way down, he had to rely on the hard soles of his boots. He lost count of the times his footing gave way and he was forced to catch himself with his raw fingers.

"Okay I understand," Jessica had said that late afternoon in the luxurious suite at the Carlyle Hotel, as she rested her head on his chest and they shared a glass of champagne. "How long are you going to be away?"

"I don't know."

"What are you going to do?"

"Travel. Maybe work a little."

"So, you're . . . leaving, it sounds like?"

For some reason, clinging to the rock in the pitch-black, in the driving rain, he smiled at the memory. They'd taken the Acela to New York City one rainy Friday morning before he left for Australia. He would never forget that weekend in Manhattan. It seemed so long ago. Walking to the Guggenheim with the patting of raindrops on the big green umbrella. The cab rides, holding hands in the back seat, her body tucked against his muscled frame. The intimate table in the dimly lit Café Carlyle, listening to the French chanteuse whose name he couldn't pronounce, unable to look away from Jessica's eyes for more than a few seconds at a time. Holding hands as they walked through Central Park. And that night, the last night, when they'd eaten out at Sistina's then practically run back to the hotel, making love for hours. It was afterwards, as they lay there on the bed, the sound of the Upper East Side echoing softly up to the thirty-third floor, honking horns, traffic, energy.

"Come back in, Dewey," she'd whispered after that, as she leaned down and kissed his muscled chest. "Please come back in. I could say do it for your country, but what I really mean is do it for me."

"I'm too old," he'd said. "There are better men for the job, Jess."

But what Dewey had really meant was: I want to live to be too old. I want to live and breathe when I'm too old to kill any longer and you are by my side and our children are asleep down the hall and we are happy.

But he didn't say any of it. He closed his eyes and imagined Jessica's auburn hair. He pictured her body, a photograph in his mind of her in a big, thick terry cloth bathrobe, the Carlyle logo emblazoned in navy blue, peeling it off as she joined him in the shower, her sculpted body, big, firm breasts, so shy at first then forgetting her pride as they stood under the big, oversized showerhead and the buckets of warm water.

"You can have any job you want, Dewey. Langley. You can return to Delta if you want. You can work at the White House."

"That's not what I want, Jess."

Then the real question.

"But why do you have to leave?" she had asked, and in that last word he had heard her voice tremble. He had looked down and seen tears on her cheeks.

Dewey hadn't responded. He had watched as Jessica rolled over and shut her eyes. After a long, long pregnant pause, she finally spoke again:

"Aswan Fortuna will never let it go," she had said. "He'll hunt you to the far corners of the earth. You can pretend you can go off and lead a simple life somewhere, but it's a dream. He'll find you."

That was why Australia. A random point on a map, far enough away that Fortuna wouldn't find him. And if, God forbid, he did, at least Jessica wouldn't die too.

Finally, as Dewey searched with his foot below for a crack to step down onto, he felt flat, hard ground. In the dark, Deravelle leaned forward and brushed his snout against Dewey's wet face. Dewey unwrapped the coat and felt for the girl. She was colder than before. He lifted the small frame and pressed his ear against her chest; he heard the faint beating of her heart. He reached for the wax raincoat with his right hand and put the coat on, wrapping her inside. He climbed atop Deravelle. On top of the saddle now, he secured the child within the coat, pressing her across his torso and chest, her small head tucked into the notch above his left shoulder, beneath his chin. Dewey guided Deravelle back from the butte, pulling the mare alongside.

If the oval-shaped butte was a clock face, they were at seven o'clock; Dewey knew that to get to the coast, they had to head straight out from the butte at two. He'd have to guess; there was no way to know exactly the circumference of the large rock structure and therefore where precisely two o'clock was.

"Are *you* feeling lucky?" Dewey whispered to the unconscious girl, gently pressing his bearded face against her cheek. "I am. That's usually a good sign."

He broke the horses left just as a furious smash of lightning hit. In front of him, he saw rolling valley for miles.

"Here we go, Deravelle," Dewey said, kicking his stallion's side, pushing the horse into a healthy trot. Trusting his master, Deravelle began a slow but steady run into the dark unknown.

"What's your name, anyway?" Dewey whispered as they moved across the wet, muddy valley floor. "I bet it's something sweet. In fact, I bet you're sweet. Can you hold on for just a little while longer, sweetheart? We'll be home soon. Just keep that big heart of yours beating, will you? Your mom'll make you your favorite dinner. What do you think? Let me tell you a story about my mom. Okay, here goes. One time my brother Jack and I got in an apple fight. We were throwing apples at each other down in the McIntosh field . . ."

Dewey spoke to her for the entire ride. By his own estimate, he said more words to the little girl that night than he'd said collectively the entire year he'd been in Australia. But the words kept coming, and he let them, stories about Castine, about his brother, stories about Boston College and the football team, the touchdown he scored sophomore year against Notre Dame, Rangers, even some stories about Delta, stories he was, technically, prohibited by law from telling anyone without top secret clearance. But he told them anyway. Eventually, when he ran out of stories, Dewey started singing to the small child.

At some point, Dewey realized that he could see at least a horse length in front of him. He kicked Deravelle, urging him on faster. To the right, in the distance, he saw the faint glow of distant lights. He turned Deravelle toward the lights. As he got closer, Dewey knew that he had found Chasvur.

After a last stand of elm trees, Dewey came into a meadow, fresh cut and wide, which swept down to a large, rambling barn.

Next to the barn, he saw the back of a pretty stone mansion which he recognized from the photos. To the right, near the stables, overhead lights shone down on at least a dozen men, sitting atop horses or else standing in the drive. Umbrellas were scattered about as the rain continued to pour.

Dewey moved across the grass meadow until, halfway across the open field, someone at the barn pointed at him. He heard yelling, and then a lone horse with a rider on top lurched from the gathered party, galloping on a brown mustang toward him.

"Oh, thank God," the man yelled as he came closer to Dewey. "You found her!"

"She's alive. But she's in shock and her forehead is badly gashed. She needs a hospital."

"Mrs. Chasvur called an ambulance," said the rider. "It's waiting."

In the pebble driveway between the Chasvur manor house and the barn, an ambulance, along with several police cars, awaited. Dewey moved into the bright lights. At least twenty people were gathered; EMTs, policemen, ranch hands. He saw Joe Sembler, standing next to one of the police officers.

The crowd moved over and surrounded them. A door on the side of the stone mansion opened and a woman with long blond hair stepped through the door and began a sprint, in bare feet, toward them. As she got closer, Dewey saw that the beautiful woman's face was red with grief. She pushed her way into the middle of the small group.

Dewey untied the coat and opened it up.

He handed the little girl down to the woman, who smiled through her tears. She took her child and embraced her tightly. She shut her eyes and rocked her limp daughter in her arms.

Joe Sembler walked toward Dewey.

"I knew you were looking for her," he said calmly as he came to Deravelle's side. "When you didn't come back, I knew you was out there."

"Who is she?"

"The Chasvur girl. Their only child."

Two EMTs stepped through the throng. One of them placed his hand on the child's neck.

"Ma'am," he said to the woman cradling her. "We need to move her."

The woman held on to the girl. She followed the EMT toward the open rear doors of the ambulance, carrying her daughter. At the ambulance, she turned to Dewey.

"How can I ever thank you?"

"You just did," said Dewey. "I was wondering. What's her name?"

"Nicola."

She climbed into the ambulance. A police officer shut the doors behind her. The ambulance ripped across the gravel and sped away from Chasvur, its red lights disappearing into the black rain.

10

U.S. ARMY WAR COLLEGE
STRATEGIC STUDIES INSTITUTE
CARLISLE BARRACKS
CARLISLE, PENNSYLVANIA

In a small office on the second floor of the historic brick building that housed the Strategic Studies Institute, or SSI, Karl Chelmsford sat staring at the computer screen in front of him. Around him, the office was a cluttered mess; three walls were lined with bookshelves, the two chairs in front of the desk were stacked high with papers and folders. The floor was covered with small stacks of books and files. Behind him, a large window looked out on the neatly manicured green lawns of Carlisle Barracks. Chelmsford, with his bifocaled glasses just a few inches from the computer screen, was mesmerized by what he was reading.

Chelmsford turned and moved to a filing cabinet behind his desk. He rifled through it, looking for a particular brown accordion manila folder. The folder, more than three inches thick, was the product of more than seven years of research. He had a copy on his computer, but Chelmsford always liked to read a hard copy of his work before anyone else saw it. After what he just read on the OCONUS DMS, the top secret communications system within the

Pentagon which he had access to, he knew this file would soon be read by a wider group of people than ever before.

The title of the working paper: "Tipping Point Kashmir: India-Pakistan War Scenarios in a Post-Nuclear Age Framework."

Chelmsford, at the age of thirty-seven, was a tenured professor at Johns Hopkins University. He had two Ph.D.s. The first was from Columbia, where his thesis concerned the creation of a divided Kashmir, its history, and the reasons why overwhelmingly Muslim Kashmir opted in 1947 to ally itself not to Muslim Pakistan, but to the Hindu-dominated India, a chain of events that led inexorably to the near-constant state of trouble and conflict between the two countries for more than half a century. Chelmsford's other Ph.D. was from MIT, where his thesis concerned the three wars between India and Pakistan and the possible implications of the next war between them, a war that would, for the first time, involve two nuclear-armed countries.

It was this thesis which brought him to the attention of General Tim Lindsay, who invited him to join the faculty of the U.S. Army War College. The War College, designed to educate U.S. military leaders, comprised military and CIA officials, as well as academics. SSI's main mission was to predict future combat scenarios and wars, so that policy makers could better understand decisions as they were being made in the heat of battle. Since then, Chelmsford had split his time between teaching at the Johns Hopkins School of International Affairs, and modeling and updating different scenarios for a future war involving India and Pakistan.

When General Lindsay was appointed U.S. secretary of state, Chelmsford had sent him a bottle of Silver Oak and a note. Chelmsford had written:

> *General Lindsay,*
> *My congratulations on your*
> *appointment. I have no doubt*
> *that you will be a truly great*

secretary of state. Please
don't take this the wrong
way, but I sincerely hope
we never have reason to talk
once you are in office,
other than as friends.
Sincerely,
Professor Karl Chelmsford

Now, as Chelmsford pulled the thick folder from the filing cabinet, he knew that war between India and Pakistan was now inevitable. He had read the entire document less than a month ago and knew it almost by heart. Still, he would try and read the entire document this morning, checking for the umpteenth time to make sure the logic of the alternative war scenarios was well-reasoned.

But he didn't have time to even complete the first page of the document. His office phone rang, three fast, high-pitched tones. He assumed it was his main point of contact at the Pentagon, Defense Undersecretary Barry Ziegler. He hit the small red button that flashed on the corner of the phone console.

"Hi, Kitty," said Chelmsford, referring to Ziegler's assistant. "I have a feeling I know why you're calling."

"This isn't Kitty," said a deep, gravelly voice. "It's Harry Black, secretary of defense. There's a chopper waiting at the barracks helipad for you. Get your ass out there. You're going to the White House. And bring that report."

Two floors below ground, under the West Wing of the White House, the Situation Room was teeming.

Nearly every chair at the large conference table was occupied. The walls of the windowless room displayed live shot video feeds, taken by aerial drones, of different battle scenes in Kashmir. On one screen, a rotating sequence of video feeds showing Skardu in Pakistan-controlled Baltistan, now firmly in the hands of Indian troops. On another screen, a similar rotating sequence of videos showing Kargil, a town in Indian-controlled Kashmir now occupied by Pakistani troops. Kargil was now the epicenter of an escalating ground and air war between the two countries.

The room was mostly silent, a few whispers and private one-off conversations the only noise, as everyone in the room stared at the video screens, transfixed by the violence.

The door flew open and the entire room turned to look as the president walked in, accompanied by Secretary of State Lindsay and Jessica Tanzer, the national security advisor.

President Allaire walked past his seat at the end of the conference table, crossing to one of the video screens. On the screen, the side of a small, grass-covered mountain was suddenly lit up by an explosion, temporarily shutting out the drone feed, which quickly recalibrated and adjusted, refocused and brought the shot back, now a scene of flaming terrain. The president walked to another screen, which had a wider vantage point, as if from an airplane. In bright yellow, the Line of Control separating India from Pakistan was illuminated in computer-generated yellow. This line ran in a jutting, zigzag pattern from the left of the large plasma screen to the right, giving the room some perspective as to where the battle was taking place. On another screen, the hundred-mile stretch of India highway through Kargil, at the center of the battle, was displayed. The plasma showed the brown and green land near Kargil. Kargil's main town area, shops, houses, and streets, were interrupted by two large clusters of flames at either end of the screen as the wide shot allowed a clear view of the battle line.

President Allaire turned and walked to his seat at the end of the table.

"Evening, everyone," said the president. "Go ahead, Jessica."

"Let's start with a status," said Jessica, looking at Harry Black, the secretary of defense. "Go, Harry."

"This is as of ten minutes ago," said Black. "Hector might have some incremental perspective from Langley, but here goes. An incident in a small village under India's control in the northern reaches of Kashmir Territory has sparked another conflict between India and Pakistan. Whoever started it, the bottom line is the incident resulted in an attack by India across the Line of Control. India destroyed a Pakistani military base in Baltistan, called Skardu, approximately twenty-six hours ago. Three Indian MiGs completely eliminated the base and Pakistan countered with a series of aerial attacks, destroying three small northern encampments beneath the LOC. India has now done a rapid deployment of more than fifty thousand troops to the area. They're trucking them up from a base to the south called Pullu. They also constructed a down and dirty airstrip along the Shyok River across the Line of Control and they're moving men frantically into the hills south of Skardu. India is now more than twenty miles into Pakistan. They're moving a lot of men and they're moving them quickly. From the hills, they're overwhelming the Pakistanis as they try and reclaim the line. Pakistan is responding by going airborne, dropping clusters of bombs at the Indians more than fifty miles to the south, including population centers. Their pilots are also attempting to destroy the Indian supply line. There are multiple engagements occurring in the skies above the Line of Control in the battle corridor. Of greatest concern, Pakistan has responded with its own incursion. Following a similar attack route as the 1999 invasion, Pakistan has moved aggressively into Kargil, Drass, Mushkoh, here."

Black stood up and moved to the screen and pointed.

"Pakistan now controls the Indian highway for at least fifty miles east of Srinagar, through Kargil. Kargil is now the flash point. Both sides are loading up with ground troops. There are dogfights occurring all over the skies above the LOC. It's getting extremely violent, and lots of people are dying. There don't seem to be any brakes, controls, or a desire on either side to calm things down. It's getting hotter and hotter."

"Why does India need to be in Pakistan in the first place?" asked Jessica. "Have you spoken with anyone in their chain of command?"

"Yes," said Black. "I've spoken twice with General Dartalia, their army chief. I've also attempted to reach General Karreff, Pakistan's top military commander, but he won't talk with us, not yet anyway.

Dartalia says the Indians will not retreat to the Line of Control. They believe Skardu, and, generally speaking, the northern territories, should be India's in any event. My guess is, they didn't expect the Pak counterattack into Kargil to come so soon and so effectively and they're holding on for future terms."

"Any movement in or around the nukes, on either side?" asked Jessica.

"Nothing," said Calibrisi. "No redeployment or movement, which we would pick up by satellite. The one thing I should point out is coming out of Beijing. The Chinese are moving men to the northern border of India-controlled Kashmir, a region called Aksai Chin."

Calibrisi stood and moved to one of the large plasma screens, pointing with his finger.

"They've annexed the only road into the area, a mountain pass called the Karakoram Highway that feeds directly into the battle area. So far they're keeping most of their men inside China. But we're detecting a big troop movement to the east, down toward northern India, here."

Calibrisi pointed at the screen.

"This has got to be on your radar screen, Tim," added Calibrisi, looking at the secretary of state.

"It is," said Lindsay. "I've spoken briefly with Secretary Chao, their foreign minister. He termed the movement of troops 'precautionary.'"

"Precautionary or not, I am frankly more concerned with the Chinese at this point than anyone else," said Calibrisi.

"What's happening on the diplomatic front?" asked the president, looking at Lindsay.

"We have every possible channel in play on both sides of this battle. I've spoken with Pakistan's foreign minister, Darius Mohan, as well as Priya Vilokan in New Delhi. There is anger on both sides, as you might imagine. Neither country wants to discuss a ceasefire. Even the idea of going back to the Line of Control was rejected by both sides. The Russians, the French, the Swiss, everyone is trying to stop this thing, but neither side is listening."

"Why are the Chinese moving men to the border?" asked President Allaire.

"In the past two months, a couple of developments have occurred that are worth reminding everyone," said Lindsay. "First, President El-Khayab spent the better part of three days in Beijing last month, meeting with President Kim. Many people thought El-Khayab might try and extricate Pakistan from the very expensive weapons deal Musharraf signed a decade ago, which obligates Islamabad to spend more than four hundred billion dollars on jets and missiles and other assorted gadgetry, in return for the implicit understanding that China will continue to protect Pakistan from aggression by outsiders."

"Why would they want to get out of it?" asked President Allaire.

"The China desk thought that the sheer cost to Pakistan was not sustainable," said Calibrisi. "The minimum purchase requirements on military hardware and technology are staggering, especially for a country whose main export is underwear."

"Whatever El-Khayab went to Beijing for, he came back with a stronger, tighter relationship with Kim," continued Lindsay. "We assume China restructured the deal. Pakistan put in a fresh order, more than sixteen billion dollars' worth of Chinese fighter jets, the first fifty of which were delivered a week ago."

"Presumably the Chinese are putting men at the Kashmir border should they need to come to Pakistan's rescue," said Jessica.

"Or if they see an opportunity for themselves," added Calibrisi.

"Yes," said Black, the defense chief. "My theater OPS desk is estimating movement of more than half a million soldiers. That's a big number. Now, let's remember that China can play around with big numbers and they can do it quickly. But still, it's a lot of men."

"What are we doing about it?" asked the president.

"I think it makes sense to start thinking about scenarios," said Jessica.

"That's why you're here," said Black, looking across the conference table at Karl Chelmsford. "What's going to happen next, professor?"

"Thank you for having me," Chelmsford said, adjusting his glasses. "I just want to explain something, and that is, my analysis predicates different scenarios for an India-Pakistan war. We then prosecute those scenarios in an implication-based framework, designed to provide you, Mr. President, and your advisors, with thoughts, ideas, possibilities, about what might make sense for America and what might not. But we are not out there in live combat theater, and policy assessments like ours, done using the best data but from the comfort of the War College and the Pentagon, have been shown to be wrong before."

"Yeah, kid, it's all guessing," said Calibrisi. "Cut to the chase."

"There are four main conclusions to the report," said Chelmsford, looking at the president, then around the table. "First, if you look at the unique geography, culture, history, and religion of the Jammu and Kashmir region, there is no convenient way to slice up the land to accomplish a fair, reasonable, or logical break. Britain did a lousy job of splitting the area up but I'm not really sure anyone could have done any better. It should have remained an independent sovereign in 1947. There are large pockets of Muslims at the southern border, near India, and there are major areas of Hindu along the Pakistan border. Many Muslims are India loyalists, but there is a growing Islamist radical presence, especially in Kashmir Valley. The biggest issue, however, is not religious; it's that neither Pakistan nor India would ever give up land voluntarily, now or in the future."

"The geography lesson is probably not necessary, Karl," said Jessica.

"It's relevant," interrupted Chelmsford. "The point is, we shouldn't waste any time trying to come up with a policy-based geographic diplomatic solution.

"Second," said Chelmsford, continuing on. "The three wars fought between India and Pakistan were intensely bloody and were conducted in a prenuclear context. There has not been a war since 1971. Unfortunately, interviews with top decision makers from both countries involved in the most recent war, revealed that both countries would have employed nuclear weapons in earlier conflicts, had they been available. That is a fact. Does that mean today's leaders are going to use nuclear devices? I don't know. Someone should be thinking about it.

"Point three," said Chelmsford. "Potentially the most disturbing. The leadership of Pakistan is a central binary to what will happen. In nearly three-fourths of our war scenarios, the presence of a military leader or a traditional politician in the Pakistani presidency is a precursor to a reasonable outcome with India, an outcome in which nuclear weapons are kept *in silo*, so to speak. However, the exact opposite likelihood scenario occurs when you place an Islamist in the Pakistani presidency. More than eighty percent of the time, nuclear weapons will be introduced to the theater.

"Fourth," continued Chelmsford, "and by far the most important conclusion. In all scenarios where nuclear weapons were introduced to the India-Pakistan theater of war, China and America ended up being dragged into the conflict. Once this happens, the scenarios become increasingly complex and unpredictable. The most daunting implication is that in nearly a third of these war scenarios, the result is nuclear exchange between the two superpowers. As the report demonstrates, this happens for a number of reasons, one of which is a scenario in which the U.S. is stretched thin, such as in another war engagement, as we are now in Iraq and Afghanistan. Because of our obligations to India, and because of our concerns about the possibility of China annexing India, we are then left with only one option: some sort of small-scale nuclear deterrent on China. We envision a number of possible reactions by the Chinese to such a threat. Unfortunately, those reactions are not uniformly predictable or even rational. This creates, as you can imagine, great uncertainty in our ability to predict outcome."

"Is there a conclusion?" asked the president.

"The main point here," said Chelmsford, looking at the president then moving his eyes slowly around the table, "is that unless America is prepared to fight China on the ground with massive amounts of manpower, over an extended period of time, we should give up on India. Or be prepared for the consequences of keeping the Chinese out of India, which by necessity involves nuclear weapons. If we allow China to take India, we should then expect dramatic destabilization of our geopolitical relationships throughout the world, as allies would obviously reconsider their military and political reliance upon the United States."

"If we did engage on a conventional basis in India, what does it look like?" asked Black.

"We worked with the China desk at the CIA and RAND to assess scenarios involving a big ground war between China and the U.S. spearheaded out of northern India," said Chelmsford. "It's not surprising, but it is, well, it's quite sobering. Under a framework in which America effectively abandons both Iraq and Afghanistan to redeploy forces into a conventional conflict with China, the war would last a very long time, in no case less than a decade. The draft would have to be reinstated. There would be casualties in the millions. Outcomes become increasingly difficult to predict. Chaos theory. At some point in a conventional war, nuclear weapons could and probably would still be introduced, taking us back to the original schematic."

The room was silent.

"Thank you, Karl," President Allaire said.

Chelmsford nodded in reply.

"The really scary thing?" said Calibrisi. "The Chinese are aware of all of this. This small goddamn conflict in Kashmir could lead to a very fast-paced series of events, military as well as political. Many of them we will have no way of even being aware of. If, for example, we cede India and China moves to exercise what will be an uncontested supremacy in the region, they will soon look to strengthen their presence within the Arabian Peninsula. That's just one example. There are no doubt others."

"I should point something out," said Chelmsford. "And I'm sorry if this sounds, well, a little dark. But the main policy implication of the fourth section of our report is that, sometimes, mere survival of American citizens should be the primary goal of policy makers."

"In other words," said President Allaire, "it might be better to allow China to take India, Pakistan, Saudi Arabia, and whatever else comes next, because at least we, as a people, survive?"

"The point is, we might not have the luxury of making that choice, Mr. President," said Chelmsford. "My team and I could be wrong. But we would argue that, if events occur along the architectural lines of what we predict, it will not be in America's power any longer to prevent one of the two nightmare scenarios. It *will be* one of the two. Either we will have to fight a nuclear war with China, or we will have to allow China to become the ascendant and sole superpower in the world. This is history in the making. It has the potential to be a big, big event, a redrawing of the map, as we call it. Hopefully, by knowing that this is the case, you around this table can act now to alter, stop, and divert the events that lead to this."

"Are there examples of the nuclear threat working to keep China away from India?" asked President Allaire.

"Yes," said Chelmsford. "But not, by our measure, in a great percentage of scenarios."

"We have to remember," said Calibrisi, "China has a long-term perspective. That perspective is that one day China will control the world."

Chelmsford reached up and wiped perspiration from his forehead, then cleared his throat.

"I must point something out," said Chelmsford. "Of this set of war scenarios, in which China and the U.S. trade tactical nuclear weapons, events do spiral out of control in virtually one hundred percent of the modeled frameworks. This leads invariably, in virtually *every* framework, to full-scale thermonuclear war between China and the United States. Nuclear Armageddon."

Chelmsford stopped speaking and sat back. He glanced at Harry Black, the secretary of defense, who nodded at him. President Allaire sat in silence for a moment, in contemplation. On the video screen just behind his head, a large orange and red burst expanded over the screen.

"Bottom line, we need to get on the phone with Ghandra," said Lindsay, the secretary of state. "We need to make him understand the implications of dragging this thing out."

"Are you suggesting we force the Indians to surrender?" asked Jessica.

"Surrender is a strong word," said Lindsay. "We need to get India to agree to a cease-fire, then pull back to the Line of Control. We involve Russia on the Pakistani side to get some reason built into El-Khayab's head."

"But you yourself are saying nobody is listening," said Black.

"Yes," said Lindsay, "but India needs to know that if this thing escalates, we may or may not be there to defend them from China. If we're not prepared to keep China out of India, using conventional or, God forbid, tactical nukes, we better tell Ghandra and his war cabinet *right now*."

"And then what?" asked Jessica. "Watch as the rest of America's allies run into China's arms? Knowing that our word is meaningless? We all at this table know how tenuous our alliance is with the Saudis. Let's not forget that Beijing has courted them over the past five years. If our military commitment to one ally is called into question, our commitment to all of our allies is called into question, and it will have dramatic impact. Why did we spend all of this time and money and brainpower creating the greatest military threat in the world, to run from it at its most appropriate and critical time?"

"But if that use leads to China and the U.S. emptying their nuclear weapons silos and destroying one another, will you then be glad we stood up for ourselves?" asked Lindsay. "We are here at the end of the day to protect America's citizens. Our children and grandchildren. I would rather have my granddaughter alive and breathing, albeit with diminished American influence in the world, than dead. Three hundred years ago, this country didn't even exist. There is nothing, there is no overarching reason, that the United States must be the world's protector. Certainly not when doing so endangers our own safety and security, as it does in this case."

"I agree that we need to get Ghandra on the line," said Jessica. "But, Mr. President, we cannot show any weakness or indecisiveness in our commitment to India. We need to simply explain to President Ghandra the very real possibility that prolonging this engagement creates incalculable risks for his own citizens, especially with a nuclear Pakistan led by a religious zealot."

"Let's get Ghandra on the phone," said President Allaire. "From the Oval. What is very clear is that no one can predict what's going to happen. We don't want the war to continue. The risks grow very quickly as long as this goes on and the crisis will soon be outside of our capability to control or influence it. We need to tell Ghandra to shut this thing down. That's the bottom line."

"In the meantime, we need to see a full strategic capability set on what we have in the theater," said Jessica. "Where is the closest carrier group. Harry, run the numbers on troops; what is the maximum number of soldiers we can put into India if necessary, how soon could we deploy, et cetera."

"On it," said Black.

"We also need better intelligence on El-Khayab," said President Allaire. "What is he discussing? Are we capturing any of his communications with Beijing, with his war cabinet? And get on the phone with Beijing. Press them. We need them to help us keep El-Khayab in a box."

The president was silent as the doors to the elevator opened. He said nothing, and walked down the thick red carpet of the West Wing to the Oval Office.

Inside the Oval Office, the president walked behind his desk. He removed his blazer, hanging it on the back of the chair next to his desk, then removed his red-and-blue-striped tie, threw it onto the same chair next to the blazer.

"I hate to sound like a broken record, but we have policies and ways of executing those policies that are tried and true, Mr. President," said Jessica. "There are legitimate, fundamental reasons we agree to protect vital interests outside of our borders, such as India. Why is it that we are having debates about basic policy underpinnings at the very time we can't afford to, at the very time these policies should form the compass points in our strategy?"

The president sat down. He closed his eyes and rubbed them.

"I need a few minutes, Jess," he whispered. She stared at him, noticed the redness around his eyes.

A strange feeling came over Jessica then. It was a surreal sense of anxiety; part euphoria, part terror. Terror because she saw the president as he was, a fallible, insecure human being; a man adrift due to the loss of his wife at a time when he needed to be in total control. Jessica understood why she was there, that she could, and would, manage the crisis for the president, if he would let her.

Jessica reached for the phone on President Allaire's desk.

"You don't have a few minutes, Mr. President."

"Good morning, President Ghandra," said President Allaire. "How are you holding up?"

"I appreciate your call," said Rajiv Ghandra, the president of India. "We're in the thick of it. So let's get to it, yes?"

"Yes, Rajiv. I'm on the line with Jessica Tanzer."

"Hi, Jessica," said Ghandra. "I trust you're well."

"Yes, thank you, Mr. President," said Jessica. "If you don't mind my cutting to the quick, what is the current status of the battle?"

There was a long pause, which Ghandra finally filled.

"It's blowing up quickly," said Ghandra. "We're losing more than five hundred men an hour. It's extremely violent, and there's no letup on either side. We are inflicting as many casualties, if not more, on the Pakistanis."

"Why is it so intense, so quickly?" asked President Allaire.

"Because we are each trying to build stable supply lines up to the battle theater. If either side lets up, what has already been put in place will be destroyed within hours. It's like building a dam in the middle of a river: you have to keep putting the rocks in place even though many are being washed away."

"Mr. President, surely this makes no sense," said Jessica. "A few incidents and all of the sudden there is a flash point with seemingly no control? Why? We've had relative stability in Kashmir for almost a decade."

"It has become, how shall we say, complex, Jessica. I can't fully impress on you the deleterious effects of the incidents at Yagulung; the rape, the massacre of this small village in the middle of nowhere, on all of my people. There is legitimate anger. This anger is built on two decades of fear that the jihadists have already created in my people. Do you have any idea how many of my countrymen have been killed over the past decade by Islamic terrorists? More than ten thousand Indian citizens! *Imagine* that. People are angry. This has set them off. I have to tell you, *I* am angry. El-Khayab is a jihadist. He's one of them. I believe we need to fight until the end. I have no interest in a cease-fire. I have no interest in moving back to the Line of Control."

"Rajiv, you know that the United States stands behind you," said President Allaire.

"Yes, thank you. I know that."

"We're prepared to step in and defend India if necessary to protect our ally and our own strategic interests in the region."

"Yes, I appreciate that."

"But our military support cannot protect you from an irrational attack by the Pakistani Army and by Omar El-Khayab. We will be coming in after millions have already perished."

"What are you saying?"

"You're in grave danger," said President Allaire. "El-Khayab is the first Pakistani president who might actually decide to use a nuclear device. Have you considered that?"

A low, soft, humorless laugh came across the phone as President Ghandra chuckled. "Considered it? Of course we've considered it. But even he is not that crazy. He knows what would happen if he launched a nuclear strike on India. Even a radical cleric as hateful as El-Khayab wouldn't do something so suicidal."

"But if he does—" asked Jessica.

"We would annihilate Pakistan," interrupted President Ghandra.

"We want you to consider a cease-fire," said President Allaire.

"The implications of this thing going on much longer are simply too dangerous. Under any circumstance, both countries lose. Potentially millions of people. India needs to be the reasonable player here."

"Thank you for your advice," said President Ghandra. "I will take it under advisement. But I will tell you that India *will not back down*. Not today. Not tomorrow. Certainly not as long as I am president."

II

KOT COPPER WORKS, LTD.
KAROO OPERATIONS
INDIA-CONTROLLED KASHMIR

At a quarter after eleven in the morning, Gautam finished his second cigarette in succession. He flicked the butt down into the wide tire track that had been left in the mud. He chugged what was left of the water in his tin cup. It was a cool day inside the mine tunnel, at least comparatively speaking; yesterday had reached a hundred degrees inside the mine. Today, the air sweltered around eighty-five. Still, it was early in the shift and his clothing was already drenched in perspiration.

"Hey, Gautam, come on, boy, break over," came a voice out of the darkness. It was Indiraman, his supervisor. Always trying to prove himself, Gautam thought. As if managing Gautam hard would somehow allow him to rise up the KOT ranks quicker.

"Yes, Indiraman, I know," called Gautam. *And fuck you, asshole*, he added, but only in his thoughts.

Gautam turned his head. To his right, as far as he could see, a tunnel ran straight off into the distance, into the darkness. The tunnel was more than fifty feet high and wide enough to accommodate three large earthmovers standing side by side. Steel girders ran like a rib cage along the ceiling of the tunnel, holding the loamy earth in place; dangling down from the girders at regular intervals were large, saucerlike halogen lights.

To the left, where the shaft was being extended down into the earth, the girders and lights had yet to be secured in place. The darkness was interrupted only by a canopy of lights surrounding the tunnel-boring machine, or "mole" as it was usually referred to.

The mole looked like a gigantic centipede, hydraulic jacks pressed against the carved-out sides of the tunnel like caterpillar legs, giving the big machine the stability it needed in order to thrust forward into the earth. The mole moved slowly but ineluctably down into the wall of dirt and rock below ground, the cutter head rotating slowly clockwise, its tungsten carbide cutting bits breaking up the earth inch by inevitable inch, creating a rough tunnel more than thirty feet in diameter. The resulting dirt—or "muck" as it was called—spilled onto a makeshift conveyor belt that moved alongside the mole, running the muck up and into piles which Gautam and his team then hauled up to the surface, where it was sifted and processed for copper, then repurposed.

The mole was the oddest and most amazing piece of machinery Gautam had ever seen. He'd gotten used to the sight of it, after nearly three years of looking at it. Still, he always found himself staring at the mole. Harrison, an older man, stood next to him, smoking a cigarette and drinking a cup of coffee.

"So fucking big," said Gautam, shaking his head. "What do you think it cost?"

"Why, Gautam?" Harrison chuckled. "Are you thinking of buying one? This cost the company fifty million U.S. dollars. That's over two hundred million rupees."

Gautam's eyes bulged. "Wow," he said to Harrison. "I guess I will have to bank a few more paychecks. Maybe they will advance me a little, what do you think?"

They both laughed. Gautam watched Harrison throw his cardboard coffee cup onto the ground, then climb into the cab of a Caterpillar R2900. Harrison lumbered the 2900 forward and lifted a pile of rock, turned, and dumped the pile into the back of Gautam's truck. In a few minutes, the dump truck would be filled and he would drive up the tunnel to the surface.

Gautam walked to the side of his truck. He smiled as he stood next to the large tire. He was more than six feet tall, yet he stood less than halfway up the monstrous tire. He climbed the ladder in front of the tire and got back into the cab. He waited in the cab for the last few arms full of muck and enjoyed another cigarette. Finally, the weight sensor chimed indicating the dump was maxed out. He moved the truck into gear and, turning carefully in the dark mine shaft, he aimed the truck back down the tunnel. He drove slowly, five miles per hour, down the winding tunnel for more than two miles. Finally, he saw the first sprinkling of daylight at the end of the tunnel.

The yellow Caterpillar rumbled out of the mine entrance. He drove the big truck down across the operations field, to the primary crusher, where the big pile of rock and dirt would be quickly crushed, sifted, ground up, sieved, and processed for traces of copper. However, most of the copper would be concentrated in a find somewhere beneath the tunnel. The KOT strategy was for the copper found in the tunnel to finance the initial land acquisition, shaft construction, and equipment purchases. After that, drilling into the surrounding rock would be mostly profit for KOT. Gautam moved the truck to the crusher, backed up the large truck, then flipped the switch that lifted the big dumper slowly into the air.

"And that's your life," Gautam said aloud, to no one. He reached for his pack of Marlboros as he sat in the cab, waiting for the load of dirt to fall out of the flatbed. He lit a cigarette. "Thirty-four more years and you will be eligible for retirement!" he yelled to no one.

He laughed. He should be grateful. It had taken every connection his father had to get him a job at KOT. The job paid well, more than $100 a day, almost all of it went automatically into a bank account he had set up with the Bank of India back in New Delhi. After all, there was nothing out here to spend the money on, except for cigarettes and alcohol, and he didn't like to drink. Still, he was twenty-two years old and more than two hundred miles from the nearest town. While KOT had constructed a makeshift town, with a few shops, four restaurants, a bowling alley, pool hall, and even a movie theater, it just wasn't the same. It was artificial. Built to make the nearly eight thousand KOT employees and their family members at Karoo feel like they enjoyed a normal life, even though they were so far from civilization.

KOT Karoo was one of seventeen different mining operations KOT had spread across India. KOT was one of India's largest mining conglomerates. Copper, zinc, plutonium, coal, you name it. Gautam had asked for the copper surface mine outside of Mumbai, but there were no jobs there. This was the only opportunity. Father had used his only connection, the son of someone whose hair he used to cut at his barbershop, who worked in the accounting department at KOT in New Delhi. He remembered listening to Father, practically begging on the pay phone outside the shop. Whenever he remembered the sound of his father's voice that day, the sound of him begging, it almost made him want to cry. He missed Father. What other father would beg in such a way for his only son?

Now he was here. In Karoo. Beautiful Kashmir. Even he had to admit that the beauty of the place was sometimes almost overwhelming, like the paintings at the museum. Behind the ugly temporary village and the industrial buildings of the mine, the dark green and blue hills spread like a painting. Snow-capped mountains formed a distant frame around them in the distance.

He lit his second cigarette in a row, put one of his work boots up on the dashboard.

"O Kashmir," he sang to himself, a folk tune from his youth, by Tansen. "May I spend my windswept life in your green embrace, my dear Kashmir?"

12

Omar El-Khayab sat in the large leather armchair behind the desk in the President's office.

The room resonated with the chants from Constitution Avenue, a main artery through downtown Islamabad, now completely shut down due to the crowds which had taken it over. In less than four days of demonstrations, the throngs of Pakistanis had grown and spread, filling the land surrounding Aiwan-e-Sadr, the presidential residence, to capacity with more than a million men and women on sidewalks, streets, and any other available space.

The chant from the angry throngs grew louder with each passing hour. The intensity of the words was palpable.

"Death to India! Death to India! Death to India!"

After only four days, more than thirty thousand Pakistani soldiers had already died and thousands more were injured.

El-Khayab sat alone in the presidential office. He didn't like the office, its size and opulence, which he interpreted in the gasps he heard as visitors walked in, in their comments about the vaulted ceilings, the gold and marble statues along the walls, the floor-to-ceiling windows, the cavernous space.

But today he would use the office. Today, the most important decision by any president in the history of the country would be made.

El-Khayab tried to imagine an image of himself, what he looked like and how he was perceived by others. He was taller than most, with long, bony fingers, a mane of white hair, his face mangled by fire and scars, covered in moles. His looks alone should have relegated him to obscurity and exile, and yet they did not. Why? he asked himself. But he knew. It was his voice. It was a sound unlike any on earth, a voice whose tone in and of itself could inspire either love or fear, even in those who didn't understand his native tongue, "the Hitler of Islam," as one writer had called him, a comparison he ignored but which he did little to dispute. It was El-Khayab's voice that he could ignite in an instant into venom. For he knew that one of his greatest strengths was the irony of his appearance, an ugly man enjoying the love of so many, a gentle man having such violent thoughts, a quiet man having such rabid supporters, a simple man complicating the world in such a dramatic way.

"Today, Omar," he said aloud to the empty room, "you will complicate the world for Allah."

El-Khayab knew that history had chosen this time and this place. It was his destiny. Islam would ascend today. He would be Allah's agent on earth.

El-Khayab had awakened that morning with a vision fresh in his mind. It was the fire that had blinded him as a three-year-old boy in Karachi, the fire that killed his parents, four sisters and one of his two brothers. So painful was the memory, he had learned to blot it out from his mind, to erase the horrible images, of inferno, bright red, orange, and black. El-Khayab realized now that the flames which destroyed his eyes were actually the beginning of his true vision. They were the fingers of Allah, taking his eyesight so that he might see.

Atta, his only surviving brother, had pulled him from the fire. They had grown up in the madrasa, without parents, with the bitter memory of his family, whom he loved so much, gone, destroyed by the smoke and flames.

This morning, Omar El-Khayab awoke to the sight of his parents, his sisters, and his brother, burning to death in the devastating inferno. But instead of the pain, this morning El-Khayab felt nothing but ecstasy. In the middle of the vision, he saw a darkened face, with no eyes. He struggled to interpret the sight. Was it him? Was it Allah? Whoever it was, he knew the sign. He knew what it meant.

He heard the sound of the large brass knocker on the door to the office. He listened as the door opened.

"Mr. President," said the voice from across the large office. "May we interrupt you, sir?"

"General Karreff," said El-Khayab, rising from his chair. "Thank you for coming on such short notice."

"Of course, sir," said Karreff.

"Is Minister Khan with you?" asked El-Khayab.

"I'm here, Mr. President." Osama Khan, Pakistan's defense minister, was a tall man, dressed in a stylish gray suit, with neatly combed black hair and a mustache.

"Ah, Minister Khan. Thank you for coming."

"My pleasure, Mr. President. Khalid el-Jaqonda, my deputy, is also with me, sir."

"Good morning, Mr. President," said el-Jaqonda.

El-Khayab listened as the three men crossed the marble floor and sat down in front of the desk.

"New Delhi started this war," said El-Khayab. "The Hindu display no sense of proportion or reason. They have insulted Pakistan for more than half a century now, claiming land which is rightfully ours. We now have a historic opportunity to reclaim it."

"Kashmir," said Khan.

"To take back that which is ours," said El-Khayab. "Nothing more, nothing less."

"Mr. President," said Karreff. "If Minister Khan is here, you obviously have a . . . well, a *design*."

"Yes," said El-Khayab, pausing. "No population centers. But people must die."

"How many, sir?" asked Khan.

"Thousands."

"Ten thousand?"

"Yes," said El-Khayab softly. The sound of the crowd seemed to grow louder, and the old cleric turned his head away from his guests, toward the window.

"Death to India! Death to India! Death to India! Death to India! Death to India!"

"How many nuclear devices do we have that are fully functional?" asked El-Khayab.

"One hundred and sixty-one," said el-Jaqonda. "These are comprised of three primary designs based on kiloton, extensibility, and size."

"My suggestion, Mr. President, is the following," said Khan. "Khalid and I shall work with General Karreff to determine a proper target. We shall then return and report back to you."

"That's not necessary," said El-Khayab. He removed his glasses. Khan flinched as he looked at what had once been El-Khayab's eyeballs, now aimed relentlessly at the window. "What value will I add to what is now an operational process? My decision is made. When you are ready, when the time is proper, then strike."

"When do you want this to occur, President El-Khayab?" asked Khan.

"As soon as possible. By the hour, our soldiers die in the hundreds. My hope is that this stops the violence. That the Hindu enemy understands our very real intentions."

"I must caution you, sir." General Karreff cleared his throat. "Please don't take this as my being in disagreement. But it is my duty to point out the pitfalls, to play a *devil's advocate*, so to speak."

"Speak, General," said El-Khayab.

"The Indian government will almost certainly respond in kind. If we have one hundred and sixty bombs—"

"Sixty-one," interrupted el-Jaqonda.

"Whatever," said Karreff. "One-sixty, one-sixty-one, two hundred, two thousand, whatever the number. If we have that many, New Delhi has twice or perhaps three times that number. We strike a remote town and kill a few thousand Indians. They strike a less remote town and kill fifty thousand Pakistani. Soon, we are aiming our weapons at Mumbai, New Delhi, Hyderabad, and they are aiming their bombs at Karachi, Peshawar, Lahore, and Islamabad."

"That is the risk we take," said El-Khayab. "There are risks in leadership. Risks in acting, in defending, in living."

"We are four days into the war," said Karreff. "Field Marshal Bolin is hurting the Indians. If land is what we want, we are laying siege to the valleys around Kargil."

"And what of Skardu?" asked Khan.

"We give them Skardu temporarily, as a distraction," said Karreff. "They are killing themselves trying to push supplies and arms to their new encampment. Meanwhile, we are laying the groundwork for a major acquisition of territory: Kargil, Drass, perhaps even as far west as Srinagar and the Kashmir Valley. We have destroyed three Indian military bases in Jammu. When we want Skardu back, we can take it in hours, not days. Let Bolin have his time. I will gather you Kashmir, Mr. President. With conventional weapons. I truly believe this."

There was a pause as El-Khayab rotated in his chair. He sat back, ran his hand across his white beard.

"He will still have his time," said El-Khayab. "Plenty of time. Bolin not only will have time, I fully expect him to keep up the current strategy."

"If we drop a nuclear bomb on India there is a very real possibility Bolin will be targeted with a retaliatory nuclear strike," said Karreff. "There's a possibility that within minutes, New Delhi will drop not one, but five or ten nuclear bombs. And then what? How do we continue to fight a conventional war when all of the sudden it is no longer conventional? When our hills and our cities are not only on fire but are irretrievable, with fallout from the nuclear devices destroying towns that we will never be able to inhabit again?"

"Spoken with eloquence," said El-Khayab. "I expect no less from my top military commander. Your candor is refreshing and it is vital to our Pakistani democracy. It is why I selected you over the others,

Persom. But the debate is now over. You must design your plan with what you have said; *the risks,* in mind. What does it mean? Strike hard. Do what is necessary to inhibit their next move."

"The Americans will urge India to hold their counterfire," said Khan. "Where would they get the troops? Iraq? Afghanistan? Be serious. The U.S. is stretched too thin to act as India's safety net."

"That's an awfully big gamble for us to take," said Karreff. "We gamble that the U.S. will have the power and influence to stop President Ghandra from retaliating. The Indian president will be under enormous pressure to respond in-kind. Let's not forget that India has the second largest standing army in the world."

"The Americans understand the implications of a retaliatory counterstrike from India," said Khan. "They will have to prevent it. Otherwise they will soon stand face-to-face with China and the largest standing army in the world."

"Yes," said Karreff, bitterness in his voice. "They will stand face-to-face with China—upon the ashes of our dead soldiers and children."

"Remember yourself," said Khan.

"Gentlemen," said El-Khayab. "Our meeting is complete. I must pray now. Take Srinagar, General Karreff, take whatever is necessary, whatever is possible. I expect nothing less. *They* expect nothing less." El-Khayab nodded at the window.

Karreff stared at the blind man. He looked down at his own hands. The palms shimmered with perspiration.

"Very well, sir," said Karreff. "It will be done."

13

88 TWENTY-FOURTH STREET, N.W.
GEORGETOWN

The doorbell to Jessica's town house rang just as she was buttoning her jeans in the bedroom. It had been a long day. A dinner she was supposed to have with her college roommate had to be canceled because of the growing crisis in Kashmir. She ran down the stairs and opened the door. Standing on the front stoop was a man holding a box, *Pizzeria Paradiso* in cursive on the top.

"Hi, Sammy."

"Hey, Jessica. Eleven-fifty."

"Well done?"

"Of course."

"Thanks." She handed him the money, then closed the door.

She went into the den and placed the pizza box down on the wooden coffee table in the middle of the room. She put the TV on. She'd Tivo'd her usuals, but instead of watching any of them, she searched through the DVR and purchased *Australia*. The movie, she knew, had been roundly panned, but she wanted—she needed—to take her mind off of Pakistan and India, if only for a few hours. Plus she knew it would make her think about Dewey. And right now, she was too tired to try and *not* think about him.

When she called him at Sembler Station earlier that day, her fingers had trembled as she held the phone. In a way, she'd been relieved he wasn't there to talk. But now she couldn't stop thinking about him, knowing he might call her back at any moment.

Her cell phone rang. On the screen, the words said, "Restricted Caller."

Is it him? she thought to herself. She reached for the phone.

"This is Jessica."

"Excuse me for calling so late, Jessica. It's Karl Chelmsford."

Jessica shut her eyes for a brief moment, disappointed.

"Hi, Karl. What is it? Can it wait until tomorrow?"

"Actually, no, I don't think it can. It concerns Pakistan. I didn't feel comfortable discussing it at the meeting today. I probably have no business saying it, but I need to. It's not part of the analysis. It reflects my own opinion."

"Why didn't you bring this up at the White House?" asked Jessica, picking up a piece of pizza and taking a bite.

"I'm an academic. I'm not a CIA operative or a military commander. Frankly, I was afraid everyone would think I was crazy."

"And you don't think I will?"

"No, you might. But I get the feeling that you wouldn't hold it against me."

"All right, you've piqued my curiosity. Tell me."

"Coup d'état."

"Coup d'état? Explain."

"I've been sitting here in my office at the Pentagon trying to figure out a way this ends peacefully and for the life of me I can't. El-Khayab is not only not going to back down, he's probably going to up the stakes. America needs to remove Omar El-Khayab."

"There are a lot of people working on Pakistan right now," said Jessica. "Right this moment. Beijing is even pitching in. On the other side of the conflict, we both know India is eminently more reasonable. They'll come around."

"What did Rajiv Ghandra say to the president when he brought up the cease-fire?" asked Chelmsford.

"The direct quote was he would never back down. But that doesn't mean he won't. We have to keep pushing."

Chelmsford was quiet.

"America has significantly toned down its attempts at regime change," said Jessica. "We've been burnt too many times. When we succeed, the country is tarnished—seen as an American puppet—then we're blamed. When we fail, we get blamed again. It's a no-win situation."

"I know," said Chelmsford. "I'm not looking for you to just agree with me then order a team into action. What I'm asking is, will you think about it? The risk, in this case, might be worth taking."

"Of course we'll think about it. Good night, Karl."

Jessica hung up her cell phone, then took another bite from her pizza. She thought of Chelmsford, the nebbish professor, working late in his office at the Pentagon. She admired him for calling. He cared. She was eating pizza and watching a B movie about Australia and Chelmsford was working, trying to figure out a way out of the India-Pakistan mess.

She put down the pizza, turned the movie off, then put on the news.

14

The seasonal winds came from the Mediterranean Sea. They blew in a southerly direction, through the low plains along the coast of Lebanon, then dispersed through canyon after canyon up through the hills above Beirut and the small town of Broumana.

On a blue stone terrace, next to a villa on Patula Hill, the breeze made the newspaper in Aswan Fortuna's hands rustle and nearly blow away. He sat down and opened the paper. The India-Pakistan war dominated the front page of the paper. He read the articles carefully, sipping his coffee. Finally, he stood and walked to a large rosebush at the edge of the terrace.

"Pakistan is going to beat India out of Kashmir," said Fortuna. His hair was combed elegantly back, longish, parted down the middle.

"And that is good, yes?" asked Candela. She was reclined on a teak chaise next to the gunite swimming pool, topless.

"Good? It's glorious, my dear." Fortuna knelt next to her. He placed his right hand on her knee, then ran his fingers up her deeply tan thigh, brushing the top of her white bikini.

"You're the only man I know who would call war glorious."

"Don't you see? If Islam is to ever be the blanket that covers the earth, the battle must begin somewhere."

"But aren't you afraid it will get out of control? What if India defeats Pakistan?"

Fortuna said nothing. He stood up and walked to the edge of the slate terrace. He counted a handful of guards, machine guns in hand, spread out along the perimeter of the property. He looked in the distance at Beirut. The sea behind it shimmered.

Fortuna walked around the pool and inside the house. Four men were seated at the kitchen table.

"What's the report?" asked Fortuna.

"Youssef was successful with the Customs employee," said Nebuchar. "We have information about what part of Australia Andreas is in."

"Is he dead yet?"

"We found out he's in Australia less than four weeks ago. We found out what part of Australia he's in two days ago. Give it some time, Father."

"*I've given it time!* It's been over a year since Andreas murdered Alexander."

"It's a big country, as they say," said Nebuchar. "There are twenty-two million people. One of them is Andreas. I have a team of seven men, all Al-Muqawama, the best Hezbollah has to offer. But it takes time."

"What are they doing?" asked Fortuna impatiently.

"Now that we know what part of the country he's in, we know he works on a ranch," said Nebuchar. "So now it's a matter of narrowing it down."

"What about the photos?"

"Borchardt sent us the photos, Aswan," said another man at the table. He pulled a manila envelope from his bag and placed it on the table. "They were taken after Andreas was awarded a medal by the U.S. president. Borchardt asked for six million dollars."

"Mother of God, six million dollars."

Fortuna pulled the photos from the envelope. There were two photos, both showing Dewey the day he was given the award. He had short hair, and wore a suit. He was big, tough-looking, handsome. One showed him smiling as he shook hands with President Allaire. The other showed Allaire placing the medal around Dewey's neck. In both photos, a pretty woman stood at the president's side.

Fortuna studied the photos. "Who's the woman?"

"Jessica Tanzer," said another man. "The national security advisor for America."

"And Youssef has these?"

"Yes," said Nebuchar.

"It's taking too much time," said Fortuna, tossing the photos down on the table.

"Don't lose your temper now, Papa. We're extremely close."

"Candela could have found him by now, for God's sake. She could've found him with a flashlight and a map. It takes you nearly a year just to find out what country he's in. All the while you've spent what, five, six, seven million?"

Nebuchar stood up, stepped toward his father, then moved his face to within inches of his father's.

"The only thing Candela is good at finding is your cock and your wallet, Father."

The three men who had been seated at the table next to Nebuchar leaped out of their chairs and pulled Nebuchar away from his father. Nebuchar struggled against them, his powerful frame hard to dislodge. It took all of them to tug him away from Aswan, and when they did, Nebuchar tripped on one of the men's boots, falling to the marble floor.

Aswan stepped forward. He looked into Nebuchar's eyes, then swung his right arm down and across Nebuchar's cheek. Nebuchar absorbed the blow, then looked at his father with hatred in his eyes.

"Whatever money you spent is not your money," Nebuchar whispered, wiping his hand across his cheek. "It was Alexander's. You spend it like you earned it."

"I want Andreas dead."

"*And he will be dead!*" screamed Nebuchar. He stood up, glared at Aswan, then turned and walked to the door.

Aswan watched him walk out of the house, then looked down at his right hand, the one with which he'd just struck his son. He shut his eyes, regretfully, for a few seconds. When he opened them, the three men at the table were all staring at him.

"Get out," said Aswan. "Don't come back until Andreas is dead."

When the men had left, Aswan turned to see Candela, standing in the doorway, her small red thong the only clothing she wore. In her hand, she held a cell phone.

"Are you okay?" she asked.

"I don't know."

"It's for you." She held the phone out. "Should I take a message?"

Fortuna walked across the kitchen and took the phone from her.

"What is it?" he asked angrily.

"Aswan, it's Khalid el-Jaqonda. Is this a bad time?"

Fortuna breathed deeply.

"No," said Fortuna. "No. I'm sorry. Khalid, I have been thinking about you. How are you?"

"Fine, fine, everything is fine. But I can't talk for long."

"What can I do for you?" asked Fortuna.

"No, Aswan, the question is what can *I* do for *you*."

"What do you mean?"

"Watch the news," said el-Jaqonda. "I told you that our day would soon come."

"You mean?"

"Just watch. And please pray for me."

15

PALM COVE
QUEENSLAND, AUSTRALIA

Palm Cove was crowded with sunbathers, swimmers, and surfers. The heat was in the eighties. There wasn't a cloud in the sky.

In front of a T-shirt shop near the southern end of the beach, a man in a blue bathing suit lay on a big orange and yellow beach towel. He was in his thirties, olive-skinned, very tan, with a mess of uncombed, perfectly blond hair, the product of a $14.99 bottle of peroxide. The effect was a slightly punkish look, a dark-skinned Johnny Rotten. He blended in, just another weirdo, at one of the most popular tourist destinations in Australia. That was the brilliance of the blond dye job. Nobody suspected Youssef was a terrorist.

Youssef's chest was wiry, gaunt, but muscular. He had brown eyes, which cast about, always searching. The eyes were as blank as stone, but they hid a fury that was reaching its boiling point.

He looked at his watch, then sat up. He walked down the beach out into the water and began swimming freestyle parallel to the beach. After five minutes, he stopped and treaded water.

In front of him, the beach was dense with sunbathers, blankets laid out in a madras of stripes and colors, umbrellas dotting the sand. Youssef searched, then caught the movement of a man. That man was walking into the water more than a hundred feet away. He was a bald man, young, in his early twenties. He too was Arab.

Soon, the two men, tourists by appearance, Hezbollah by training, were treading water next to each other more than fifty yards from shore.

The younger man waited for Youssef to speak.

"Well, is it done?" Youssef asked.

"Yes," said the bald man, whose name was Ahmed. "Basil collected a list of all of the ranches near Cairns. Youssef, there are more than thirty."

"Thirty? Fuck me."

"He could be at any one of them."

"Thank you, professor fucking dildo head."

"Sorry, I—"

"Button it," said Youssef. "We need to think now."

"I've mapped out the ranch locations," said Ahmed. "We could literally just walk up and ask—"

"No! You stupid fuck. That's not what we're going to do. We need to surprise him. If we walk up to the wrong ranch and ask for a man named Andreas and he's not there, what do you think will happen, jackhole? How long do you think he will then hang around, Einstein? We can't do anything that will tip him off."

"Well, you seem to be a genius, so how do we find him, boss?" asked Ahmed.

"Patience," said Youssef, treading water. "And don't wise off to me, fuck ball."

"Sorry."

"Stop apologizing," said Youssef.

Youssef dipped his head beneath the water for a moment, then re-emerged.

"Most of the ranches are north of here," said Ahmed. "Starcke, Hope, Cooktown, Yarradan, Aurukun, Lakeland."

"Good. We have seven men so we divide up the towns. Everyone goes out tonight, tomorrow night, every night until we see something or hear something. We go to the bars. We drink. We stay until we find him."

"Maybe we fuck some chicks?"

"No, we don't 'fuck some chicks,'" said Youssef. "At least, you don't. You're too fucking ugly. Now me, that's a different story. Will you look at some of that ass up there on the sand?"

Youssef nodded toward the beach.

"Unreal, brother."

"But even *I* am not going to do that," said Youssef. "We are single-minded until we kill this Chevrolet-driving asshole. It's inevitable now. We look around. We listen. We will see him. There's no other way. If we meet ranchers, we talk with them. No mention of Andreas. We need to spread out. If we see him, and we have a clean kill, we take it. If not, if we find out where he is, we wait and all move together."

"Understood," said Ahmed.

The two terrorists treaded water in silence, next to each other, staring at the beach in front of them.

"It's only a matter of time now," said Youssef.

"It's Allah's will," said Ahmed.

"No, Allah has nothing to do with it, you silly idiot. Grow up. There is no such thing as luck in what we do. If you think like that, you will die."

Youssef dove under the water, emerging a few feet away and began swimming backstroke down the beach.

"If you weren't my brother I would drown you and let the sharks eat you," said Youssef hatefully as he swam away. "Try not to do anything stupid."

16

Dewey woke up after lunch. He went into the bathroom and splashed some water on his face. He put on the clothes and went downstairs. Sitting on the kitchen island in the ranch house was a note:

> *Dewey,*
> *Cold steak in the fridge.*
> *A woman named Jessica called,*
> *said it was important.*
> *Joe*

Dewey went to the refrigerator, opened the door, and saw a blue and white porcelain plate with a big steak on it. He walked to the sink, picked up the steak with his right hand and took a big bite. He left the plate in the sink then walked outside into the pebble stone circular driveway, eating the cold steak like a candy bar.

At the stables, he found Deravelle. He brought him outside, sprayed him down with cool water and scrubbed the stallion from head to toe. He toweled him off and brushed him down, then fed him before putting him back inside the barn. He took one of the ranch horses, an older mustang named Buzz, and rode back out to the fence line he'd cut the night before. He fixed the fence then returned to the ranch. By then, it was nearly dinnertime.

Dewey walked down across the manicured green lawn that spread for a quarter mile to the bunkhouse. The lawn looked like a large green rectangle, bordered by white horse fence. Behind everything, in the distance, the dark blue of the ocean sat like a backdrop, miles in the distance, dark mercury that framed the vista.

The bunkhouse was a large, simple building, three stories tall, white clapboard with navy blue shutters. It stood a few hundred yards across from the Sembler house. Inside the bunkhouse, thirty-five bedrooms held the ranch hands, who ranged in age from eighteen to sixty.

Dewey heard music as he approached, country music coming from the stereo in the great room on the first floor, a large open room with couches, chairs, a big kitchen, a couple of pool tables. The room was crowded with men when he walked in through the screen door. It was Saturday, and most men were back at the bunkhouse. On Saturdays, drinking usually began right after dinner. That was followed by an evening in town, at Cooktown's restaurants and bars.

"Dewey!" yelled one of the men when he walked in through the door. It was Talbot, one of the younger ranch hands. He was seated on one of the couches, a beer in his hand, his face layered in dirt. "The man of the hour!"

Someone turned down the music. Then another hand, Bill Zachary, leaped on top of the pool table. He stood with a pool cue in his hand. From the way he wobbled slightly, Zachary had clearly already had a few beers, like most of the others.

"Everyone," bellowed Zachary, waving the cue through the air. "Let's give a big one for Dewey! A fucking hero! Good job, old man!"

The gathered ranch workers all cheered and clapped. Talbot stood up and handed him a beer. Dewey smiled.

"Thanks, guys. I couldn't have done it without you."

As the thirty-odd ranch hands gathered around him, Dewey retold the story of saving Nicola Chasvur.

"Where'd you learn to climb rock like that?" one the men asked when he'd finished the story. "Nighttime? In the rain?"

"You would've done the same thing," said Dewey. "Every one of you. You'd be surprised what you're capable of when your back's against the wall. A lot of it was just plain old luck."

"Luck, my ass," said Zachary.

For the next hour, they cranked the music, played pool, and relaxed. At some point, Dewey felt a pat on his back and turned to see Talbot.

"You up for a night on the town?" he asked.

"Sure," said Dewey. "Let me grab a shower."

17

CHAKLALA AIR FORCE BASE
RAWALPINDI, PAKISTAN

At 2:46 P.M., a Chinese-made F-7 fighter jet, painted in the light green colors of the Pakistani Air Force, barreled down the 8,900-foot runway at Chaklala Air Base in Rawalpindi.

This PAF jet was one of a series of fighter jets taking off at steady intervals from Chaklala, now the main staging area for the air war. All of them, a smorgasbord of F-7s, Mirage 3 and 5s, A-5s, F-16s, and JF-17s, were weighted down with air-to-air and air-to-ground missiles. Their primary mission was dumping missiles on the Indian Army supply lines in the Kargil area. An increasing number of jets were being sent directly east, toward Srinagar, Kashmir's largest city; PAF was attempting to divert Indian resources so that the Kargil area could be fortified by Pakistan and used as the staging ground into Srinagar. But the going was tough for the PAF pilots. Already, seventeen Pakistani jets had been shot down.

But on this day, at this hour, one particular F-7 fighter jet was different from the others. It looked the same, same light green paint job, same gold star on the rear wing, and beneath the left wing of the jet, the normal payload was strapped; three surface-to-ground missiles. But beneath the right side of the jet, something different had been attached: A single, roundish, polished steel bomb. It looked like a slightly elongated, very large football. On its nose, an unusual appurtenance; a black cube the size of a shoe box that extended out in front of the bomb.

This piece of hardware was a thirty-four-kiloton nuclear bomb.

Inside, the bomb held weaponized plutonium, trapped in an ion-free, airtight alloy capsule spiked through with a sophisticated, altitude-sensitive trigger mechanism. The bomb and its trigger mechanism had been designed by Osama Khan and his team of nuclear engineers. It was neither the largest nor the smallest of Pakistan's nuclear weapons. It was not the newest technology, nor the oldest. Of the one hundred and sixty-one in the Pakistani nuclear arsenal, this particular bomb was average. But, it was reliable. The trigger mechanism had been thoroughly tested, the fissile material ratio was known and dependable.

The Chengdu F-7 climbed quickly to 12,000 feet, aiming northeast toward the LOC above Kargil. At Drass, however, when the jet should have veered slightly south, toward Kargil, Captain Ranala, the pilot, kept the flight path northeast. After several minutes, he pulled the throttle back, moving the F-7 to more than nine hundred miles per hour, climbed to 21,000 feet and arced north.

At the Indian Army's Northern Command headquarters, Lieutenant Ashwan Miri, an intelligence officer in the battle operations group, stared at his radar screen. Miri tracked Pakistani jet movements into the war theater, and, based upon the trajectory of those inbound fighters, dispatched the routes to the appropriate missile battery for targeting. The job was largely an automated one, thanks to the sophisticated SIGINT system designed by Lockheed Martin and Raytheon. Miri's job was to move his cursor to the flight line, then simply click the mouse three times, at which point the computer would pick up the trajectory and push the assignment for the incoming jet to a missile battery, based on proximity to the predicted target of the fighter and supply of weapons at the batteries, as well as the altitude and speed of the inbound jet.

Miri picked-up the Pakistani F-7 as it crossed the LOC. The in-bound jet formed a pattern they had seen many times, swooping down to the Indian Army supply lines attempting to get weapons, fuel, and troops to Kargil. Miri triple-clicked the tracking protocol on the F-7 as it crossed the LOC. When the F-7 didn't turn when it was supposed to, above Kargil, Miri did not notice, for the jet's flight path had already been locked down by the SIGINT system, assigned to a battery; the bright red path on Miri's screen was now gone, the dull blue just another line he did not need to pay attention to.

More than four miles in the sky above Karoo, Captain Ranala listened as the target system inside the jet chimed monotone. He smiled nervously, flipped the steel cover cap off the launch button, moved the red safety button to the left. He paused a brief moment, only a moment, then he depressed the green button. He listened as the nuclear bomb roared to life, felt a slight bump beneath the right side of the jet as the weight of the nuclear device was freed from the body of the F-7. Ranala maneuvered the fighter jet to the left and up, directing the plane higher in the sky then turning back toward Rawalpindi. Outside the window to his right, there was a black trail of smoke, wavy and quickly dissipating behind the increasingly small object that roared through the cold blue sky toward the ground, toward Karoo.

18

KOT COPPER WORKS, LTD.
KAROO OPERATIONS
KASHMIR

The afternoon sun, high in the sky, beat down on Gautam's forehead as he stood next to the portable toilet, just a few yards from the sluice station. He finished a cigarette and realized that he had already smoked an entire pack today. He shook his head as he dropped the butt to the ground and stepped on it.

"You're going to kill yourself, Gautam," he whispered.

The chemical smell from the portable toilet made his stomach turn. And yet, every day, at the end of his shift, he stood here and had a cigarette before walking down the gravel hill to the small mining town of Karoo. The smell was disgusting, but it reminded him of the smell in the alley behind his father's barbershop in New Delhi. How many times did his father make him go out with leftover na'an from dinner the night before, and give it to the homeless men who slept in the alley?

"Why do we feed them?" Gautam would ask his father. "They urinate on the walls. They smell. They're worthless bums."

"We feed them," his father would say calmly, "because we are human beings together. If I was ever in their position, I would want to know that someone cared enough to bring me a piece of bread.

Gautam, do you really want to live in a world where a man won't even spare a piece of bread for another man?"

Gautam smiled at the thought. Smiled at the strange comfort he had learned to gather from the daily ritual at the mine, of standing next to the toilets and thinking about his father.

He walked to the side of the truck, picked up the small water bottle and took a sip. He leaned against the big black tire of the Caterpillar dump truck, waiting. Finally, he heard the rumble from the opening in the tunnel, the last dump truck of the day.

"Hey, Gautam, son of a bitch," Blackmon yelled, a big smile on his face, from the passenger side of the vehicle. The big truck came to a stop and Blackmon opened the door.

"Jump down, you dumb motherfucker," Gautam yelled, laughing at his best friend.

"Yeah, will you take care of me if I break my legs, asshole?" Blackmon said. He opened the door to the truck and reached for the ladder that would take him to the ground.

"I will take care of Rasha," Gautam yelled.

"Hey, watch it," Blackmon said as he climbed down the big steel ladder of the truck. "She probably couldn't handle you, what with that enormous pecker."

Gautam laughed, screwed the cap back on the water bottle. "Got any ciggies?" he asked.

"Where are yours?"

"Finished them."

"You're going to die from those," Blackmon said. He climbed off the bottom of the ladder, looked up at the cab. "All set, Kalif!" he yelled to the driver, who was out of sight. As the Caterpillar rumbled down the gravel road toward the primary crusher, Blackmon took a pack of cigarettes from his pocket, tossed it to Gautam. "There you go, Smokey the Bear."

"Thanks," said Gautam.

Gautam took a cigarette from the pack and handed it back to Blackmon. He puffed greedily and felt the familiar tug of the smoke filling his lungs.

As Gautam exhaled, his eye caught something interrupting the clear azure sky. He looked up. A small black object. He looked away, not registering the sight, then looked back as his mind processed the fact, unexpected and abnormal, that something was happening, that something was about to happen.

An object is dropping from the sky, he thought to himself.

His eyes affixed to the object as it dropped from the sky and grew larger. He slowly raised his cigarette to his mouth and took another drag. Had the mine works not been so noisy, he would have heard the faint whistle of the bomb as it screamed through the afternoon sky.

Blackmon finally noticed that Gautam was silent, motionless, transfixed. He followed the trajectory of his friend's stare, glancing up at the sky, at the approaching object, now plainly visible. It was a bomb, descending down upon them.

That was the last action, thought, the last moment the two friends shared. The bomb covered the final few thousand feet and was then above them. For the smallest part of a second, Gautam felt as if he could reach up and touch the object, catch it even. Had he lived, he would have remembered not feeling fear in that last second before the bomb hit.

Even though their eyes followed the bomb's flight path, even though they stared at what would be the epicenter of the crater created by the nuclear device, Gautam's and Blackmon's minds did not even have the time to process the sensations that came next; the intense white heat, and blinding light that was created in that moment. The blast tore across the land and air and the two friends were immolated into vapor before their brains could process the awesome sight, the incredible pain, the ending of it all.

In point of fact, the bomb detonated ten feet above the ground, its sophisticated altimeter sensing the approaching terrain and sending an electronic signal to the trigger mechanism. The twenty-eight-kiloton charge was more than twice the power of the bomb dropped by the United States on Hiroshima in 1944.

The bomb immediately destroyed the small town of Karoo and

everything in it; every human being, every building, truck, piece of mechanical equipment—everything. Its insatiable appetite for oxygen, created just milliseconds after the initial detonation, sucked air like a tremendous vacuum. The mine works collapsed as the air was sucked from the entrance to the mine shaft, crushing the structure in a violent instant.

In the seconds following the blast, oxygen fed the heat and soon a vast ball of fire ricocheted across the landscape in every direction, then jumped skyward. The mushroom cloud. What started in white and blue turned a painted red and orange as it cooled, still wildly hot but diminishing as the air above Karoo tempered the nuclear heat of the radioactive atoms.

In the minutes immediately following the detonation, the mushroom cloud climbed into the blue sky. A rainbow of color crossed black smoke. It stretched half a mile across and arose quickly as its interior hungered for air, which it sought by stretching up and out, the temperature diminishing with each passing moment, the cloud growing, until soon the cloud was at an apex, still held together by the flames, stretched wide and far, a stunning sight, had anyone been able to actually see it. But nobody saw the cloud. All 8,390 inhabitants of Karoo were dead.

And then the mushroom cloud's edges started to tear apart and dissipate. The killer wind drifted aloft in the innocent sky, the destruction of the deserted area just beginning as the fallout settled into the ground, to lie there for a quarter millennium to come.

19

At the Indian Army Base in Leh, Sergeant Noree noticed a bright green spot on the radar screen in front of him. He reached out, tapped the screen with his right index finger, thinking there was a malfunction, but the spot would not go away.

"Lieutenant Ka'ash," said Noree. "Come quickly."

The watch officer, Lieutenant Rasher Ka'ash, walked from his desk and stood behind Noree, leaning in and looking for himself at the screen.

"Where is that?"

"South of here. Karoo, the village."

"The mining town?"

"Yes, sir."

"What is it?" asked Ka'ash.

"I don't know. Technically, if the system is functioning properly, it's telling me this is some sort of fingerprint event."

"Fingerprint—"

"Electronic. A bomb. A big bomb. But it can't be."

"Why not?" asked Ka'ash.

"They don't make bombs that big."

"Check it out," said Lieutenant Ka'ash. "Get a jet over there."

Leh, more than fifty miles north of Karoo, was the closest military facility to the war front. The dispatch team at Leh was heavily involved in the fighting for Skardu, managing the early coordination of the battle and now spearheading the movement of troops into Skardu, working with the command operations center in Udhampur to coordinate. The temporary military hospital at the base had more than five hundred beds, twenty doctors, sixty nurses, and was already overcrowded. Leh also served as IAF's primary rescue and reconnaissance point, running choppers to the front lines, where injured soldiers were picked up and shuttled back to the hospital.

Sergeant Noree studied his screen for a few seconds. When he saw an IAF jet heading back toward the base, he leaned forward, pressed the COMM link.

"Targa Six, this is Leh dispatch," said Noree.

"Go, dispatch," said a voice on Noree's headset.

"Detour east," said Noree into his headset. "I'm programming in the sequence. You'll see it in two."

"Got it," said the pilot. "What am I looking for?"

"This is a visual recon," answered Noree. "Just check it out."

Inside the IAF Su-30MKI attack jet, the pilot punched in the new coordinates, heading across the cloudless sky at seven thousand feet, at more than one thousand miles per hour. The jet flew along the snowcapped peaks of the Ladakh Range heading south. The pilot banked and aimed the jet toward the ground in order to get a better view. He pushed the jet to 1,200 miles per hour, scorching across the deserted, rocky, green and white terrain of the Indus Valley.

The pilot flew toward the V-shaped canyon between Stakna Mountain and Shakti Mountain. For the first time, the pilot realized something was wrong. Between the mountains, as the plane came closer, he saw nothing but black. The pilot moved the throttle back, slowing the jet. Ahead, it was unmistakable now, the sky was black and rising like a wall, stopping at a horizontal line beneath the top of the mountains.

The jet flew past a last peak and into the open valley. He gasped.

"My God," he whispered out loud when he could finally collect himself.

"What?" asked Noree over the headset.

The valley just beyond Stakna and Shakti was on fire. Where there should have been lush green and brown valley, the ground was a plain of low-flung flames and smoke as far as the eye could see. But most shocking of all was what floated above the burning plain, the signature mushroom cloud of an atomic blast. The cloud hung in the air as if in slow motion, a gargantuan cloud of dark gray, red, and black, the top of the cloud arched and round, the bottom a tornado that was connected by flames to the ground.

The pilot forced himself to look away from the mesmerizing sight. He stared at his navigation screen. Karoo was still more than a mile away.

Inside the jet's cockpit, the heat sensor chirped. Instinctively, the pilot banked right, away from the scene.

"Targa Six, I repeat," barked Noree. "What do you have?"

"You're not going to believe this," the pilot said quietly, still stunned. "I think they dropped a nuclear bomb. I'm putting it on video."

The pilot flipped a switch on the dash of the jet. Circling, he again aimed the nose of the Su-30MKI at the mushroom cloud.

"Are you getting that?" the pilot asked.

"Keep filming. I'm patching it to New Delhi."

20

The Cooktown Hotel was a rectangular, slightly dilapidated, tan clapboard building that looked like something out of the old West. It had a second-floor verandah that wrapped around the street-facing sides of the hotel and jutted over the sidewalk below. The hotel was centrally located, popular, but also a tad run-down, the rooms small and plain. There were better places to stay in Cooktown, better places to drink, and better places to eat. Still, it was an institution, a stone's throw from the beach and the Coral Sea.

Inside the hotel's restaurant, called the Top Pub, Jamil sat alone at a chipped and scratched brown Formica table. The restaurant's dozen tables were half filled with tourists. The waitress walked from the kitchen to his table and placed a plate down in front of him. On it sat a pickle, some potato chips, and a thick sandwich on rye bread.

"There ya go," she said. "Vegemite sandwich with a tomato, no onion."

"Thank you," said Jamil. He'd ordered the sandwich upon her recommendation. Jamil knew the Vegemite was without question the worst dish on the menu, yet he pretended to be oblivious. It was meant to be somewhat of an insult, an inside joke, a putover on the stupid Arab tourist.

Jamil smiled and politely examined the sandwich. He looked up at the bar a few tables away. The bar was empty except for a pair of college students, longish hair and tie-dye, one male and one female, who were chatting with the bartender, a short man with wildly unkempt, overgrown curly hair and a big handlebar mustache. The bartender had a thick Australian brogue and was engaged in conversation with the two college students. As he spoke, he kept looking over at him.

Jamil tried not to stare back at the bartender. He picked up the Vegemite sandwich and took a big bite. The taste was like an old sweaty sock; salty, a hint of seaweed or rotten meat; soggy but grainy; disgusting. Some people liked it, particularly if you'd grown up with it, as many Australians had, but a newcomer to Vegemite usually had a different reaction, primarily nausea. More than one customer over the years, upon trying Vegemite for the first time, had outright puked on their plate after taking a bite.

Of course, this is precisely why the waitress had recommended it. It's why the bartender kept looking over. Jamil knew all this. But after growing up in a poor madrasa and sometimes going for days without food, then spending a year at Hezbollah's Jaffna camps, eating whatever was fed to them by their sadistic al-Muqawama captains, he could eat anything. With a grin on his face, he powered down the sandwich, then licked the soupy brown Vegemite that spilled over onto his fingertips. He left the chips and the pickle on the plate.

"Lookie there, will you," said the waitress, smiling at Jamil after he'd finished. "Would ya like another?"

"No, thanks. I'm stuffed. But my compliments to the chef."

"Would you like your check?"

"I'm going to have a beer."

"Foster's? It's very good."

"Sounds good."

Jamil nodded, laughing to himself. Even he knew Foster's was considered piss water by Australians.

Jamil had spent the morning with Ahmed, driving to the village of Lakeland in the north. He left Ahmed at the Lakeland Downs Motel then doubled back to Cooktown. After arriving in Cooktown, he walked up and down the main street then down to the pier. After lunch, he'd get a hotel room somewhere, maybe right here or someplace slightly more run-down. The harder the environment, the worse the food, the more he felt himself sacrificing, the more proud Jamil became. If he didn't need to occasionally make a phone call in private, Jamil would've been happy to sleep behind a tree. He was gaunt, but all muscle. After running IEDs across the Iranian border to Iraq the last four years, Australia was cake.

In Jamil's backpack was more than a hundred thousand dollars Australian, and he had no problem spending it. He knew Aswan Fortuna was a billionaire. Being cheap was about self-abuse. It was about reliving the sacrifices others had made in the name of Hezbollah.

"Here you go," said the waitress, sliding him a pint of beer. "One Foster's, super large. Enjoy that for a bit, how 'bout."

"Thank you."

Jamil sipped the beer and stared at the rows of liquor bottles behind the bar. He listened to the two students and the bartender. They were describing the surfing off of Melbourne to the bartender and he was giving them directions to a local surfing spot he thought they would appreciate. Of course, Jamil wondered if he was fucking with them too. He had no doubt that if *he* asked for a decent surfing spot, within five minutes of getting in the water he'd get eaten by a shark.

Jamil grinned to himself, drinking slowly and biding his time. *We will win,* he thought to himself. *For every ounce of hatred you have for us, we will burn a pound of flesh. Look down upon me. Call me whatever you want. But soon I will make you pay. Your children, your grandchildren; the day is coming.* These were the thoughts that got Jamil through the Vegemite, through the glass of warm, watery Foster's.

He'd been in Australia for nearly a month now, searching for the the American, Andreas. He was prepared to stay as long as it took.

He remembered Ahmed's words as he left him at the motel

entrance: "Don't mention his name. Don't ask questions. People already suspect you of being a terrorist. You're a tourist. If you hear or see anything, Tweet immediately."

Jamil sat at his table and sipped his beer. Beneath his windbreaker, he felt the silencer on his HK USP .45 caliber handgun jabbing into his left side, beneath his armpit. Eventually, the students left the bar. The bartender wiped down the bar with a blue rag and walked in and out of the kitchen, whistling the entire time.

Later, a pair of middle-aged men, both sunburned, came in and sat at the bar. They spoke with the bartender about the Great Barrier Reef. The bartender clearly liked the two tourists, who were drinking gin and tonics and laughing. Jamil ordered a second beer, still eavesdropping. These two were easier to listen in on; Cockney accents from working-class Britain.

"So what do people do around here, besides work the tourists?"

"There's a bunch of stations inland," said the bartender. "Mainly cattle. Just wait around. The hands get awfully thirsty around dinnertime. They'll try and push you right offa those stools too."

"I heard a story about a rancher saving a little girl's life," said one of the tourists. "They were talking about it at the hotel."

"Happened at Chasvur, twenty minutes north of town," said the bartender. "One of the ranchers climbed a sheer rock face in the pitch-black."

Jamil heard the words and felt a chill run up his spine. He stepped to the bar.

"Pardon me," Jamil said to the bartender, interrupting his next story. "Did you just say that a man climbed a cliff in the dark to save a girl?"

"A two-hundred-foot-tall cliff. But that wasn't the half of it. He did it during a driving rainstorm. Climbed straight up Percy's Ledge. Bare-handed. An American, I heard. Tough son of a bitch."

Jamil stared for an extra moment at the bartender. He was about to ask, Who was it? The words were on the tip of his tongue. But then, he realized, he didn't need to ask.

128

21

CHURCH ROAD
NEW DELHI, INDIA

More than five hundred miles south of the Kashmir war front, the air in downtown New Delhi sweltered. The sun beat down relentlessly on the city, on the crowds of people walking, lining the streets, sitting in cafés. Near the Kendriya Bus Terminal, a ruckus ensued along Church Road as the bright red and blue lights appeared in the distance followed soon thereafter by the high-pitched tone of the sirens.

At the lead, several police officers on motorcycles cleared the boulevard of people, forcing them off to the sides of the road. Soon, the motorcade came barreling down the road, cruising at more than sixty miles per hour, the sirens piercing the air.

The motorcycles were followed by vans that contained sophisticated equipment that enabled secure communication between the inhabitants of the vehicles in the motorcade and other parties, such as the Indian Ministry of Defense. Following the vans, four black Range Rovers, lift gates opened, gunmen strapped to the backs, their automatic weapons out, cocked to fire. After the Range Rovers, long, dark limousines were interspersed with more large SUVs.

Inside the seventh vehicle, a long, black, heavily fortified Mercedes-Benz limousine, President Rajiv Ghandra sat in the backseat.

Ghandra, at fifty-four years old, looked younger than his age. He had brown eyes that were framed by a chiseled face and a sharp nose. Ghandra's longish black hair was parted neatly in the middle. He wore a dark gray suit, a stylish blue button-down shirt, and a blue and red tie. The one unusual aspect to his demeanor, a thin scar above his right eye, only added to the allure that made Ghandra so popular, especially with women.

A former IAF pilot, Ghandra had been elected to Parliament at the age of thirty-one. Now, in his second term as president, he looked as calm and serene as he did the first day of his presidency, completely unflappable, supremely confident, totally laid-back. He stared out the darkened, bulletproof glass of the limousine. His elbow was propped on the armrest, his hand formed into a fist that his jaw now rested on as he studied the crowds.

"Rajiv," said the man next to him, "you should read this before you go on television."

The man speaking was Indra Singh, India's minister of defense. A short, dark-skinned, bald, stout man with an unruly mustache across his pudgy face, Singh had served in the IAF with Ghandra. The two men were also best friends. Singh was the only member of Ghandra's cabinet allowed to call Ghandra by his first name.

"Did you hear me?" Singh repeated. "The casualty count approaches twenty thousand. They'll ask you about that. You don't want to look unprepared."

Ghandra glanced at his friend, who sat poring over the papers in front of him.

"Thank you," said President Ghandra. "Do you think I'm a fucking idiot? The last thing I will talk about is body count."

"Why? Are you crazy? This will be watched by the entire country. The death count is mounting, and all at the hands of El-Khayab. Our countrymen need to become angry. We need their support."

"They're already angry. *Look at them.* Be careful how much you stoke the fire because if it gets too hot it will burn the house down."

130

"Telling the people that casualties are mounting will rally them, Rajiv."

"The casualty count is at a pace that scares even me. If this war is ever going to end, there will need to be some sort of diplomatic settlement. If we get the Indian people too upset, that will be a practical impossibility."

"Your mind is obviously made up," said Singh.

"I need you to fight the war in Kashmir." Ghandra patted his friend on the knee. "I don't need your advice on communicating with the people of India. Had I relied on your political advice, I wouldn't have been elected dogcatcher of Chennai."

"What do you really think of my advice, Mr. President?" Singh laughed. He folded his papers and looked out the window. The crowds were packed tight as they came closer to the capitol building. "Still, I'm worried by what you say. We've acquired more than ten thousand square miles of Baltistan in less than three days. Are you suggesting we go back to the Line of Control?"

"We're in the process of possibly losing Kargil and the Mushkoh Valley," snapped Ghandra. "Have you forgotten that? Pakistan now has as much leverage as we do. Maybe more."

"We're not going to lose Kargil," barked Singh defensively, reaching up and loosening his tie. He was sweating and he wiped his brow with his sleeve. "Northern Command has it under control, or will soon."

"At what cost?" asked Ghandra. "Our boys are dying by the hundreds every hour."

"Would you negotiate back to the Line of Control?" asked Singh. "What if you knew we were going to retake Kargil, which we will, I assure you. Would you give up what we've taken in Baltistan?"

"To get Kargil back, yes," said Ghandra. "We've taken Skardu and its mountains and yak herders, all the while ceding much more important territory. If we don't watch out, El-Khayab is going to march right into Srinagar and then where are we? This thing has to cool down at some point."

"Your words concern me, Mr. President."

"Why?" asked Ghandra, a tinge of anger in his voice. "Do you think I don't have resolve? Of course I do. Who authorized the movement toward Skardu? I'm just realistic. Did you read the remarks by the president of France? He's right. At some point, self-defense becomes suicide. Kashmir is beautiful but the only thing we've acquired is a few million tons of copper, some cornfields, and yak milk. Do we really need all of this? The Line of Control has served as an effective buffer."

"So tell the prime minister to call the insane one and negotiate a settlement," said Singh. "I don't completely agree with you, but I support you. If that is to be our destiny, then let's save some lives."

A loud ringing noise reverberated in the back of the limousine. On the right door, the phone came to life, flashing red. A second later, Singh's cell phone chimed loudly.

Ghandra reached over and pressed a button on the console of the car phone.

"Mr. President, General Kashvili."

"What is it, General?"

"I'm sorry to report, sir, the Pakistanis have dropped a nuclear bomb."

At Parliament House, Ghandra's motorcade entered the underground parking garage, quickly moved in a 180-degree arc, and reexited the building. The motorcade sped up, moving back in the opposite direction. A minute later, the motorcade was joined overhead by a pair of black Mil Mi-35 attack choppers, guarding from the sky. The motorcade barreled down Church Road back toward the Presidential Palace, Rashtrapati Bhavan.

Five minutes later, in an underground parking lot beneath Rashtrapati Bhavan, Ghandra and Singh climbed from the back of the Mercedes limousine. Met by a line of armed soldiers, they walked to a waiting elevator then descended six stories to a secure room designed to withstand a nuclear blast, the "Security Room."

Gathered in the room was President Ghandra's war cabinet: Priya

Vilokan, the prime minister and head of the country's Nuclear Command Authority; General Praset Dartalia, the chief of army staff, India's highest-ranking military officer; Guta Morosla, the secretary of the Research and Analysis Wing; Vijay Ranam, the home secretary; and Rajiv Channar, the national security advisor. An assortment of other aides were also in the room. The large conference table was filled with phones, coffee cups, and computer screens. The walls of the large, windowless room were lined with plasma screens. A series of workstations were staffed by military personnel monitoring Karoo from various altitudes and perspectives.

As Ghandra and Singh entered the room, it went silent. He removed his tie and tossed it to an aide. He stepped to a large plasma screen on the wall displaying a series of grainy black-and-white photographs taken by the pilot of the mushroom cloud over Karoo.

The occupants of the room watched Ghandra as he stared at the photos on the screen. Indra Singh soon joined him.

Finally, Ghandra spoke. "Let's hear what you have."

"Yes, sir," said General Dartalia, the chief of army staff, India's top military officer. "We believe the bomb was dropped by a Pakistani jet, approximately thirty-seven minutes ago. It was dropped on a remote part of Kashmir, a small mining town called Karoo, population around eight thousand. The town's inhabitants are presumed dead."

"Do we have any reports of more bombs?" asked Ghandra.

"No, sir," said Dartalia. "That doesn't mean they're not coming. We're monitoring by satellite and by radar from every military base in Kashmir and across the LOC. If Pakistan drops another bomb, we'll know immediately."

Ghandra finally looked away from the screen, turned to the large conference room table. He walked to his seat at the end, nodded at an aide, indicating that he wanted a cup of coffee.

"Why?" asked Ghandra as he sat down, wiping perspiration from his brow with his shirt sleeve. "What happened? Is it the first part of a larger strike?"

"It's surgical," said Morosla, the head of RAW. "A message. If they were truly attempting to harm India, why select this location?

They wanted to go all the way and detonate a nuclear weapon, but in a place we wouldn't care enough about to come back and wipe out their cities."

"It makes no sense," said Ghandra.

"El-Khayab is insane, we all suspected it," said Singh, the minister of defense.

"They're gauging our response," said Morosla. "If we don't respond, this could embolden them. They could launch another, then another."

President Ghandra sipped his cup. He stood up as he did so, then slammed the cup down on the table, spilling coffee all over the table.

"So what's your counsel?" asked Ghandra.

"Before I review military options, I recommend we put between ten and fifteen Tupolevs in the air, armed with nuclear-tipped missiles. This will serve as a precaution while we formulate a more appropriate response. We would position these bombers in a high-altitude circuit at the border. This way, should El-Khayab have more nuclear devices on the way, we can decide then if we are to use these weapons and will be in a position to do so immediately. This is solely your decision. Unlike a normal tactical defensive position, the movement of nuclear weapons requires an executive order from the president of India."

Ghandra polled his war cabinet. There was no dissension.

"Get the Tupolevs in the air, General," said Ghandra.

Dartalia picked up a phone on the table. "Air Marshal Barbora, this is General Dartalia. I am authorizing protocol four with WAC being the command operative."

Dartalia repeated the command, then reached forward and typed a series of numbers into the console. He hung up the phone and returned to the table.

"Go on, General," said President Ghandra.

Dartalia picked up an electronic remote and aimed it at the large plasma screen on the wall. The black-and-white photo of the bomb was replaced by a topographical map of India and Pakistan. He clicked the remote again and the lines that defined the borders of the two countries appeared in bright orange on the screen. The word "China," at the northern border of Kashmir, appeared ominously in red.

"The following war scenarios have been developed and regularly updated over the past decade," said Dartalia. "These are hypothetical scenarios, and are intended to predict what will happen under three alternative responses available to India."

General Dartalia clicked the remote. A large red dot appeared on the screen, where Karoo was located.

"Option one," said Dartalia. "Under this scenario, India responds proportionally, an eye for an eye, dropping a nuclear bomb on a remote village in Pakistan."

He clicked the remote. A bright green dot appeared on the map, above a village in southern Pakistan.

"This is the hypothetical bomb footprint of our first nuclear device, dropped on a village in south Pakistan."

He clicked the remote again.

"At this point, as you can imagine, Pakistan responds," continued Dartalia. "The cycle is joined. Pakistan strikes a larger area, perhaps two bombs this go-round, higher-density population centers. India counters, again proportionally, as we recognize we cannot let the Pakistanis gain the advantage. Soon, within hours, the two countries are literally emptying their nuclear arsenals."

The screen showed a progression of green and red dots until the map was consumed in green and red dots representing the nuclear bombs.

"Ironically, the fastest destruction of the two countries comes from this kind of proportional, incremental attack framework," said Dartalia. "By attempting to control ourselves and limit damage, we end up inflicting the most destruction in the quickest time frame possible."

"Option two." He clicked the remote. The screen erased the colored bomb prints, except for the single red dot over Karoo. "Under this scenario, India recognizes the implications of responding. India plays the adult and doesn't counterattack. We rely upon the United Nations, diplomacy, and conventional military power to respond to the attack on Karoo. The results will surprise I think everyone, as they surprised me."

He clicked the remote. A radius of red dots burst onto the Indian portion of the map.

"New Delhi's lack of response is taken as a sign of weakness. Pakistan moves with a decisive second wave intended to wipe us out, and they do so. Under this scenario, as you see, we manage only moderate counterdamage as we were unable or unwilling to move decisively and the Pakistanis remove much of our nuclear arsenal in a brutal second wave."

General Dartalia clicked the remote. The screen was again wiped clean.

"In addition, under option two, we believe there's another potentially dangerous outcome if India does not counterattack immediately."

He clicked the remote. From the top of the screen, red lines with arrows at their tips shot down across the screen from China.

"China moves to annex India," continued Dartalia. "The Chinese would manufacture any variety of reasons; to maintain order, to prevent Pakistan from doing further damage. But the bottom line is, China covets India and would see a lack of response by India to the Pakistani nuclear attack as weakness, as well as a sign that the Americans have chosen to avoid being dragged into the theater. To move into India with large numbers of ground troops would be easy for the Chinese. Already, they have more than half a million troops along the Aksai Chin. Unfortunately, this is another very real scenario."

Dartalia reached down and picked up a bottle of water, took a large gulp, then walked back to his place at the conference table.

"Option three," he said, looking at Ghandra.

Dartalia clicked the remote. Pakistan was quickly illuminated by a progression of green dots that soon overtook the plasma screen. Over India, a few red dots appeared.

"Under scenario three, we move to erase the Pakistani threat. We launch a full-scale nuclear counterstrike, targeting large population centers, military-industrial complexes, transportation assets, power grid, water sources. We wipe Pakistan off the map. We bomb them, as they say, 'back to the Stone Age.'"

Dartalia paused. He sipped from his water bottle.

"As hard as it might be to contemplate the thought of destroying an entire country," continued Dartalia, "the bottom line is that under option three, India limits its own casualties to under one million citizens. There will be some damage due to fallout that drifts back into the southern and western regions of India as well as casualties from the few nuclear devices Islamabad will get off before we destroy the rest. But even so, the losses are relatively insignificant. Now, as for world opinion and other such matters, I have no comment. That's not what I'm paid to think about. But there's no question that, from a military perspective, option three has the greatest likelihood of success. It is the best *military* option for India."

Dartalia stood in front of the screen for several moments then walked to his seat at the conference table and sat down.

"Thank you, General," said President Ghandra. He looked around the table, his eyes settling on Indra Singh, the defense minister. "This isn't acceptable. There have to be other options. Why would El-Khayab up the stakes like this?"

"We need to strike back immediately," interrupted Singh, looking at the president. "There's no use contemplating *why* he did this. He did it. It's that simple. And right now, a delayed response by you, Mr. President, will be misinterpreted."

"I agree with Indra," said Priya Vilokan, the prime minister. "There are geopolitical issues at play here. If we don't hit back—hit back immediately, hit back hard—we're sending a message to El-Khayab and to Beijing. We're saying, come into our land, kill our people, use your most fearsome weapons, your nuclear weapons, it's okay. We'll fume and get angry, but in the end we will do *nothing*. In turn, this message spreads. It has unintended consequences. It will be seen by the Chinese, hungry at our northern border. We must respond, even if we do not want to. That's the point. We *must* respond, President Ghandra."

The prime minister pounded the table with his fist. His face flushed red with anger.

"Even if we decide that the response is proportional, an eye for an eye, even if we select a random town somewhere in the northern territories, we *must* do something," continued Vilokan. "To not fight back is simply too dangerous to our own people. It will harm India for generations to come."

President Ghandra stared at his prime minister, considering his words. He looked to his left, at the oldest man in the room, Vijay Ranam, the Indian home secretary. "And you, Vijay? What do you think? Next to Indra, you're the biggest hawk in India."

"It's a difficult question," said Ranam. "There's no clear-cut answer. Every choice has pitfalls. I'm the only man in this room who fought in the last war with Pakistan, in 1971. We won that war. I met General Arora on the second day of the war. I will never forget him. He was a warrior. I'm a warrior. I fear what happens if we do not hit back, and hit back with overwhelming force."

"A full retaliatory strike?" asked Ghandra.

"Yes, Mr. President. Option three."

"What of the diplomatic ramifications?"

"Our obligation is to the people of India," said Ranam. "Without question, we will be condemned. Just as America was after Hiroshima. But El-Khayab dropped the first bomb. He struck first. Karoo is our Pearl Harbor."

"We'll be wiping out tens of millions of people."

"More than a hundred million, sir," said Dartalia, "to be accurate. Which is far fewer than if we do nothing."

Ghandra leaned back in his chair. It was a surreal feeling. The world had yet to learn of the nuclear strike. The calls had yet to start pouring in. It was the proverbial calm before the storm. But they would start soon. Soon the world would know that the Pakistanis had changed the course of human events, and done so in dramatic fashion.

"I want to look at a detailed operational plan for option three," President Ghandra said, looking at Dartalia. "You have one hour."

22

DEFENSE INTELLIGENCE AGENCY
DEFENSE INTELLIGENCE OPERATIONS
  COORDINATION CENTER
LEVEL G, ROOM 400
THE PENTAGON
WASHINGTON, D.C.

Four minutes after the detonation of the bomb at Karoo, Defense Intelligence Operations Coordination Center—DIOCC—had picked up the atomic fingerprint of the event.

Occupying a large, windowless suite of offices on the basement level of the Pentagon, it was DIOCC's responsibility to gather and coordinate all relevant information coming from sources across the globe; relevant intercepts from the National Security Agency, CIA, Homeland Security, NORAD, other units of Defense Intelligence Agency, Interpol, MI6, and other foreign intelligence sources. DIOCC's job was to synthesize raw information, and then get the national security apparatus, including the Department of Defense, briefed and moving.

DIOCC had been focusing on the war in Kashmir; nine analysts were tracking developments in the theater of battle between India and Pakistan, around the clock. Still, what Lieutenant Myles Heddeke saw coming in from NORAD, a live-feed satellite shot from an

AWACS lofting 32,000 feet over India, left him momentarily speechless.

Recovering, he said quietly, "I got something." Then, noticing that no one heard him, "Hey, I got something. I think someone dropped a fucking nuke!"

"What do you got, Myles?" asked a middle-aged woman with short-cropped blond hair, Major Anne Callaway, who walked quickly from her desk to Heddeke's desk.

In front of Heddeke sat two large plasma screens, bolted to the cement wall. The central screen collected data from different sources. The right screen showed a topographical map grid, isobars in bright green, a geographic layout of the area around Karoo, in amazing detail. In the middle of the grid pattern, a bright red ball was spread out like cotton candy.

"India-controlled Kashmir," said Heddeke, pointing his finger at the screen. "East of the Line of Control. Near a village called Karoo."

"DOE just confirmed," said a man two desks down from Heddeke. "They're estimating a thirty-four kiloton blast."

"Okay," said Callaway, stepping back, pointing to a young officer across the room. "Let's get this up the tree. This is top priority, to the President, SECDEF, Langley, NSA, et cetera. Immediately."

Callaway picked up the phone.

"Control."

"Get me the president."

President Allaire was seated at the cherrywood breakfast table in the White House residence, reading *The Wall Street Journal*. The phone on the wall rang loudly. He put down the piece of English muffin in his right hand and hit the button for the speakerphone.

"Yes."

"Mr. President, this is Major Anne Callaway at DIOCC. Pakistan dropped a nuclear bomb on India, sir."

"When?"

"Approximately five minutes ago, sir."

"Has India responded?"

"Not yet, Mr. President."

"Is it isolated? Are there more?"

"So far this is the only bomb we've picked up. It was presumably delivered via jet so it will be hard to know whether it's isolated or not for a few minutes."

"How big?"

"Thirty-four kiloton."

"Where?"

"A small town called Karoo in Kashmir."

"How many people."

"We don't know that yet."

"Okay," said the president. "Major, I want you to stay on the line. Control, get the secretary of defense and the rest of the national security directorate over here. *Immediately.*"

President Allaire stood up and pushed the last bite of English muffin into his mouth, ran out of the kitchen, past several attendants, to his office within the personal residence. He knew he had precious few moments. Behind the desk, he hit a red button.

"Yes, Mr. President," the female voice said.

"Get me President Ghandra in New Delhi," said President Allaire. "And find Jessica. I need her up here."

The president stood behind the small, elegant desk, looking out the window, the Washington Monument in the distance. He had to think clearly now. He stared at the black phone in his hand.

After less than a minute, the warm voice of Rajiv Ghandra came on the line.

"Mr. President."

"Rajiv, I'm deeply sorry for what's happened."

"Me too," said Ghandra, a trace of bitterness in his voice. "As you can imagine, I can't talk for long."

"How many casualties?"

"Eight to ten thousand. We won't know for a few hours."

"I'm urging you to hold off retaliation until we can analyze the strike and discuss with various back channels what has happened and why," said Allaire.

"My country is under attack," snapped Ghandra, his voice rising. "It's time for New Delhi to conduct its own war council. At this point India and America's interests are not necessarily aligned."

"You're wrong. They *are* aligned. The actions you take in the next few hours impact the U.S. I'm asking you to take the time to properly analyze the options before you."

"What is there to analyze?" asked Ghandra, exasperation in his voice. "The Pakistanis dropped a *nuclear bomb*."

"Is it the only one?"

"We don't know."

"Was it a rogue group within the Pakistani military?"

"Again, I don't know."

"Are there more bombs in the air right now?"

"We're looking and right now the answer is we don't know."

"If you launch a retaliatory strike immediately, even though the facts and circumstances surrounding this first nuclear device are as yet unknown, and Pakistan counters, by dinnertime India and Pakistan are both gone," said Allaire. "Give America time to help India figure out what is best for India. This could be an isolated attack by a crazed El-Khayab. It could've been done by a rogue within Pakistan Armed Forces. It will inflame the world. China will share your anger, as will Russia and the rest of the civilized world. Your job, your duty, is to do what is best for India."

The phone console was silent for a moment. President Allaire looked up as Jessica came sprinting into the room.

"I am told that I need to move my location. I will need to call you back."

"Do I have your commitment, Rajiv, that you'll give the U.S. adequate time to help you develop a strategy?"

"I cannot do that. However, I will take your advice to heart."

"I'm getting on a plane within the hour," said Allaire, glancing at Jessica, who shook her head. "I'll be in New Delhi in approximately ten hours. I expect the Indian government to hold off a counter-strike until then."

The phone was silent.

"Rajiv, there is no practical difference between launching nuclear weapons right now and waiting until the end of the day. None."

"If they drop more nuclear devices—"

"If Pakistan drops more nuclear bombs all bets are off," said Allaire. "I'm not asking you to commit suicide. I am asking you to give us—India and America together—time to figure this out. The best solution might in fact be a nuclear counterstrike. But let's make that determination with the benefit of information more than ten minutes old."

The console was again silent. Then, Ghandra cleared his throat.

"I'll wait, President Allaire," said Ghandra finally. "Unless something occurs in the interim which requires our immediate action."

"Thank you, Rajiv," said President Allaire. "We'll be airborne in less than an hour. In the meantime, we'll go to work. See you in a few hours."

President Allaire pressed the button on the phone, ending the call.

"I know you've already made up your mind," said Jessica, "but the president of the United States cannot fly into a war zone that's under nuclear attack."

"Good point," said Allaire as he gathered his briefcase and some files. He smiled. "Better wake up the vice president and tell him to push back his tee time."

"I'm not kidding."

"Neither am I. I'm going to New Delhi. This is why I was elected. This is why America is looked to by the people of the world. If I die, I die doing what I'm supposed to be doing."

143

23

LION'S DEN PUB
COOKTOWN

Lion's Den Pub was crowded. As late afternoon gave way to evening, the pub was packed with locals and tourists. Opened in 1875 to serve workers from the now defunct Lion's Den Tin Mine, the pub had a kind of grubby, disheveled, beer-soaked charm, a place where you could have a pleasant conversation with a stranger from another country, but where you also wouldn't be surprised to see a girl stand on top of the bar, remove her shirt, and start dancing.

At a picnic table in the corner sat six men. Despite their best efforts not to do so, they looked serious, their eyes darting about the room nervously. In the middle of the table was a pitcher of beer.

A strange-looking man with spiked blond hair walked into the pub, eyed the table, then pushed his way through the crowd.

"Could you have picked a place any more inconvenient?" asked Youssef, staring at Jamil. He sat down and grabbed a glass, filled it with beer, then chugged half of it quickly. "And by the way, where did these fucking Aussies learn to drive? I have never seen so many shitty fucking drivers in my goddamn life."

"Youssef, you said find a place near Cooktown," said Jamil, "but out of the way."

"Whatever," said Youssef. "It doesn't matter. Okay, let's get to work."

Youssef took a pack of Dunhill reds from his coat pocket. He lit one and blew smoke into the air.

"Mind if I have one?" asked one of the men at the table.

"Sure," said Youssef. "Next time, buy your own goddamn pack. What do I look like, a fucking charity?"

A buxom, red-haired waitress approached the table.

"Another tank of Victoria's?" she asked, looking at Youssef.

"Sure," said Youssef.

He waited for the waitress to leave.

"Did you see those butter bags?" he asked, polling the table as he pretended to squeeze a set of imaginary breasts. "Mamma mia. Okay, where's the list?"

Ahmed pulled a piece of paper out from his pants pocket.

"It's a list of bars around here," said Ahmed, "like you asked."

"Good."

"We'll cover each bar in Cooktown. Jamil and I each will have to cover two bars."

"What if he doesn't go out?" someone asked.

"Then we go out tomorrow night," said Youssef. "And the next night. And the night after that. We need to be patient."

Youssef took a big sip from his glass, then pulled a photo from his back pocket. It showed Dewey; the same photograph Nebuchar had obtained, of Dewey receiving the Medal of Freedom.

"This is him," whispered Youssef. "Andreas. Dewey Andreas. Pass it around. He might not have short hair anymore. He might have a beard. He's big."

The photo was passed around.

"This is important: if you see him, Tweet. Then the rest of us converge. He was Delta Force. He's trained and he's dangerous. I don't want any one of us to take him one-on-one if we don't absolutely have to. We need to surprise him, then overwhelm him."

"What if he suspects one of us?"

145

"If he suspects you, or if he starts to leave, then kill him. Most likely he'll be drinking and we'll have time. Don't act obvious. Don't be nervous. You're a tourist, remember. Just Tweet, let everyone else know where you are, then we'll kill him. No problems. Got it?"

The six men at the table nodded.

"As for the rest of you, when you get the message, move. We're getting close. Nebuchar thought it would take us six months to find him. We've been in Australia for just over a month. One fucking month. Let's finish the job. Then we can go home."

Youssef emptied the rest of his beer, poured another one, then pounded that one as well. He stood up.

"Don't fuck up," he whispered, then grabbed the photo from Jamil's hand. He placed it on the table, then took the last of his cigarette and pressed the burning ember against the photo, burning a hole in the middle of Dewey's forehead.

24

Dewey opened the drawer on the small table next to his bed. He pulled out a black-and-white photo of Jessica, taken from a newspaper article. She had a serious look on her face, but he could also see a hint of her pretty Irish grin. Dewey had other photos, photos of Jessica and him together, but for some reason he liked to look at the newspaper clipping.

He walked down the hallway to the phone. He looked around then dialed the phone number he'd committed to memory. The phone clicked several times, then, after several moments of scratchy silence, the phone began ringing.

"White House," said a female voice. "How may I direct your call?"

"Jessica Tanzer."

"Hold."

Another ring, then a male voice:

"Office of the national security advisor, how may I assist you?"

"Jessica Tanzer, please."

"May I ask who's calling?"

"Dewey Andreas, returning her call."

"Hold, please."

Dewey waited on hold for nearly a minute, then the phone beeped.

"Dewey," said the slightly faint voice of Jessica.

"Hi, Jess."

"I can't talk for very long. How are you? How's Australia? Sembler Ranch?"

"Station."

"Station?"

"Sembler Station. They call them 'stations' down here."

"Why?"

"I haven't figured it out yet. But I certainly intend to."

Jessica laughed.

"It's nice to hear your voice," she said.

"Yours too. Where are you? The reception is terrible."

"I'm on a plane," said Jessica. "I need to be quick. I'm sorry."

"What's up?"

"The CIA picked up information. Aswan Fortuna knows you're in Australia. He has people in-country. They're searching for you, paying people off, that sort of thing. You're not safe."

Dewey felt a small surge of adrenaline.

"How close are they?"

"Australia Federal Police turned a two-man cell outside of Melbourne. They had a trunk full of cash and a manila folder on you. Photos. Two ex-Al-Muqawama."

"Al-Muqawama?"

"Hezbollah. They both committed suicide before AFP could extract any information. There's also evidence of a team in Sydney trying to buy off ONA agents."

"When was all this?"

"The Melbourne cell was a week ago. The Sydney incident was two days ago."

"So it sounds like they're not very close."

"Dewey, that's two cells. There could be a hundred. Let me send a plane to get you."

"I'm as safe here as anywhere. He's going to look for me wherever I am."

"He's not going to leave it alone."

"So kill him. You know where he lives. You can take him out if you're that worried about it."

"You know it's more complicated than that. We kill Fortuna and all of the sudden there's ten billion dollars in the war coffers of Hezbollah, Al-Qaeda, Hamas, and all the rest of them."

"Jess, you know I understand how things work. We just disagree on this one. If you want to beat our enemies we need to kill them. America can't be afraid to kill. It's that simple. We need to kill as many of them as possible as often as possible."

"Why didn't you use one of the aliases Hector gave you?"

"I'm not going to hide."

"You *are* hiding."

Dewey looked down the hallway behind him, thinking he'd heard someone come up the stairs.

"Thank you for the warning. But you don't need to worry about me."

"Maybe I *want* to worry about you."

Dewey paused, in silence.

"Are you still there?" she asked.

"Yeah." Dewey heard footsteps on the stairs at the end of the hall. Talbot leaned his head around the corner.

"You coming?" Talbot asked.

Dewey ignored the question.

"Well, that's why I called," said Jessica. "I have to run."

"I'll let you know if they kill me," said Dewey.

"You think it's all a joke. That's fine. Laugh your way through life. Then you can look back in fifty years, alone, and think of all the great laughs you had. Goodbye."

"I don't think it's a—"

"Take care, Dewey," interrupted Jessica. The line went dead.

Back in his room, the noise from the other ranch hands, drinking, playing pool, partying on this Saturday night, came from the great room a floor below. Dewey pulled his boots on, put some money in his pocket, then got down on his knees in front of his clothes bureau and ran his hand along the underside. He felt a slight rise from the edge of a piece of duct tape. He ripped the duct tape off and pulled out a .45 caliber handgun. Colt M1911. He hadn't looked at it or really even thought about it since he taped it there the day he moved in more than a year ago. He ripped the duct tape off the butt of the weapon.

He reached back under. Next to where the handgun had been, he found another piece of tape. Dewey pulled out a long, eight-inch black steel Gerber combat blade. He glanced at the knife, black and silver with a patina of scratches. On one side, his initials were engraved. On the other side, one word: "Gauntlet."

Standing, he opened the top drawer of the bureau, reached in back, and removed a worn leather knife sheath that he fastened to his left ankle.

He heard footsteps. Then a knock at the door.

"Yo, beauty queen," said Talbot. "Everyone's left. You ready?"

Dewey tucked the handgun into the small of his back. He strapped the knife to his left calf inside the sheath. He put on his leather coat. He stepped to the door and opened it.

"Let's hit it," said Dewey.

Cooktown was a small beachside town that sat along a meandering strip of white powder beaches and rocky coast. Just offshore, the Great Barrier Reef crested less than ten miles away. The town attracted mainly British, European, and Asian tourists. A main strip ran for a mile through the middle of Cooktown. On one side was the water. The boardwalk above it was crowded with people out for a stroll. On the other side of the street, facing the beach, shops, restaurants, and bars were open.

Talbot drove the F-150 the length of the strip. Finally, he pulled onto a small lane about halfway up the strip and parked. Dewey and Talbot walked several blocks to a crowded bar called Whitey's. Talbot pushed his way to the bar and ordered a beer.

"What do you want?" the bartender asked.

"Two Jacks and a beer."

A pair of seats opened up and they sat down. Dewey looked about the room, seeing mostly couples.

Talbot was a large Aussie with short blond hair, a deep tan, and a constant smile on his face. At twenty-four, he'd worked Sembler Station for nearly five years, signing on after graduating from high school in Cairns. Talbot and Dewey chatted about the ranch, while Talbot kept his eyes trawling for females. Soon, he started a conversation with a stunning Australian woman. She moved between Talbot and Dewey, speaking with Talbot. After a few minutes, she turned from Talbot and attempted to engage Dewey in conversation.

"Hi," she said. "Fun place, isn't it?"

Dewey pretended not to hear her.

When she turned back to Talbot, Dewey glanced in her direction. Her long brown hair framed a distinct face, golden tan, freckles, a sharp nose, stunning blue eyes; aristocratic beauty. The more Dewey ignored her, the more she focused her attention on him, until, finally, Talbot found himself being completely ignored. He looked around and found a Frenchwoman, in her forties, with long blond hair and a slightly wrinkled face. Soon, the woman was standing between Talbot's legs, next to the bar.

"Looks like your friend found his soul mate," said the young Australian woman.

Dewey looked up from the wood of the bar, glancing to his right at Talbot. He smiled but said nothing.

"Is there a reason you won't talk with me? I won't bite. Promise."

"It's not you."

He stared down the bar, keeping his eyes low, watching the line of people.

"Then why won't you look at me?"

"I did," said Dewey, looking into her eyes. "You're too young for me."

"I'm not looking for a relationship. I'm looking for an intelligent conversation."

"Well, you've definitely come to the wrong place."

"Where in the States are you from?"

Dewey sipped his Jack Daniel's, then nodded to the bartender and ordered another along with a beer for Talbot, who was face-to-face with the Frenchwoman, giggling and kissing.

"Oh, really," the young beauty said, over Dewey's shoulder. "That part. Hmmm. I really like that part of the States. So beautiful."

Dewey flipped the bartender some cash. "Whatever she's having," he said to the bartender, nodding to the girl without looking at her.

"No, thank you," she said as the bartender looked at her for her order. "I don't let guys buy me drinks who aren't willing to speak with me."

"Whatever." He took the cash, left a few dollars' tip, then put the rest in his pocket.

After several minutes, the young woman leaned in, against the bar, and pushed her face in front of Dewey's.

"You have very blue eyes," she said, smiling. "My name is Charlotte."

Charlotte's face was now just a few inches from Dewey's. Her eyes were as blue as sapphire, her lips red and voluptuous, her beauty simply dramatic at such a close distance. She shook her head back and forth, staring into his eyes, a quizzical look on her face.

"I've been on the cover of Australian *Vogue* twice. I received double firsts at Oxford. And yet I can't get a word out of you. You really do intrigue me."

"Trust me, there isn't anything here to be intrigued about."

"I'll be the judge of that. Isn't there anything nice you can say?"

"I like your name."

"It was my great-grandmother's name. Thank you."

"Do you want that drink now?"

"Sure. Grey Goose and water, lime."

She remained in front of him. She seemed slightly inebriated.

"So are you going to tell me where you're from?"

"Maine. Do you know where that is?"

"Yes. I've been there. L.L. Bean's. Mosquitoes."

Her eyes were warm. She brushed her hand on his right knee then left it there.

"I'm from farther up. A town called Castine."

"What brought you here?" Charlotte removed her hand from his knee, reached up and took a sip from her drink.

"A job, that's all."

"Station hand?"

"Yes."

"What station?"

Dewey smiled but didn't answer. "Where are you from, Charlotte?"

"Melbourne," she said. "Have you been there?"

"Sure."

"By the way, name please? Wait, let me guess. Chet? No, not Chet. Bill? Boris? Bart? Bleck? Blick?" Charlotte giggled. "Jim? Jim-Bob? Jim-Bob. I knew it. Okay. I give up."

"Dewey."

"Dewey? Dewey. Okay. I like that. Probably the first and last Dewey I'll ever meet. Actually, I love it."

"What are you doing out here?"

"We have a station. It's called Masters. That's my last name."

"I've heard of it."

"We come out here in the summer. At least, I do. I have two older sisters. They don't really come anymore."

"Why do you come?"

"The quiet," she said, sipping her drink. "I like to ride. Mostly I like to be off on my horse. Hearing nothing. Seeing no one."

Dewey smiled. "I like that too."

Charlotte leaned down, put her face near Dewey's, leaned forward, made a slightly awkward, goofy smile, then moved forward and kissed him on the lips. She stayed there for one, then two, then five seconds. She moved her head back.

"Oh, Dewey, why can't you be at our ranch? I could just stare at you all day."

Dewey tasted lime from her lips and smelled the warmth of her breath. He reached his right hand out and placed it on her hip. He looked again at the stunning blue of her eyes.

Behind her brown hair, in the mirror of the bar: a glint.

His attention was drawn behind her.

The momentary freeze of one eye. Darkness, dark eyes, a glint in one man's black eyes, one instant: *anger.*

He processed the sight. Reflected in the mirror was a man. He stood near the back wall, staring at Dewey.

25

Six stories below ground, Jessica stepped out of the elevator. President Allaire and President Ghandra both waited for her to exit before them. Hector Calibrisi from the CIA, Tim Lindsay, the secretary of state, and Harry Black, the secretary of defense, stepped out next, followed by a pair of Deltas, who had been on board since Andrews.

In the hallway stood four armed soldiers from India's Special Protection Group, rifles clutched chest high, pointed sideways.

The group walked down the corridor and into the Security Room, equivalent to the White House Situation Room; a top secret, highly secure room beneath the Presidential Compound where the most important discussions in government took place. Ghandra's war cabinet was already waiting inside the Security Room as President Allaire stepped inside.

Jessica glanced up at Calibrisi as they came to the end of the hallway just outside the entrance to the Security Room. He grinned at her. His smile, at that moment, sent a warm calm through her body.

Jessica knew, as did Calibrisi, that the coming meeting was nearly incalculable in its importance—and its danger. Its outcome could serve to bring the two nuclear powers, India and Pakistan, back from the brink of mutual destruction. Alternatively, the meeting could lead to the destruction of both countries and the involvement of the United States in a broader theater war that would inevitably involve China.

"Here we go," Jessica whispered to Calibrisi before entering the Security Room.

"Let's make this quick," Calibrisi said quietly to Jessica, "before El-Khayab drops one on the building."

"*Not* funny, Hector."

The flight to New Delhi had taken ten hours. They traveled on a specially designed Gulfstream G650—faster than production models, and designated as Air Force One due to the president's presence aboard the craft. Luxurious on the inside, the jet had souped-up Rolls-Royce engines, room for extra fuel, and was equipped with a variety of systems designed to cloak its presence in the air, including low-probability-of-intercept radar, specialized radios, laser designators as well as state-of-the-art active defenses and electronic countermeasures.

Throughout the flight, the plane had been surrounded by three U.S. fighter jets—one in front, two behind—at a distance.

The Security Room, six stories beneath the Indian presidential offices, was hot and humid, despite the air-conditioning. As they took their seats, Jessica glanced quickly into the faces of Ghandra's war cabinet. A palpable mood of anxiety clouded the room. Jessica sensed anger, confusion, and exhaustion. Worse, beyond the fatigue, she sensed helplessness, as if the Indian president and his war council did not know what to say or do.

But then, as she moved to the empty chair at the table that was reserved for her, next to President Allaire, Jessica had a stark, fleeting, but powerful realization. Deep down, despite the confidence of her demeanor, despite the carefully planned agenda she, Lindsay, Calibrisi, and the president had worked out on the plane, Jessica realized that she felt helpless as well. This was uncharted land. It was the unknown. So many lives depended on them making the right decision. What was the right decision?

It was precisely this moment the president had looked to Jessica for. This was the crisis she'd been born to face. This wasn't a dream, a book, or a Hollywood movie. This was history being made. Future generations would study the decisions that were about to take place in this sweaty, crowded conference room six stories below the crowded New Delhi streets.

Would Jessica sit silently, take the middle ground of anonymity and mildness? Or, would she help to solve this crisis? Was she a leader?

Trust your instincts, Jessica told herself. *Trust yourself, Jess.*

"Thank you for coming," said President Ghandra, sitting down next to President Allaire. "I wish it was under different circumstances."

"Me too," said President Allaire. "Thank you, all of you, for agreeing to meet with us. I know that you've held off taking action, and I appreciate that."

"To the contrary, Mr. President," said Indra Singh, India's minister of defense. "The Indian government has taken action, and we should update you. First, we've scrambled seventy-two Indian Air Force planes, all armed with nuclear bombs, and these planes are now in the sky. We have also taken those mobile units near the western border and positioned them—"

"Indra, we spoke three times on our flight over," said Jessica. "You never said a thing about this."

"I don't know how secure these transmissions are," interrupted Singh. "We cannot take the risk that Pakistan or China is eavesdropping."

"Let's cut to the chase," said President Allaire, looking at Ghandra. "Has India made the decision to retaliate?"

"Yes," said Ghandra.

"How many bombs are we talking about?" asked Allaire.

"We have seventy-two planes in the air," said Singh. "Each plane holds two devices. Plus the mobile units positioned at the border. India has one hundred and eighty nuclear devices ready to go."

"That would—" began President Allaire.

"Wipe out Pakistan," interrupted Jessica. "Completely, I imagine."

"India has been attacked," Singh began.

"Be quiet, Indra," barked President Ghandra, staring at his minister of defense and oldest friend. He paused, looked blankly down at the table, then turned to Allaire. "If you came here with the expectation that you could convince India to not respond, you've wasted your time, Mr. President. To not respond is not an option. It would be suicide."

"We cannot be pacifists," added Singh, "as you in America might wish us to be. India will not swallow the casualties in Karoo so as not to drag America into a theater war."

"I have not stated an opinion," said President Allaire, anger rising in his voice. "And I don't appreciate you ascribing an opinion or philosophy to me, my people, or my words. America understands that, for New Delhi, not responding is not an option. We agree that to not respond is not an option. Unlike India, America is a country that was born in blood. Our freedom was won with the barrels of our shotguns. We were the country that first dropped nuclear bombs in a foreign land. We are the country that has protected our allies, including India, with the threat of our nuclear arsenal, for more than half a century. So don't any of you sitting in this room think or imply that you know more than we do about protecting India's vital interests, about warfare, or about nuclear weapons. India is about to bite off a responsibility and a set of results whose import and consequence you have no experience with. You simply have no idea how powerful the decision you are making is. This is a real decision and getting it wrong could result in the annihilation of hundreds of millions of people in India, Pakistan, China, and perhaps beyond. Yes, perhaps even in America."

President Allaire trembled as he finished speaking, staring at Indra Singh, then Ghandra.

Jessica felt a shiver move up her spine. She had never seen President Allaire so forceful.

"If you came here to insult us, Mr. President—" said Ghandra calmly.

"This is how allies, how friends, speak to one another," said Allaire, "when one of them is about to alter their own history in such a dramatic and potentially lethal way. You are not about to build an airport. You're not passing a budget, building a dam. You are, all of you, none of you having slept for days, about to make a decision that will wipe out millions of innocent people. And my only point is *not* that you shouldn't do that, but that to say you've already made that decision—without the debate and counsel of your closest ally, the one country who has done this before—is insanity. This meeting should be the one before you make the decision. Not after. Do you understand that? Are you so prideful that you can't admit that you need our help in this decision?"

President Ghandra held his hand in the air. The room became quiet again.

"We are starting off on the wrong foot, Mr. President," Ghandra said. "You're right, we should hear you out. But the clock is ticking. Our silence will only embolden Pakistan. Even worse than Pakistan is China. It lurks like a hungry snake at the border. Furthermore, it would be unwise for you to believe that anything you could say, or do, at this point would alter our sentiment. We are unanimous on this point. India must strike back with nuclear weapons, and we must do so in an overwhelming fashion. This is the only way we can preserve Indian lives."

"This is the very situation that diplomacy was meant for," said Tim Lindsay, the U.S. secretary of state.

"Oh, for God's sake," said Singh, exasperated. "Diplomacy. Everyone wants to talk diplomacy."

"I fought in two wars, Indra," said Lindsay calmly. "I've spilled plenty of blood and I know you have too. I'm willing to do it. But let's take a step back. Let's talk about what diplomatic options, if any, exist."

"Well, Mother Teresa is dead," said Singh. "How about we send, what's his name, from American television, Barney? He can fly to Islamabad and meet with El-Khayab."

"That's funny," Lindsay said flatly, staring at Singh. He turned to Ghandra. "But I ask you, President Ghandra, why not at least try? There is no reason not to try. America, the Chinese, Russia, Europe; the free world is ready to help."

"Say we are successful," interrupted Ghandra. "We prevent more nuclear weapons from being dropped. We keep China at bay. What happens in six days? In six months? Six years?"

"We deal with it then," said Lindsay.

"There won't be a then," said Singh. "Not with the terrorist-sympathizing United Nations, and duplicitous France and Russia, our fair-weather friends."

"Diplomacy is acknowledging our fundamental weakness," interrupted Ghandra calmly. "Read your own report, Secretary Lindsay. It states very clearly that the pursuit of a diplomatic solution will be seen as weakness. Inaction. And this will only invite more peril for my people. If we fall into the lull of a would-be diplomatic solution, we expose ourselves and we rely upon the word of a country and a man who just dropped a nuclear bomb on our people."

"The complexity of your decision is compounded by China," said Jessica. "Privately, they acknowledge the necessity of a hard response. But if India's response goes further than what they believe it should, there will be consequences."

"They have publicly condemned El-Khayab," interrupted Singh. "Privately, they believe the man is insane."

"Indra, have you spoken with anyone in China?" asked Jessica.

"Yes," said Singh.

"How recently?"

"Wednesday."

"Two days ago?" said Jessica. "I've spoken with my counterpart in Beijing no less than eight times since Wednesday. You are absolutely incorrect if you believe China thinks President El-Khayab is insane. China and Pakistan are as tight as peas in a pod. And you are mistaken, by the way, if you believe El-Khayab *is* insane. I wish he was, but he's not. Furthermore, what the Chinese say publicly is irrelevant. Frankly, what they say even privately is irrelevant too. They keep their own counsel. But there are three things that you can be sure of. One, China backs Pakistan over India in this conflict and in any conflict; you are a threat, Pakistan is a weak sister that does what they tell it to. Two, China covets India and its natural resources, particularly in the north. Three, China will respond to opportunities that are created, and they will do so quickly. This is the most important thing to remember. For Beijing, the current conflict represents an opportunity.

"If India alters the chemistry of the region by launching a full-scale nuclear counterstrike," continued Jessica, "China will alter its outlook on the region. So you drop, you said, a hundred and eighty nuclear devices? You destroy Pakistan, okay. I understand. But then how many weapons are left in your arsenal? A few dozen? China has more than five hundred warheads. And unlike India, which has to strap most of its warheads to the underside of an airplane, the Chinese have but to press a few buttons to send their nuclear warheads raining down on this city and every city in India. And trust me, they will do it. And they will probably only need to drop half a dozen nukes before everyone in this room surrenders, or, more likely, you're dead, and the group that follows you amid the terrible carnage surrenders."

The room was silent. Everyone stared at Jessica, and she felt their eyes upon her. A tense silence hung over the room. She glanced at President Allaire, who returned her look with a slight nod.

"So tell us, President Allaire, Secretary Lindsay, Mr. Calibrisi, Ms. Tanzer," said President Ghandra, "what should we do?"

The room was silent.

"We believe we should pursue an aggressive multilateral diplomatic solution," said President Allaire. "We should engage Europe, the UN, China, and Russia. We should give it a week, perhaps two. I will personally manage the crisis, along with Secretary Lindsay."

Jessica glanced at President Ghandra, whose eyes stared down at his lap and his hands that were crossed on top of it. Ghandra shook his head slightly, then looked at Singh, his minister of defense. They exchanged glances. Ghandra's eyes then moved to Priya Vilokan, his foreign minister.

"Thank you, President Allaire," interrupted Ghandra. "And thank you all for coming. We have listened to you. America is our greatest friend, and today reminds us why. Our shared desire for freedom and peace for our people ties us together. But today you have told us nothing we do not know. Your ideas are ones we've considered and rejected. We rejected them because they will not work. India faces its gravest hour. Diplomacy is the equivalent of not responding. If you don't believe me, ask Neville Chamberlain. Indra and I thought you would come here with an argument for a proportional nuclear counterattack. We would have rejected that too, but at least it would have made some sense."

President Allaire smiled. He reached out to his coffee cup and took a final sip, drained the cup, then put it back on the conference table.

"The Pakistanis have dropped a nuclear bomb on our country," said Singh, leaning forward, pounding the table with his right fist, his face red with emotion. "More than eight thousand Indian men, women, and children are dead today. And for what reason? Because they are Indian. That is all, nothing more, nothing less."

"That's a slippery slope," said Lindsay. "If you strike Pakistan, how many innocent people will die? How many men, women, and children for the simple reason they happen to be Pakistani?"

"Honestly, I don't care," barked Singh. "Don't lecture me with your American sanctimony, Mr. Lindsay. You live on an island. This is the fourth war we've fought with our enemy. They pursue us always, the desire to exterminate India running like a fever in the blood of every man, woman, and child in that godforsaken country. What we do today will resonate for generations. This war cabinet will be condemned, but our children, our grandchildren, and their children and grandchildren, will live in peace from the vile Pakistanis. I am willing to die a condemned man, condemned by the

Americans, by the history books, if it delivers freedom for future Indians."

"One man made the decision to drop the bomb on Karoo," said President Allaire. "And for that you will exterminate a people."

"That one man happens to be the president of the country," said Vilokan. "The democratically elected president of his country. The representative of a majority of his people. In fact, nearly seventy percent of his people."

"We told you of our concerns three years ago," said Singh. "A team from RAW flew to Langley and practically begged for your help."

"We saw the threat of El-Khayab long before he was elected," said Guta Morosla, secretary of the Research and Analysis Wing, India's version of the CIA. "Even then, before he was elected, before he was even a candidate. And what did you do? You scoffed at us. Now we're living with the results."

Jessica looked down at her hands, clasped together on the table in front of her. She separated them for a moment. She watched as they trembled like leaves in a mild breeze, then reclasped them so nobody else could see.

Jessica knew the meeting was over. She knew the meeting was over before they even got there. Ghandra and his war cabinet had already made up their minds. Could she blame them? No. It was an impossible situation. To not respond to Pakistan would likely result in an uprising by the very people who had elected Ghandra, as well as more bombs from Pakistan, and quite possibly an invasion by China. To respond with a proportional strike would only lead to a series of nuclear strikes that wouldn't stop until Pakistan and India were both destroyed.

She looked from her hands to President Allaire. His face was expressionless. Ashen. To Allaire's left, her eyes found Ghandra. His normal confidence was gone. His brow appeared furrowed. He kept rubbing his eyes. Jessica knew that on some level the decision to kill so many people, regardless of who they were, enemy or not, was tormenting him.

She looked at Hector, who glanced at his watch. He looked pissed off. He wanted to get out of there and had already written off the meeting.

Trust yourself, Jess. She heard the words, her own words, inside her head. *Trust yourself.*

"I have an idea," Jessica said, interrupting the silence of the conference room.

26

Khoury pushed his way to the back of the crowded bar. He leaned against the wall and fumbled for his iPhone. He could practically feel his heart in his throat. Nervous sweat coursed down his back. His eyes darted between the iPhone and the man at the bar, the man he tried hard not to stare at, the American.

I found him Whiteys Bar

Khoury felt for his silenced Glock, tucked into his pants at the belt.

Should I shoot him here? he thought to himself. *I have a clean shot. Answer me, Youssef.*

Khoury waited a minute, then a second minute. It seemed like an eternity. He watched as the American threw back a shot of whiskey, then a second. His eyes alternated between the iPhone and Andreas. *Answer, Youssef.* Finally, a Tweet appeared, from Youssef.

Whats he doing?

Drinking

Did he see you?

No

Is he leaving?

No. talking to girl. He has a beard and long hair

WAIT. everyone to whiteys NOW! kill him if he tries to leave

Khoury put the iPhone in his pocket. He stood at the rear wall, trying to blend in, as he had been trained to do, watching the man he'd spent so long searching for.

27

RASHTRAPATI BHAVAN
NEW DELHI

All heads in the Security Room room turned to Jessica. She looked around the table, met Calibrisi's surprised eyes for a brief moment, then President Allaire's, and finally settled on President Ghandra's.

"Go on, Jessica," said President Ghandra.

"Coup d'état," Jessica said.

She waited a moment and let the words sink in. Then she continued. "We design and execute the removal of Omar El-Khayab. America handles it. We remove the cancer. We install someone who will work with India. In the meantime India maintains its war stance. You keep your planes in the air. You fortify the northern border with China by moving troops to the area. You prosecute the war front in Kargil and Baltistan."

She paused and leaned forward. The room was silent.

Finally, Indra Singh shook his head.

"Oh, sure, that should be easy," Singh scoffed, waving his hand in the air. "We never thought of that. Just pop off El-Khayab. Jessica, that is, how do you say it, a mission impossible. We've been targeting El-Khayab since before he was elected. He is better guarded than even you, President Allaire. It is simply not a viable option, and certainly not within the time parameters we have to work with."

"How many foreign leaders has India removed from power?" asked Jessica.

Singh was silent.

"How many?" she repeated.

"The answer is, not a one," said Calibrisi.

"The United States has removed three foreign leaders in the last twenty years," said Jessica. "There are no guarantees, but we know how to do it."

"It will take too much time," said Singh. "We don't have the time."

Jessica stared at Singh, whose face was red with anger. She turned to President Ghandra.

"Will you give us the time?" she asked, looking into Ghandra's eyes.

"No, that is not an option," said Singh. "India has not—"

"Shut up, Indra," said President Ghandra sharply. He turned to Jessica. "How much time are we talking about, Jessica?"

She looked at Harry Black, then Hector Calibrisi.

"At least two weeks," Calibrisi said. "Three would be optimal."

"One week," said Jessica, turning to Ghandra. "We need a week, Mr. President."

Ghandra glanced around the conference table. Singh was shaking his head, apoplectic. He moved down the line of his advisors and asked each one of them to give his opinion. Every member of Ghandra's war cabinet was against delaying the nuclear strike.

"If it had even a prayer of working I might reconsider," said Morosla, the secretary of RAW. "But it won't work."

After polling his cabinet, Ghandra turned to Jessica. He smiled warmly at her. He seemed to have regained his composure and calmness that she so admired.

"Two days," Ghandra said, overruling his cabinet. "You have forty-eight hours to remove Omar El-Khayab from power." Ghandra pointed at the clock on the wall. "It's noon. Two days from now, unless Omar El-Khayab is gone, we will begin our attack."

"Thank you," said Jessica. She looked at the clock, then at President Allaire. He stared back at her without expression.

"After that, we destroy Pakistan," said Ghandra. "Unless they strike again in the interim. In which case we will destroy them not in days or hours, but in a handful of seconds."

Jessica nodded. She said nothing. She glanced at her silver Cartier tank watch. It was exactly noon local time. She felt a tightness in her stomach as she watched the second hand on her watch move around the watch face. *Forty-seven hours, fifty-nine minutes, forty seconds, and counting . . .*

28

Do you want to come back to the ranch?" Charlotte asked. "I have my own carriage house. It's very private."

But Dewey was no longer listening to Charlotte.

The olive-skinned man with the Afro at the back of the room glanced around nervously. Whoever it was, he had found what he was looking for, and it was Dewey. Dewey recognized that. He saw it in the hatred, in the way the man's eyes darted about constantly, settling back on him every few moments. Dewey knew when someone had come to kill him.

Dewey removed his hand from Charlotte's hip, lifted his left leg, and felt for the dagger sheathed against his calf. Reflex: making sure it was there. His brain sharpened, his muscles tensed. He felt the steel of the Colt at his lower back. A fever of warmth invaded his veins.

"I decorated it myself," said Charlotte, still talking about the carriage house at her family's ranch. "I cleaned it out and painted it. It used to be a barn for the old owner's prized stallion. I think you'll like it. It's very cozy."

The killer was young, early twenties. He wore an orange polo shirt with the collar popped up. He'd marked Dewey a minute ago, five minutes ago, half an hour ago. He stared, unaware that Dewey could see him in the mirror behind the bar.

"Of course, we can stay for a few more drinks," said Charlotte. "I just don't want you to get into trouble. Wink, wink."

Dewey reached behind him and felt the .45 caliber handgun tucked into the small of his back, beneath the windbreaker. He stood up.

"I'll be right back."

Charlotte arched her head to the side, made a fake disappointed look, then smiled. "Sure, Dewey. I'll be here."

Dewey looked quickly at Talbot, who was deep in conversation with the Frenchwoman. He turned and pushed quickly through swarms of people to the door. There, in the glass of the door, he caught a glimpse of the bright orange shirt. The killer was following. Dewey had surprised the killer with his abrupt move.

He stepped outside onto the crowded sidewalk. It was still hot and he felt sweat pouring from his chest, wetting his shirt. He needed to move fast now. He jogged one block, then went left. He moved away from the strip, down empty sidewalks, past small houses. He jogged past car after parked car, beneath the glow of streetlights.

Looking at windshields as he moved, Dewey searched for a reflection, a sign the young killer was following behind. In the driver's side window of a pickup truck, he caught a glimpse of the orange shirt. The killer, trying to keep up, was running too fast.

Almost sprinting now, Dewey turned the corner. He reached into the small of his back, pulled out the Colt M1911. From his front pocket he grabbed the silencer and screwed it into the Colt's nozzle. Sweat rained down from his head and chest as he sprinted for his life. In a block, he took a hard right down another street. He crossed the street, then ducked behind a sedan and watched. The killer, following Dewey's turn, appeared and looked around. His left arm moved up to his face. Dewey heard his panicked voice, words barked into a cell phone.

How many are there?

Dewey took off again, picking up his pace, looking in front of him for others, running as fast as he could down the sidewalk.

He hit the next intersection sprinting. He heard the scratch of the terrorist's shoes on the pavement, charging after him down the sidewalk.

Parked at the far corner, Dewey saw a white van and caught a silhouette moving toward the back of it. Trapped between two killers, he looked around quickly for a third man but saw nothing. He ran down the middle of the street for the front of the van, then ducked in front of it just as the terrorist with the orange shirt rounded the corner. Dewey crouched in front of the van's grille. He listened for the sound of footsteps behind the van as he waited for the orange shirt to appear.

Dewey waited, gun cocked. The killer with the orange shirt appeared, running into the road, then down the middle of it toward him. Dewey waited another second, then two, watching the killer come toward him, oblivious to the fact that he was waiting for him in front of the van, hidden behind the back bumper of a pickup.

Dewey steadied his arm, then squeezed the Colt's trigger, firing a silenced bullet across half a block into the killer's chest, knocking him backward. The body dropped into the middle of the street. A pool of blood quickly spread onto the black tar as the terrorist was killed.

Dewey turned. He looked around again for others as he listened for the other killer, the one at the rear of the van.

Dewey crouched and waited. He heard the terrorist begin to move along the passenger side of the van. Dewey remained in a crouch, close to the blacktop. He ducked and looked beneath the van. He saw the silhouette of two legs stepping slowly toward the front of the van.

Dewey waited. One second, ten seconds, then fifteen. He waited in a crouch at the front for nearly half a minute. Drops of sweat cascaded down his face, drenching his hands, arms, legs, and shirt. He heard the faint scratch of movement, denim, a leg shifting in space, just a whisper. He looked up. Above his head, the black tip of a silencer emerged from behind the edge of the van.

Dewey lunged, grabbing the killer's weapon just as bullets started to fly from the machine gun's silencer. Dewey felt the heat of the gun barrel, but held on. A shower of slugs struck a windshield across the street, shattering it. Dewey pulled back sharply and ripped the weapon from the killer's arms. The hail of bullets ceased as Dewey threw the machine gun to the blacktop. The startled terrorist was frozen in place for a second, then reached for Dewey's neck. He slammed his knee into Dewey's abdomen. His fists struck wildly. A fist hit Dewey's mouth and Dewey tasted blood. The killer hit him again, a sharp punch to Dewey's chest, the blow absorbed by a wall of muscles.

Dewey turned, his back to the killer for just an instant, then wheeled his left foot in a vicious roundhouse kick to the Arab's stomach. The terrorist was knocked back a few steps, moaning, clutching his chest. Dewey followed the kick with a fierce swing to the Arab's face, crushing the killer's nose, blood exploding out everywhere. Another strike, this time Dewey's left fist to now-cracked ribs. The terrorist fell backward onto the sidewalk, and reached inside his pocket, pulling out a cell phone. Dewey reached down and tore the cell from the man's grip before he could say something. Frisking him, he found a handgun in the killer's ankle holster and removed it. Incapacitated, the Arab grunted from the pain.

Dewey stood over the man. He needed to move quickly, before someone discovered the corpse of the other man, the thug in the orange shirt, in the middle of the road. He tucked his handgun into the small of his back and reached for his knife. As the terrorist struggled to breathe, Dewey knelt atop his chest and stuck the tip of the combat blade into his mouth. He pushed the blade in, vertically, so that the jagged teeth along the upper blade ran across the top of the terrorist's mouth, against his upper teeth, and the razor-sharp blade of the knife was pressed into the man's lower teeth.

Slowly, Dewey pushed the blade down into the killer's mouth. He stopped when it was a few inches in. The knife now propped the terrorist's mouth wide open. Biting down or struggling in any way was futile; the blade would sever the man's tongue and lip. Both men knew that one last push by Dewey and the knife could easily go straight through to the man's spine, killing him. He writhed in pain, as blood poured like water from his lips and mouth down his chin. In the pale glow of a distant lamppost, the terrorist's brown, bloodshot eyes looked up at Dewey, helpless.

With the thick steel blade propping the man's mouth open, Dewey reached into the man's mouth, feeling the molars until one loosened. He tore the fake tooth from the mouth and looked at it quickly. The cyanide pill was the size of a pinhead.

The terrorist was silent.

"Talk and I'll let you eat the cyanide," said Dewey. "Don't talk and I'll tie you up. The police will find you. You'll be at Guantánamo in a day or two. They'll torture more information out of you than you ever thought you knew. Aswan Fortuna will exterminate your family by the end of the week out of revenge."

The killer grunted.

"How many?" demanded Dewey. He glanced down the sidewalk both ways, an eye out for any others, but saw no one. "*How many?*" Dewey pushed the blade half an inch further in. The terrorist grunted, gagging.

"Seven," the man said awkwardly as the blade held against his lips and teeth.

"Where are the others?"

"Coming. Nearby."

"How close are you? Do you know where I live?"

The terrorist shook his head. "No. But they have your friend from the bar by now. They'll find out from him and go there next."

"If they harm anyone—"

"It's too late. He's a dead man."

Dewey shook his head back and forth as his anger boiled over. It took everything he had to restrain himself.

"Al-Qaeda?"

"Hezbollah."

"Are your instructions to kill me or take me back to Beirut?"

The terrorist shook his head, back and forth again.

"Kill." The edges of the terrorist's mouth flared up at each end, a slight grin.

Dewey stared at the young terrorist. It was time.

"Break my neck," whispered the killer, as if sensing Dewey's thoughts. "Please. A soldier's death."

Dewey leaned forward. He placed his left hand on the side of the man's neck. With his right hand, he grabbed the man's forehead.

"Aswan will never stop," whispered the young terrorist.

Dewey said nothing.

In a swift motion, Dewey ripped the man's forehead to the side as he held his spine steady. The dull snap of the terrorist's neck echoed down the empty street.

Dewey stood up and walked back to Main Street. He walked past shop windows, a diving store, a bikini shop, until he saw the neon sign a block away: WHITEY'S.

His eyes were drawn to the street in front of the bar. A chill ran from his ankles up his back. Across the street from the entrance stood two men. Short-cropped hair, one was in a black windbreaker, the other in a red, white, and blue warm-up jacket, watching the entrance to the bar like wolves. It was in their eyes.

Dewey looked for others. Seeing no one else, he turned and walked away from the bar. He took his time, a tourist out for a stroll. After two blocks, he crossed to the elevated boardwalk above the beach. He went to the railing, next to a couple, kissing and oblivious. Dewey leaned down, jumped through the railing slats and onto the sand ten feet below the boardwalk, his feet striking first. He rolled and then looked up. The couple was still kissing, unaware.

Dewey walked, hidden in the dark recess of the overhanging boardwalk. When he reached the place where he knew the two men were waiting, he pulled the silenced Colt from his back.

Dewey paused. The terrorists were swarming. The first had seen him, and now that knowledge was disseminated through the group. He realized now the danger in which he'd inadvertently placed Talbot, not to mention Charlotte.

He stepped away from the darkness so that he could see the

boardwalk above him. Hidden by the shadows, he watched another couple standing against the railing, holding hands, their backs to the ocean and to him. Behind them, Dewey could see the tops of the shoulders of the two killers, and their heads, which shifted about as they searched for him. He raised the .45. He aimed it in the only open space he could find that had a direct angle: between the legs of the young girl, now leaning toward the boy and kissing him. The taller terrorist leaned in, whispered something in the other killer's ear. Dewey squeezed the trigger. The bullet tore through the humid air and the terrorist's head jolted left, a millisecond later the left side of his skull exploded outward toward the car traffic. The man crumpled, falling awkwardly to the sidewalk at the feet of the other terrorist.

The other Arab shuddered as he stared at his dead partner and tried to process what had just happened. Momentarily confused, he struggled to regain his composure and began to look for the source of the bullet. Dewey, invisible in the darkness, steadied his firing arm and aimed. Before the man could collect himself enough to run, he triggered the .45 again. A silenced bullet whistled through the same space and struck the terrorist in the right eye. His body was jerked violently backward, thrown into the air, pummeled in a roll onto the crowded street.

Dewey ran down the cool sand of the beach, beneath the protection of the boardwalk. After several hundred yards, he climbed up from the beach, back onto the boardwalk, and sprinted toward the bar.

Behind him, the sound of screams ricocheted across the crowded street. Sirens pealed in the distance. People ran in every direction, trying to get away from the violence.

At Whitey's, Dewey opened the door to the crowded bar. It was loud, and the drunken crowd had no clue about the chaos just outside the door. He pushed through the crowd, looking for Talbot, but he was gone. He looked for Charlotte. He saw the back of her head, the long brown hair, halfway through the room. Her arm was held tightly by a tall man with long black hair, who was forcing her from the bar stool. He had her arm twisted behind her back and with his other hand he pressed what was almost certainly a handgun against her side. The boisterous, drunken crowd was oblivious to it all.

Dewey pushed hard through the crowd, elbowing aside anyone in his path. One man, a large, overweight tourist in a bright yellow golf shirt, sunburned, pushed back, yelled an obscenity at Dewey, but Dewey simply raised his right arm and brushed him to the side. By the time Dewey reached her and her abductor, Charlotte was near the door. Dewey reached down to his ankle and pulled the knife from its sheath. He approached the terrorist from behind, slipping past a blond woman giggling with her friends.

Dewey wrapped his right arm around the killer's front, plunged the knife between his third and fourth ribs, yanked sideways, and ripped the blade through the man's heart. Just as quickly, he pulled the blade out. The killer grunted, then tumbled to the hardwood of the barroom floor. Dewey left the killer in a bloody clump on the ground.

The blond woman looked to her right. Her laughter turned to shock as she saw the terrorist falling to the ground and she screamed. The crowd split and several more screams pierced the air as people realized a killing had just taken place in front of them.

Charlotte stared at the dead man on the ground. Then her eyes drifted up to Dewey's arm, covered in crimson, his hand clutching the blade. Her fear was pure and innocent and there was nothing he could say, there wasn't time. Dewey grabbed her hand and pulled her toward the door.

"What's happening?" Charlotte whispered slowly.

"Where's Talbot?" Dewey pulled her past a line of patrons, frozen in fear, out through the front door onto the street.

"They took him. Just now. Two men."

"Where's your car?" he asked calmly.

She pointed and they walked quickly down a side street as the sound of sirens, now coming from all directions, filled the night air. The sidewalk was emptying quickly now, as people ran from the scene of the dead men in the middle of the street. Charlotte caught sight of the two dead terrorists, lying in the street across from the bar, blood pooled on the blacktop. She audibly gasped.

"What are you going to do to me?" she asked.

"I'm not going to hurt you, if that's what you're asking," said Dewey as he led her away.

"You just killed a man."

"Yes."

"Why?"

"He was a terrorist," said Dewey as he directed Charlotte down a side street, toward where she had pointed.

She tried to pull away from him, but he held her hand tightly with his clean hand. In his right hand, now covered in blood, he pulled the .45 from the small of his back. They were a block off the main street and Dewey glanced around, searching for other terrorists who might have marked him.

"It's hard for you to understand this," Dewey continued. He stopped in a shadow, scanned the darkened side street quickly with his eyes, then looked at Charlotte. "There's a war going on. It's mostly invisible to you, but that's an illusion. Tonight, you're seeing the real world, Charlotte."

"My head is spinning," she cried softly. "I'm scared."

"Where's your car?" he asked.

Charlotte pointed to the next block. Dewey picked up the pace, keeping hold of her arm.

"I need you to do something for me, Charlotte."

"What is it?"

"I need you to trust me."

A low yell came from down the street. The voice was unmistakable: Talbot. Then, a door slammed, an engine started, followed by the screech of tires. Dewey turned his head and saw the flash of the car's red lights crossing the road less than a block away as it tore away.

"How many men did you kill?" Charlotte asked.

"I've killed five men tonight," said Dewey, running now, still holding her arm. "Those men were all part of a team that came here to kill me. That man would've tortured you for information, then killed you. All because you spoke with me."

"Why do they want to kill you?"

"I killed one of their leaders."

They reached a black Porsche. "Is this yours?"

"Yes," she said.

Dewey pointed to the car in front of the Porsche, a sedan.

"Climb under that car," said Dewey. "Wait for the police to arrive. Don't move until they get here."

"Who are you?" Charlotte asked as she looked at Dewey one last time. "You're not a rancher."

"No," Dewey said as he quickly surveyed the dark street, his blood-soaked hand clutching the steel of the Colt in front of him, cocked to fire. "I'm not a rancher."

29

The Gulfstream G650 tore into the sky over New Delhi. Within five minutes, the jet was at 18,000 feet, flying through a thin cloud line, tearing back home at 700 miles per hour, protected by an invisible triangle formed by a lead F/A-18 U.S. Navy war jet, and trailed at each wing by two more Navy fighter jets.

The small cabin of the jet contained eight leather seats, a leather sofa, a work area with a table, and an aft bedroom. President Allaire, Secretary of State Lindsay, and Jessica occupied the table. Harry Black, the secretary of defense, and Hector Calibrisi, the CIA director, sat in leather seats. Two Deltas and two Secret Service officers were in the leather seats closest to the front of the plane. A couple of aides, who had stayed aboard the jet during the meeting in New Delhi, were seated in the back of the Gulfstream.

"I'm not sure if you deserve a pat on the back or a kick in the ass," said Lindsay, looking at Jessica. "We didn't discuss the concept of a coup. As you know there are significant political considerations."

"She bought us time," said Black. "Your arguments were not working. In fact, they were antagonizing the Indians, Ghandra especially."

"Oh, I don't know about that," said Lindsay. "We were progressing them."

"Bullshit," said Calibrisi. "If you had kept talking Ghandra would have started dropping bombs just to get you to shut up."

"I'm not going to dignify that comment," said Lindsay, shaking his head. "Look, I was three feet away from Allende in 1973 when we removed him. My point is, there are serious consequences from a coup. There are consequences if we're successful and if we fail. We haven't debated it much less tried to figure out those consequences. That's my point."

"There is nothing that a coup could do, successful or not, that is worse for America than for India to proceed on its present course," said Jessica. "We know what will happen if they retaliate with nuclear weapons. Pakistan, the sixth-most-populous country in the world, will be effectively wiped out. In addition, let's assume Pakistan is more capable of launching a counterstrike than the scenarios suggest. Tens of millions of Indians, perhaps hundreds of millions, will also die. It will be a humanitarian crisis on a scale that has never been seen before. And that's before China is brought into the mix. We can threaten China all we want but the fact is, America will be unable to deploy troops in time, or in quantities, sufficient to deter the Chinese. We're spread too thin in Iraq and Afghanistan. Are we really ready and willing to stop the Chinese with our own nuclear weapons? I mean, come on. Will we start nuclear war, a war that could lead to nuclear Armageddon, over India?"

"Removing Allende and installing Pinochet required more than a year of planning," said Lindsay.

"You make a valid point," said Calibrisi. "But an irrelevant one. We don't have a year. We have less than two days. We play the cards we've been dealt."

"Jessica bought us time," said the president. "If Ghandra didn't like you, Jess, the answer would've been no. He gave *you* two days. Probably a credit to the trust you built during your visit last year. Tim, this is a pointless debate. We have forty-six hours. We *are* going to take down Omar El-Khayab. Failure is not an option. The questions before us now are who and how."

"Who is obvious," said Black. "SEAL Team Six or Delta."

"That's not at all obvious," said Calibrisi. "This isn't a military exercise. Special Operations Group, Mr. President."

"What the fuck does that mean?" asked Black.

"I'm on your side, Harry. But we can't take the risk that a member of SEAL Team Six or Delta is captured. This is a CIA job. This is a tight kill team operation with deniability, black-on-black. Special Operations Group is untraceable. If, God forbid, one of them is caught, America will not be implicated."

"You're naïve if you think they won't know Special Operations Group is American," said Black.

"A captured American soldier will bring the wrath of the Muslim world to our doorstep," said Calibrisi.

"It's already at our doorstep," said President Allaire. "Come up with a plan and let's move."

"Am I the only person here who thinks this is a terrible idea?" asked Lindsay. "We should redouble our efforts to give diplomacy a chance."

"This is grown-up time, Mr. Secretary," barked Black. "The time for diplomacy ended when that nuke dropped. The question before us now is who is going to give us the best chance of removing Omar El-Khayab."

"We need to make the call," said Jessica, impatiently.

"We have less than forty-six hours," agreed Calibrisi. "The team, whoever it is, needs time to plan. If it's CIA, Political Activities Division needs to plot the targets. For chrissakes, we don't even know who we would install in place of El-Khayab."

"Indra Singh was right," said Black, leaning back, closing his eyes in resignation. He rubbed the bridge of his nose. "El-Khayab is going to be impossible to get to. Add to that the basic fact that his countrymen love him. We just don't have enough time. I'm sorry. It's a suicide mission."

President Allaire stared at Black, then Jessica. His face flushed red. He was angry.

"We're going in!" yelled President Allaire, exasperated. "Giving up is not an option! I don't like what I've heard. Neither of you is giving me a hell of a lot of confidence."

"I'm not trying to give you confidence," said Calibrisi. "This is a Hail Mary at best. Leveling with you, Mr. President."

President Allaire stood up. His face still colored red, his nostrils flared in anger. He took a sip from his bottle of water. Then, he hurled the bottle down the row of seats, where it struck the back of the cockpit door and fell to the ground.

"Goddamn it!" Allaire barked. "The clock is ticking."

"You need to make a call," said Jessica.

"*I don't like the choices!*" shot back the president. "Harry, where would a Delta team come in from?"

"Afghanistan," said Black. "Kabul. It'll be patchwork. I'll be pulling them from another operation."

"Will any of them have coup experience?" asked Allaire.

"No."

"What about knowledge of Islamabad?" asked Allaire.

"Yes, that won't be a problem."

"What about CIA paramilitary?" asked Allaire, looking at Calibrisi. "You mentioned Special Operations Group. Where are they? How long to get a team in here?"

"We'll stitch a team together out of Iraq, Afghanistan, and Europe. On the ground in eight to ten hours."

"Same question," said Allaire. "What about coup experience?

"We've been out of the coup business for some time, Mr. President," said Calibrisi. "That being said, these guys are good."

"Not good enough," said the president, still angry, shaking his head.

The president took a deep breath, walked toward the back of the plane. He turned near the tail end of the seat rows, walked back to the conference table. He sat down.

"Okay," he said calmly. "I'm looking for a needle in a haystack."

"If you ask me, we use Delta out of Kabul," said Jessica. "At least they could get started soon."

"But is there anyone out there better than what we have?" asked President Allaire. "What about MI6? Mossad? Private contractors? I know that's crazy, but—"

"That's not your profile here," said Black. "No other country is going to have any better options than America. Hell, they would have the same exact debate we're having right now but with dramatically inferior options."

"As for hiring a private kill team," added Calibrisi. "As someone who does that from time to time, I can tell you that will not work. This must be a team of Americans. Patriots. Because when the shit hits the fan, they need to be willing to die for their cause. And that's the bottom line."

"I agree," said Black.

The president nodded and looked at his watch. "Very well," he said. "Hector, it's CIA. Your operation. Your mission. Harry, give 'em whatever he needs. Get going."

Calibrisi nodded at President Allaire. He looked briefly, blankly, at Harry Black. Then his eyes moved to Jessica's. He stared for a moment into her eyes.

The president started to walk toward the front of the plane.

Calibrisi grinned to himself, then cleared his throat.

"There is someone, Mr. President," Calibrisi said. "I hadn't thought of him until now, until this very moment."

The president turned. He looked at Calibrisi. "Who?" he asked. "Does he work for the CIA?"

"No, he's not CIA," said Calibrisi. "But he's American and a patriot. The one person alive who would make this, well, maybe a little less than a Hail Mary."

"Who?" Allaire asked, impatience in his voice.

"I'm sorry, Jess," Calibrisi said, looking into Jessica's eyes. He turned to the president. "Dewey Andreas."

30

Talbot sat in the middle of the backseat of the M5, which sped at more than eighty miles an hour away from Cooktown. His head rested against the seat cushion. Blood coursed from his now broken nose, from his mouth, and from the back of his head.

"What's the name?" the odd-looking, blond-haired terrorist screamed from the front passenger seat. He struck Talbot again in the head with the butt of the pistol, this time harder, at a spot just above his temple. More blood.

The first strike—the one to the back of the skull—in a quick moment, altered everything. Talbot was extremely dizzy, nauseous, and tired.

On some level, even though he didn't know the words "subdural hematoma," Talbot knew he was about to die. When he had been forced at gunpoint from the bar and into the backseat of the BMW, Talbot still harbored some hope that he would escape from this bizarre episode with his life. But the blow to the head had changed everything. He felt tired, a dull, deep pain that was too severe, and a wetness of blood flowing down his back, which he knew was coming from his skull.

"Where do you work?" said the blond, yelling at him in a fervent, high-pitched voice. "Just give me the name of the ranch and we'll drop you at the hospital."

"You hit him too hard, Youssef," said the driver, looking in the rearview mirror. "He's going to die before he tells us the name."

"Fuck off," said Youssef. "Drive the car and shut your piehole."

Youssef aimed his pistol at Talbot's right knee and fired. A slug tore into the front of his knee, ripping a hole in the jeans and splattering bone and blood.

Talbot screamed and felt himself coming back from the gauzy brink of unconsciousness. He felt the intense, sharp, searing burn of the bullet in his leg. It focused him. He could do this. *Hold on*, he told himself.

"Start talking," screamed the blond terrorist from the passenger seat. "You fucking dumb fuck, start talking."

The blond reached to Talbot's jacket and found his wallet.

"What kind of name is Youssef?" asked Talbot, breathing hard, sweat mixing with blood on the front of his face.

"It's a beautiful name," said Youssef, pulling apart the wallet. "Now shut the fuck up unless you're telling me the name of the ranch."

"What'd he do? Why do you want to hurt him?"

"Andreas killed someone," said the blond. "Tonight he's going to die."

"What's the name of the fucking ranch?" yelled the driver.

"I have something," said Youssef. "Who is this?" He held up a photo of a girl with short brown hair and freckles. It was Talbot's little sister, Lolly. "Cute kid. Your little sister?"

Talbot groaned as pain from his legs enveloped him.

"And here's an address," said the terrorist, holding up a small slip of paper. "Cairns. Archie Street. What is it?"

Talbot started to cry.

The blond trained the gun at Talbot's head.

"Cairns is a few hours from here," said the terrorist, looking back at Talbot. "If you die before you tell us the name of the ranch we will simply go to Cairns. Believe me, I will kill anyone and everyone at this address. This cute little girl; maybe I'll rape her before I kill her."

Talbot felt a surge of fear, and nausea, at the man's words.

He glanced into the eyes of the man who'd just shot him. Youssef. No emotion. Cold, dark pools of hatred stared back at him. The terrorist said something in a language he didn't understand, then moved the nozzle of the weapon slightly left. Fired another shot, this one into the left kneecap, and this time the pain was incredible, it struck like an electric shock down Talbot's leg in the same instant a wash of blood and bone arced from the knee into his mouth and eyes.

"Someone's behind us," said the driver. "He's getting closer."

Dewey pulled the Porsche out of the parking spot on the side street, accelerated, burst forward in a fifty-foot quick sprint, then, at the intersection, yanked back on the emergency brake; the car rotated into a 180-degree turn. He pressed the accelerator to the ground and the sound of the screeching tires ripped the air. Within a few seconds he had the Panamera tearing down the road—toward the men who had just abducted Talbot—at more than a hundred miles an hour.

In two blocks, he cut a sharp left, then accelerated down a street headed away from town. Small bungalows, homes with tidy grass lawns, lined the narrow streets, now dark. Dewey throttled the sedan as fast as it would go, barely under control.

There was but one way to get to Sembler, but the terrorists were headed in the opposite direction. Talbot hadn't given up the name yet.

Once the Arab at the bar had seen Dewey, he set off a swarm. First in the street, and now. They were on him. Events were on him. He struggled to focus on the chase at hand. He wished he'd had one less drink.

Jessica's phone call saved his life. Yet even with the tip, Dewey had still underestimated the scope, the seriousness, the size, hell, even the very *existence* of the cell. A seven-man incursion was no small matter. The planning involved in getting the team into Australia, post-9/11, was impressive. They were running an expensive, elaborate mission.

This cell was different, more sophisticated, like a special forces team, prepared to move quickly and attack en masse.

He should not have come with Talbot tonight.

He pushed the accelerator down, looked at the speedometer. Nearly one hundred and twenty miles per hour. The street merged with two others and soon he was on Route 81, heading out of Cooktown proper. He had to reach the terrorists' car before they killed Talbot.

Tough son of a bitch, Dewey thought. Talbot was his closest friend at Sembler, like a younger brother. *Why did you put him at risk? It's not his battle.* He cursed himself: *You arrogant asshole. Underestimating the enemy.* He slammed his fist down onto his thigh, trying to control his anger at himself.

He felt the blood on his right hand—from the terrorist he'd stabbed at the bar—drying, getting sticky. He wiped it across his jeans.

He looked ahead and saw, for the first time, a glimpse of light from the escaping vehicle.

The BMW surged forward as the driver pressed the accelerator to the floor.

"I'll tell you the truth," said the blond killer, looking into Talbot's eyes. "You're going to die. Whether you tell us or not. But if you tell us, we'll have no reason to go to Cairns and kill your family. We would only go there to find out the information which you already possess. The name of the ranch."

"Say it," said the driver, without looking back. "Spare your family."

Youssef trained the weapon at Talbot's head, between his eyes. He held up the small photo of his young sister.

"It's very simple," Youssef said calmly. "You have the choice. Either Andreas dies or your sister dies."

Talbot stared back into the killer's eyes. He thought of Lolly. She would be nine this June. He loved Lolly so much, his little sister; she made everyone who knew her happy.

Talbot then understood he was living his last moments on earth.

He would miss Lolly's birthday party. That is what Talbot thought about as he stared down the black hole at the end of the pistol's silencer, felt the word arise from his throat, the last word he would ever say or hear.

"Sembler," he said.

Youssef stared at Talbot and slowly his mouth formed a smile. He pulled the trigger, the bullet entered Talbot's skull between his eyes and ripped a simple, dark hole. The back of Talbot's head blew off, raining blood, skull, and brains in a splash across the rear window.

"Turn right on the mine road," said Youssef, thinking of Ahmed's map showing the locations of the different ranches, which he'd memorized. "We need to head north."

"Okay," said the driver. He had both hands on the steering wheel, the gas pedal fully depressed. The speedometer read one hundred miles per hour. "By the way, whoever's behind us is getting closer."

Dewey watched as the sedan's brake lights went on. He had moved to within a few hundred feet of the car, the Panamera's power—and his reckless driving—enabling him to make up the distance between the two vehicles in a matter of minutes.

The BMW broke right, down a different road, the mine road. Dewey knew the road. It went north, back toward Sembler.

Dewey turned hard. The Panamera's tires screeched as it slid into the end of the road, following.

He slammed the accelerator down and moved into the dust wash trailing the terrorists, getting closer. The terrorists' car sped furiously down the dark road ahead of him. It was a fast car and the driver knew what he was doing.

Dewey floored the accelerator, tearing down the dirt road. The lights in front of him started to flicker through the dust trail as he came closer. He floored it, then reached to his left for his Colt.

The butt was sticky with drying blood. The powerful Porsche gained on the BMW; it was much faster, and Dewey no longer cared if his reckless speed caused him to flip over. The lights of the BMW grew brighter through the dust. Then the Panamera slammed, hard, into the back of the M5. Dewey kept the gas pedal down, holding the Porsche against the terrorists' sedan. Both vehicles were moving now, bumpers locked, at more than ninety miles per hour. The air was filled with choking dust and the sound of scraping metal.

Dewey heard automatic-weapon fire from the car in front of him. Shots sounded above the engine din. The staccato beat of the weapon was soon met by the tinking of steel as the Panamera was hit by bullets. The windshield shattered as lead hit the glass. Dewey ducked to avoid the line of slugs, swerving to the right. The BMW burst ahead, but Dewey accelerated, cutting the distance between him and the first car.

"It's him!" screamed Youssef as the lights from behind came closer. "I see his face!"

Youssef grabbed an UZI and turned to face the oncoming car, holding the submachine gun out the window. He pulled the trigger back and fired just as the car slammed into the rear of the BMW, kicking him backward against the dashboard.

"Fuck!" he screamed, righting himself, then aiming at the back window and firing. The glass shattered and he kept firing at Andreas.

Dewey ducked low, toward the center of the Panamera. With his right hand, he took his handgun from the passenger seat. He leaned against the center console. He held the weapon up, his foot drilled against the gas pedal. Dewey aimed his weapon at the car in front of him, toward the sound of the bullets. He had to move his head up for a brief second and he spied the terrorist, leaning into the middle of the sedan, blond hair, a sadistic smile on his face. He saw the silhouette of the short submachine gun, a black smudge across the hazy, dirt-filled space between the two vehicles.

Dewey fired blindly at the speeding BMW.

Youssef held the trigger and fired at Andreas's car, but Andreas had ducked. The terrorist kept firing, waiting for him to stick his head back up.

The Porsche slammed again into the rear of the BMW, but Youssef was ready this time, and braced himself.

"Faster!" yelled Youssef.

He heard gunfire from the Porsche. He saw the pistol, the hand firing blindly in his direction. Then, like being struck with a baseball bat, Youssef was hit. A bullet struck him in the right arm, kicking the UZI from his hand. His entire body lurched backward into the dashboard, then settled awkwardly, headfirst, into the passenger seat.

The firing stopped. Dewey glimpsed up again. The blond gunman was gone, only the driver remained.

Dewey sat up. He pushed the gas pedal against the ground. In the distance, past the silver sedan, he glimpsed the road ahead, and could see, to the right of the road, a large tree at a bend in the road. He felt the silver sedan's brakes engaging, trying to slow down in order to turn and avoid hitting the tree. Dewey pressed the pedal, hugging the terrorists' back bumper. He kept the heavily damaged front end of the Porsche locked against the rear bumper in front of him.

Dewey glanced through the front of the sedan. The big tree at the corner came closer and closer. As they approached the sharp corner, he slowed for a moment, then two, then a third second, before slamming his foot on the pedal and accelerating. He slammed into the back of the BMW, against the sedan's brakes. The power of the Panamera was too much for the BMW. He did not let up on the pedal. Dewey focused on the tree line ahead of the terrorists' car. He concentrated on not letting the bumper of his car become detached from the BMW. The trees grew larger. They were about to hit. Still, Dewey kept the accelerator pressed to the ground.

"Later," Dewey whispered.

Dewey flexed the gas pedal one last time then ripped the emergency brake back at the same time he moved the wheel hard right. The Porsche cut right, away from the BMW, just as the M5 crashed head-on into the thick oak tree straight off the road. The shattering of metal combined with screaming. Then there was silence.

Dewey straightened the Panamera then stopped. He turned the car around and drove back to the destroyed silver BMW.

Dewey climbed out and stepped to the side of the vehicle. Sweat poured down his face and chest. He knelt down and looked in the window on the driver's side. The Arab was crushed between his seat and the steering column. His brown eyes stared out blankly ahead. Blood trickled from his nose and ears. In the passenger seat, all Dewey could see was one of the other killer's legs. Sprawled across the backseat was Talbot's corpse.

Dewey walked back to the Porsche. He climbed in and drove. He needed to find the police.

He needed to get out of Australia.

31

SOUTHERN AIR COMMAND, INDIAN AIR FORCE
TRIVANDRUM, KERALA
INDIA

The Gulfstream G650 landed at the Indian Air Force's Southern Air Command, on the southwest coast of India, four hours after leaving New Delhi. After coming to a stop at the end of a long runway, with the dark blue water of the Arabian Sea visible from every window, Jessica Tanzer and Hector Calibrisi stepped off the plane.

They climbed into a waiting Land Cruiser with the IAF logo on its side. The SUV drove quickly along a service lane between runways, coming to a stop next to a long, black windowless plane with a large saucerlike disk sitting on top: an E-3 AWACS. AWACS, Airborne Warning and Control System, was America's surveillance, command-and-control, and communications war room for tactical and defensive missions anywhere in the world, almost all operated by the U.S. Air Force. This one, however, belonged to the CIA.

At the base of a set of portable air stairs stood two plainclothed men holding carbines. Between them was a smiling bald man in his late forties, dressed in a coat and tie, as anonymous and generic-looking as a high school teacher. This was Bill Polk, deputy director of the CIA's National Clandestine Service and director of the Special

Activities Division (SAD). He ran the two branches of SAD: Special Operations Group (SOG), CIA's paramilitary units across the globe; and Political Action Group (PAG), in charge of deep-cover political, cyber, and economic activities. Polk was in charge of planning the coup.

"Hi, Hector, Jessica," said Polk above the din of the idling jet as Jessica and Calibrisi walked quickly from the SUV to the stairs. "Welcome to Kerala. Do you two have time to do a little sightseeing?"

"Still the funniest hit man I know," said Jessica. "Any word from Australia?"

"Nothing," said Polk, following them up the stairs. "But they're on it. I have a man on his way up from Melbourne and Aussie Federal Police is all over it."

"We have ten minutes before we need to be back on Air Force One, so let's make this quick," said Calibrisi. "What's the plan for meet-up with Andreas?"

"Well, if we can find him, we're going to put him on an Aardvark out of a RAAF base below Cairns," said Polk. "I have one waiting on the tarmac for him. We'll head south and meet him somewhere en route."

One of the two agents who followed Polk up from the tarmac shut and sealed the door, then knocked twice on the wall just outside the cockpit.

Polk, Calibrisi, and Jessica moved past a bank of six workstations, filled with intelligence officers, to a conference table. Calibrisi and Jessica sat down across from Polk.

"Where are we on the plan?" asked Calibrisi.

"I'm trying to design something quickly," said Polk. "If you gave me a month, or even a week, I would feel a hell of a lot more confident."

"Let's hear what you got," said Calibrisi.

"We're focused on three elements of the coup," said Polk. "One, the team. Who do we send in. How many. We're building an all-star list. The Iraq-Afghan theater actually means we have more choices; I assume I can pull someone off an active mission?"

"Yes," said Calibrisi.

"I'm not sure how you want to select the final list, but I think we give Andreas options, then let him choose."

"Agreed," said Calibrisi.

"We're constructing a list of Delta, SEAL, and Special Operations Group," said Polk. "I'm picturing a three- or four-man team. I'll bring them over the Qu'ush, down the Khyber Pass, through Peshawar down into Rawalpindi."

"How long is that going to take?"

"From the time we drop them near the Afghan border, six hours," said Polk. "We have a couple of private contractors we work with. They'll be hidden in a supply truck. We also have assets in Europe and UK."

"What's the second option on the team?" asked Jessica.

"You mean if Fortuna's goons have already gotten to him?" asked Polk.

"I meant if he won't do it," said Jessica.

"If he won't do it, we'll send in four PMOOs," said Polk. "That's the best I can do."

"'PMOO'?" asked Jessica.

"Paramilitary Operations Officers," said Polk, pausing. "Otherwise known as killers."

Jessica nodded. "Thanks for the clarification."

"Don't mention it," said Polk. "Same infiltration design; my guy from London, three agents over the Qu'ush. I'll deploy out of Qatar into Bagram, chopper to the border."

"Who do we replace El-Khayab with?" asked Jessica.

"That's our second focus area," said Polk. "Obviously, it can't be a jihadist, but that shouldn't be hard. The key here is: who will the line military hierarchy follow? I don't know the answer to that question yet, but I will. Four of those guys you passed," said Polk, nodding at the midcabin workstations, "are Political Action Group. They're sifting through the upper ranks of Pakistan's military leadership. We'll have some options."

"Once you start the ball rolling on one of these coups, all of the generals and commanders who didn't get selected start conspiring," said Calibrisi. "They all think they'd make a great *el presidente*."

"We need to get very smart on back-channel relationships," agreed Polk. "We could unwittingly tip off El-Khayab without even knowing it. Khan, their Minister of Defense, has deep ties down through PDF. We have to be real careful here. We need someone willing to be a fucking dictator. Of course, being a dictator doesn't usually inspire loyalty from your coworkers."

"What's third?" said Jessica, looking at her watch. "Our *el presidente* is about to leave without us."

"Third is ground plan," said Polk. "We need to figure out who we're replacing El-Khayab with before we can design the OP. But we can get a head start on some parts of it. We know we'll need weapons, transportation, money. We have an agent working on that end of it inside Rawalpindi, building the cache, getting cars, food, money, everything. By the way, can I get one of you something to drink? Coffee, Coke, water, a Mojito?"

"No, thanks," said Calibrisi, laughing. "We have to get back."

One of Polk's agents leaned out from one of the workstations and snapped his fingers.

"What is it?" asked Polk.

"NSA is picking up some chatter from Cooktown," said the agent. "Two Arabs shot in the middle of the town."

"Cooktown is where Dewey's ranch is," said Jessica, concerned. "Who is NSA listening to? If they found him—"

"Calm down, Jess," said Calibrisi. "All we know is two Arabs are dead."

"In Cooktown!"

"Did you have the chance to warn him about Fortuna?" asked Calibrisi.

"Yes," she said. "But he shrugged it off."

"Get on the phone with whoever's in charge down there," said Polk. "Let them know what they're dealing with."

"I just spoke with Australia Federal Police," said the agent. "They've got a chopper en route to Cooktown."

"That's not good enough," said Polk. "We need this guy alive. Call AFP back. Get hold of Archibald McCleish. He runs the place. Tell him I told you to call. They need to manage the local police in Cooktown. If there are bodies dropping, the locals are going to start panicking. We have to make sure some cop doesn't accidentally put a bullet in Dewey Andreas's head."

32

MAIN STREET
COOKTOWN

Jay Haynesworth climbed out from the front passenger seat of the black police sedan.

A crowd of more than a hundred people had gathered behind yellow police tape. The mood was hushed in the wake of the violence.

Haynesworth pulled aside the black tarp that hung from stanchions. Behind it was a group of police officers. On the street, a pair of bodies lay next to each other, aligned almost perfectly, as if they had decided to lie down together and take a nap right there in the street. The two men were young, each with short hair. The man on the left wore jeans and a gray T-shirt that had a hole the size of a golf ball surrounded by blood. The other wore khakis and a polo shirt. His mouth and chin had been blown off. Beneath his head, a reservoir of blood ran toward the drainage grate at the sidewalk.

"Touch anything?"

"No, sir," said a deputy. "Nothing."

"Is there any reason we don't start cleaning the scene up?"

"I don't think so, Jay. We catalogued the evidence and took photos."

"Pick 'em up. Clean up the street. Where's the next one?"

Haynesworth walked down the sidewalk half a block. The sign

for Whitey's had been turned off. Another policeman stood at the door. The smell of cigarettes and beer filled the musty air. The bar was empty. In the middle of the floor, another corpse lay, long greasy hair, a goatee and mustache, jeans, white T-shirt, leather jacket, leather boots. The man lay in a pool of blood. Across the chest, a gash, still fresh, oozed red.

"Where are the witnesses?"

"In the trailer," said a policemen. "They didn't see the stabbing. But they saw the guy who did it."

"What's he look like?"

"Big fella, long hair. He grabbed a young woman and ran."

Haynesworth exhaled loudly, whistled.

"Whoever did this is probably halfway to Timbuktu by now. Let's hit the corpses on the side street."

Haynesworth tried to act calm, but inside he felt as if he was drowning. He'd been police chief in the small resort town for more than a decade. Yet tonight marked the first murder on his watch. *Murders, plural*, he thought to himself. He felt discombobulated, as if his little dinghy had inadvertently struck the tip of an iceberg.

Haynesworth and his team walked beneath the streetlights. Halogen spotlights on tripods stood in the middle of the street. Near the corner, a crowd was gathered next to a white van.

A dark-haired man lay on his back, in the middle of the street his left leg bent awkwardly beneath his torso. White jeans, tennis sneakers, an orange polo shirt. He'd been shot square in the heart and his front was covered in blood.

Haynesworth walked to the van and knelt down on one side of the dead man. He wore jeans, New Balance running shoes, a blue T-shirt with a Nike logo, leather jacket. His mouth and face were covered in blood. Next to him, on the ground, sat a long machine gun with a screw-on suppressor.

Haynesworth reached out and lifted the man's head, which moved easily, limply, like a doll's head.

"Broken neck."

He stood up just as an officer came running.

"Mickey's got a guy pulled over on eighty-one who matches the description of the killer."

"Tell Mickey not to touch a fucking thing until I get there."

Youssef opened his eyes. He felt sharp pain in his head and neck. He tried to move his legs. They still worked, but he was sandwiched between the dashboard and the passenger seat, upside down. His head was pressed to the carpet in front of the seat. He smelled gasoline. He couldn't see, there was only darkness.

I'm alive, he thought.

He moved his left arm and felt for the door handle. The door made a groaning noise as he pushed it open. Youssef crawled out the door and onto the ground. His neck hurt badly. He crawled slowly, resting every few feet. Finally, he made it to the back of the destroyed M5. A single taillight still blazed. He looked at his right biceps, where the bullet had hit. It was still bleeding and it hurt badly. From the elbow down, his hand was coated in blood.

Youssef pulled his knees forward and stood up. Pain inhabited every ounce of his body. Yet he knew that he needed to get out of there. He knew that if they found him he would spend the rest of his short life on the southern coast of Cuba, in a jail cell, in a place called Guantánamo.

For more than a minute, he leaned against the badly dented fender. He felt tears in his eyes. He knew he was the last one. They would soon find him. They would pump him for information, torture him.

You must move, Youssef.

He moved back to the front of the car, reached in, opened the glove compartment, and found his cell phone. Quickly, he pressed a number and held it down. He put the phone to his ear and waited. After more than half a minute, he heard the phone ringing.

"What is it?" It was the voice of Nebuchar Fortuna. "Is he dead?"

"No," said Youssef.

"What's wrong?"

"I've been shot."

"What happened? *Speak!*"

"He killed the entire cell," said Youssef. "Everyone except me."

"Where is he?"

"Gone."

There was a long silence.

"Can you get to Brisbane?" asked Nebuchar.

"I don't know," said Youssef, looking at the bullet wound on his arm.

"Get there. I'll make arrangements to get you out of Australia."

Youssef grabbed his handgun off the front seat, an Arcus 98 DA, bought in Bulgaria several years ago. He felt for his wallet, finding it in front of the seat. He walked slowly around to the other side of the car, leaned in and grabbed the neck collar of the driver's T-shirt, ripping it. He took the material and wrapped it around his right arm above the bullet wound, then tied it tight. He found his leather jacket in front of the passenger seat and put it on.

Youssef started walking back down the mine road. Then he turned and walked back to the car. He ripped another long strip from the dead man's shirt, found a small, flat stone on the ground and tied the end of the shirt around it. He opened the gas tank and tossed the stone in, keeping the other end of the cotton material in his hand. Taking a lighter from his pocket, Youssef lit the end. He watched as the strip of rag caught fire. The flames moved quickly down into the gas tank.

Youssef again started down the mine road, toward Route 81. He counted the seconds out loud: "One, two, three . . ." When he said the word "eight," the sky lit up and a loud explosion concussed the air. Turning, he watched as flames engulfed the M5. He stared for a moment, then turned and kept walking, staying a few yards off the road so that he could hide if anyone came.

Haynesworth sped away from Cooktown, south on Route 81. He flipped on the siren of his police cruiser. He stepped hard on the gas. Soon, he was moving at eighty miles an hour down the dark street.

He saw flashing police lights a half mile ahead.

Haynesworth felt his heart beating. He looked at his handgun, on the seat, Smith & Wesson .45 caliber. Other than at the firing range, he'd never actually used it.

Haynesworth slowed down, moving behind the mauled Porsche and another police cruiser. He came to a stop. He reached for the handgun, then stepped out of the car. He aimed his gun at the Porsche as he approached.

One of his patrolmen stood at the side of the dented Porsche, his 12-gauge shotgun aimed at the driver.

Haynesworth came to the side of the car. Seated in the front seat was a man, sweating, his brown hair messed up. His beard and the front of his shirt were covered in blood.

"Step out of the car with your hands up."

Slowly, the door latch clicked. A worn brown leather boot emerged first. Then, he stepped out of the car, hands above his head. His right arm was covered in blood.

Haynesworth moved the gun closer.

"Put your hands on the car," he said calmly. "Now."

He placed his hands on top of the car.

Haynesworth reached for handcuffs from his waist belt.

"Put your hands behind your back. I'm going to put handcuffs on you. Then I'm going to pat you down. You understand?"

"Yeah." He moved his hands behind his back.

"What's your name?"

"Dewey Andreas."

"I have you ID'd at Whitey's," said Haynesworth. "Someone saw you kill a man there. We've found four more. One shot not far from the bar. Another with a broken neck. So that makes, what, five tonight?"

"There are a couple outside of town. The road to the mine. They're terrorists. Hezbollah. They came here looking for me."

"Why are they after you?"

"Before I answer you, you need to send a car to Sembler Station," said Dewey.

"Why?"

"If there are any still alive, they'll go there next, looking for me."

Haynesworth became aware of the incessant beeping of his radio. He stepped backwards, keeping the .45 trained on Dewey. At the side of his police cruiser, he reached in and grabbed the mic.

"This is Haynesworth. I've got the suspect."

"Captain," interrupted the dispatcher. "I have an emergency call I'm patching into you."

"Who is it?"

"It's Federal Police."

"I need to call them back."

"It's Archibald McCleish," said the dispatcher. He didn't need to tell Haynesworth who Archibald McCleish was. Everyone knew. McCleish was the commissioner of AFP, the top officer for Australia's top law enforcement agency, the country's equivalent to the FBI.

"Is this Haynesworth?" came a gruff voice over the radio.

"Yes."

"This is Archie McCleish."

"Yes, sir. What can I do for you, sir?"

"There's a man you need to find. He's in Cooktown. Likely, he's in the middle of these killings."

Haynesworth smiled, glancing at his patrolman who stood guard behind Dewey.

"Yes, sir. I'm already on top of it."

"American. Goes by the name Dewey Andreas."

"I already have him."

"You . . . have him?"

"I just slapped the cuffs on him. He killed about half a dozen people tonight."

"Take the cuffs off," ordered McCleish. "Right fucking now."

"Don't take this the wrong way, Commissioner, but I'll need an explanation—"

"I don't need to give you a goddamn explanation. This investigation became AFP property an hour ago. Got it? But I'll give you one anyway. Those dead men are terrorists. That man there, who you have handcuffs on, stopped them before they killed a bunch of people."

Haynesworth looked at his patrolman.

"Got it?" he said to McCleish. "Get out to Sembler Station," he whispered to his patrolman, hand over the mic. "Make sure everyone's safe. Bring backup."

The patrolman nodded and jogged back to his squad car.

"After you get the cuffs off, drive him to Cooktown Airport. There's a chopper there waiting for him."

"What's the chopper for?"

"None of your fucking business. Now get the bodies cleaned up. Brent Holder from my office will be up there by sunrise. He'll run the investigation. Get moving."

33

IN THE AIR
EN ROUTE TO ROYAL AUSTRALIAN AIR FORCE,
TOWNSVILLE BASE QUEENSLAND

At Cooktown Airport, Dewey climbed aboard a Sikorsky S76 helicopter that lifted immediately into the darkness. Once airborne, one of the pilots turned and pointed to his ears, instructing Dewey to put on a headset. He put them on and was greeted by Jessica's voice.

"Are you all right?" Jessica asked when they were connected.

"Yeah, I'm okay," he said, staring out the window of the chopper. "Have they gotten to Sembler yet?"

"The ranch is secure. I'm sorry about your friend. Were you close?"

"We were friends."

"I'm sorry, Dewey."

Dewey stared into the cockpit of the chopper, at the backs of the heads of the two pilots, trying to control his anger.

"I told you Aswan Fortuna wouldn't let it go," she said.

"And you were right. I should have listened. Is that what you wanted to hear?"

"No," said Jessica. "Do you think I like being right? You have no idea what it's been like wondering when he would find you."

"I'm sorry."

"I'm glad you're alive."

"You saved my life, Jess," said Dewey. "I owe you one."

"Joe Sembler told me how you saved the little girl."

Dewey stared out the chopper's back window into the dark sky.

"Are you still there?"

"Yes," he said, clearing his throat."

There was silence on the radio for several seconds.

"Promise me something," Jessica said.

"What?"

"We're going to ask you to do something."

"Who is?"

"The president. Hector Calibrisi. Me."

"Where exactly am I being taken?"

"You're flying to an Aussie Air Force base near Cairns. When you land, there'll be a secure phone line."

"So it's serious."

"Yes," she said. "But will you promise me something?"

"What?"

"Promise you'll come back alive."

Dewey was silent.

"Dewey, promise me. I know it's just words. Please promise me you'll come back alive."

"I promise."

After landing at RAAF Base Townsville, Dewey was shown the way to a bathroom, where he cleaned up the dried blood on his arms, face, and chin. He was given a fresh T-shirt, then was escorted to an empty office. He shut the door, then went to the phone and picked up the receiver.

"Hold for NSA Tanzer."

A moment later, the phone beeped.

"Hi, Dewey," said Jessica. "I've got Hector Calibrisi and Bill Polk on the line. You know Hector; Bill is the deputy director of National Clandestine Service and runs CIA paramilitary."

"It sounds like you've had a rough night," said Calibrisi. "We just read the first AFP report. You stacked up some body count."

"Let's cut the bullshit," said Dewey. "What do you guys want?"

"We need your help," said Calibrisi.

"I told you all I was out. I said that more than a year ago."

"Can we at least take you through the situation we have on our hands?"

Dewey sat down in a beat-up leather desk chair. He put his boots up on the steel desk.

"Sure, let's hear it," he said.

"Have you followed the news over the past few days?" asked Calibrisi.

"No," said Dewey.

"Pakistan dropped a nuclear bomb on a remote mining town in India," said Calibrisi.

"I did hear that. El-Khayab. How many people were killed?"

"More than eight thousand," said Jessica.

"India now believes it must counterstrike," said Calibrisi. "We just left New Delhi. The Indians intend to drop most if not all of their nuclear weapons stockpile on Pakistan."

"I can't say I blame them."

"The problem is, if India moves ahead with this attack, we believe China will seek to assert itself," said Calibrisi. "Partly as a response to the destruction of a key ally, partly because they covet the natural resources in northern India. If that happens, America *will* defend India. But our options are severely limited. We could try to deter China with ground troops, but we're already spread thin in Iraq and Afghanistan. That leaves us with only one option: deterence with tactical nuclear weapons."

"If we allow China to walk into India, our strategic security alliances across the globe will be altered dramatically," said Jessica. "Our allies would quite simply no longer trust us. China will become the ascendant superpower. In places like Saudi Arabia, this will have real, material impact on the U.S."

"And, of course, if we use nuclear weapons—or even the threat of them—to keep China out of India, all bets are off," said Calibrisi. "Things could spiral out of control very, very quickly."

"Have you attempted to explain this to the Indian government?" asked Dewey.

"We spent an hour doing just that," said Jessica. "A nuclear bomb was just dropped on one of their towns. They understandably don't care what we or anyone else thinks at this moment. They're in shock and they believe they're at grave risk of further attack."

"New Delhi believes if they don't hit back, they run the real risk Pakistan strikes again or China invades anyway," said Calibrisi. "If India is seen as a weak sister, they're vulnerable."

"If India strikes back, it could be a matter of hours before we're at war with China," said Jessica.

Dewey sat back in the leather chair and closed his eyes.

He remembered standing in the hotel room in Cuba more than a year ago, staring out the window at downtown Havana, when they'd asked him to come back to America to help stop the terrorists who had launched the attack on U.S. soil. He had refused to help. And despite the fact that he ended up returning and helping to stop Alexander Fortuna, he still felt shame for saying no when they first asked him. He opened his eyes and looked at the ceiling beams and the fluorescent lights of the office at the RAAF air base.

"What do you need from me?" asked Dewey.

"We asked New Delhi to delay their counterstrike," said Calibrisi. "New Delhi has given us two days to remove Omar El-Khayab from power. That was six hours ago."

"*Two days?*" asked Dewey, incredulous. "That's not a lot of time."

"No, it's not."

"Have you designed the OP?"

"We're working on that right now," said Polk.

"Who's running the OP?" asked Dewey.

"The concept was that it would be you," said Calibrisi.

Dewey was silent. He'd known the answer before he even asked the question. He ran his thumb along his upper lip, which was slightly swollen from the terrorist's punch.

"I'm flattered," said Dewey finally. "But you need some young turks. Delta, SOG, SEAL. That's what you need. I'm getting old."

"You're the one we want on this," said Calibrisi. "As for being too old, tell that to the dead Hezbollah up the road there in Cooktown."

"The elements are simple," said Polk. "Infiltrate with a tight kill team. Access the one who can deliver the military leadership and infrastructure. Then remove the cancer."

"Let some younger guys have a turn, Hector. That's how they learn."

"I hear you, but this isn't an educational opportunity," said Calibrisi. "The stakes are too high. If Omar El-Khayab isn't removed in forty-two hours, the consequences are unimaginable."

"We need a veteran in there who will react in-theater to what's going to be a fluid, raw, and highly lethal operation," said Polk.

"You're not a very good salesman."

"I'm not trying to sell you. We have a crisis and you're the best solution."

Dewey looked down at his leather boots. The left one was covered in dried blood, which he noticed for the first time.

"I'm expendable," said Dewey. "Why don't you just say it. If they catch me, you have deniability."

"That's not why we want you," said Calibrisi. "We can get deniability in other ways if that's what we wanted. Contractors. Even Special Operations Group can go in sanitized. But that's not what we want. We want a highly talented soldier and a patriot, in that order. I know you, Dewey. I saw what you did after Capitana. We all did. You're a unique young man, whether you want to admit or not. Your country needs you."

Dewey's mind raced as he listened to the voices coming over the phone. Calibrisi had a warm, deep voice, with a slightly Hispanic accent. He liked Calibrisi. He trusted him. After Dewey killed Alexander Fortuna, it was Calibrisi who asked him to come and work at

Langley. Then, when Dewey was leaving for Australia, Calibrisi had given him covert identification, which he'd never used. But still, he remembered the gesture.

"There's something we didn't tell you about Omar El-Khayab," said Calibrisi. "Something you should know."

"What?"

"El-Khayab was created by Aswan Fortuna," said Calibrisi. "Plucked him out of obscurity, funded his rise in Pakistani politics, and paid for his presidential campaign. The same money that paid for the bullets that killed your friend Talbot tonight got Omar El-Khayab elected president of Pakistan."

Dewey stared at the fingers on his right hand, scratching a small flake of dried blood from the cuticle of his ring finger. Just the word—Fortuna—made his adrenaline spike. Dewey eyed the worn patina on the butt of his M1911. After a long, pregnant pause, he moved his right boot from the desk down to the ground, then his left. He stood up from the big leather chair. He glanced around the large, empty office, at the walls covered in framed photographs of old Australian warplanes. He ran his fingers through his long, sweaty hair. He picked up the .45 caliber gun from the desk and tucked it into his belt. A smile slowly appeared on his face.

"I'll do it. But there's one condition."

"What is it?" asked Calibrisi.

"After it's all over, if I survive, you give me Aswan Fortuna's location and you let me put a bullet in his head."

"You got it," Calibrisi shot back.

Dewey hung up. He looked at his watch. *Forty-two hours.* He exited the office, walked down a dark corridor, then out onto the tarmac, still black under the night sky. He saw an F-111 in the distance, its lights on, the canopy open. "Aardvarks" they called them back home, but here they nicknamed them "pigs." He walked quickly to the side of the plane and climbed up the air stairs.

At the top of the stairs, Dewey looked at the young Aussie pilot and nodded.

"You Andreas?" the pilot asked.

"Yeah," said Dewey. "I assume you know how to fly this fucking thing?"

The pilot laughed as Dewey climbed into the second seat and the canopy glass descended, the wheels bounced forward and the fearsome engines on the back of the attack jet roared to life.

34

ROUTE 81
CAIRNS, AUSTRALIA

Youssef had walked less than a half mile when the first police cruiser came barreling down the mine road. He saw its lights in the far distance. By the time it approached where he was, Youssef was lying facedown in the dirt thirty feet off the road. He waited as the police car sped by, then stood up and continued walking down the road toward Route 81. Two more times, Youssef was forced to hide. After twenty minutes of walking, he reached the end of the mine road and went right on Route 81, walking along the dirt apron ten yards off the road, ducking whenever a car approached from either direction.

His arm hurt badly, but he didn't think about it. Youssef had been trained in pain attenuation. He knew he was lucky to be alive. He thought only of getting to Brisbane. He also thought about Dewey Andreas, picturing the look on the American's face as he drove the car just behind the BMW. There was no fear in the man's eyes, no emotion, just steel determination. Youssef would never forget the look.

Youssef walked south along Route 81 for more than an hour. Then he stopped. He waited just off the road, crouched, out of sight, as several cars passed by. When, in the distance, he saw the lights of a semi, he stepped toward the road and held his thumb out. The first eighteen-wheeler passed him without slowing down, as did the second and third. In between trucks, he would crouch out of sight, lest one of the cars traveling on Route 81 turned out to be a police car. The fourth semi slowed down and stopped to pick him up.

"Where ya headed?" asked the driver as Youssef climbed into the cab.

"Cairns."

"Hop in," said the bearded, overweight truck driver, eyeing Youssef's leather coat and bottle-blond, spiky hair. "You a surfer?"

"Yes," said Youssef. "Thanks for stopping."

Youssef closed the door and the truck rolled forward, south on 81, toward Cairns.

They drove for two hours. The radio played country music and they talked only briefly, Youssef asking the driver about what he was carrying, where he was from, and other polite small talk, all of it forgotten almost as soon as the words came out of the burly driver's mouth. When they came to a traffic light near Lake Mitchell, just north of Cairns, Youssef took his Arcus 98 DA 9mm handgun out of the pocket of the leather coat and fired a single round into the side of the truck driver's head.

Youssef pulled the dead driver toward the passenger side of the cab, then climbed over him. Taking off the leather coat, he inspected the bullet wound in his arm. He was in pain, but it was tolerable. The bleeding had stopped. Examining the wound for a few moments, he found a hole at the back of the biceps where the slug had exited.

With his right boot, Youssef pushed the corpse down in front of the passenger seat. When the light changed back to green, he shifted the semi into first gear and started to drive toward Brisbane.

35

QANNABET BROUMANA ROAD
BROUMANA, LEBANON

Nebuchar Fortuna drove his bright orange Lamborghini Gallardo LP 550-2 "Valentino Balboni" through the winding hills above downtown Beirut taking the hitchbacks at speeds that caused the tires on the €180,000 sports car to squeal. He took a right down an unmarked road and was soon at a heavily fortified set of iron gates. He honked the horn twice. After an armed guard identified him, he drove through the gates. He parked in the circular driveway in front of a rambling villa, slammed the car door behind him, and went inside.

Gathered in the living room, on sectional sofas in a square, two men sat.

"What is it?" asked a small, bald man in the middle of the sofas, dressed in khakis and a green short-sleeve button-down shirt.

"None of your affair, Pasa," said Nebuchar. "I must speak with you alone, Father."

"He's my guest," said Aswan Fortuna. "Speak. Nobody's leaving."

"Dewey Andreas is alive."

"So what's new?" asked Pasa. "The son who couldn't shoot straight."

"Shut up," said Nebuchar, not even looking at Pasa. "My father may abuse me. You may not unless you would like to taste blood in your mouth."

"Big threats," said Pasa.

"Calm down!" barked Aswan. "Both of you. What happened?"

"We finally found him. They saw him at a bar and moved on him. But somehow he killed most of the cell."

"How?" whispered Aswan, incredulous. "How could this happen?"

He sat back, staring icily at Nebuchar.

"You manage to fuck up everything," said Pasa from the sofa.

"It was your men, Pasa, you fucking Hezbollah midget," said Nebuchar, turning to his father. "Half of the cell Pasa here delivered from Bekaa. So we can start pointing fingers or we can just figure out what to do next."

"What to do next? They're all dead! The cell is dead and you're asking what to do next?"

"They're not all dead. Youssef survived."

"What would you do next?" asked Pasa.

"Build another team. A clean team. Send them back to Australia to dig for information. This is a long-term struggle, and we can't give up."

"Another team?" said Aswan, as bitter laughter erupted from his mouth. He sat back and ran both hands through his long, silvery hair. His tan shirt was unbuttoned, and he placed his hands nonchalantly across his chest.

He stood and walked calmly around the square sectional sofa. On the wall hung a photograph. It was a photo of a handsome young man in a lacrosse uniform, the word Princeton on the jersey. The player's hair was wet with perspiration. Eye black was painted in stripes beneath each eye. The photo was of his dead son, Alexander; the chosen one, the one he had loved; the one Dewey Andreas had killed.

Aswan stared for a moment at the photo, then stepped slowly back toward Nebuchar.

Pasa laughed as he watched Aswan.

"What's so funny?" asked Nebuchar.

"You are," said Pasa, still laughing. "Both of you. You're in love with a dead man. You spend your life chasing ghosts."

"I told you to shut the fuck up, Pasa," warned Nebuchar, his eyes flaring in anger.

"Perhaps *you* should shut the fuck up now," said Pasa. "If I had handled this little project, Andreas's skull would have been stuffed and mounted above the fireplace long ago."

Nebuchar pulled out his Glock .45 G.A.P and aimed it at Pasa's head.

The pistol cracked loudly as a single bullet tore into Pasa's right eye and ripped a hole through the eye, kicking his entire body backward.

"I warned you."

Aswan looked, stunned, at the dead man on his couch, then at his son.

"You do realize that is the number three man in all of Hezbollah, yes?" asked Aswan.

"Was," said Nebuchar.

"I can't guarantee your protection."

"Since when have you ever protected me?"

36

The F-111 swooped in and landed on the main runway at Paya Lebar Air Base. The jet taxied to a stop next to a large, black windowless plane with a Frisbee-like object on top, the CIA's E-3 Sentry AWACS.

The sun was out. Dewey looked at his watch: 7:15 A.M.

A set of portable air stairs was rolled quickly to the side of the F-111.

"Thanks for the lift," said Dewey.

"Anytime," said the pilot. "Good luck."

Dewey climbed down and walked fifty yards across the cement tarmac, where a bald man in a coat and tie stood, holding two Styrofoam cups filled with coffee. As Dewey approached him, he extended one to him.

"Hi, Dewey," said Polk. "I'm Bill Polk. Welcome to Singapore."

Dewey took the coffee cup, but said nothing. He ascended the air stairs into the A-3, followed by Polk. The jet's door closed and within two minutes the mysterious-looking black plane was barreling down the runway at Paya Lebar.

At the conference table on the big plane, Dewey was joined by

Polk, who sat across from Dewey, and two other men, Will Drake, an operative within the CIA's Political Action Group, and Van Bradstreet, an operative from the CIA's Strategic Operations Group.

Both Political Action Group and Strategic Operations Group were divisions of the CIA's Special Activities Division. The two divisions were the Kevlar-tipped front edge of the CIA bullet. Its members were the elite of the elite. PAG managed political, cyber, and economic analysis as well as covert offensive activities involving the manipulation of various political, economic, and technological systems within foreign countries. PAG's members were drawn heavily from elite graduate programs at Ivy League schools. They tended to be brainy, multilingual, highly intellectual, out-of-the-box thinkers who enjoyed solving problems—and causing them.

SOG was the CIA's front-edge paramilitary force; the first guns into foreign land. SOG operatives were drawn primarily from Delta and SEAL, and were smart, secretive, and brutally tough. During missions, SOG operatives carried no identification or articles of clothing that could identify them as American.

Drake, a senior-level case officer, was leading the analysis of who to replace El-Khayab with. Only twenty-nine, Drake had been pulled away from his honeymoon in Morocco. Drake knew the Pakistani military hierarchy, and Polk needed him.

Van Bradstreet, the SOG operative, was designing the operation along with Polk, as well as handling logistics for getting the team in place and supporting them once they were in-country.

"We have three hours to Bagram," said Polk. "Let's talk about your team first."

One of the CIA operatives on board brought a plate with a turkey sandwich on it over and placed it in front of Dewey.

"Thanks," said Dewey. "Give me a rough summary of the time line, will you?"

"Sure," said Polk. "Van, what do we have?"

In front of Bradstreet was a laptop. He punched a few keystrokes.

At the end of the conference table, a large plasma screen on the wall lit up. On it was a map of the Afghanistan-Pakistan border.

"It's six A.M.," said Bradstreet, pointing at a clock on the cabin wall. "We have until noon tomorrow to take out El-Khayab. That's thirty hours."

"Okay," said Dewey.

"We'll get you to Bagram by noon," said Bradstreet, pointing to a red marker on the map where the U.S.'s Bagram Airfield was located. "From Bagram, we're going to chopper you to Gerdi, a little shithole near the Afghan-Pakistan border, here."

Bradstreet pointed to another marker, just to the left of the bright yellow line that ran through the mountains demarcating the two countries.

"Gerdi to Rawalpindi will take anywhere from six to twelve hours depending on border searches, traffic on the Khyber Pass, and other unforeseen shit. Let's call it nine hours. By late evening, you'll be in Rawalpindi, next door to Islamabad. From there, you'll have twelve hours to find El-Khayab's replacement, move troops into position, and take out El-Khayab."

"Chopper to the border?" asked Dewey. "Daytime? Have things calmed down up there?"

"No, they haven't," said Bradstreet. "Taliban are everywhere. But we should be okay."

"The main concern during the chopper ride is getting hit by a surface–to-air," said Polk. "Joint Special Operations Command is running a border incursion to the north. JSOC has two separate platoons from the 101st Airborne working across the border twenty miles above Gerdi, hopefully dragging any Taliban in your flight path out of the area. You should be safe."

"What about the border crossing?"

"It'll be tricky," said Bradstreet. "But so will the ride down the Khyber Pass. In addition to the main checkpoint at Torkham, we'll need to worry about the ad hoc checks the Terries are doing along the highway to Peshawar."

" 'Terries'?"

"Taliban. They're stopping trucks with increasing frequency. If they find you, they will kill you. With your eyes, your looks, we're gonna need to conceal you. Let me take care of that."

"How?"

"We have a relationship with a trucking company owned by a midlevel Taliban. I recruited him myself. You'll be hidden in a compartment in the back of the truck. I've done it. I was the first to ride the route, and I've ridden the route now six times."

"So the same guys America's been fighting for a decade are going to deliver us to Islamabad?" asked Dewey.

"The Taliban's like any organization," said Polk, smiling. "There's always some bad apples. It's just that their bad apples are our good apples."

Dewey raised his eyebrows.

"Not every Taliban is a fuckhead," said Bradstreet. "This guy's not bad, just corrupt. I've been to his house. He's a survivor. As for the run down the Khyber Pass, we have an understanding: if he ever once fucks me, I will light him up from the sky with one of our Reapers."

"How much do you pay him?"

"Fifty thousand bucks a load. If we stay on schedule, you'll be in Peshawar by dinnertime, and Rawalpindi sometime late tonight. What happens next is somewhat dependent on who we install as president."

"Okay," said Dewey, between bites. He glanced at his watch. "Let's talk about the team."

Polk emptied his coffee cup, then crushed it in his hands.

"It's a four-man job," said Polk. "Depending on who we select to replace El-Khayab with, there will be at least one, maybe two multistage assaults. If I were there, I'd want some extra hands to carry the load."

"I want Deltas," said Dewey. "On the size of the team, I want to understand the design of the incursion before we decide on how many men I'll need. At least two, maybe three. My gut tells me two."

"That's awfully thin."

"It's the way I like it."

"Okay."

Bradstreet took a stack of manila envelopes and held it out.

"Here's the list of Deltas we have in theater," said Bradstreet. He pushed the small stack of folders toward Dewey. "That's Iraq and Afghanistan and one guy in the UK. JSOC is standing by on our orders. You should review the group right now. We're going to be scrambling to get whoever you select to Bagram in time to make the Khyber run work."

"Got it," said Dewey. He started flipping through. "Do you have former Deltas in here?"

"Yes," said Bradstreet. "Everyone's in there, including a couple of guys who are private contractors now."

"Okay," said Dewey. He opened the first folder.

There were sixteen Deltas or former Deltas in either Iraq or Afghanistan. Dewey flipped through all sixteen files before going back for deeper dives. The ages ranged from twenty-four to thirty-six. The photos told him little, but they were interesting to look at nevertheless; they all looked different. Three were black, a couple were Hispanic. One looked Arabic. The rest were white. Some were big, others looked smaller and more academic. The only trait they all had in common was the look in the eyes. Blank, far away, detached, wary; mean.

Dewey opened the manila folder on the Arab-looking Delta:

Millar, Alex
DOB: 9-17-87
POB: Karachi, Pakistan

Dewey read on. Millar had been born in Pakistan, the only son of a history professor at the University of Karachi. Millar's mother had died in childbirth, and his father had never remarried. Originally, his name was Arshad Mehr, but his father had had it changed when they emigrated to the United States in 1998, at the age of ten. He'd grown up in Chicago. His father had joined the faculty at the University of Chicago, becoming a professor of Near Eastern languages. Millar had gone away to boarding school, attending Groton School, then went to West Point. After West Point, Millar had joined Rangers, then been recruited into Delta. He was only twenty-five, but that didn't worry Dewey. Dewey liked the way he looked; he would blend in. He also knew Punjabi and Urdu, two of the main languages in Pakistan.

"Millar," said Dewey, pointing to the photo of the Middle Eastern–looking Delta. He looked at Bradstreet. "This says he's on a JSOC consignment to Langley out of London. First question: Why?"

"We're assessing him for Special Operations Group," said Polk. "London is just an address; he's doing a lot of traveling. He's young, but last week he successfully killed a midlevel Hezbollah IED builder named Saa who'd been running a small bomb school. Millar handled it by himself. Went in as a recruit and they bought it. He was inside the house for three days, picking up intel on how they're making them and where they're sourcing materials, who's paying. Then he killed Saa and two others, destroyed the building. It was a smooth operation."

"Can you get him here on time?" asked Dewey, looking at Bradstreet.

"Yes," said Polk. "Just try not to get him killed. These guys who can speak the language are worth their weight in fucking gold."

Dewey finished his sandwich as he looked through the remaining files. He stopped on one file in particular that was thicker than the others, mainly because he found its contents entertaining.

Iverheart, Rob
DOB: 8-1-1979
POB: Los Angeles, California

The photo on the cover showed a blond-haired, good-looking man with a beard and mustache. Iverheart grew up in Bakersfield, California, attended public schools through high school, then went to USC. It took Iverheart six years to graduate from USC; his files showed that he'd gotten into trouble on numerous occasions while at USC; twice for fighting, one time even getting arrested for disrupting the peace. He was suspended for a semester, the third and last time he'd been suspended from USC. The file showed a series of letters between Iverheart's uncle, who was on the university's board of trustees, and the then-president of the university. It was clear that political influence had kept Iverheart at USC. He graduated with a 1.8 GPA.

Attached to Iverheart's transcript there was a notarized "Letter of Understanding" signed by Iverheart in which he agreed, after his disrupting the peace arrest, that if he was allowed to continue as a student at USC, he would enlist in one of the four branches of the U.S. military upon graduation. Iverheart had done so, enlisting in the army. Inside the army, Iverheart was assigned to the 82nd Airborne out of Fort Bragg, North Carolina. Iverheart graduated first in his training class at Bragg. But what caught Dewey's eye was the fact that Iverheart won the boxing championship at Fort Bragg while in the 82nd Airborne. He beat the four-time Bragg boxing champion, a Delta who weighed twenty-five pounds more than him. Iverheart had been selected for duty in Colombia, setting up kill teams deep in the jungles of the country and helping train the Colombian Army in the methods of interdiction and jungle warfare. One evening, while on leave in Cartagena, Iverheart had been at a bar and saw a man whom he recognized as a high-level member of the North Coast Cartel named Papa Rodriguez. Though off duty, Iverheart had nevertheless followed him, tracking him first to an apartment in Cartagena, then the next morning, into the jungle. Iverheart's initiative led to the capture not only of Rodriguez but also the discovery of a new cocaine processing facility and the arrest of a dozen other cartel operatives. He was asked to join Delta a week later.

"I like this guy," said Dewey. He pushed the file toward Polk.

"Rob Iverheart," said Polk. "He's running around Kabul somewhere."

"Let me get someone on that," said Bradstreet, standing up and walking toward the front of the plane.

"Let's discuss leadership inside Pakistan," said Polk. "I want to patch Hector and Jessica in."

Polk nodded to Drake. He picked up his phone and dialed. In a few seconds, he placed the handset down and put the speakerphone on.

"Hector, Jessica, are you both on?" asked Polk.

"Yes," said Jessica. "You have me here."

"Me too," said Calibrisi. "What's the latest?"

"We need to talk about succession," said Polk. "Who we're going to install as the next president of Pakistan."

"All right, before we start, I want to make something crystal clear," said Calibrisi. "The most important qualification for the next president of Pakistan is not whether or not President Allaire likes him, Jessica Tanzer likes him, I like him, or if he's a good guy or not. This is an *operational* decision. Who can we install by noontime tomorrow. That's it. This is not highfalutin geopolitical strategy. It's tactical on-the-ground feasibility. Dewey, you're the one who has to execute this. So listen carefully and make sure you're comfortable getting the job done with the limited amount of time you have."

"Got it," said Dewey.

"What do we have, Will?" asked Calibrisi.

"Three options," said Drake, leaning back in his chair. "First, General Persom Karreff." Drake punched his laptop. Photos of an olive-skinned man with longish gray hair and glasses, a military uniform on. "Karreff was the number two at ISI, then he ran Special Services Group until earlier this year when El-Khayab promoted him. He's a career soldier; grew up in Rawalpindi, went to Pakistan Military Academy, then the Command and Staff College in Quetta. He's smart and noncontroversial. He's Muslim, but as far as we know, he's not a jihadist."

"So what's the problem?" asked Dewey.

Drake looked at Polk.

"I don't have a problem with Karreff," said Polk. "Hector does."

"That's right," said Calibrisi over the speaker. "Look, on the positive side, Karreff is obviously capable. He controls the military. He knows the ranking hierarchy because he put them there. They're loyal to him. He's gotten rid of the Zardari loyalists in the upper ranks. More important, he's kind of a Renaissance man; he loves Paris, wine, women. He has a mistress. In other words, he would, I think, fancy himself presidential material. He understands how the world works and my guess is he has no interest in fighting a nuclear war with India."

"Why don't you like him?" asked Dewey.

"I've met Karreff at least a dozen times," said Calibrisi. "Despite the fact that he's running the armed forces, he's weak. He's risen because he doesn't offend people. It's why he was selected. Khan, their defense minister, selected him, not El-Khayab, because he knew he could manipulate him. This worries me. Either he agreed to the dropping of the bomb on Karoo or he didn't. If he did agree with it, he's not our man. If he disagreed with dropping a nuclear device but didn't stop it, then it's worse. If we ask Karreff he'll read the situation, agree to do it, then back off before the confrontation that will need to take place with El-Khayab and Khan. You and your team would be highly vulnerable at this point. In fact you'd be dead, and you wouldn't even know it. The other thing is, even if Karreff were to go through with the coup, a more ambitious general is going to put a bullet in him. It would only be a matter of time. And if that guy is not the guy America puts in there—if it's a jihadist like Osama Khan—we could in fact be in a worse predicament than we are today."

"Keep moving, Will," said Polk.

"The second option is the man who runs Special Services Group," said Drake. He typed again and the photos of Karreff were replaced by a picture of a younger man, in his forties with short-cropped black hair and dark skin, tough-looking. "Itrikan Parmir. He's young and talented. Very ambitious. His mother, believe it or not, is Indian, born in Punjab. My guess is he's extremely pissed off about the bomb that was dropped on Karoo. Parmir was an SSG commander during the early years of the Operation Enduring Freedom, and one of the good ones. He and his men have killed literally thousands of Taliban. Some of the more corrupt members of armed forces have targeted him; he was shot by a Pakistani lieutenant in 2009 while on convoy outside of Landi Kotal. The bullet struck him in the chest, but he had armor on."

"What'd he do?" asked Dewey.

"He stabbed the guy in the throat," said Drake.

"He's got balls," said Polk. "I would go with him. He'll not only have no problem working with the U.S., with making peace with India, but he also understands the politics inside PDF."

"It sounds like he has enemies," said Dewey.

"Everyone has enemies," said Polk.

"I like Parmir," said Calibrisi. "We've studied him for several years now. He's a rising star. The only reason Khan didn't have him shot like he did so many others who had been loyal to Zardari is because he needs him. He's one of the best field commanders Pakistan has."

"So let's get this over with," said Dewey. "He sounds fine. Let's get on with designing the operation."

"There's a problem," said Bradstreet.

"What?" asked Polk.

"We can't find him," said Bradstreet. "As of yesterday morning, when we started tracking replacements for El-Khayab, we've been unable to locate General Parmir. Last known whereabouts was Lahore a little over a week ago. We might get lucky here; Lord knows we have a ton of feelers out there. But we just don't know where the fucking guy is."

"Who's the third option?" asked Dewey.

"The third option is the commanding field marshal prosecuting the war against India," said Drake. He punched up another photo on the plasma screen, this one a black-and-white head shot of a Pakistani man with longish dark hair, slightly messed up, his face a little jowly, and a mustache. "Xavier Bolin. He's popular with the grunt-level troops, less so with the upper ranks. Career soldier who came in as an enlistee. He grew up in a poor neighborhood in Karachi. He's kind of a street thug, if you know what I mean. But, he's not a jihadist. In fact, we know from NSA wiretaps that he despises Omar El-Khayab."

226

"What's the issue with him?" asked Dewey, holding the photograph and studying it.

"First of all, he's as corrupt as they come," said Drake. "For several years, Bolin has been working with a contracts officer on his own staff to manufacture fake contracts payable to a dummy corporation, which he, of course, approves. The Ministry of Defense pays them. Bolin has stolen more than thirty million dollars, it's sitting in a Swiss bank account. He's not the first to do it. But it is troublesome."

"He wouldn't be the first scumbag America worked with," said Dewey.

"And he won't be the last," said Calibrisi.

"Can he deliver the upper ranks of the military?" asked Jessica.

"Yes," said Drake. "He's feared. If he would work with us, the hierarchy, for the most part, will go along. Those that don't would, no doubt, die a very quick death."

"The goal here is someone who will make peace with New Delhi," said Calibrisi. "Bolin will make peace. The other stuff is window dressing. I don't see how Bolin's corruption could endanger the mission."

"We might have to pay him," said Drake.

"That's not a problem," said Calibrisi. "Dewey, you're authorized to offer him whatever you want. Ten, twenty, thirty million."

"So other than the fact that he's a dirtbag, what's the problem?" asked Dewey, leaning back in his chair.

"In this case, the problem is, we *do* know where he's located," said Bradstreet. "He's moving between encampments in the Mushkoh Valley, around Drass, in the middle of the battle theater. He's running the war. It's a logistical nightmare just getting you there. Then there's the assault. That won't be easy either. He's going to be extremely well guarded."

Dewey closed his eyes and rubbed the bridge of his nose, deep in thought.

"What are you thinking?" asked Polk.

"I think we should focus on Karreff," said Dewey. "If we have to go to the war front. We're going to be pressed for time."

Dewey looked up at the clock. It was 7:30 A.M. The thirty hours he'd started with was already down to twenty-eight and a half. He watched as the red second hand swept quickly across the clock face.

"So you want Karreff?" asked Calibrisi over the speaker. "That's fine. You're the one who's running the operation. But we have to disclose something to you. There's evidence showing that before Karreff was appointed head of the armed forces, when he was number two man at ISI, that he was helping the Taliban."

"So what?" said Dewey. "Sounds like we're already working with the Taliban."

"The people we're working with aren't trying to kill Americans," said Calibrisi.

"Karreff supplied Taliban with mines that were used on roads in Afghanistan," said Polk. "Roads used by U.S. troops. In 2006 alone, he authorized four different shipments of mines."

"Now, did Karreff order the mines be used on U.S. troops," said Calibrisi, "or did he simply turn a blind eye to some of the collaboration that was going on, and that is still going on, between Pakistan and the Taliban? That we don't know."

"NSA has one recording of a cell phone call that took place between Karreff and an unidentified Taliban operative in which Karreff tells him to quote 'warm the snows in Kabul,'" said Drake.

"Let me get this straight," said Dewey. "Karreff supplied bombs used to kill U.S. troops?"

"Or knew of them being supplied," answered Drake.

"This might surprise you but I don't have a problem with it," said Calibrisi. "It's not disqualifying, in my opinion. The fact that he's weak is. No one is clean over there, Dewey. No one. Next to Iran and Syria, Pakistan is the most corrupt place on earth. The generals and politicians in these countries have been pulled in different directions for so long, conflicting directions, by greed and money, religion and politics. Frankly, even by us. At some point, there's no moral compass. Having one just gets you killed. We're deluding ourselves if we think we're going to find Abe Lincoln over here. Even if Karreff did help the Taliban, it doesn't matter. We have a larger goal here. At the end of the day, we're trying to save U.S. lives by not having to fight a war with China."

"I'm not going to risk my life for a guy who helped kill U.S. soldiers," said Dewey. "Period. End of statement. Let's go find Bolin."

There was a long silence in the room, interrupted only by the steady din of the E-3's engines.

"You realize this means a trip to the war front?" asked Calibrisi.

Dewey was silent.

"It also means we'll have to kill Karreff," said Bradstreet. "He has too many generals that are loyal to him. If he's alive, he could create real problems."

"The schedule is getting tighter," said Jessica. "Do we know where Karreff is?"

"Yes," said Bradstreet. "He'll be in or around Islamabad and Rawalpindi."

"Twelve hours to take out Karreff, then go and find Bolin," said Calibrisi. "You okay with that?"

"Piece of cake," said Dewey.

37

BATH & RACQUETS CLUB
CLARIDGE'S HOTEL
MAYFAIR, LONDON

Alex Millar pushed open the thick glass door and stepped onto the brightly lit squash court. He was half an hour late for his match.

"Where the fuck were you?" Goodale asked. "Five more minutes and I would've DQ'd you."

Millar didn't know his opponent, but he knew of him. Tim Goodale was a brash American and reigning club champion. At Yale, he'd won two NCAA championships. Everyone knew he was the best player at Bath & Racquets. Everyone, that is, but Millar.

Millar had learned to play squash in Karachi, winning the Pakistan ten-and-unders at age seven, eight, and nine, before he and his father moved to Chicago. He'd played through high school, dropped it in college, and when he was assigned to London, he'd picked the game back up.

Millar and Goodale were supposed to have started their match at four. It was the semifinals of the Bath & Racquets annual club championship. Goodale was the heavy favorite. Millar was unknown, but en route to the semis, he had dispatched a former British Open champion. A lot of people at the club were wondering who the quiet American with the nasty backhand was.

"Nice to meet you too," said Millar, placing his racquet cover and warm-up jacket in the front corner of the court.

Goodale moved to the left and snapped a shot to the forehand court, which Millar hit back.

"Look, I wouldn't be such a dick except I have dinner with a lingerie model," said Goodale, pounding the ball back to Millar. "I'm going to have to drop you in three so I'm not late. Don't take it personally."

The two players hit the ball back and forth for the next five minutes, getting warmed up. The small white ball was a blur; Goodale and Millar moved in rhythm, anticipating each other's next hit and rallying in a series of perfectly executed shots. By the time they started practicing serves, a crowd of more than twenty people had gathered in the gallery to watch.

"I heard you beat Bern," said Goodale.

Millar didn't respond.

"Thanks for doing that. He actually made me work for the cup last year. I might not have to break a sweat this year. You warmed up?"

"Yeah," said Millar.

Goodale served first. From the forehand court, he hit a high, soft lob that landed in the back corner and didn't bounce so much as a foot.

Goodale 1, Millar 0.

"Nice serve," said Millar.

"Get used to it."

Goodale swatted a serve from the left, hard, into the forehand court. Millar caught it behind the tee and put the ball high and right, into the back corner. Goodale caught it near the back wall and hit a crushing shot into the front left corner an inch above the tin, which Millar anticipated and met halfway between the tee and the front wall; he snapped it into the corner, where it died.

Goodale 1, Millar 1.

The first game lasted half an hour, with long rallies, as two athletes in prime condition played as if their lives depended on the outcome. Goodale took the first game 9–6. Millar took the next two, 9–7, 9–4.

The crowd had grown to more than fifty people, and with every point, a small eruption of clapping or cheering arose from the crowded gallery. Goodale took the fourth game 14–12. After a long water break, the two players caught their breath near the front of the court before beginning the deciding fifth game.

"I take back what I said," said Goodale, drenched in sweat, leaning over and stretching out.

"Which part?"

"The part about Bern. The part about dropping you in three."

"No worries."

"I gotta ask, though: who the fuck are you?"

"No one."

"No one? Where'd you go to school? What do you do?"

"West Point," said Millar. "I work for Boeing." His London cover.

Goodale studied the tough-looking American. "Boeing? Yeah, right."

Millar shot Goodale a look. His laughter stopped as he registered the threat in Millar's eyes.

"I meant, awesome," said Goodale. "Great planes."

Millar shook his head, then laughed.

By halfway through the fifth game, every point was greeted by raucous cheers from the crowd, which was now beyond capacity. With the score tied at 5–5, an insistent beeping noise rang out from Millar's cell phone in the front corner of the court. He walked to his racquet case, pulled out the phone, and read the message:

6:22 PIA 177 to ISL

Millar looked at his watch. It was 5:50.

"What is it?" asked Goodale.

"I have to be at Heathrow in thirty-two minutes."

"Sucks for you."

"No, actually, it sucks for you. I need a ride."

––––––––

Rob Iverheart lay on top of a long, flat rock on a bluff above the Dori River, southeast of the U.S. Kandahar Airfield. In front of him, resting on an adjustable bipod, was an Accuracy International AX .338 long-range rifle.

Iverheart waited. He'd been waiting now since before midnight.

He and five other Deltas had been on their patrol for two days now. Iverheart and his team were working off a piece of intelligence suggesting that two high-ranking officials from the Haqqani network, insurgents closely aligned with the Taliban, were in the area east of the village of Arghistan.

The Delta team had picked up fresh boot tracks the previous afternoon on the west side of the Arghistan River. Moving several miles downriver toward Pakistan, where the Arghistan turns into the Dori, they had found cigarette ashes put out on the side of a rock. Likely, the Haqqanis had drifted back into the mountains to the south, toward Pakistan. Nevertheless, Iverheart and his team hoped that the Haqqanis were simply waiting them out.

Iverheart was on a bluff, as was another Delta sharpshooter a half mile to his left. The four other members of the team had crossed the Dori the night before and worked their way behind the insurgents. The goal was for the four forward Deltas to find and kill the insurgents, or else push them back to the Dori, where Iverheart and the other shooter were waiting.

At a few minutes after noon, one of the Deltas on the far side of the Dori spoke:

"I'm coming north at position longitude four-nine. I got something about two hundred yards in front of me."

Doyle, his teammate, was describing a location to his right, on the south side of the river. Iverheart studied the landscape with his binoculars.

"Should you fire a few rounds?" asked Iverheart. "Flush him out."

"Let me get closer. He might be coming your way anyway."

Iverheart adjusted his position. He checked the weapon, then resumed studying the land behind the riverbanks. The area Doyle was describing was more than a half mile away.

After more than twenty minutes of silence, Iverheart saw a flash of movement.

"Where are you, D?" asked Iverheart.

"Moving north."

"Did I just see you or did I see one of these Haqqani fuckers?"

"Not me. I'm out of sight."

Iverheart put the binoculars down and lay behind the rifle, adjusting the Schmidt & Bender telescopic sight. He quickly found the area where, with the binoculars, he'd just seen movement.

"I want a confirm from each of you," said Iverheart, adjusting the bipod ever so slightly as he continued to pore through the telescopic sight. "Is everyone out of my firing line?"

"Yes," said Doyle. The other Deltas all confirmed they were out of sight.

"Okay," said Iverheart. "Hold your positions."

Iverheart studied the small steppe upon which he'd seen movement.

"Iverheart, this is Colonel Field back at Firebase Gecko," said the voice on his earbud.

"Yes, sir," said Iverheart. He steadied his head upon the rifle's cheek piece, watching the landscape through the sight, looking for more movement, multitasking.

"You're to get back five clicks. You'll be picked up by a chopper. You're going up to Bagram. They'll brief you en route."

"What about my team?" asked Iverheart.

Iverheart saw something flash in the scope. He adjusted the sight focus. *There.* Two figures, just the head of one on the right, the entire body of the other, dressed in tribal garb, on the left holding a rifle. They were crouched behind a rock. At this distance, they looked like specks of dust.

"Just you, Robbie," said Field.

"I've got two targets," said Iverheart. "Everyone stay low."

Iverheart moved his finger to the trigger. He pumped it. Dust shot out from the rock to the left of the first insurgent's head. Before the man realized he was being shot at, Iverheart fired again. This .338 caliber slug hit him in the head, dropping him to the ground. The other figure moved his head around in a panic, not knowing what had happened. Iverheart triggered the weapon again. His bullet hit the insurgent in the chest; Iverheart could see a red splash of blood on the rock as the body tumbled to the ground.

"Bull's-eye," said Iverheart. "Gotta go, fellas."

38

Polk gave Dewey a tour of the AWACS. The windowless cabin looked like the inside of a submarine. The walls were lined with large plasma screens displaying a dizzying array of images: the Kashmir battle theater, Fox, CNN, Al Jazeera, BBC, state news feeds from New Delhi and Islamabad.

In the middle of the cabin, spreading for more than a hundred feet and occupying a substantial rectangular block of the cabin's space, eight large workstations were abuzz with activity. Each workstation had multiple plasma screens tiered on the walls and was staffed by a CIA analyst wearing a headset.

"The key to all of this is information," said Polk. "Knowing precisely where your target is. That's what this team is here for. You're the surgeon, Dewey. This E-3 is your X-ray machine."

Dewey glanced at Polk. He liked him. He was no doubt smart. And yes it *was* like surgery. But Polk was going to be in the relative comfort of a plane flying thirty-five thousand feet above the ground while he was going to be up to his eyeballs in alligators. Dewey wished he could fast-forward an hour or two. He wanted to get going.

At the first workstation a male analyst was seated before two large plasma screens that showed a black limousine, from different angles overhead, moving quickly through a crowded city street.

"That's Karreff." Polk pointed at the screens.

A pair of screens displayed live drone feeds taken from the sky showing Karreff's limousine, in remarkable detail, moving along a crowded street. A different screen displayed the technical GPS details of Karreff's movement in longitudinal and latitudinal detail, green and blue isobars on black screen. The CIA analyst's eyes stayed glued to his screen; he spoke every few moments into his headset.

"He's online with the UAV pilot, who's somewhere in Iowa, and with an agent we have on the ground in Islamabad following Karreff," said Polk. "Someone at Langley is probably on there too. DoD and NSA too. Each one of these guys is hooked into between four and a dozen other people. Network effect. We don't want to miss anything and we don't want anyone else to miss anything that will end up inadvertently fucking up the mission or costing you your life."

At the next workstation, a female analyst was chattering rapidly into a headset. Her words were in Hindi. Dewey counted seven screens in front of her. Most of the screens displayed news channels from inside India, which she was monitoring. Another screen displayed a middle-aged Indian male to whom she was talking rapid-fire.

"This is our India desk," said Polk. "She's interfacing with CIA New Delhi as well as with RAW, India Defense Ministry, Army, CIB, and a few others. Langley and the Pentagon are on there too. We'll keep track, in real time, of President Ghandra and the New Delhi war cabinet, making sure they don't launch a nuclear counterstrike either ahead of time or before you're out of there. You'll be COMMed into her feed."

Dewey nodded. The woman, who was in her thirties, with red hair and glasses, smiled politely then turned back to the screen.

At the third workstation, another female analyst, this one in her forties, with blond hair, sat in front of four screens with a rotating series of images. One screen looked like a checkerboard, with round objects in red and black, spread in tiny dots across the screen. Another screen looked like satellite photos of green and brown terrain, a yellow line running across the screen.

"Here we're tracking Pakistan's nukes and their borders," said Polk. "Those screens are being shared in real time by a team at the Pentagon and Langley. We want to know if Pakistan makes another move. Right now, we're working to pinpoint and track as many Pakistani nuclear devices as we can through radiological imprint. Once we do that—once we have a nuclear bomb identified and located—we can monitor for any sudden movements. The fact is, if the Pakistanis drop another device, all bets are off, and India will move to obliterate the country. If we see Pakistan moving any bombs, you'll know before New Delhi."

At the next station, a young Asian male sat in front of a wall of screens, speaking rapidly into his headset. The screens showed detailed images of what appeared to be mountainous topography, with snow-capped mountains and stretches of green and brown valley. Dewey leaned forward and could see movement, illuminated in red, like bugs.

"China desk," said Polk. "We're watching troop activity along the Chinese border with Kashmir. The Chinese have moved more than half a million soldiers to the border. We want to know if they increase that number or if they start to move troops across the border into Kashmir."

Dewey followed Polk to the next workstation. There, the screens displayed satellite images of mountainous terrain.

"This is the infiltration route," said Polk. "After we chopper you into Gerdi, we'll keep a steady eye on you down the Khyber Pass, through Peshawar, to Rawalpindi. We'll have a Reaper overhead. If we have to, we can take out anything we're worried about from overhead, though, of course, we'd prefer not to. Technically, we're not supposed to be in their airspace. Over the cities, they can detect us. Over the Qu'ush, their systems are simply not good enough and we take advantage of it."

They stepped to the next workstation. A young, pretty woman with long brown hair was speaking into a headset. She turned and smiled, mouthed the word "Hello," then turned back to a wall of plasma screens. Two of the screens showed a satellite feed, from two different angles, of a small white building in amazing detail. It looked like a cement hut. Dewey watched for a few seconds as a man walked out onto what appeared to be a deck off the hut; he could make out the dark outline of a machine gun.

"Here we're watching Field Marshal Bolin," said Polk. "Like a hawk. It's her job to keep track of where he is, in real time."

Another screen displayed green and red isobars on black: a GPS tracking protocol on Bolin to match the visual feed.

"Where is he now?" asked Dewey.

"Drass," said the analyst. "A town in India-controlled Kashmir. Bolin has set up a temporary war command in the foothills. I'll figure out the best route for you and your team to approach, that is, if Bolin is still there."

Bradstreet came over from the conference table.

"We're thirty minutes out," he said. "Let's nail down the last details."

At Bradstreet's words, Dewey felt a sudden spike of anxiety. The plane made a slight starboard arc. He glanced around the cabin and realized that everyone was not only working for him, they were also watching him. He stayed cool, hiding from all the simple fact that he was beginning to worry.

The words, from training so long ago, came to him then: *Break the mission up into minutes and miles. Don't get overwhelmed. Act like you've been there before.*

Dewey took a deep breath and followed Polk back to the conference table.

"Iverheart is at Kandahar Airfield," said Bradstreet. "I'll get him up to Bagram for meet-up. He's fully briefed. Millar's on a PIA flight to Rawalpindi from Heathrow."

Bradstreet typed into a keyboard. A map popped up onto the plasma screen.

"Let me run through the details of the operation, Dewey," said Bradstreet.

"Okay," said Dewey. He took a sip of coffee.

"You and Rob'll be stowed in the back of a semi," said Bradstreet, pointing to the map displayed on the screen. "You'll ride to the capital through Peshawar, about three hours. South of Peshawar, you should be safe. You'll be incommunicado until you get to Rawalpindi, but we'll be tracking you. The truck might get searched but they won't discover the trapdoor, and even if they do, you'll be armed. Do whatever you can to avoid being captured. If the Pakistani Army captures you, you're going to be locked up for a long time and you should expect some rough treatment. If regular Taliban find you, you're dead. It's that simple. So be ready."

"What weapons can we bring on the trip?" asked Dewey.

"Handguns. That's it. You'll get what you need in Rawalpindi."

"Okay. Keep going."

"Once you're in Rawalpindi, you'll be dropped off at a warehouse about a mile east of the train station, which is in a neighborhood called Saddar. Meet-up is a bar called Al-Magreb. It's in kind of a slum, owned by a guy who we pay to keep his mouth shut. It's a real dump. You'll know it because the door is bright yellow. Meet-up is after nine P.M. That's when Millar should be there."

"Got it."

"Outside of Al-Magreb, you'll exit, take a right, walk three blocks, then take your third left, here." Bradstreet used a pointer to illuminate a place on the map. "Memorize the route. You'll be looking for a woman in a burka. She'll approach you. Her name is Margaret Jasper. She's American. The clear word is 'whisper.' Margaret'll say it to you. Remember, you won't have communications yet. You need to listen to her. She'll be your first contact with us in at least five or six hours. A lot could change."

"So she says 'whisper,' what next?" asked Dewey.

"If she says 'whisper,' you're operational," said Bradstreet. "It means everything is cool. Follow Margaret. She has the weapons, communications, transportation, money, a little food and drink, everything. Once you go live on COMM, we'll be back in touch, obviously.

"From Saddar, you're going hunting for General Karreff. He'll be in one of four places. He has a couple of homes, a mistress, and he works late. If he's still at Northern Command HQ, that will be a problem. We're counting on him being in a less secure environment."

"What if he's at the base?" asked Dewey.

"If he's at the base, we'll send you straight out to Bolin," said Polk. "We'll take the risk that we can force a regime change through him."

"All three of Karreff's other possible locations are apartment buildings. We'll give you the lay of the land when you're online in Rawalpindi; the number of guards, what floor he's on, that sort of information."

"Got it."

"After you get rid of Karreff, you'll drive here," said Bradstreet, pointing to the map. "In the hills north of Islamabad. There, a chopper will take you and your team to the war front to find Xavier Bolin."

"Whose chopper is it?"

"It's ours," said Bradstreet. "We slipped it into Pakistan two days ago. It's in a barn up there. The pilot is a writer for *The Washington Post* who also happens to be CIA paramilitary. It's a low-observable, stealth Black Hawk."

Dewey nodded. "What time will he be live?"

"By the time you step foot in Al-Magreb," said Bradstreet. "So whether you take out Karreff or not, you'll have a chopper at your disposal."

"Good."

"The chopper'll drop you off as close to Bolin as he can. We'll determine what the best route is as we get closer to the event."

"Does Bolin speak English?" asked Dewey.

"Yes," said Polk. "But Millar is fluent in Urdu just in case."

"Once you're at Bolin's location, then it's up to you in terms of how you assault, when, and, of course, what you say to convince him," said Bradstreet.

"Use some of that legendary Delta charm," said Polk.

Dewey stared blankly at Polk.

"Assuming he agrees, next step will be having Bolin reach out to India's war command," said Bradstreet. "We could be pressing time by then and we don't want them to get an itchy trigger finger."

"It all sounds straightforward," said Dewey.

"There is a scenario you need to be aware of," said Bradstreet. "Let's go back to Al-Magreb for a second. What does Margaret say if everything's cool?"

"Whisper," said Dewey.

"Exactly," said Bradstreet. "If however, Margaret says the word 'thunder,' it means get the hell out of there. It means the operation was blown or New Delhi is moving sooner than we anticipated. Steal a car and head east, into Kashmir. Take Margaret with you. She's a messenger only so she won't know about the full operation until just before it begins. Get over the Line of Control with your team before India strikes or El-Khayab finds you."

39

At a quarter after twelve in the afternoon, beneath an overcast gray sky, the black CIA E-3 Sentry landed at the U.S. Air Force's Bagram Air Base near Kabul. The plane stopped at the end of the runway. A set of air stairs was driven to the side of the big plane as the door opened.

Bradstreet was the first down the stairs, followed by Polk, then Dewey.

Less than twenty feet away, a heavily modified Sikorsky MH-60M Black Hawk idled, the attack chopper's rotors cutting through the air, blowing sand and gravel across the cement tarmac.

Standing next to the chopper was Iverheart, long black hair, a mustache and a layer of stubble on his face, dressed in jeans and a T-shirt, a flak jacket on. He was six feet one, not quite as tall as Dewey, and his hair was not the blond from the photo. Across his chest, aimed at the ground, was a Colt M203 carbine combo assault rifle and grenade launcher.

He took a few steps toward Dewey, Polk, and Bradstreet.

"Rob Iverheart," said the soldier, looking at Polk, Bradstreet, then Dewey. "You must be Dewey."

"Yeah," said Dewey as they shook hands. "How you doing, Rob?"

"Not bad. Thanks for asking me to come along."

"I'm not sure you should be thanking me."

"I'm going to get you two dropped off," said Bradstreet. "I'm still waiting on confirmation that your third team member is on the PIA flight out of Heathrow. I won't have it until we're in Gerdi. If he's not on the flight, I'll volunteer, Dewey."

Dewey looked at Bradstreet with a blank expression on his face. He nodded. "Well, it's either you or Polk."

"I'm almost sixty years old, Andreas," said Polk, laughing.

"Sixty's the new forty. Besides, it always helps to have someone on your team you can outrun."

Everyone laughed. Dewey looked at Iverheart.

"You ready?" asked Dewey.

"Yeah," said Iverheart. "I'm ready."

"See you on the other side," said Polk.

Dewey turned and walked toward the chopper, followed by Iverheart and Bradstreet.

Dewey noted the Black Hawk's M-240 machine guns bolted to the side of the chopper, along with half a dozen AGM-114 Hellfire air-to-surface missiles strapped to the rails. He climbed into the cabin, followed by Iverheart and Bradstreet. On board were two gunners from the 101st Combat Aviation Brigade, who would be manning the M-240s.

Both pilots were helmeted and goggled. One turned and looked for an acknowledgment that they were ready to liftoff. Bradstreet gave him a thumbs-up. The speed of the rotors picked up, grew louder, and the chopper bounced. Then it lifted into the balmy sky above Bagram.

"Put these on," barked the crew chief, pointing at helmets dangling along the wall at the back of the cabin.

Dewey sat back against the wall, Bradstreet and Iverheart to his left. He watched the Black Hawk gunners belt themselves in, then set up behind the big machine guns.

"You guys First Battalion?" asked Iverheart.

"Yes, sir," said the crew chief.

"How's the hunting?" asked Iverheart.

"It's been a tough month, sir," said the gunner. "We lost a chopper a week ago."

The chopper ride began above brown, rocky terrain, with long steppes of flat fields, farmed by locals. Soon, as the chopper flew deeper into the mountains east of Bagram, the hills became increasingly steep. The chopper ascended. Dewey moved behind one of the gunners. The mountains were jagged and teeth-like and they looked like they went on forever. This was the Hindu Qu'ush, a mountain range that stretched to the Himalayas. It was spectacular but desolate; a stunning vista of snowcapped peaks too numerous to count. In the wake of 9/11, it had been the home of Osama bin Laden, and it was easy to see why. There were too many peaks, hillsides, and rocky outgrowths to count and they went on for as far as you could see.

"It's about a hundred miles," said the crew chief, looking back at Dewey. "We're going to try and avoid the villages. These fuckers'll still be out here though. We're also gonna shoot up high, above ten K. We should be fine, have you there in thirty."

The pilot steered the Black Hawk high up into the sky, and the temperature aboard the chopper dropped. Within fifteen minutes of takeoff from Bagram, they were flying at ten thousand feet, moving a hundred and eighty miles per hour to the east. The gunners slid the doors to the chopper shut. It was still loud inside the cabin, but there was no wind.

Both of the gunners were young and had 101st Airborne tabs on their chests. The gunner on the right sat against the front of the compartment. He pulled a pack of cigarettes out and lit one. After he smoked it down to the filter, he reached to his left, slid one of the windows open, then flicked the butt out.

Dewey glanced at the other gunner, who was slightly older and had removed his helmet. Neither was older than twenty-one or twenty-two years old.

"How long have you guys been running ops out of Bagram?" asked Dewey.

"I been here going on six months," said the gunner who'd been smoking. "For the last month, daylight duty, so that's slightly more fun though you tend to get shot at more."

"How's it going?" asked Dewey.

"Okay. They're like fuckin' rabbits. Terries keep multiplying."

"What about the Reapers?" asked Bradstreet. "Are they helping?"

"All we see are the aftereffects," said one of the gunners. "Don't get me wrong, we gotta be using 'em. UAVs are helping. But we get the fallout. If a village is hit, and some kid gets killed, we're the ones who see Allah's wrath, so to speak."

Bradstreet, to his left, was holding his hand to his ear; he had a COMM bud and he was speaking quietly with someone. He turned to Dewey.

"Millar's in the air," he said quietly. "He left London ten minutes ago. He's briefed. He lands sometime after dinner. We're almost at Gerdi."

Dewey leaned back and zipped up his jacket. He put his hands in his pocket and felt a small, round object. He pulled it out and looked down at his fingers. It was the cyanide pill he'd popped out of the terrorist's mouth in Cooktown. He put it back in his pocket.

The sound of the main rotor pulsing the air became a steady din, monotonous and calming in its own way. Dewey sat back and tried to clear his mind. He thought, for whatever reason, of Australia, of the little girl, Nicola Chasvur. He looked down at his fingertips, which were still a little raw from the climb up the rock face.

Dewey turned back to the window. To the south, behind them now, the crags settled into a long valley of rounded green hills that spread out for miles. A thin black strip meandered down the middle of the long valley, the Kunar River. In the distance, beyond the green and brown valley, the low tan and brick buildings of Jalalabad were tiny dots, like building blocks, in the receding distance.

The next miles went quickly, and Dewey felt the chopper begin to descend.

The Black Hawk moved lower and the gunners opened the doors, taking up positions on the M-204s. The wind came into the cabin, furiously at first. The chopper slowed as they descended down into the air just atop snow-covered crags of mountain. They cruised over gray and black ledge at more than one hundred and fifty miles per hour, the high whirring no doubt alerting anyone who might have been below.

Suddenly, the low cracking sound of distant gunfire could be heard over the chopper blades. The gunner to the port side of the chopper opened fire, pulsing the big machine gun at a distant bluff, blindly.

"Some punk with a Kalashnikov," said the gunner after several short bursts of machine gun fire. "If he hit us it would barely dent the side of the chopper. There's no way I'll hit him but you never know. Kind of satisfying knowing you might."

He fired another volley down into the rocky bluff.

After several more miles, the pilots began to tilt the Black Hawk toward the ground, until they were barely a hundred feet above the craggy, brown hills northwest of Gerdi. The chopper was as visible and vulnerable now as it would ever be. The gunners held the M-204s with both hands, targeting the ground with the nozzle of the big weapons, waiting for signs of attack from below. None came.

They passed over a series of clay huts that grew into a small hillside neighborhood of handmade buildings; wood and mortar huts and outbuildings. Finally, after passing one last stretch of brown hills, the chopper arced hard to the left and then descended toward a clearing, at its center a warehouse, roofless, charred long ago by fire, now abandoned.

In the middle of a dirt parking lot, a small group of men stood in a loose semicircle. They were dressed in white, with brown vests and black headdresses. Each man held a Kalashnikov and watched as the chopper circled and came closer to the ground, then touched down.

"Don't put the cannons on them," barked Bradstreet.

The gunners both turned.

"You sure?" asked one of them. "Those are Taliban, sir."

"Trust me," yelled Bradstreet. "Take the guns off them. *Now.*"

Both gunners, simultaneously, raised the nozzles of the M-204s, aiming them at the sky.

Behind the group was a long, beat-up tractor-trailer with strange-looking letters in Urdu, like hieroglyphics, and a hand-painted picture of a walnut.

Two of the men on the ground broke away, walked to the truck and opened the back door.

Bradstreet stood as the rotors settled into a slow churn. He patted one of the pilots on the shoulder.

"I'm coming back," said Bradstreet. "Two minutes."

Bradstreet climbed from the chopper and jumped down to the brown dirt. Dewey followed, then Iverheart.

Bradstreet, Dewey, and Iverheart walked toward the group of men. They were young, Dewey noticed, all of them in their late teens or early twenties. One of them, with long hair and a beat-up Kalashnikov slung over his shoulder, stepped forward. He dropped a cigarette to the ground as he walked toward Bradstreet.

"Hello, Van," he said with a heavy accent, extending his hand.

"Afternoon, Mainiq," said Bradstreet.

Mainiq's demeanor was serious. He was large, at least six feet four tall, and broad-shouldered. Dewey noticed he had only a few teeth, and the ones he did have were brown and yellow. He looked tough, mean even.

Dewey felt an odd chill running up from his spine.

"Mainiq," said Bradstreet, "this is your cargo."

"Hello," said Mainiq, nodding.

Dewey stared back, emotionless. "Hi," he said.

"What's your name?" asked Mainiq.

"You don't need to know our names," said Dewey.

"Fine, fine. Whatever. Where is the money?"

Bradstreet pulled a yellow envelope from his coat pocket. "Here's twenty-five thousand. You get the other seventy-five when they're both safe on the ground in Rawalpindi."

"Yes," said Mainiq, taking the envelope. "They will get there nice and safe, like I always do. Let's go. We need to get going. Follow me."

He led them to the back of the eighteen-wheeler. Inside, another man held a flashlight. Dewey climbed up into the back of the truck, followed by Iverheart. Mainiq climbed up after them.

"See you guys soon," said Bradstreet, remaining at the back of the truck.

Bradstreet gestured to Dewey with his hand, and Dewey knelt down.

"If they do get pulled over, it's *Lord of the Flies* time," said Bradstreet. "These guys won't protect you, so be smart. Stay alert. Kill what you need to."

Dewey nodded. He and Iverheart were led down the long, open tractor-trailer. Stacks of large burlap bags stood on both sides of the trailer and had a strong, musty smell. At the front of the dark trailer, Mainiq reached his hand up toward the corner of the trailer and pushed a bolt. Then he reached to what appeared to be the flat, dirty front wall of the trailer. He pulled and a thin door opened up.

"Here," said Mainiq. He handed Dewey a flashlight. "There are bottles of water. Also, if you need to go to the bathroom, there's a pail."

Dewey flipped the flashlight on and aimed it into the dark compartment. The space behind the false wall occupied the entire front of the trailer. Dewey stepped in; it was no more than two feet wide, and smelled of urine partially hidden by some sort of cleaning solvent, as if somebody had tried to clean it. There were two chairs, one on each end; folding lawn chairs. He saw the bottles of water and the tin pail.

Dewey climbed into the space, followed by Iverheart.

"We'll be in Peshawar in three hours," said Mainiq. "After Peshawar, we're safe. We'll pull over and you can come sit up front. We'll try to be quick. We have been searched many times, I have to tell you. But they've never found this yet."

40

PESHAWAR

Sometime later, after hours of bone-rattling bumps in the road which seemed like they would go on forever, the truck stopped. Dewey heard the back of the trailer open. At the side of the door, a bolt was moved and the trapdoor opened. The ugly face of Mainiq appeared in the dim opening.

"We're through Peshawar," the Talibani said in barely understandable English.

They'd made it down the Khyber Pass without incident. It was getting dark outside as Dewey and Iverheart climbed down from the back of the truck. They had pulled over on the side of a remote, single-lane dirt road. Low brown hills without much vegetation spread out on both sides of the deserted road. There wasn't a house, another car, a soul in sight.

They climbed inside the cab. Dewey and Iverheart sat in the middle, between the driver and Mainiq.

"Two hours to Rawalpindi," said Mainiq.

Dewey didn't trust people generally, but when it came to Mainiq, he got a particularly bad feeling. But Dewey did trust Bradstreet. Still, he kept his right hand on the butt of the .45 holstered beneath his shoulder.

The truck began to move down the road and they drove for several miles, through a sparsely populated area south of Peshawar. Music played on the radio; some sort of Pakistani folk music with high-pitched guitar.

At some point, a set of headlights appeared in the side mirror. The driver shifted and said something to Mainiq in Urdu.

Dewey glanced at Mainiq.

"What's going on?" asked Dewey.

Mainiq said nothing, instead studying the side mirror as the vehicle approached from behind.

"Mainiq," said Dewey, louder this time. "What the fuck is going on?"

"No worries," said Mainiq in barely understandable English. Then, to the driver, Mainiq said something that Dewey couldn't understand.

The truck lurched forward as the driver abruptly floored the gas pedal. Dewey glanced at the speedometer; the orange hand moved as the truck went from sixty to sixty-five to seventy kilometers per hour—only about forty-five miles per hour. *Too slow*, Dewey thought.

The lights, coming from behind, drew closer. Dewey craned his neck forward and looked in the driver's side mirror. He saw a black pickup truck coming on quickly.

Dewey pulled the weapon from his shoulder holster.

"No, no, it's okay," said Mainiq, holding his hand up to Dewey. "They're just passing."

"Do you know them?" demanded Dewey.

"No. I don't think so."

"Who the fuck are they?"

"They're passing. They're just driving by."

Dewey glanced at Iverheart, then nodded. Iverheart withdrew his weapon, a SIG Sauer P226 9mm pistol, and aimed it at the driver. In the same moment, Dewey trained his Colt on Mainiq.

"Nothing personal," Dewey said to Mainiq. "See what they want, then let's get the fuck out of here."

The black pickup raced alongside the truck. It swept by them, swerved in front of the truck, and slowed down, blocking the road just fifty feet ahead.

"It's okay," said Mainiq calmly, holding his hands up, ignoring the gun aimed at him. "It's okay. Let me talk. They're punks. It's nothing."

The driver braked and slowed the truck down. It came to a halt just behind the pickup.

In the flatbed of the pickup, two men sat, dressed in similar tribal garb as Mainiq and the driver. Both held Kalashnikovs, which they trained on the cab.

Mainiq opened the door, but Dewey grabbed his arm before he could climb down.

"If you fuck with us," said Dewey, "the first bullet's got your name on it."

Mainiq nodded, still calm. "It's okay. I would not betray Mr. Bradstreet. I will take care of it."

Dewey and Iverheart watched from the cab as Mainiq walked in front of the semi and approached the black Toyota pickup. The passenger door on the pickup opened and a short, thin man, older, with a gray and black beard, climbed out.

Dewey moved to the window. He glanced at Iverheart, who still had his gun on the driver. "Keep your weapon on him."

Dewey held his weapon aimed straight ahead, just out of sight of the people in the road.

Mainiq marched to the short, wiry man and began to speak loudly to him in Urdu. The man yelled back and soon they were arguing. Mainiq leaned forward, into the older Pakistani's face, and yelled at him. They looked as if they would come to blows.

"What are they saying?" asked Dewey, looking at the driver. "*What are they saying?*"

"Argue," said the driver in broken English.

"Yeah, no shit Sherlock. *About what?*"

"Don't know, man."

Mainiq was stabbing his right index finger into the air just in front of the man's face as he yelled.

Iverheart looked at Dewey.

"This is gonna get ugly," Iverheart said.

"On my lead," said Dewey.

One of the gunmen on the flatbed fired his rifle. The crack of gunfire was shocking and loud. The bullet hit Mainiq in the chest. He was propelled backward by the force of the Kalashnikov, his tan shirt splattered in blood. Mainiq tumbled backward onto the dirt apron next to the road, dead.

"*No!*" screamed the driver, next to Iverheart.

The older one who'd been arguing with Mainiq, started screaming at the man who'd just shot Mainiq.

Dewey had no idea what had just happened. And he didn't want to know. But he did know this was spiraling in the wrong direction.

He raised his Colt, moved it outside the window, and fired a round. The bullet hit the gunman in the chest, throwing him backward and down onto the bed of the pickup. He fired again. This bullet struck the other gunman in the side of his head. He was kicked sideways, falling next to his dead colleague in a wash of blood.

The older man stood for a moment in shock, staring into the back of the pickup. He looked up at Dewey, then reached for a weapon at his waist. Dewey pulled the trigger again. The bullet tore into the man's chest, knocking him backward and to the ground.

The pickup driver stepped on the gas, flooring it to get away.

To Iverheart's left, the driver started screaming.

Dewey pumped the trigger as fast as his finger would flex. The rear glass of the pickup shattered and a slug caught the driver in the back of the head. The pickup slowed down and, as the dead driver slumped over the wheel, turned left and wandered off the road, stopping a few feet off the pavement.

The driver was screaming uncontrollably now.

"You want me to . . . ?" asked Iverheart looking at Dewey.

"No. Just kick him out."

Iverheart reached over and opened the door.

"Out," he said.

The driver climbed down and began running toward the hills. Iverheart shut the door, then moved behind the wheel.

"So much for a bloodless coup," he said.

41

Millar stepped off the PIA jet and walked through the crowded terminal at Benazir Bhutto International Airport. At the immigration security checkpoint, he presented his passport.

Millar looked younger even than his twenty-four years. He had medium-length black hair and a good-looking face. He didn't stand out. He was handsome but not head-turning handsome. He blended in, especially here, where he was from, Pakistan.

Millar had a French passport with the name Jean Milan on it, supplied by CIA London station. Had the security desk at Benazir Bhutto been wired into Interpol or any other multinational, real-time security database, the name Jean Milan and the passport would have checked out. Milan, according to his passport, was French; according to his visa papers, a reporter for *Le Monde*.

However, the lack of an advanced security database forced the better security people at Benazir Bhutto to rely more on instinct. As Millar's passport was stamped, Parakesh, the customs officer overseeing airport security, did a double take. There was something about Millar that made the customs agent look twice, then a third time, at him. Perhaps it was the way Millar carried himself; he walked in the unmistakable manner of an athlete—or a soldier. Maybe it was the trained manner in which he ignored Parakesh's inquisitive look. To a junior customs agent, Millar wouldn't have set off alarm bells. But Parakesh was a veteran who came to customs from ISI. Benazir Bhutto represented his final promotion after a career of risky work in more challenging environs, including ten years in Peshawar. Overseeing security at the airport for Pakistani customs was supposed to be an easy job, a coveted nine-to-five gig at the highest pay level within government. But that didn't mean Parakesh's instincts had disappeared.

As Parakesh reached for the small microphone clipped to his lapel to call for one of his deputies, Millar realized he'd been marked.

Fuck, he thought to himself.

He walked through the terminal and saw a restroom sign down the terminal hallway in the direction of baggage claim.

Millar walked to the crowded baggage claim area, despite the fact that he hadn't checked any baggage. There were hundreds of people packed densely into the windowless area near the carousels. He stood behind an old man in a black beret. He looked back at the terminal. Within thirty seconds, he saw the gray-haired customs agent who'd stared at him at the security checkpoint. Out of the corner of his eye, he watched as the agent surveyed the crowd, found him, paused a second too long, then continued looking around. He then made eye contact with another agent; this one young, tall, uniformed in dark green.

Millar was trained in evasion. Losing the two Pakistani customs agents would've been easy. But Bradstreet's instructions were clear: *"If they mark you at the airport, it's imperative that you get back on the first flight out of Pakistan, or cut off the problem at the airport. Do not infect the operation."*

Millar waited a few more minutes in the baggage claim area, then walked to the restroom. He went to the last stall and set down his bag. Flipping a small steel hinge on the bottom of the case, he opened up a hidden compartment, removed a switchblade, and tucked it in his right hand.

He heard the door to the restroom open. He put his shoe on the toilet and flushed it, then opened the door. Standing next to the sinks was the younger agent. He stared at Millar as he moved to the sinks. They were alone. Millar set his bag down next to the sink and turned on the faucet.

"Papers," the officer said.

Millar reached into his coat pocket and pulled out his passport. He offered the passport to the officer.

"Here," said Millar.

As the agent reached for the passport, Millar grabbed his wrist and swung it violently behind his back, then moved his left hand over the agent's mouth to muffle the scream that came a second later as he snapped the arm at the elbow. Still covering the agent's mouth with his left hand, Millar pressed the release button on the switchblade in his right hand. He jabbed the blade against the officer's neck, pressing the sharp steel into the trachea but not breaking skin. When he knew the officer would not scream any longer, he released his left hand and took the walkie-talkie from the officer's belt.

"Calm now," said Millar in Urdu, holding the walkie-talkie next to his mouth. "Tell him to come."

The agent struggled to speak, tears of pain from his broken arm ran down his cheeks. "Tell who to—"

Millar yanked back on the switchblade, cutting the officer's neck a half-inch. He winced in pain as blood spewed forth from his neck.

"You know who," said Millar quietly. "If you want to live, tell him to come. Calm now."

Millar pressed the walkie-talkie button.

"Parakesh," the officer said. "In the restroom."

Millar dropped the walkie-talkie, then ripped the blade across the officer's neck, severing the trachea. He dragged him to the last stall and threw his body inside. Millar moved back to the door and stood behind it. There was a long streak of blood across the light blue linoleum, but there was nothing he could do about that. The door opened. In stepped Parakesh. He glanced about the restroom, saw the blood on the ground, then desperately reached for his weapon. He caught sight of Millar in the corner, in the same moment Millar lunged at him, plunging the blood-soaked switchblade into his chest, through the heart, killing him. Millar dragged the corpse to the last stall and threw it on top of the other agent, who was rapidly bleeding out. Blood flooded the restroom floor. Millar stepped to the sink, grabbed his bag, and left the restroom. Within two minutes, he was out of the terminal and sitting in the back of a rust-covered taxicab.

"Where to?" asked the driver.

"Saddar," Millar said in Urdu as he wiped blood from his hands onto his pants. "Al-Magreb."

42

Less than thirty miles from the Line of Control, the darkness of evening was punctured by small gas-fired lanterns at every street corner, dangling over crowds upon crowds of Pakistanis.

As midnight approached, Rawalpindi, Pakistan's fourth-largest city, teemed with noise and tension. War with India raged less than a hundred miles away, at the mountain-ringed canyon near Kargil, India-controlled Kashmir Territory.

They stood about in the humid night air. Pakistani men, shoulder to shoulder, smoking cigarettes, drinking espresso, tea, and chai. Arguing. Next to cafés overflowing with yet more people, as decrepit automobiles and jammed buses blared horns and raced recklessly through uneven streets.

The entire city, the entire country, was on a knife's edge. The anger of the city's devout Muslims fueled a sense of uneasiness that seemed palpable and menacing.

Dewey moved through the dark, crowded streets. Taller than most, he nevertheless attracted little if any attention. He walked quickly through the crowded, grimy streets of the Saddar District, the lower-class neighborhood in east Rawalpindi, mostly slums and working class. His eyes surveyed with trained wariness in front of him as he moved.

Dewey had learned long ago that it wasn't just what you looked like that attracted attention. It was how you carried yourself. How you moved. Tonight, he moved with stealth quietness, cloaked in the unkempt clothing and general dishevelment of a drifter, a freelance journalist, a tourist from the West, a mountaineer on his way to climb K2, a lost soul who somehow ended up here in Rawalpindi. There were many of them floating around.

Saddar was a dangerous place, among the poorest neighborhoods in all of Rawalpindi. But with that danger, that lawlessness, came anonymity and to a certain extent freedom for this lone traveler.

Dewey moved past crowds upon crowds of men for whom the war with India unleashed years of pent-up anger. Sweat drenched Dewey's shirt as he moved. It poured unabated down his face, down his thick chest, it was everywhere.

He and Iverheart had arrived an hour before, then split up so as not to attract attention.

Dewey's Colt was holstered beneath his left armpit, a black suppressor screwed into the end of the weapon. It bulged slightly at his spleen. At Dewey's right calf, his Gerber combat knife lay sheathed.

Dewey assiduously avoided eye contact. Tension was high now, and with tension came suspicion and paranoia.

Dewey occasionally felt the dark eyes upon him as he walked down uneven streets of stone and decaying mortar. Past crowds of men, past restless throngs of student radicals, out smoking, talking to one another about the war with India.

Just look away, he implored them silently. *I am just passing through. Look away . . . look away.*

Saddar's streets reeked, a medley of stinging aromas, the smell of human sweat, meat cooking on open flame pits. Horns blared above a din of car and bus traffic. Voices were raised louder than they should've been. Street vendors competed for space with clusters of men, smoking feverishly, drinking espresso, arguing.

"No, it couldn't be true!" a man yelled.

"It is," said another, "and praise Allah for it!"

Dewey knew what they were all talking about. Were the reports true? Had Pakistan really dropped a nuclear bomb on India?

Yes, it's true, Dewey thought as he moved silently past the heaving, angry throngs. *You people are within a hairsbreadth of being incinerated and you don't even know it.*

As he stepped by street vendors hawking meat and vegetables, past the occasional woman covered anonymously head to toe in burka, past young boys out way too late, yelling playfully at one another, past old men sitting at cafés, the words came into his head. The three syllables that sent crystalline fear up the spine of every illegitimate two-bit dictator in the world.

Coup d'état.

Dewey glanced at his watch: 9:55 P.M. The hour was at hand. They had little time now. Fourteen hours, five minutes. Then India would turn Rawalpindi and every other city and town in Pakistan into a glass parking lot.

The temperature in Rawalpindi hovered at around one hundred degrees, unseasonably hot.

Dewey walked with his head down, trying not to meet the eyes of passersby, finally spying a small yellow doorway from across the crowded street. He crossed the uneven, cracked pavement, maneuvering carefully between speeding cars and buses, approached the yellow tin frame, reached a hand out then pushed the door in. There was no sign on the small establishment.

He entered the illegal pub with his eyes down, silent, trying not to be noticed by the people inside the pub. It was at the seedy outskirts of the Saddar. Unnoticed as he stepped inside, Dewey glanced quickly around the place. Dimly lit, half empty, anyone in there too drunk to notice another scraggly-looking Westerner.

In the back corner, Dewey took a seat at an empty table. The stench was almost overwhelming, urine from the bathroom, which didn't have a door on it, combined with old Murree beer and wine, spilled on the floors, never really cleaned up properly, no ventilation. It was 10:00 P.M. He was an hour early. He sat with his back to the wall. He pulled a pack of cigarettes out from his pocket, lit one, looked around. When the waiter came, he ordered whiskey.

Iverheart walked in and stole a quick glance at Dewey, then sat at a table near the left wall, across from the bar, and ordered a beer.

It was 11:05 P.M. and still no sign from Millar. Another ten minutes passed, still nothing.

Dewey ordered a beer; one whiskey was enough, even though he wanted another. He remained in the back of the pub. Iverheart caught his eye. They both knew what the other was thinking: *Where is this fucking guy?*

Finally, at 11:45 P.M. a tall man walked in, drenched in sweat. He looked like one of the locals, but there was something different about him. His black hair was cropped close. His dark eyes roamed the bar, then met Dewey's: it was Millar.

Dewey put money down on the table and finished his beer. Standing, he walked through the bar. Iverheart and Millar fell in line behind him as he walked to the door.

On the rough-hewn stone sidewalk outside the bar, the three Americans walked down the street toward an alleyway. They were dead silent, no words.

In a block, a woman in a burka passed by. Her eyes stared out from the dark shroud for a moment too long.

"Whisper," she said in perfect English.

Margaret. Dewey nodded.

She turned, started walking, and fell in line at a distance. After a block and a half she turned into a side alley. The team followed her down the alley. Darkness made it hard to see her. They followed her down a meandering series of sidewalks, doors bolted, windows shuttered.

In a doorway next to a dilapidated garage, they ducked inside behind Margaret, then shut the door quickly behind them. Inside a small, windowless room, Margaret flipped a light on. She pulled her hood back. She was black, pretty, her face covered in sweat, a small, roundish nose framed by a short, curly Afro. She was no more than twenty-five years old. She smiled at Dewey.

"Hi," she said. "I'm Margaret Jasper." She had a faint southern accent.

"Hi, Margaret," said Dewey. "What's the update?"

"You're running late," she said. "We have a hard location on Karreff. So the plan is on, but you need to move."

"What about Bolin?" asked Iverheart.

"Bolin's still in the Drass aerie," said Margaret. "Here's your cache. I put food, drink, IFAK, in the car."

Arrayed across the dirt floor were three HK MP7A1 compact submachine guns with suppressors, three tactical vests packed with extra magazines holding 4.6x30MM Fiocchi CPS "Black Tip" slugs, and .45-caliber slugs. Three handguns were laid out, all Colt M1911s, suppressors attached to the ends. Three pairs of ATN FIITS14 night vision goggles. A supply of hand grenades. To the side, a long, thin duffel bag, unzipped, revealing an already converted Desert Tactical Arms "Stealth Recon Scout" .338 Lapua Magnum sniper rifle with AAC Titan-QD suppressor and L-3-Renegade-320 thermal sight, already mounted.

In the fluorescent light of the windowless garage, Dewey looked at Iverheart and Millar.

"We're watching Karreff from across the river," said Margaret. "He's with his mistress. We estimate eight to ten guards outside the apartment. There are two apartments on his floor but the other one is unoccupied."

"Why were you late?" Dewey asked, looking at Millar.

"They marked me," said Millar, wiping his brow. "At the airport. The passport held but a customs agent marked me and didn't let up. He and a backup followed me."

"Where are they?" asked Dewey. "Did you lose them?"

"I killed them," said Millar. "They're in a bathroom stall at the airport. They'll be found soon."

"We'll monitor ISI and capital territory police for any activity coming out of the airport," said Margaret.

Dewey, Millar, and Iverheart each leaned down and picked up a vest and weapons. The extra grenades and ammo Iverheart stuffed into a duffel bag.

Margaret reached down and picked up a small plastic box, then opened it. Inside were three small black objects that looked like gumdrops. She held the case out to Dewey, then Iverheart and Millar.

"They're waiting for you," said Margaret.

Dewey placed one of the COMM buds in his right ear.

"Hey, guys," he said quietly.

"Dewey," said Bradstreet. "Are you all there?"

"Yes," said Dewey.

"How was the trip in?"

"Fine," said Dewey. "You're going to need a new delivery man."

"What do you mean?"

"We were ambushed south of Peshawar. Your man was shot and killed. We had to kill a few locals."

"Look on the bright side, Mainiq," Polk chimed in, "you saved Uncle Sam seventy-five grand."

"What about witnesses?" asked Bradstreet.

"Not an issue," said Dewey. "Now give me an update. We need to move."

"It's just past midnight. So you have time, but it's getting tight. As we discussed, you need to take out Karreff before you go and find Bolin. Margaret will give you the layout of the apartment building."

"Okay."

"After taking out Karreff, you'll drive north. That's where the chopper is. Millar knows Rawalpindi and is briefed on the location of the chopper."

"What about India?" asked Dewey. "Are they committed to the time frame?"

"They're not backing off," said Polk over the COMM bud. "Noontime tomorrow. You have less than twelve hours now."

Dewey looked at Margaret. "What do we know about Karreff's security team?"

"They're all Special Services Group," said Margaret. "Karreff handpicked them. These are not security guards or even regular army. They've been killing Taliban in the Hindu Qu'ush for the past five years. That said, they won't be expecting visitors. Before the war with India, we watched them on four separate occasions during Karreff's overnights. They play cards, smoke cigarettes, and talk. Still, you just need to be aware: SSG is not a pushover group."

Margaret pulled a piece of paper from her pocket and unfolded it. It was a floor plan of the apartment building.

"The apartment is on the sixth floor," said Margaret, pointing to a corner apartment.

"On the nights you watched," asked Dewey, "where were the guards posted?"

"They had three men on the sixth floor, one on the first, and some men in the stairs," said Margaret. "We'll be monitoring from a safe house across the river. If we see movement before your attack, we'll call it off."

Dewey looked at his watch: 12:18 A.M. He glanced at Iverheart and Millar, then Margaret. He smiled at her. "Nice work. Thanks for your help."

"My pleasure, Dewey. Good luck, guys."

They followed Margaret through a small doorway, down an enclosed walkway, ducking their heads at the low ceiling height. They emerged into a garage bay. In the bay was an Isuzu minivan, rust-covered and layered in dents.

They climbed in. Millar took the steering wheel. Dewey rode shotgun. Iverheart threw the weapons duffel in back, then climbed in. Margaret pulled her burka back up, then opened the garage door. Millar hit the gas, exited the small garage, turned right, and punched the old vehicle down the thin, dark street.

43

A teenager was the first to step into the bathroom. The boy's name was Rasim and he was fourteen years old. He'd gone to the airport with his mother to meet his father, who was returning from London. He walked over to the urinals and, as he did so, looked down. He had a strange sensation then, realizing that he was standing in a pool of blood. For several moments, he stared in silence at the dark crimson that covered the linoleum. Then, he screamed.

Rasim ran out of the bathroom, yelling hysterically. Just outside the doorway to the restroom, his high-pitched yelp caused most of the hundred or so people in the baggage claim area to turn. Rasim looked around, his mouth open, and tears began to drip down his cheeks. He saw his mother, who was walking quickly toward him. He sprinted at her, bloody tracks following him, left by his shoes, across the cement floor of the terminal.

"What is it?" Rasim's mother said as he fell into her arms. Involuntarily, he kept yelling. Then he pointed toward the restroom door.

Two airport customs agents heard the screaming and approached the door. The first, a stocky, short man in a tan uniform, pulled his handgun from his waist holster.

"Don't let anyone in," he said to the other agent. "Call Colonel Parakesh and then the ambulance."

He held his gun out, trained at the door, waited a few seconds, then pushed the door in, weapon raised. He stepped into the restroom with the weapon aimed straight ahead, then let the door close behind him.

From the terminal, he heard the security siren begin to sound, loud then soft, loud then soft.

The agent's eyes registered the riot of blood covering the linoleum, deep maroon, almost black. His eyes followed the pool at the center of the room along its edges. It was coming from the stalls in the corner of the restroom. He inched forward, toward the stalls.

"Hello?" he said. "Anyone here?"

He pressed the microphone attached to his lapel.

"Have you found Parakesh?" he asked.

"*No,*" said the other agent. "*He hasn't responded.*"

The agent stepped gingerly into the sheen of wet blood and moved to the last stall, his eyes tracing the simple stream that coursed from beneath the stall door. At the stall, he reached out and pulled the handle back, swinging the door open. Lying in a contorted pile, he saw Parakesh. Beneath him, wedged against the toilet, he saw another body, Uruquin, another customs agent.

He pressed the mic on his lapel.

"I . . ." he whispered. He let the button go and tried to gather himself. He tried again. "I . . . I found them. Parakesh and Uruquin. They're dead. They've been murdered."

"*Shall I—*"

"Radio DIG Sahi at Capital Territory Police," he said. "Tell him there's been a double murder at Benazir Bhutto. Tell him Colonel Parakesh is among the dead. Then shut down the airport."

44

The minivan moved along the small, dark streets of Rawalpindi, dodging pedestrians as they walked in the night. Dewey glanced at his watch: 12:32 A.M.

Millar drove in silence. They crossed a bridge into the southern edge of the large city and at Jinnah Road went left. They took Jinnah for several miles, through the heart of Rawalpindi. Even at this late hour, people were gathered late into the night. After a few more miles, they went right onto Iqbal Road, then took another right onto College Road and finally a left onto a small, dark street called Gowal Mandi.

The sky was clouded over. Off the main boulevard, there was only ambient light.

"There," said Dewey, nodding to a large, white stucco apartment building, more than a dozen stories high.

In front of the building, three black Range Rovers were parked. An armed soldier stood at the door, weapon raised. He registered the minivan as it passed.

"Why don't they just hang a fucking sign?" asked Iverheart.

Millar drove past the apartment building without slowing down. He went six blocks south, then took a right, weaving back through the alleyway behind the row of apartment buildings.

Millar parked the car next to a row of garbage cans several hundred feet south of the apartment building.

Dewey, Iverheart, and Millar climbed out of the van. Each man was now stripped down to T-shirts. Shoulder holsters held their handguns, in front, they each carried MP7A1 submachine guns, nine-inch Gemtech suppressors screwed into the nozzles to soften the noise. Dewey flipped off the safety on his weapon, the others followed his lead. They pulled the ATN night vision goggles down, then flipped them on.

They walked quickly down the alleyway, MP7s aimed forward as they moved quietly along. Dewey led the team along the back edge of the alley, hugging the shadows, shrouded in darkness.

The men were soaking now in the intense humidity.

Dewey smelled cigarette smoke. He held up his right hand. At the rear entrance, more than a hundred feet away, was a small orange ember.

Dewey pointed at Millar.

Millar lifted his goggles to his forehead, then raised the sniper rifle to his shoulder. He turned on the thermal sight. He took a few seconds to set the target through the red dot laser optic atop the weapon. Then he pulled the trigger. The slug hit the soldier dead center on his forehead. The force of the bullet ripped most of his head off while kicking his body backward, into the air, for a brief second before he tumbled into a pile.

They ran quickly down the alley toward the back door to Karreff's apartment building. Behind the corpse of the dead Pakistani soldier, Dewey found a handle, but the door was locked. He pulled a snap gun—a device for picking locks—from his pocket and picked the lock.

Dewey entered first. Behind the door, a set of stairs led the men down into a darkened, musty-smelling basement-level room. Dewey moved quietly into the room, his goggles on, the machine gun out in front of him.

Iverheart and Millar followed Dewey into the room. Through the door, into the basement's hallway, then a set of stairs. Dewey cracked the door to the stairs and listened for nearly an entire minute. It was silent. Then, overhead, he heard the faint sound of chuckling. He stepped into the landing and found the light switch panel next to the door. He stepped back out into the basement hallway and closed the door slowly and silently.

"We have two men on the stairs outside Karreff's apartment," whispered Dewey. "What else do we know, Van?"

"You have one man on the first floor," said Bradstreet into Dewey, Iverheart, and Millar's earbuds. "The rest of the crew is upstairs, floor six."

"We'll take out the first-floor man, then take the elevator two floors above and two floors below Karreff," whispered Dewey. "Alex, you kill the lights on my signal, then Rob and I will take out the guys on the stairs. We'll wait for you, then move on the main floor."

Dewey and Iverheart climbed the stairs in silence. At the first floor, Dewey cracked the door open. A lone soldier, the one who'd been positioned outside, stood in the apartment building's foyer. Dewey nodded to Iverheart, who held the door while Dewey moved his MP7 to his shoulder and aimed. He looked through the Zeiss red dot optic on top of the weapon, setting the small dot on the soldier's cheek. The weapon made a dull thud as it fired.

Dewey dragged the dead guard to the stairwell entrance while Iverheart pressed the elevator button.

Dewey slung the MP7 over his back and pulled the Colt .45 from his shoulder holster as they stepped into the elevator. Dewey pressed the buttons for the fourth and eighth floors, two floors above and two floors below the sixth floor where Karreff was with his mistress.

The elevator doors closed and they began to move.

"COMM check," said Dewey, holding his earbud.

"Check," said Iverheart.

"Okay here," said Millar.

Millar opened the door to the basement level landing of the stairwell and stepped inside. He could hear voices coming from above. He moved to the light switch panel, then pulled his goggles down over his eyes.

At the fourth floor, Iverheart stepped off the elevator. Next to the elevator was a light switch, which he flipped off, darkening the hallway.

He pulled his ATN night vision goggles down over his eyes and moved to the stairwell door, waiting for Dewey. He extended the butt of the MP7, locked it in place, then moved the fire selector to full auto.

"I'm in position," said Iverheart into his earbud.

"Okay," said Dewey as the elevator doors opened on the eighth floor. "Hold on."

Dewey stepped off the elevator. He flipped off the light switch, pulled down his goggles, then moved to the stairwell door. He extended the butt of his weapon, then moved the fire selector to full auto.

"On one, we enter the stairs," whispered Dewey. "Nice and calm, Once we're inside, wait for me to give the go. Alex, don't kill the lights until I give you the signal."

"Got it," said Millar.

"Three, two," whispered Dewey, "one."

Gently, Iverheart pulled the door to the stairs open, then stepped into the stair shaft at the fourth-floor landing.

The voices of Karreff's guards were louder now; they jabbered on distracted, oblivious.

With his back against the wall, submachine gun in his left hand and aimed out in front of him, Iverheart moved silently up the stairs.

Dewey entered the stairwell at the eighth floor. He pressed his back against the wall, then moved down the stairs, feeling along the wall with his fingertips, in his right he held the MP7, suppressor jutting forward, trained down the empty stairwell in front of him.

He could hear the voices of the two soldiers echoing up the stair shaft. Their voices helped to cloak whatever noise was coming from his movement down the stairs.

At the seventh-floor landing, between iron bars on the stairwell bannister, Dewey eyed the red of one of the soldier's berets.

"Rob," Dewey whispered.

"In position," whispered Iverheart.

"Alex."

"Ready."

"On one, kill the lights," said Dewey.

Iverheart felt perspiration dripping from his hair and face. His heart was racing now as he waited for Dewey to start the count. He aimed the MP7 out in front of him. He placed his right foot on the first stair, readying for the sprint up to the guards.

"Three," whispered Dewey into the earbud. "Two, one."

The stairwell went black. Iverheart sprinted up the stairs, leaping three steps at a time, guided by his night vision goggles. His silenced MP7 was trained in front of him as he climbed.

He heard a panicked voice, then the faint thuds of weapon fire from above.

As he rounded the last corner before the sixth-floor landing he came upon one of the guards, running blindly down the stairs.

As the stairwell went dark, Dewey stepped to the railing, weapon forward, his finger on the steel trigger.

Dewey examined—through night vision goggles—the landing one floor below.

The soldier with the beret was looking about frantically, his world having gone abruptly black.

Dewey aimed his weapon at him and fired. The soldier was

knocked back onto the landing, where he tumbled to the ground. The other guard panicked, running down the stairs toward Iverheart.

As Iverheart made his way up the stairs, one of the soldiers came into view, clinging to the railing and moving down. Iverheart fired his silenced submachine gun, striking the soldier in the chest. The man fell, then rolled down stair after stair until his body stopped at Iverheart's feet.

Dewey moved down the stairwell toward the landing. He came upon the soldier with the beret, contorted against the wall. He didn't need to check and see if the man was dead; the right side of his face was missing.

"Clear," said Dewey.

"Clear," said Iverheart.

Millar's footsteps came faintly up the stair shaft. He joined Dewey and Iverheart at the sixth-floor landing, stepping by the corpses of the soldiers.

Dewey flipped a small light of his MP7 on, then removed his ATN goggles, which Iverheart and Millar did as well. In the dim light, he looked at the two young soldiers. He showed no emotion, but he felt it. For a brief moment, Dewey had a surge of feeling he'd long ago forgotten; the brotherhood of being a soldier.

"Nice job with the lights," whispered Dewey, trying to keep the mood light.

"Thanks. It's one of my specialties."

Dewey smiled at Millar. He was focused, but calm. He made it look easy, as if he'd been born into black-on-black operations. Dewey looked over at Iverheart. His eyes were as black as coal. Yet, they had something about them, a slightly mischievous aspect; Iverheart, it almost seemed, was having fun.

A noise came over a radio on the belt of the dead guard, words in Urdu.

"Their captain's checking in," whispered Millar. "We need to move."

"How many are down?" asked Bradstreet.

"Four," said Dewey, "including one in the back alley."

"You got three more dudes," said the Bradstreet over the COMM. "Maybe four."

Dewey moved to the door, the suppressor on the end of the MP7 aimed at the ceiling. Iverheart and Millar crouched to their knees on each side of the door, weapons ready.

The radio squawked again, the voice more insistent this time.

"They're looking for a response from the guy on the first floor," whispered Millar.

Millar swung his MP7 around. He extended the stock of the submachine gun, locked it into place, then moved the fire selector to full auto.

"You're entering at six o'clock," said Margaret on the COMM. "Karreff's apartment is at midnight."

"Quickly and quietly," whispered Dewey. "We don't want the general to hear us."

Dewey nodded at Iverheart. Slowly, Iverheart pulled the door ajar. Dewey pressed the silencer's tip against the small crack that soon appeared as Iverheart eased the door open. Light flashed into the stairwell.

Dewey saw the green of a uniform just inside the door. He spied brown eyes, short-cropped black hair, the silver black steel of an UZI SMG. Dewey moved the suppressor's tip up a few inches. He pulsed the trigger of the MP7 just once. The soldier's body catapulted violently, hit the wall, then crumpled to the floor.

Iverheart yanked the door open.

Dewey went right. A tall Pakistani soldier turned and sprinted, running desperately toward the corner of the hallway.

Dewey charged at him, submachine gun out and firing full into hail. Silenced bullets tore the wall; the bullet line approached the escaping soldier just as he rounded the corner, out of sight.

Dewey ran in pursuit of the fleeing soldier, trying to stop him before he could alert Karreff.

A moment after Dewey charged right, Iverheart and Millar moved left. Two more soldiers were standing in the corner, smoking cigarettes.

They barely had time to register the death of the first soldier.

Millar stayed low, in a crouch, his silenced MP7 in front of him. Iverheart was trailing just behind, silenced MP7 aimed just inches above Millar's head.

Millar fired first, putting a hole in the first soldier's forehead. The second man raised his UZI and fired wildly as he turned and ran down the hall toward Karreff's apartment.

Millar charged down the corridor and dived just before the corner. He rolled with the machine gun in his right hand out in front of him. He landed on the hard linoleum in the same instant he pulled the trigger of the MP7.

The fleeing soldier was halfway down the corridor, still sprinting. Slugs from Millar's weapon struck his back and he tripped up and rolled. Iverheart hurdled Millar and came upon the soldier, who he thought was dead. The soldier suddenly turned his weapon and fired. A slug passed by Iverheart, but one hit Millar, grazing his neck. Iverheart fired the silenced MP7 into soldier's neck, killing him.

In the opposite side of the apartment building, Dewey dropped the submachine gun to the ground as he ran, pulling his handgun out as he hit the corner and dived. Bullets tore the wall to his right, just above his head, as he lunged, rolled, and fired. The soldier stood firing at shoulder height, but Dewey was on the ground and his first shot hit the soldier in the forehead, killing him instantly.

"Clear," Dewey whispered.

"We're clear," said Iverheart.

Outside the entrance to Karreff's apartment, they inserted new forty-round magazines into their MP7s.

"You're hit," whispered Dewey, pointing at Millar's neck.

Millar had a clean, inch-long gash at the juncture of his neck and shoulder where the bullet had grazed him. Blood coursed down his neck. The collar of his gray T-shirt was quickly turning dark red.

"I'm fine," he said.

"We'll sew it up in the car," said Dewey.

"Karreff's awake," Margaret said over the COMM. "He may have heard something."

Iverheart pulled a snap gun from his vest. He moved to the door, pushed the tip of the snap gun into it, then pulled the trigger. He turned the device and pushed the door in, quietly.

Iverheart stepped into a long entrance corridor, followed by Millar then Dewey, who shut the door behind him. The apartment was big and eerily quiet, save for music—classical violin—playing somewhere in a distant room.

"What's he doing?" asked Dewey, whispering.

"He was getting a book," said Margaret. "You're still clean."

Dewey looked at Millar, pointed at his neck wound, then nodded toward the kitchen. Millar nodded and stepped away to clean up the fresh wound.

"Is there a suture in the IFAK?" whispered Dewey.

"Yes," said Margaret. "Two. There's also some *Quik clot*."

Dewey moved toward a doorway at the far end of the living room. His MP7 was in his right hand, tucked against his side. He opened another door, which led to a dimly lit hallway. The music was louder now. At the end of the hallway, the bedroom door was ajar. Light spilled from the room.

The sound of violins combined with the quiet murmur of voices.

Dewey reached out with his left hand and placed his fingers against the wood frame of the door. He pushed the door in.

On the king-sized bed, a beautiful dark-haired woman lay reclined. She was dressed in a pink nightgown. The woman sat back against a large red pillow. A reading light attached to the white headboard articulated over her shoulder. She wore reading glasses. Her long black hair had specks of gray.

Karreff's mistress was a large woman. Her cheeks were red and round. Her body spilled against the nightgown's fabric. But she was still beautiful, that was clear, her face elegant, her nose sharp and perfect. She looked up at Dewey as he stepped forward into the room, handgun raised, silencer jutting out toward the bed. The look of shock on her face paired with a sudden gasp. She attempted to gather the breath to scream, but fear gripped her throat and she could only quiver as she stared up at Dewey.

Karreff lay next to her, on his side, resting on his arm as he read a book. Karreff's hair was receding, gray and black, combed neatly to the side. He looked older than the fifty-two years of age he was. Karreff was a thin man and tall. His feet stuck out the end of the bed from beneath the black bedsheet.

Karreff's eyes followed his mistress's, looking up at Dewey as he entered the bedroom. But if her look was one of stunned shock and fear, Karreff's was one of calm, acceptance even. He remained relaxed on his arm, his sole reaction an involuntary jerk to his right. He casually removed his reading glasses with his right hand as he looked up at Dewey.

In that brief moment, it was obvious that this was not some sort of typical affair. Whatever Karreff had with the woman was something different. He'd left the war front this night to be with her, to talk and listen to Mozart.

"Please spare her," said Karreff calmly in perfect English. "She's innocent."

Dewey knew there could be no witnesses. One phone call from Karreff's mistress and the entire mission would be over before it started.

"Margaret, can we rendition a witness?" asked Dewey without removing his eyes or the track of the silencer from Karreff.

"Yes," Margaret answered.

"Meet us in the alley."

Dewey aimed the silenced MP7 at Karreff's naked chest. Karreff held up his right hand.

"Just tell me," Karreff whispered. "Are you American?"

Dewey stared at Karreff. He nodded at him, then fired. A silenced bullet hit Karreff between the eyes. The blunt force of the slug jerked his skull backward. Karreff's large frame rolled off the bed.

Dewey looked at Karreff's mistress.

"Do you speak English?"

"Yes," she said.

"Get dressed," said Dewey. "Now. Don't say a word. If you want to live, don't say a word. Do you understand?"

She nodded her head up and down as she wiped tears from her cheeks.

45

BENAZIR BHUTTO INTERNATIONAL AIRPORT
ISLAMABAD

Deputy Inspector General Wafeeq Sahi of the Capital Territory
Police Department stepped into the cordoned-off area outside the
restroom at the now-empty Benazir Bhutto Airport.

Behind him, in addition to an assortment of assistants and deputies, followed the executive director of Benazir Bhutto Airport, a
short, pudgy man named Karim Gola, who was dressed in a light gray
suit. He was attempting to get Sahi's attention, though Sahi wasn't
listening.

"We now have more than a dozen flights circling in the sky overhead," pleaded Gola. "Outside the terminal, more than three hundred people are waiting to get in. This disruption—"

Sahi entered the restroom, stopped a foot inside, and looked
down at Gola. He held his hand up, indicating that Gola was not to
take another step.

"You have two dead men in your airport," said Sahi. "Federal
agents. We'll have this cleaned up as soon as we can. In the meantime,
I suggest you make arrangements through PAF to take any planes low
on fuel into another part of Chaklala until you're back open."

Sahi stepped into the restroom. He nodded to one of two police officers standing inside the room, indicating he wanted the door shut behind him.

A sheet of plastic had been laid on the floor, on top of the pool of blood that covered most of the linoleum. The bodies of Parakesh and the other customs agent, Uruquin, were next to each other in the center of the room. A woman in a white coroner's jacket knelt between the two corpses. She'd stripped the uniforms off the dead mens' upper torsos and was taking photos. The stab wounds were gruesome. On Parakesh, a half-foot-long horizontal incision across his chest. On Uruquin, a ghastly slash across the neck, his head nearly detached.

"Hi, Chief," said the coroner without stopping what she was doing. "Both are homicides, obviously. Nothing exotic, just a very sharp blade."

"How recent?"

"Within the hour."

"Was it the same blade?"

"I don't know. Most likely. Does it matter?"

Sahi shrugged. "Probably not."

He looked at one of his deputies.

"Want me to dust it?" asked the deputy.

"What's the point?" said Sahi. "There are millions of prints in here. See if you can find any bloody ones, I guess. We'll cross-reference them with ISI database."

He turned to a customs agent at the door.

"Get me whoever's running security at the airport now that Parakesh is dead. And get these bodies cleaned up."

In a windowless conference room a floor above the terminal, Sahi and two of his deputies sat at a large table with the airport's now senior security official, a uniformed agent named Muhammed Hasni.

"Any witnesses?" asked Sahi.

"None that we know of," said Hasni.

Sahi looked at one of his deputies.

"Get a few men interviewing taxi drivers," said Sahi. "Did anyone pick up any strange passengers? Anyone injured or bleeding? While you're at it, have someone back at HQ working the hospitals; see if anyone arrived within the last hour with a knife wound or other injury."

"What's our profile, Chief?" asked one of Sahi's deputies.

"I don't know," said Sahi, shaking his head, bewildered. "Let's do an inventory. This individual killed two experienced security men, then dragged them into the corner of the bathroom. Parakesh used to be ISI; I knew him. He was a hard-ass who spent years fighting Taliban in Peshawar. These were precise, efficient kills. So that tells me this is not some sort of punk. This guy is strong, efficient. And clearly after something; otherwise why did he need to kill two federal agents? Maybe Parakesh suspected someone coming into the country and tried to stop him? I just don't know. It seems pretty clear this was done by a professional."

"Professional?" asked Hasni.

"Intelligence agent or special forces. Mossad, CIA, MI6. A foreigner."

He paused and removed his glasses.

"What about passenger manifests?" asked Sahi, looking at Hasni. "I assume we can get at those?"

"Yes," said Hasni. "Immediately."

"Is the airport linked into the ISI mainframe?" asked Sahi.

"No," said Hasni.

Sahi shook his head. "Let me make a call. I want you to cross-reference the names of arriving male passengers during the two hours leading up to the discovery of the bodies against the ISI database. If anyone is on the ISI list, you tell me immediately."

"Got it."

"If nobody sets off the ISI alarm bells, let's look for someone young," said Sahi. "Someone who could be a foreign agent. American, British, European, Russian, Chinese. Get me a list of any foreign males who arrived in the last two hours."

"What are we going to do with the list?" asked one of his deputies.

"It depends on the size of the list," said Sahi. "If the group is small enough, we'll put out an all points bulletin."

"Why do you think he killed them?" asked Hasni.

"The question is not why he killed them," said Sahi, standing up. "The question is, why is he in Islamabad?"

46

Aswan Fortuna and another man stepped into the lobby of the Damac Tower in downtown Beirut, near the marina. Damac Tower was brand-new with marble, steel, and glass. Modern art hung on every wall. But what was most noticeable about the lobby was none of these; it was the security desk—an elegant but intimidating four-foot-high wall of steel, over which flowed a small waterfall and behind which stood two large men in black uniforms, guns prominently holstered at their waists.

Fortuna and his bodyguard showed IDs, then walked to the back of the lobby and into an elevator.

His bodyguard was young, dressed in a long, shiny black leather coat, with a shaved head and a few days' worth of stubble. Beneath the leather coat, he carried two weapons. In his shoulder holster was a CZ 75 P-07 DUTY 9mm handgun. Tucked into his pants, at his front waist, was a subcompact Glock 33 .357 magnum. He walked in front of his boss. Fortuna wore a blue linen button-down shirt and jeans. As always, Fortuna was unarmed.

They rode the elevator in silence. When it stopped on the

twenty-eighth floor, they stepped directly into the only apartment on the penthouse floor of Beirut's most exclusive address.

It was a sprawling, open apartment. Glass was everywhere, and the midday sun, the smells and sounds of the Mediterranean, all made it feel like a beach house.

"Wait here," said Fortuna, nodding at a white leather Barcelona chair near the entrance. He stepped into the living room. Glass walls encased a space that was at least a thousand square feet. The floor was concrete. The only furniture was a pair of bright orange leather sofas, each at least ten feet long, facing each other near the far corner of the room, and, in the middle of the room, a stone sculpture of a reclining nude woman done by Rodin. The view was nothing but black ocean and blue sky.

Seated on one of the sofas, smoking a cigarette, was Nebuchar Fortuna. He was wearing only a pair of red underwear. Nebuchar said nothing as his father approached. He watched as his father crossed the room and stood next to the sofa across from him, staring out the window at the sea.

"What a view," Aswan said, shaking his head back and forth, as if in disbelief. "Magnificent. How much did this place cost you?"

Nebuchar took another drag but said nothing.

Aswan sat on the leather sofa across from Nebuchar. For several moments, he stared at his son, then attempted a smile. Still Nebuchar had no reaction other than to continue puffing on his cigarette, then ashing it carelessly on the cement floor. Finally, Fortuna leaned forward.

"I'm sorry, Nebbie," he said. "What more can I say? I would like to think that if you were the one who'd been murdered, and Alexander hadn't been able to find the killer, that I would have struck him, too."

Nebuchar looked at his father with a cold glare, then took another puff on his cigarette.

"Now we both know that isn't true," said Nebuchar. "And even if it was, a man who would strike his son is no man."

"How would you know what it is to be a father?"

"I don't. Hopefully, I never will."

"Now, don't say that. You'd be a good father."

"Stop the flattery, Papa. Why did you come here? To blame me for Andreas getting away?"

Fortuna stood up and moved to the opposite sofa, next to Nebuchar.

"First and foremost, I came here to apologize." Aswan reached out and awkwardly patted Nebuchar on his knee. "I'm very sorry for striking you. You know my temper."

Nebuchar nodded. "Okay, great, is that it?"

"That's not it. I realized something this morning."

"And what is that?" asked Nebuchar, a malicious smile on his face. "Did you finally realize that the only reason Candela fucks you is because of your money?"

Nebuchar laughed at his own joke. Aswan remained silent until his son had finished laughing.

"Perhaps you're right," said Aswan, controlling his anger at his son's remark, "but I would rather be making love to a twenty-three-year-old model than a bottle of gin, like you do every night."

Nebuchar nodded. He stared at his father for several moments. "Don't worry, Father, I fuck whatever I want. I just don't have to pay for it, like you."

"Enough. Can we stop this? I didn't come here to insult you or to be insulted."

"Yes, fine. What do you want?"

"I came to tell you that I straightened it out with Hassan Nasralla," said Aswan. "You'll make a payment to Hezbollah to atone for killing Pasa. He wasn't happy, but he also didn't like Pasa very much."

"How much?"

"Ten million euros."

"Is this why you came here, to collect the money?"

Aswan Fortuna paused, then reached his hand out and placed it on his son's knee.

"I realize what a bad father I've been to you. I'm sorry."

Nebuchar looked down at his father's hand on his knee.

"I want to talk to you about the money," said Aswan. "The money that Alexander left us, the money that funds jihad."

"A billion?" asked Nebuchar. "Two?"

"Twelve billion."

Nebuchar sat up. He leaned forward, incredulous, taking another cigarette and lighting it. "I knew it was more than a billion, but—"

"Yes. Your brother was a prodigy."

"Yes, he obviously was. Unlike me. Is that what you're thinking, Father?"

"No, it's not what I'm thinking. I'm getting old. I'm making you trustee, Nebuchar. You'll have a fiduciary relationship to the funds. You will have access to the money, and, as you will come to understand, you will take on the responsibilities of the money. There are many people who depend upon the money, many groups."

"Groups? Hezbollah?"

"Hezbollah, Al-Qaeda, Lashkar-e-Taiba, Taliban, Hamas, Islamic Jihad, Muslim Brotherhood. These are the main ones. But there are dozens of others you don't know about. We fund splinters; a small group who breaks off from Al-Qaeda, for example, we will back them. We don't choose sides and we don't tell them what to do, as long as the group believes in violent jihad."

"How much did we spend to sponsor them last year?"

"Last year, the total was six hundred and eighteen million dollars. Much of that paid for IEDs used in Iraq. The details are all in here."

Fortuna handed the folder to Nebuchar.

"In addition, we fund more than nine hundred madrasas throughout the Middle East, Africa, Europe, and Indonesia. That number is growing."

"What is that number?"

"Last year, we spent almost two hundred million on the schools. That's our future. If I could spend more, I would."

"How does this all happen?"

"Ah, yes, it sounds complicated. It *is* complicated. Alexander designed it all. There are three primary agents: one in Moscow, one in London, one in Dubai. They handle the disbursement of funds.

They're paid monthly from different accounts. These accounts are in banks all over the Middle East and Europe, even a few in Russia and Canada. Accounts are set up automatically each month based on a sequential series of numbers. For example, three accounts every month are established with an account number that is your birthday followed by the date the account is established. These new accounts are funded by the oldest accounts, which are wound down. It's automated."

"Will the money eventually run out?"

"I don't think so," said Aswan. "The money is invested, also automated. The financial institutions are selected by the three agents."

"Are they aware of what you're doing?"

"Yes, of course. They're believers. But the institutions themselves are oblivious. As for the recipients, they are largely successful in masking where the money comes from. It's always the challenge. The CIA, MI6, Interpol, are constantly on the trail. Because it's so dispersed now, we are able to suffer the loss of one account. Lashkar-e-Taiba, for example, has accounts all over the place: Montreal, Moscow, Dubai, UAE, despite the fact that the money is used exclusively in Pakistan."

Nebuchar flipped through the folder.

"Your brother was indeed a financial genius," said Aswan. "Alexander's greatest gift to jihad is that he guaranteed its funding into the distant future. Perhaps until its ultimate victory."

"What do you want me to do with this?" he asked, holding the folder open.

"Put it somewhere safe. Learn it. Ask me questions. It's time for you to begin to play the role that you must play, Nebuchar. And I must begin to teach you. I must also begin to treat you like a son. We have a great deal to be thankful for."

Nebuchar stared at his father. He smiled.

"Would you like to share a glass of wine, Papa?" asked Nebuchar.

"Yes, that would be nice, Nebbie."

47

Margaret met Dewey, Iverheart, and Millar in the back alley and took Karreff's mistress. With her was a pair of men, both dressed in bishts.

"Who are they?" asked Dewey.

"Cleanup crew," Margaret said.

"Check the basement and the stairwells," said Dewey. "And get rid of the Range Rovers out front."

Iverheart drove the minivan and turned out of the alleyway behind the apartment building, retracing their path back to Jinnah Boulevard.

Dewey glanced at his watch. Nearly 2:00 A.M. He sat in the back of the minivan. Millar sat to his right, bouncing his left leg up and down, the adrenaline flowing.

"How bad is it?" Dewey asked, looking at Millar's neck.

Millar pulled the blood-soaked neckline of his dark T-shirt down. The wound was covered by a small dishcloth soaked with blood.

Dewey reached up, flipped on the light of the minivan, then pulled off the towel.

The bullet had penetrated the skin and muscle at the very juncture of the neck and shoulder line. A small, black hole was ruptured and torn, blood coursed out.

"Half an inch and it would've hit the carotid. You're lucky you're not dead."

From a small brown duffel bag, Dewey removed the IFAK. Inside was a small plastic package which he ripped open. He took out a presutured needle.

Dewey looked at Iverheart in the rearview mirror.

"Pull over."

Iverheart turned the minivan into a parking lot, next to a squat cement building, now dark. He extinguished the vehicle's lights.

Millar leaned his head against the front seat so that Dewey had a clear view of the wound beneath the overhead light.

Dewey took the sutured needle and stuck it into Millar's neck, puncturing the skin beneath the bullet wound.

"Oh, fuck," groaned Millar. "That hurts."

Dewey pulled the needle through the skin, stitching up the wound. In less than two minutes, Millar's bullet hole had been crudely sutured.

Dewey placed the needle back in the IFAK. He removed a small tin canister filled with clotting agent. Dewey took a large pinch of the powder and sprinkled it on the wound. Millar flinched as he spread it around the suture. Dewey placed a large bandage over the wound and taped it securely to Millar's shoulder.

"Let's go."

Iverheart drove to the eastern section of Rawalpindi by Raval Lake, which they could see in the distance, illuminated by the moon. After several more miles, Iverheart took a left onto an unmarked dirt road, then took a right into a deserted field. There they saw the sudden, sharp metallic outlines of the Black Hawk.

Iverheart parked the minivan. The pilot started the chopper. Within two minutes, they were airborne.

The Black Hawk flew across the dark sky at nearly two hundred miles per hour. It stayed low, at less than five hundred feet, moving to the east, toward the war front in Kargil. The chopper flew in darkness, the pilot relying on instruments and night vision technology.

Dewey stepped into the cockpit and tapped the pilot on the shoulder.

"ETA?" asked Dewey.

"Forty-five minutes," said the pilot.

"We need to move drop-off," said Bradstreet over the COMM bud. "I'm sending the coordinates right now."

"Why?" asked Dewey.

"You've got heavy air fire in the corridor east of Drass all the way to Kargil. The National Highway is getting worse. Both sides are blowing everything out of the sky. You need to drop off farther back in the Pakistan supply line."

"Is Bolin still at the target?"

"Affirmative. Bolin hasn't moved, but you do not have a clear flight path. I don't want you to get shot down."

"What about the approach to the building?"

"Target is a high point-of-view structure. A house at the edge of Drass on the front side of a hill. Your team needs to come up from the south. There's a reservoir at the base of the hill. Target is due north from the reservoir, straight up the hill, maybe a mile."

Dewey looked at his watch: 4:10 A.M. He moved into the cabin.

Millar reached into his vest and removed a small tin. He quickly spread black on his face then passed it to Iverheart, who did the same, followed by Dewey. Millar handed Iverheart and Dewey each a small plastic packet no bigger than a cigarette pack. Inside, raw protein in thick, agarlike syrup form, enough nutrient to sustain them for a week, if necessary.

After flying for a half hour, the pilot reached his hand up and showed five fingers outspread, closed it, then opened the fist again: ten minutes.

They checked their weapons and packed ammunition and grenades into the pockets of their vests.

Dewey stared out the chopper window. The peaks of the Himalayas were visible in sudden, sporadic bursts of light from mortar fire in the valley beyond.

A bright light flashed beneath them. A burst rocked the chopper, kicking it violently sideways.

Out the right window, the horizon was increasingly dominated by orange and red flare-ups as the chopper moved closer to Drass. The steady sound of detonations could be heard across the night air as fires burned on distant hills.

The outline of the battle was illuminated by fires. This was the heart of the battle—epicenter of the rapidly escalating war.

Dewey leaned forward.

"The drop-off has been moved," said Dewey over the din of the rotors. "We're going to need to hijack a vehicle."

"Is there a contingency?" asked Iverheart.

"Contingency?"

"If Bolin's not there."

"The contingency is to get the hell out of Kashmir."

The chopper's nose arced down and shifted left. The chopper flew over a tree line, then a cluster of small huts in a village now consumed in flames.

Another loud blast ripped the air. The chopper bounced hard. A mortar burst more than a mile away, its reverberation strong enough to send a shock wave through the chopper.

They passed over a mountain ridge and a great valley lay in front of them.

Like a curtain being opened, the combat theater spread out before them across the shelf of the dark valley.

Dewey stood, leaned into the cockpit, and registered the sight.

The battle lines spread for at least ten miles in two long corridors east to west. India was in the far distance, Pakistan closer. In between the two lines of combatants, the valley was dark.

In the orange light of the mortar fire, batteries of Pakistani soldiers were visible from above. Soldiers gathered in groups behind mortar cannons staged every hundred yards or so. There were thousands of men, spread out in a line as far as the eye could see.

Behind the front line, a supply highway wound east into the mountains. Trucks, troop carriers, fuel tankers, and other machinery rumbled along, the small yellow headlights flickering in a line that stretched back toward Rawalpindi.

A mortar blast hit the Pakistani supply line. The line of vehicles, like an ant trail, was lit up in the sudden burst of light. A constellation of flames came next. Several vehicles were now consumed by fire. One gas tanker burst into spectacular red and gold flames.

The chopper moved in a straight line parallel to the supply highway, closer and closer to the front. It bounced and heaved as high-altitude winds roiled the air.

Dewey glanced at Millar and Iverheart. Their faces were now darkened in black war paint. Millar had changed from his bloody T-shirt into a long-sleeve shirt.

They had completed the first part of the mission, but time was running out, and they all knew it. In addition to the looming Indian deadline, there was now the added set of complications that would soon be created by Karreff's disappearance. Despite Margaret's clean-up crew, his absence would inevitably trigger a reaction, most likely defensive in nature. Perhaps moving El-Khayab into hiding. Or, if the Pakistanis thought his disappearance was part of an operation, perhaps another nuclear strike on India.

Dewey tried to put the time pressure out of his mind. He needed to be calm. He needed to show confidence, for it was confidence above all that would enable Dewey and his team to insert themselves like a scalpel into heart of Pakistan's war command.

The pilot waved Dewey forward.

"I need to put you guys down," the pilot barked over the din of the chopper. "There's shit flying everywhere."

"Put it down over there," said Dewey, pointing to the line of trucks headed toward the front. "Just off the supply line."

The chopper swung right and descended toward the Pakistani supply highway. Within a minute the Black Hawk was hovering above the ground.

Dewey, Millar, and Iverheart pulled their night goggles down. Iverheart reached out and opened the door to his right. Dewey leapt from the chopper, followed by Millar and Iverheart.

Seconds later, the chopper lifted back up into the dark sky, turning north and disappearing. They were on their own.

48

RASHTRAPATI BHAVAN
NEW DELHI

President Ghandra looked out the two-story window onto the square in front of Rashtrapati Bhavan, the presidential palace. Hundreds of small flames danced in the blackness, candles mostly, along with the occasional burning fire, a Pakistani flag being lit up or else a photograph of Omar El-Khayab being torched. He looked at his watch. It was past four in the morning.

There was a knock at the door, then, before he could say anything, Indra Singh entered.

"It's four in the morning," said Ghandra. "Why are you still awake?"

"Why am I still awake?" Singh asked rhetorically in disbelief. "Your country is on fire, Mr. President. Is there anyone alive who isn't awake?"

"The crowd has grown larger."

"Gate thirty-five is a bloody mess," said Singh, referring to the entrance into Rashtrapati Bhavan. He walked into the spacious living room. He placed his leather briefcase down on the leather sofa and sat down. He was sweating profusely. "The crowd is like rabid wolves. Since when are *we* the enemy?"

"What do you mean?" asked Ghandra.

"What do I mean?" asked Singh, incredulous. "The only reason they haven't stormed the gates of the palace is because of the twenty thousand men that General Nair has placed between them and you."

Ghandra stood at a window, looking down on the square in front of the palace. The square was packed with people, most holding candles.

"How many people are there?" asked Ghandra.

"Nair estimates one hundred thousand. It felt bigger. You're isolated up here, Mr. President. You can barely hear them. A group of young thugs attempted to flip over my limousine. They want to know why we haven't counterattacked El-Khayab."

Ghandra turned from the window.

"Did you tell them about the coup?" asked Ghandra, grinning.

"You think it's funny!" yelled Singh. "There are riots in Hyderabad, Bhopal, Chandigarh, and Mumbai. In southern Delhi, someone burned photos of you at a demonstration."

Ghandra walked from the window to a large mahogany cabinet, where he turned a key and opened the doors. Inside was a bar. He poured himself a glass of Beefeaters. He walked to the sofa and sat down at the opposite end of the sofa from Singh.

Ghandra took a big sip from his glass of gin, but said nothing.

"I told you the anger would rise," said Singh. "You didn't listen. The people of India want answers. You sit here isolated from it all while the people of India wonder if they even have a leader. With each passing minute of silence, they become more bitter and more embarrassed. 'Has Rajiv no pride?' my own wife asked me."

"If I had listened to you, I would have gotten the people of India so riled up that any sort of peaceful resolution would have been impossible. At this moment, they would be tearing down the palace. If I had listened to you, Pakistan would no longer exist and there would be hundreds of millions of people dead in both countries. We would probably be dead too, Indra. Your advice grows more foolish and idiotic by the hour. Get some sleep. The Americans are on schedule and the coup is going to work."

"And if it doesn't?"

"If it doesn't, we will attack."

"The irony, Rajiv," said Singh, "is that your desire for a coup d'état in Pakistan could lead to a coup in your own country."

"Is that a threat, Indra?"

"No, it's a plea from your oldest and dearest friend," said Singh, leaning forward, his face contorted and red with emotion. "Your own military is questioning your strategy. They talk openly of your will-power."

"And what would you have me do?" asked Ghandra.

"Hit back. Launch the nuclear attack right now! Apologize to the Americans later. El-Khayab is laughing at us right now. Osama Khan is painting the targets for the next attack. These men are radical jihadists. They want to push it further."

Ghandra stared down into the clear liquid in his glass. He lifted the patterned crystal glass to his lips and bolted the rest of the gin down.

The sound of breaking glass caused both men to jump up from the leather sofa. A rock smashed through the window just to the left of where Ghandra had been standing, then rolled on the green and red oriental carpet.

Ghandra stood up, stepped around the sofa, and walked to the rock, leaned down, and picked it up. It was approximately the size of a baseball.

"A good arm, perhaps we can recruit him to play for the Daredevils," he said, referring to New Delhi's professional cricket team.

Singh stared at Ghandra for several moments, then smiled.

"You're not going to change your mind?" asked Singh calmly.

"No, Indra, I'm not. There are eight hours left. Let's give America the time it needs."

"You know I support you, no matter what," said Singh. "I would never voice my doubts to anyone but you. When my wife said that to me, I yelled at her. I will need to buy her flowers for the names I called her. I'll think of ways to redirect the anger of our citizens. In a few hours, we'll make an announcement about our progress in Baltistan, something to quell the unrest."

"I'll call Jessica Tanzer. It's time for a report from the Americans anyway."

"Rajiv," said Singh. "If America has failed . . ."

"If America has failed, we will proceed with the original plan."

49

BRISBANE GRAMMAR SCHOOL
BRISBANE, AUSTRALIA

Youssef pulled the semi into the parking lot at the Brisbane Grammar School, rolling the eighteen-wheeler to the darkest spot in the empty lot. It was ten o'clock at night, eighteen hours after he hijacked the truck north of Cairns. He shut off the lights, then the engine.

The truck's driver lay crumpled in a bloody mess in front of the passenger seat. While being caught with the dead body in the truck would likely put him in an Australian jail for the rest of his life, Youssef thought the risk of being seen removing the body was even greater, so he left it there. In the humid Queensland air, the corpse had started to smell. Youssef's solution to that was to open the windows and breathe through his mouth.

In the darkness, he climbed down out of the cab of the truck, then walked across the deserted playing fields. He could smell the fresh-cut grass. For a brief moment, the smell intoxicated him.

Youssef had grown up in Damascus, but when his parents died he and his younger brother, Ahmed, were sent by their grandfather to an all-boys boarding school in Scotland called Hampden Public. Hampden Public was one step above reform school. Most of its students were from somewhere in the United Kingdom, and had been kicked out of better private schools. For a brief moment, the smell of the grass reminded Youssef of Hampden Public, of its big, open fields and brick buildings. He thought of Ahmed. The smell of the grass brought back a wave of bittersweet emotion.

As he walked across the dark grass, Youssef recalled his last day at Hampden, only a month after he'd first arrived. It was the day a Scottish boy named Simon had pushed Ahmed down a flight of stairs, breaking both of his arms, as well as his nose.

"Did you do anything to him?" Youssef had asked, standing over the infirmary bed, horrified, crying as he looked at his badly injured younger brother. "Did you say anything to provoke this?"

"No," said Ahmed. "Nothing, Youssef. I swear. I don't even know this person."

"Did he apologize?"

"No. He laughed. They all laughed."

At dinner that evening, Youssef had gone directly to the silverware cabinet. After picking up a butter knife, he'd walked through the dining hall, searching for the boy who'd pushed Ahmed down the stairs. When he saw Simon, a tall senior, sitting at a table with his friends, Youssef had approached the table. He hid the dull butter knife behind his back.

Everyone at the table had ignored him as he stood there, waiting to speak.

"Excuse me," Youssef had finally said to Simon, interrupting his conversation. "Are you the one who pushed my brother down the stairs?"

Youssef recalled the surprised look on the large boy's face, followed by the toothy smile, the food in his mouth visible as he looked at Youssef.

"What about it, *Mohammed?*" he'd answered in a thick Cockney accent, to the amusement of his friends. "Yeah, I might have. He shouldn't a been getting in my way."

Without saying anything, Youssef had raised the butter knife in his right hand, then swung it down as hard as he could. It ripped through Simon's blue blazer, through the button-down shirt, then plunged four inches deep into Simon's neck. Youssef remembered how the blood had spurted out like a garden hose. Ten minutes later, despite the best efforts of a variety of teachers and kitchen staff, Simon lay dead on the dining hall floor. He had never heard someone scream as loud as Simon had that day.

The next few months were a blurry haze of policemen, detention centers, lawyers, mental hospitals, psychologists, foster homes, jail cells, until he and Ahmed ultimately ended up in an orphanage outside of Cairo. But he would do it all over again. The moment he swung that knife blade was the moment he became a man.

The memory raced through his mind as he walked across the football fields, toward the lights of the houses in the distance. He started crying. He'd always been there to protect Ahmed. He'd driven for eighteen hours, and every time the thought of his younger brother crept into his mind, he pushed it away. He'd treated Ahmed like a dog, he knew, but he was the only relative Youssef had. He wondered how Andreas had killed Ahmed. Youssef closed his eyes. Right now, he had to focus on getting out of Australia. He wiped the tears from his cheeks, then pushed the thought of his brother completely away.

At the far end of the fields, he climbed over a wooden fence, then went right on Toombul Road. He then took another right and walked into the parking lot of the Novena Palms Motel. He knocked on the door of unit twenty-two.

"Youssef," said an older man with a beard and glasses, who opened the door. "Sit down. Take off your coat."

The man inspected the wound on Youssef's right arm, poking it with his finger, even sniffing it.

"It's not infected yet," he said. From the table, he took a syringe. "This is an antibiotic, just in case." He stuck the needle into Youssef's arm.

After the man bandaged his arm, Youssef went into the bathroom. He leaned into the tub, turned on the faucets, put on a pair of rubber gloves, then took a bottle of black hair dye and rubbed it through his hair, turning it black, then dried it. He removed the gloves, then put on a striped button-down shirt the man had brought.

"Sit down," the man ordered.

He took photos of Youssef.

"There's food over there," said the man as he looked over the photos, deciding which one was best. "Crackers, fruit, and cookies. Eat while I do this."

"Why the passport?" asked Youssef. "I thought Nebuchar had arranged for a private plane."

"A charter," said the man as he worked on the fake passport. "They will inspect your passport before takeoff."

Half an hour later, a black Camry pulled into the Hawker Pacific Flight Center at Brisbane Airport. The car drove onto the tarmac and up to a shining dark blue and white Hawker 4000 jet. Youssef climbed out of the car and walked over to the Hawker's air stairs. At the base of the stairs, a young man in a light green Australian Customs and Border Protection Service uniform was waiting. He inspected Youssef's passport, then stamped it without asking any questions.

"Have a nice flight," said the man.

Youssef climbed up the airstairs, nodded at the pilots in the cockpit, then sat down in one of the leather seats in the back of the jet. When the jet was airborne, Youssef opened his cell phone.

"I'm in the air," he said, running his hand through his short, spiky hair. "Thank you for making the arrangements. See you in Beirut."

50

Deputy Inspector General Sahi, Agent Hasni, and four other Capital District policemen, as well as a pair of customs agents, reconvened in the second-floor conference room at Benazir Bhutto Airport.

"I ran the manifests," said Hasni. "For the three hours leading up to the discovery of the bodies, there were eleven arriving flights. Eight were domestic, three were from outside Pakistan. I ran all eleven manifests, a total of one thousand nine hundred and forty-four passengers."

"What did ISI flag?" asked Sahi.

"None of the passengers set off the ISI watch list," said Hasni. "So I focused on the three international flights. There was a Thai Airlines flight out of Bangkok, and two PIA flights, one out of Chicago, the other London. On those three flights, there were four hundred and eighty passengers. Three hundred and eighty-one were Pakistani. I eliminated them, as you suggested. We can always go back to the bigger list."

"Yes, yes. Go on."

"Of the ninety-nine foreigners, forty-two were men. I removed anyone under twenty and over fifty. This reduced the number to twenty."

Hasni pushed a short stack of papers toward Sahi.

"And here they are, Inspector," said Hasni.

Sahi started to flip through the small stack of papers. Each sheet was a photocopy of the individual passenger's passport entry page, along with photo, and entry customs visa form, in which each passenger is required to list their profession, duration, and purpose of visit.

Sahi analyzed the pages, quickly separating ones he felt were improbable from individuals who looked, at least hypothetically, like they could have killed the two men. Out was a group of four men from Colorado who were climbing K2, three doctors from Canada who were traveling to Baltistan to volunteer for a month at a rural health clinic, and several others with equally disqualifying backstories.

It did not take long for Sahi to narrow the group of twenty down to three: the first was an American from Chicago who was an executive for a U.S. defense contractor called Sallyport. The second was a Chinese man from Shanghai who worked for a Chinese pharmaceutical company called Pleineir. The third was a journalist from Paris, a correspondent for *Le Monde* named Jean Milan.

"Get these out immediately," said Sahi, pushing the three sheets of paper to one of his deputies. "Police, border patrol, customs, TV stations, hospitals, newspapers, hotels, military. I want these men brought in for questioning."

Back at Capital Territory Police HQ, Sahi closed his office door. He studied the three sheets of paper. Of the three photos, it was the photo of Jean Milan that Sahi found himself going back to again and again. The man simply didn't look French. He looked Pakistani. Sahi went to his computer and searched the CDP database, found a number, then picked up his phone.

"*Oui,*" said a groggy voice with a French accent. It was Pierre Toloph, Islamabad bureau chief for *Le Monde*. "*Qu'est-ce que c'est?*"

"Mr. Toloph, this is Deputy Inspector General Sahi from Capital Police. Can you answer me a question?"

"What time is it?" asked Toloph in a thick French accent. "Do I need counsel? Jesus, it's four thirty in the morning!"

"You don't need a lawyer and you can go back to sleep," said Sahi, "if you answer me one question."

"Yes, yes, ask your question, Inspector."

"Who is Jean Milan?"

"Jean Milan? Why do you ask this? How should I know?"

"You don't have a correspondent working for you named Jean Milan?"

Toloph was silent for several seconds, then hung up the phone.

51

DRASS
INDIA-CONTROLLED KASHMIR

The air was cooler in the Mushkoh Valley than in Rawalpindi. They were more than twelve thousand feet above sea level now.

Through a night vision monocular, Millar studied the Pakistani supply line in the distance. Then they moved.

The air was thin and they ran at a good trail pace, seven-minute miles, one by one behind Iverheart, negotiating the boulders and cracks in the ground. They stopped on a bluff just above the supply line.

In the distance, the sound of a truck could be heard coming toward the front.

Millar stared through the monocular.

"Fuel truck," he said as he studied the eighteen-wheeler rumbling toward them in the distance.

Dewey looked at his watch: 4:55 A.M.

They moved down from the ridge above the road as the truck approached.

"You're shooter," Dewey said to Iverheart. "We'll fall in after you take out the driver from here."

Iverheart swung the rifle from across his back to his front, then lay on the ground, unfolding the DTA SRS. He got down on his stomach, setting the rifle on the ground. He turned on the Renegade thermal sight.

On the hill, in pitch-black, Iverheart adjusted his ATN goggles. Through the goggles, the truck was illuminated in glowing shades of green. Iverheart, on his stomach now, placed his finger on the trigger of the sniper rifle, and flipped his goggles up, then looked through the Zeiss optic on top of the rifle aligning the truck's path. He would have to hit a target moving at more than thirty miles per hour.

Dewey and Millar lay on their stomachs a few feet off the road.

The fuel truck rumbled closer, its engine louder, its headlights increasingly large as it approached, oblivious to the coming ambush.

A low crack whipped through the air as Iverheart fired from the hill. The round passed ten feet above Dewey and Millar as they waited on the cold ground. The slug hit the young driver in the skull, spraying blood across the back window of the cab. The truck jerked off the road, then slowed to a stop.

Dewey ran to the truck and opened the cab door on the driver's side. He reached up, pulled the dead Pakistani soldier from the cab, and dragged the corpse to the side of the road, more than a hundred feet, out of sight.

Iverheart arrived, sniper rifle slung over his shoulder.

Back in the truck, Dewey and Millar brushed broken glass from the seat, then took an old rag and wiped blood and brains from the seat and windows of the truck.

"We got company," said Iverheart from the ground next to the truck.

The lights of an approaching troop carrier flickered less than a quarter mile behind them.

Dewey took the wheel. Millar climbed into the passenger seat and moved to the middle. Iverheart climbed into the cab next to Millar. Dewey hit the gas and the large truck began to move. He steered it back to the supply road.

The truck gathered speed and was soon moving quickly down the supply road toward the war front. Dewey steered a straight path east for more than five miles. The sound of mortar fire grew louder as they closed in on the front. The pace of the bombing seemed to uptick as dawn neared.

When the sky was dark, the lights of the truck illuminated little more than the road in front of them. But the fires revealed an altogether different scene; a violent, chaotic beauty, composed of red and orange, framed by the ridgelines of the Ladakh Range, far in the distance behind the Indian front.

Dewey kept moving toward the front, down the supply road. They passed several departing Pakistani Army vehicles—empty troop carriers, flatbeds, a few fuel trucks.

"Dewey, it's Van," came the voice in Dewey's COMM bud. "UAV says you want to break right as soon as you can now."

Dewey moved his night vision goggles down over his eyes. He reached in front of the steering wheel and shut the headlights off. He turned right and eased the tanker truck off the dirt supply road. He kept the gas pedal floored, moving at the same pace, in darkness, across flat terrain, avoiding the occasional bush or boulder. They drove for several miles, parallel to the battle front at their left.

"You're approaching the reservoir beneath the village," said Bradstreet over the COMM. "You're good on foot from there."

Dewey downshifted, then eased the truck to a gradual stop. They climbed out of the truck. To the left was a large pond with a small shack at its edge. Dewey surveyed the hill above with the monocular. In the distance, the sharp incline of a mountain base sprang vertically skyward. Several hundred yards up was a village.

"Why hasn't India razed it yet?" asked Dewey, tapping the bud in his ear.

"They think it's abandoned," said Bradstreet. "They don't want to destroy the town if they don't have to. Remember, this is Indian soil."

Dewey glanced at his watch: 5:25 A.M.

The sky was stunning; the stars looked as if you could reach up and touch them. To the east, the horizon was turning gray as dawn approached. The light illuminated the mountain village; white cement and mortar flashing like an aerie above the fray of the battle.

Millar led a fast-paced run toward Drass. As advertised, he was in excellent shape, and it showed. The twenty-four-year-old kept them running, even in the thin, high elevation air, at a grueling six-minute pace. Dewey brought up the rear, behind Millar and Iverheart. The air burned his lungs. The steady pounding of mortar cannons filled the air. They stopped to catch their breaths at the base of the mountain, a few hundred yards below where Bolin and his commanders were overseeing the battle. Despite the temperatures, now in the forties, they were all sweating profusely.

Dewey adjusted the settings at the side of his ATN PS15-4s. The village of Drass sprouted in low, square buildings up the side of the mountain. The village was dark. A terrace jutted out from the hill above them. He saw movement on the terrace.

"Ten o'clock," said Iverheart.

"I see it," said Dewey. "You guys see the building?"

"Yeah, I got it," said Millar.

"We're counting fifteen to eighteen people," said Bradstreet. "No one below the building but there is a guard posted at the front door."

"I'll torch one of the buildings below the terrace," said Dewey, pointing. He looked at Iverheart. "You come with me. We'll assault from the terrace. Alex, when you hear the bomb, move in hard from the front."

Dewey reached into his back pocket and removed a photograph. He flipped on a low light on the underside of his MP7, and aimed it at a black-and-white head shot of a Pakistani man, longish hair, dark, slightly overweight, a mustache.

"That's Bolin," said Dewey. "Whatever you do, don't kill him."

They moved up the hill, through a quarter mile of walnut trees and flat grazing plots carved onto steppes. They split up beneath the terrace. Dewey and Iverheart moved to the side of the house and hid beneath the eastern precipice of the terrace. Millar went around the other side of the house and crouched at the corner of the building, just out of sight from a soldier guarding the front door.

The sky was rapidly growing light as sunrise approached. Dewey could clearly see now, for the first time, the Ladakh Range across the valley. For as far as he could see in either direction, the dusty plain was interrupted by a sporadic line of vehicles, tents, and men, thousands of small clusters spread out for miles. Orange and red bursts lit up the line every few seconds. For the first time, Dewey could also clearly make out the front of the Indian line, its presence indicated by the dotted red of mortar rounds, fired toward Pakistan.

"Here we go," said Dewey, speaking into his COMM bud.

"Ready here," said Millar.

Dewey took a grenade from a pocket on his vest. He pulled the pin then hurled the grenade at a wood and stone hut down the hill below the terrace. The blast ripped the hut. The sound was thunderous as the cloud of smoke and debris plumed. The building was incinerated; fire and flames engulfed the small structure.

Shouting came from the terrace as soldiers ran to see what had happened.

Dewey kicked in the door that led to the terrace.

In front of him stood five soldiers. Dewey registered the faces, recognized no one. Then he triggered his MP7, cutting down a man who was clutching an UZI.

Iverheart entered behind Dewey, shooting a second soldier.

Dewey pumped a cartridge into the chest of a tall, overweight soldier, while in the same moment Iverheart killed the remaining pair of soldiers.

Another soldier burst through the terrace entrance, his hands gripping a Kalashnikov. He aimed it at Dewey, who was sideways to him, oblivious to his entrance.

Millar heard the explosion in the same moment he felt the ground tremor beneath his feet. He moved around the front of the building. A soldier at the door turned, but Millar fired his MP7, hitting him in the chest, dropping him.

He opened the front door. The room was filled with mattresses pushed to the side and stacked. He burst through the room to another door. Shouting came from the room, then gunfire from the deck. He stopped at the door, flipped his goggles off his head, then booted the door in.

He entered a large brightly lit room. The haze of cigarette smoke hovered like a cloud. A wooden table was surrounded by more than a dozen men in military uniforms. The soldiers were staring at the door to the deck, their eyes following one of their soldiers, charging toward the deck, Kalashnikov in hand.

At the sight of Millar, confusion swept over the men at the table. They swiveled between the terrace door, and him, now standing at the opposite end of the room. Eyes moved between Millar and the black steel of the submachine gun in his hands, now aimed at their heads, and the Pakistani gunman running toward the terrace.

On the terrace, Iverheart was momentarily stunned by the approaching soldier, whose Kalashnikov was now trained on Dewey. Recovering, Iverheart fired his MP7, swinging it around, trying to intercept the soldier. His bullets blew a line of dusty holes in the stucco next to the doorway just as the gunman began firing at Dewey. A slug struck the gunman in his chest, sending him crashing to the floor against the doorjamb.

Inside, the commanders watched as their soldier was blown backward in a hail of bullets.

At the far side of the table, one of the generals grabbed a pistol from his belt holster, but Millar cut him down with a quick burst from the MP7 before he could fire, throwing him back against the wall to the shock of his colleagues.

Millar trained his silenced submachine gun at the table of military commanders. Wearing a blank expression on his blackened face, he covered the table slowly with the end of the suppressor; every man in the room knew what the price would be if they tried to move.

Iverheart moved in through the terrace door, stepping over the dead gunman now lying in a contorted pile on the ground. He took up position to Millar's left, weapon trained on the generals.

The war hierarchy stood in silence, unable to move.

Only one man remained seated. He was a large man, his hair slightly long, with a bushy mustache. He wore a khaki green military uniform, the chest and shoulders a medley of green, red, blue, and gold tabs. He held a cigarette in his hand. He had a big, bushy mustache. The man stared at Iverheart, then at Millar, impassive and calm, despite the intrusion. His eyes shot to the terrace door.

Dewey stepped over the blood-soaked corpse of the dead soldier.

Dewey's face, what was visible of it beneath the dark beard and long, sweat-soaked brown hair, was black with war paint. Only his blue eyes stood out in the light of the room.

Dewey stepped slowly into the room, his demeanor calm, his confidence clear to every man in the room. At the center of the room, Dewey stopped. His silenced MP7 was aimed menacingly in front of him. His face was expressionless.

Dewey's eyes focused, along with the tip of the silencer, solely on the man seated directly in front of him, the man with the mustache, Field Marshal Xavier Bolin.

After several moments, Dewey spoke.

"We don't have a lot of time, Field Marshal Bolin," he said.

Bolin took a drag on his cigarette, then moved it away from his lips. His hands tremored as he ashed on the table.

"What do you mean?" Bolin asked, his voice calm but trembling slightly.

"India will launch a retaliatory nuclear strike on Pakistan," said Dewey. "This strike has but one purpose: wipe Pakistan off the map. Three quarters of India's nuclear stockpile is either in the air or launch ready at the border as we speak. Karachi, Islamabad, Peshawar, Lahore, Rawalpindi; every other city and town in this country: gone."

Bolin moved his cigarette to his mouth, his hand shaking slightly. He took a long puff, then exhaled.

"What do you want me to do about it?" asked Bolin.

"With America's help, you become the next president of Pakistan," said Dewey. "Today. Right now. India stands down. You make peace."

"What about General Karreff?"

"He's dead."

"El-Khayab?"

Dewey said nothing. He didn't have to.

Bolin finished his cigarette, then stubbed it out on the wooden table. He cleared his throat. He looked around the table at the other generals and military men. To a man, their faces remained blank, part fear, part shock.

"And if I say no?" asked Bolin.

Dewey paused. He waited several seconds, motionless. He kept the MP7 trained on Bolin. Finally, he spoke.

"You say no, I empty this SMG into your head. Then we disappear into India and get the hell out of here before it's all incinerated."

"In other words I don't have a choice."

"That's right."

Bolin breathed in, a sharp gasp, but said nothing. He leaned forward, staring down at his hands, now clenched together on the table.

Finally, he looked up at Dewey.

"So it's happening right now?"

Dewey stared at Bolin. He raised the silencer and aimed it at the ceiling.

"Yes, Field Marshal," said Dewey. "Coup d'état."

52

Omar El-Khayab walked into the cabinet room. The conference table that dominated the room was surrounded by his war cabinet. A dozen different conversations were going on, the voices creating a din inside the large room. Led by his brother, who gripped the blind cleric's right forearm, El-Khayab sat in a chair at the end of the table.

It was 7:30 A.M.

"Good morning, everyone," said El-Khayab in a hushed tone as he entered the room.

The talking around the table ceased.

Outside, the chanting continued, despite the early hour.

"Death to India! Death to India! Death to India! . . ."

"So what now is the report from the war front?" asked El-Khayab. "General Karreff?"

"General Karreff isn't here yet," interrupted Darius Mohan, Pakistan's foreign minister, a hint of anger in his voice. "More important than the war front, I think, are the implications of the nuclear bomb that was dropped at Karoo."

"All in good time, Darius," said El-Khayab. "Where is General Karreff?"

"President El-Khayab," interrupted Mohan, refusing to yield. "Your decision to drop a nuclear bomb on India, for which you consulted exactly no one, is creating great pressure for me and my entire ministry."

"And I take it you don't like this pressure, Minister?"

"Answers are being demanded of me, sir," said Mohan. "We cannot simply stonewall the world. It has been a day and a half and we have said nothing."

"And there has been no response," interrupted a tall, thin man with a grayish goatee, Afro, dark glasses, Pakistan's minister of defense, Osama Khan.

"No response?" asked Mohan, incredulous. "The world has condemned us! Even our allies have condemned us. The United Nations is expected to slap sanctions on us today; wide-ranging, highly punitive sanctions that will effectively isolate Pakistan."

"The surgical utilization of the nuclear device has done precisely what we wanted it to do," said Khan. "It has flushed out the fundamental weakness of our Hindu enemy. They don't respond because America will not let them."

"America has no control over New Delhi," barked Mohan. "New Delhi has put their bombs into the sky. Have they not, Minister Khan?"

"Yes, Darius," answered Khan, calmly glancing about the table. "They cruise along the borders of our country at twenty thousand feet, like birds, but nothing drops. Have you noticed that? Rajiv Ghandra is paralyzed by fear."

"We need to reach out to Washington and to New Delhi," demanded Mohan, his voice rising. "Moscow, Paris, Beijing; our allies are demanding answers. We are allowing a small incident in Kashmir to explode in our faces."

"This small incident has created a historic opportunity," answered Khan.

"It has endangered every man, woman, and child in Pakistan," said Mohan. "We must seek a peace. We must do it now, before it's too late!"

"It's precisely now when we must press on to destroy our enemy," said Khan. "They have demonstrated their weakness and indecision to the world. This is Islam's time. We have been chosen—"

"Stop this empty rhetoric!" screamed Mohan. "Do you realize what is occurring right now, as we speak, in New Delhi? At the Pentagon? We've thrown a rock at a bee's nest and the hornets are now swarming around us. We are all going to die if we don't act to stop it!"

El-Khayab stood up from his seat.

"*Traitor!*" he screamed, his voice inflecting to a high pitch, lashing the air like a viper fang. He swung his cane down onto the table, violently smacking the wood, snapping the cane in half from the force of his swing. "*Impertinence! Get out!*"

"You've placed Pakistan in the crosshairs of America and China!" shouted Mohan, standing, refusing to yield. "We're enemies to neither but we will soon be destroyed by both!"

"*Arrest him!*" shouted El-Khayab.

Two soldiers moved toward Mohan.

"Arrest me," said Mohan contemptuously as the two guards grabbed his arms. "But let the heavens witness it was I who fought to prevent—"

"*Be quiet!*" shouted El-Khayab.

"—the annihilation of Pakistan!"

Mohan was pulled from the table and dragged out the door.

El-Khayab stood in silence for more than a minute. The chanting from Revolution Square seemed to grow in its intensity.

"*Death to India! Death to India!*"

Finally, El-Khayab cleared his throat and leaned forward.

"General Karreff?" El-Khayab whispered, anger threading his words. "Is he here yet? When will we have our report from the war front?"

"I've called the general three times now," said el-Jaqonda. "I still have no answer. I will try again."

The black cell phone in front of Khan rang. He reached forward and picked it up.

"Excuse me," Khan announced to the table. Khan flipped the

phone open, placed it against his ear. "What?" he said into the phone.

"Minister Khan, this is Field Marshal Bolin."

Bolin held the phone against his ear with his right hand. In his left hand, a cigarette burned. Through the thick sheaf of smoke that filled the cabin of the helicopter, Bolin stared into Dewey's eyes.

Dewey held another phone against his own ear, patched into the same call.

"Where's Karreff?" asked Khan, urgency in his voice.

"General Karreff is delayed at the front," said Bolin, exhaling. "He's ordered me to return to the capital to give the report."

"When will you arrive?"

Dewey held up two fingers.

"Two hours," said Bolin.

"President El-Khayab awaits."

"I'll be there as soon as I'm able, Minister Khan."

He flipped the phone shut.

Dewey looked at Bolin. "Perfect," he said.

Dewey glanced at the two other Pakistani generals in the chopper, then looked out the window. He counted two more choppers, moving across the sky, bearing west, toward Rawalpindi. Millar and Iverheart were each inside one of them, keeping an eye on the commanders from the war front traveling with them.

Dewey's submachine gun lay across his lap, his hand casually across the weapon.

Dewey nodded at Bolin's cigarette.

"Would you like me to put this out?" asked Bolin.

"No," said Dewey. "If you don't mind, I'd like one."

Bolin smiled, then handed a pack of Gitanos to Dewey. Dewey removed a cigarette, then Bolin extended a lighter.

"Thank you," said Dewey. He took a long puff, then exhaled. "Are you ready?"

Three black Alouette III SA-319B choppers swept over the eastern edge of Rawalpindi, landing on the tarmac outside PAF Chaklala Air base.

The base occupied more than ten square miles of territory, spread out in an ordered pattern of plain-looking tan and green buildings, barracks, landing strips, lines of fighter jets, helicopters, and assorted other structures.

The choppers landed in the middle of an asphalt landing strip adjacent to a cavernous corrugated steel hangar.

The two generals seated next to Dewey and Bolin descended from the chopper. Bolin started to follow, but Dewey stopped him, placing his hand on his knee.

"Hold up," said Dewey.

Bolin sat back. He lit another cigarette.

After the other commanders had departed the chopper, Bolin shut the door behind them.

"What is it?" asked Bolin.

"Let them wait. You're the next president of Pakistan. You need to start acting like it."

"You know what you're doing," said Bolin, puffing on the cigarette.

"Yes," said Dewey. "The only danger right now comes from your own commanders. Ambition. 'Why Bolin? Why not me?' You need to keep your eyes open. You need to *take* power. Right here, right now. If anyone opposes you, they need to be removed. Either they're with you, or they're dead. Failed coups are caused by weakness at the top, guys like you thinking it's your charm and personality carrying you to power. Successful coups are accomplished through strength and fear, the barrel of a gun and loyal men at your side. In a year or two, you can turn Pakistan back to democracy. But right now, it's all about strength and fear."

"Your men can't carry their weapons," said Bolin. "Some will see it as a threat. Or worse, they'll think I'm a puppet."

"Not an option. Let me explain something to you. The reason

317

you're here right now, and not lying on the ground with a hole in your head, is because of America. When your commanders see us standing behind you inside that hangar, the thought in every head in that room will be Persom Karreff. Right now, me, my team, the United States of America, we're an extension of you. Like it or not, we are your greatest asset."

"Then what? You stay and babysit? Get me to buy American war jets and tanks? Tell me when I can blow my nose?"

"Is that why you think we're here? Do you really think we care what kind of jets you fly?"

"Of course."

Dewey laughed and shook his head.

"Field Marshal Bolin, if we don't remove Omar El-Khayab by noon, India will destroy this country. India will turn Pakistan into a radioactive sandbox. And when they do, it's highly likely China will move on India. America will be forced to respond. I'm here because America doesn't feel like fighting a war with China. Get it? You, Pakistan, even India for that matter, you're all a sideshow. I don't care what kind of jets you fly. President Allaire doesn't care what kind of jets you fly. To be honest, I don't even care who steps up and helps us take out El-Khayab. But the fact is, you were chosen. You have the loyalty of the troops and the midrank commanders. You aren't religious and we know of your dislike of El-Khayab. You owe America peace with India, that's it. Peace and stability. You can buy jets from the Devil as far as I'm concerned. But the war stops. And El-Khayab is a dead man. Got it? We'll be gone by sunset."

318

53

President El-Khayab stood next to a window that looked out on Constitution Avenue. The chants came in steady bursts now.

"Death to India! Death to India! Death to India!"

"They've gathered earlier than usual," said Atta. "I heard the chant until the middle of the night."

El-Khayab remained silent.

"They support you," said Atta. "You've struck a great blow."

"I've begun something whose ending I cannot foresee, brother," said El-Khayab. "I don't like that feeling."

"Then foresee it," said Atta. "What do you want it to be?"

"Ummah," said El-Khayab, "united under a caliphate. But is it Pakistan that is meant to start it all? Is it me who is meant to be the caliph?"

"It is you, brother. It is your time. It is our time."

The door to the president's office opened at the far side of the room. Khan, the Pakistani defense minister, and his deputy el-Jaqonda, walked in the room.

"Hello, Mr. President," said Khan.

"Has Bolin arrived?" asked El-Khayab.

"He's at Chaklala. He will be here momentarily."

El-Khayab turned back to the window.

"Mr. President, we're at a crossroads."

"Speak."

"It is irrational for New Delhi to not react," said Khan. "I'm told that last night, in New Delhi, more than a million people gathered. They burned effigies of you. They chanted, 'Death to Pakistan.' More than eighty people were crushed to death in the protest. The Indians are enraged."

"What is your point?"

"They will react, Mr. President," said Khan. "Today, tomorrow, who knows. What I mean to say is if we don't continue to make the choices we desire for Pakistan, we will be the ones forced to react. New Delhi will assert itself. Frankly, it shocks me that they've done nothing so far."

"What are the choices you speak of?"

"The lack of Indian counterattack, especially in light of the pressure from Ghandra's own citizenry, this can only be seen for what it is: America. America is somehow preventing New Delhi from counterattack."

"Yes, I agree with you, Osama," said El-Khayab. "Have we won?"

"No," said Khan. "But we have it in our power to win. I believe we must now up the ante. Now. Today. This minute. We must follow our first strike with a larger wave of bombing."

"You mean . . . ." said El-Khayab.

"Yes. More nuclear bombs, inside the Indian homeland. We have prepared a briefing sheet."

Khan nodded to el-Jaqonda.

"We assessed two separate options," said el-Jaqonda. "Option one would be a series of surgical nuclear strikes, spread out in a variety of geographies, west, south, and north. We contrasted that with a concentrated use of the same weapon set. Under this option, we selected New Delhi as the target. The design here would be to harm the focus of government, create more widespread political chaos, but leave most of the country unharmed. Potentially open to a new form of government in the near future."

"Under the second option, we create an opportunity for political change," added Khan. "We open the door to a different kind of government, perhaps Islamic. At the very least, we create unbelievable, durable chaos."

El-Khayab rubbed his bearded chin with his left hand as he contemplated what he had just heard.

"And tell me, Khalid, how many people would die?"

"In both scenarios, we recommend the use of twelve additional devices," said el-Jaqonda. "Under option one, between four and five million people would die. Under option two, a strike on New Delhi alone, with the same weapon set, we estimate a death toll of just north of ten million people."

54

Six stories below ground, President Ghandra exited the elevator and turned toward the Security Room. Immediately, he heard shouting coming from the conference room down the corridor. He walked slowly down the brightly lit corridor toward the room where he knew his war cabinet awaited, listening to the angry voice of Indra Singh excoriating someone.

"You'll do nothing of the sort!" shouted Singh. "It's not your decision. *You* were not elected president!"

"Control yourself, Indra!" The voice of Priya Vilokan, India's prime minister and head of the Nuclear Command Defense.

"This is treason!" screamed Singh. "Have you been meeting in secret?"

"It's not treason, you crazy bastard!" came another voice, Guta Morosla, the director of RAW, the Research and Analysis Wing, India's CIA.

Ghandra stepped into the frame of the door.

On one side of the table was Singh, standing, his face beet red. Across from him sat General Praset Dartalia, the head of Armed

Forces. Morosla and Vilokan were seated at the far end of the conference table.

Singh's anger was directed at Dartalia. His sleeves were rolled up and he was leaning over the table.

Dartalia sat calmly, reclined in the chair. His eyes shot from Singh to Ghandra, standing in the doorway.

"President Ghandra," said Dartalia.

"May I ask what this is all about?" asked Ghandra.

There was silence in the room.

"Indra?"

"Tell him what you told me," said Singh, looking at Dartalia. "Go on."

"There is movement afoot," said Dartalia. "Near mutiny. Generals in Strategic Forces Command. A large contingent of commanders in Punjab. Everywhere there is discontent."

"'Movement'?" asked Ghandra.

"The upper ranks of the Indian Armed Forces believe you're weak," said Dartalia. "That the coup is a subterfuge."

Ghandra walked to the table and took a seat next to Dartalia.

"Subterfuge?" Ghandra asked. "What do you mean, Praset?"

"They're worried that when noon comes, and the coup hasn't happened, that America will have yet another excuse for delaying the counterattack on Pakistan," said Dartalia. "And you will do what they say."

"So what would be your plan?" asked Ghandra. He looked at the clock on the wall, then pointed. "It's nine in the morning, General. Thus far, as we're all aware, the team of American special forces have killed Persom Karreff and have succeeded in infiltrating the war command of Field Marshal Bolin. Haven't we been attempting to find Bolin's war command?"

"Yes, Mr. President."

"Well, the Americans found him," said Ghandra. "They convinced Bolin to step into the Pakistani presidency. With three hours left, they have only to remove Omar El-Khayab."

Dartalia rubbed the bridge of his nose.

"What is it?" asked Ghandra.

"May I speak frankly, sir, without being yelled at?" Dartalia asked, looking at Singh.

"Yes, of course."

"My loyalty is to India, Mr. President, and therefore it is to you, as the elected leader of our country. I will not go along with any attempts to remove you. I am on your side, Mr. President. But I must warn you, if noon comes and Omar El-Khayab is still in power, if India does not then strike Pakistan with the full weight of its nuclear arsenal, I fear your administration will be over. There will be a coup, but instead of Islamabad, it will be in New Delhi."

55

CHAKLALA AIR BASE
RAWALPINDI

The hangar at Chaklala Air Base sweltered in the morning sunlight.

Inside, more than forty men were gathered. All wore military uniforms. The group included most of the commanding hierarchy of the Pakistani Army, Air Force, and Internal Security. The group stood inside the cavernous enclosure, in front of a Chengdu JF-17 "Thunder" attack jet. Inside the hangar, the temperature had already reached one hundred degrees.

Suddenly, the steady purr of the approaching choppers buzzed the air. Through the open-air side of the large building, the group watched as three black Alouette III SA-319B choppers swept across the blue sky from the east and came in for a landing in front of the hangar.

From each chopper stepped a group of military commanders who were part of Field Marshal Bolin's Kashmir theater war command. A pair of men also emerged, unrecognized by the group, high-powered automatic weapons at their sides. Each of the strangers wore jeans and a T-shirt and had black war paint on his face. One was tall, an American. The other looked Pakistani.

The generals and other military leaders in the hangar exchanged glances nervously.

Bolin's men entered the hangar and moved into the gathered crowd.

"What's going on?" more than one commander asked.

As instructed by Dewey, none of Bolin's war command answered.

The two strangers moved to the side of the hangar. Each man stood in silence, weapons aimed toward the ground, faces expressionless.

Several minutes later, the side door to the farthest chopper from the hangar opened. Out stepped Field Marshal Bolin, followed by another man carrying a submachine gun. This third outsider had long brown hair and a beard and mustache. He was tall. His chest was broad, barreled, his arm muscles tanned and ripped. Though Bolin was the ranking officer, the most decorated soldier in the entire Pakistani military, it was the stranger who commanded the gaze of every officer in the hangar. At his side, he carried the same weapon as the others: MP7A1. As with the others, a long, black silencer was screwed into the nozzle of the weapon.

Bolin walked inside the hangar. The plainclothed stranger walked beside him, then joined the other strangers at the side of the hangar.

Bolin stepped into the group of generals, which formed a loose semicircle in front of him.

Bolin looked about the semicircle in silence, meeting the eyes of every man in the group, saying nothing. After completing the arc, he removed his pack of cigarettes, took one, lit it, then took several puffs.

Finally, he spoke.

"It's time, my friends," said Bolin quietly. He took a puff and exhaled. "You're here because you've given your life to Pakistan."

Bolin's voice grew louder.

"Each of you has risked your life, untold times, to preserve and protect our country. You've done this for your families and for Pakistan."

Bolin's voice showed, in turns, confidence and a hint of anger.

Above all else, it showed the resolve of a man not used to losing nor to wavering; the resolve of a strong man, battle-tested, a warrior.

"Many of you, like myself, have fathers and brothers who fought for our country and died. My own father died in the last war with India. I know that most of us have similar stories of pride and pain that come with being the defenders. We all have children and grand-children who someday will stand here, on this very ground, acting to do what they believe is best to preserve and protect Pakistan."

Bolin paused. The commanders were silent.

"Today," he said, steel in his voice, "we take back our country."

Bolin took a large puff on his Gitano, then blew into the air.

"More than half a century ago, the Indians took Kashmir. They stole it. We all know that. But in the name of that mistake, that terrible legacy, will we see our entire country annihilated? Will we watch as an interloper comes into Pakistan and turns the theft of Kashmir into the destruction of our children, our land, and our future?"

He paused. He again glanced around the group.

"Field Marshal Bolin," said one of the generals, a tall man in the back of the gathered group. "Where is General Karreff?"

"General Karreff is dead," said Bolin. "Today, I ask for your allegiance and your loyalty. I want your support. If you cannot give that to me, I ask that you leave. You will not be hurt, but you cannot stay in this country. You'll receive safe passage out of Pakistan, along with your family. But you cannot enjoy the freedom and security that will once again be ours if you're not willing to help win it back from the evil forces that have threatened us with eternal darkness."

Bolin stared at the general who had asked the question.

"You have my loyalty," said the general.

"Mine too," said another to the right. Soon, the group had all expressed their support.

"Thank you," said Bolin. "Now we have work to do."

Dewey watched Bolin's speech, standing next to Millar and Iver-heart.

"How's the cut?" he asked quietly.

"It's fine," said Millar.

Dewey felt a small vibration in his pocket. He removed a small silver device slightly larger than a credit card. He read the words as they scrolled across the top of the card. He placed it back in his pocket.

Dewey stepped in front of Millar and Iverheart.

"Do you recognize Isa Garali?" Dewey asked, looking at Iverheart.

Iverheart searched the crowd.

"Yes," said Iverheart. "Back left. Third from the left. Short guy with a red beret."

"Got it. Who is he?"

"He runs ISI. Inter Services Intelligence, the CIA here."

When Bolin finished speaking, he signaled to Dewey.

"Watch my back," whispered Dewey.

Dewey walked to the group of generals. Millar and Iverheart followed him, but stood back, at a short distance. Dewey stepped into the middle of the group.

"Who is this?" asked one of the generals, looking at Bolin.

"This is someone from the United States. He's here to help us."

"We don't need the help of the Americans. We know whose side they're on."

"He's right," said another general, shaking his head. "Are we to be a 'puppet regime' of the United States, Xavier?"

Several men nodded agreement, shaking their heads in disgust.

Dewey glanced across the group of generals, gathered in a loose semicircle around him and Bolin.

"I'm not here to choose sides," said Dewey. "I don't work for India. Frankly, I could care less who wins your war. But when nuclear bombs start dropping on American allies, we start paying attention. You, in this hangar, you all constitute Pakistan's military leadership. And what you need to understand is that your boss, the president of Pakistan, dropped a nuclear bomb on an American ally. When you do that, there are repercussions."

"*This has nothing to do with America!*" yelled one of the generals.

"Field Marshal Bolin, is this the man who killed Persom Karreff?" asked a different general.

Dewey paused, he glanced back at Millar and Iverheart. He turned back to the circle of Pakistani generals.

"Who sent you here?" another general asked.

"Let the man speak," said Bolin.

"I'll keep this brief, because we don't have a lot of time," said Dewey. "You can listen to me or not, that's your choice. But I know you're all men who care deeply about your country. And your country is facing its gravest hour, whether you care to admit it or not. If Omar El-Khayab isn't removed and replaced by noon, the country of Pakistan—your cities and towns, your families, your way of life—all of it will cease to exist. India *will* destroy Pakistan. New Delhi will not ignore the destruction of Karoo, nor will they respond proportionally."

"*How do you know this?*" yelled one of the generals.

"IAF has seventy-four planes in the air as we speak," said Dewey. "Each of those planes is carrying two nuclear bombs. That's almost a hundred and fifty nuclear bombs. In addition, there are at least two dozen mobile units at the border. In about two hours, those bombs are going to fall from the sky like rain. Pakistan will be wiped off the map. After India destroys you, we believe China will attack India. The U.S. won't allow that." Dewey paused. "You asked why I'm here? I'm here because America would rather put a bullet in Omar El-Khayab's head than fight a war with China. It's that simple."

The gathered commanders stared at Dewey, in shock. He glanced at Bolin.

"*If this is true, we must attack first!*" shouted a commander in the back. "*Before India strikes!*"

"It's too late for that," said Dewey. "Before you could get even one nuclear bomb in the air, India would act. The die is cast."

Dewey watched the hushed crowd of generals.

"But even if you could surprise New Delhi, why would you?" Dewey continued. "So you can inflict the damage first? So that both countries are destroyed instead of just Pakistan? You're all patriots. You all care about your homeland. The solution is not to destroy India, General. The solution is to make peace."

Finally, a short, bearded general in the front raised his hand.

"Who sent you here?" the general asked.

"The president of the United States sent me."

He looked into the eyes of the gathered generals, scanning the semicircle of men, as if defying the gathered group to do something, to leave, get mad, anything to show their disapproval at his words, but no one moved so much as an inch.

"Now there's not a lot of time," Dewey continued. "I'll get you out of this mess, but you all need to shut the fuck up and listen. You want to live? Do exactly as I say."

The gathered commanders stood in silence, shocked by Dewey's candor, mesmerized by his words, awed by his physical presence, his big arms and chest, his height, the way the weapons on him—a handgun in his shoulder holster, the MP7 at his side—looked as if he'd been born with them.

"The most important thing right now is loyalty," said Dewey calmly. "Not only is it important that you're loyal to Field Marshal Bolin, you must demand loyalty from your line officers. Loyalty equals stability. Disloyalty equals chaos."

Dewey looked at the group of generals, who stared at him, some contemptuously, others nodding, coming around. He reached to his shoulder holster and abruptly removed his silenced Colt M1911, raised it and aimed it at one of the generals, a short man in a red beret, Isa Garali.

"What the hell are you doing?" barked Bolin.

Garali, in the red beret, stood motionless.

"This man is in charge of ISI," said Bolin.

"I know who he is," said Dewey, the weapon extended in front of him. "Isa Garali." Dewey stared into Garali's eyes. "Five minutes ago, this man sent a text to Osama Khan."

With his left hand, without moving the aim of the weapon, Dewey removed the small silver device from his pocket. He handed it to Bolin. Bolin studied the small device. His eyes shot from the device to Garali, whose eyes now darted about nervously.

"'Bolin. Coup,'" read Bolin aloud.

A slight tremble shuddered across Garali's body. His eyes blinked nervously.

"By the way, General, he never got the message," said Dewey.

Dewey pulled the trigger, just once. A bullet hit him in the chest. Garali lurched backward and fell to the ground.

Dewey glanced across the gathered commanders. He holstered his weapon, then waited.

"This isn't a game," said Dewey finally. "You need to put your country in front of your own personal interests. Garali didn't do that, and now he's dead. If you step out of line, you should expect what just happened to him to happen to you."

The generals listened as Dewey continued.

"Some of you were involved in the Musharraf coup," continued Dewey. "This is different. Nawaz Sharif was not popular. El-Khayab is. We need to anticipate widespread civil unrest. That's manageable. What's not manageable is fracture within Pakistan's military hierarchy. If you aren't united—the men in this room—you'll trigger a civil war.

"One of you, maybe more than one of you, is looking around right now and wondering, 'Why isn't it me?'" said Dewey. "You're thinking, 'Why Bolin?' Bury the thought. Because you won't win. You'll end up with a bullet in your head, just like Garali. You need to be united. Being a soldier means you care about something bigger than yourself. It means you care about your country. I know you all care about Pakistan. Right now, your country is at risk. You men gathered here, Pakistan's military leadership, you're the only hope your country has right now. For your country, I'm asking you to be soldiers. To unite behind Field Marshal Bolin."

"How can we trust the United States?" barked one of the generals.

"I'm not a diplomat," said Dewey. "I don't care if you trust me. I'm telling you the way it is. You have one shot at saving Pakistan. And it's right here, right now."

"He's right," said another general. "Listen to the man."

"What's next?" asked Bolin. "What do we need to do?"

"The first phase of the coup is command and control," said Dewey. "That's now through El-Khayab's removal. It should be relatively straight-forward, like removing a lightbulb. We go in, remove El-Khayab, then replace him with Field Marshal Bolin. Easy. This should be a light battalion. No more than a couple hundred soldiers. The group that accompanies Field Marshal Bolin should be SSG. We need to move right now. Get the soldiers outside the hangar immediately. We'll need to coordinate tightly with whoever is in charge of the president's security. We want to do this with as little bloodshed as possible."

"What do we do with El-Khayab?"

"El-Khayab is removed from the premises," said Dewey. "We're not going to treat him roughly at the palace. He'll disappear once he's outside the compound, but while there are still people loyal to him lingering around, we treat him like a little kitten. We want the story to be about saving Pakistan, not about killing an old blind man we disagreed with. Once he's off premises, India will demand proof that he's dead. Also, we need to remove Osama Khan. He gets a bullet. Today."

"Colonel Martu has oversight of SSG and El-Khayab's security detail," said Bolin. "Reach him immediately."

"Yes, sir," said Lerik, one of his generals.

"Phase two is control and transition," said Dewey. "It begins when El-Khayab is removed and Field Marshal Bolin takes jurisdiction over the military and the other branches of government. A few hours. Legal formality of the regime change will occur, proper authorizations, that sort of thing. This is the most vulnerable stage of the coup. Any jihadists, El-Khayab loyalists, or disloyal line commanders within your ranks could try and do something irrational. You need to kill off these threats immediately. No mercy. Access to Field Marshal Bolin should be severely restricted.

"The Field Marshal's main job during this phase is meeting with parliamentary leaders and negotiating a truce with India. America is doing what it can to prevent India from attacking, but you will still need to descale tensions. That's just a fact. The war in Kashmir has to end; you can't have a smoldering side fire while the change of government is taking place.

"During the transition, it's *imperative* that the media be kept completely in the dark. That means corralling reporters and, more important, photographers. We need to limit information coming out of Islamabad, at least until this afternoon, following parliament's acceptance of Field Marshal Bolin's presidency. That means cutting off electricity and communication links to Al Jazeera, AP, CNN, Fox, BBC, and any other network. Just do it. We can apologize later. Also, if possible, we need to cut off access to Facebook and Twitter. We can help with that.

"Finally, we need to get people inside their houses and we need to shut off visitors, at least for a few days. I assume Pakistan has some sort of martial law protocol."

"Yes," said Bolin.

"That's what we'll use," said Dewey. "Shut down all border crossings for at least forty-eight hours. The point is, we want to send a signal that you are in charge, you're organized, and you will do whatever it takes to consolidate and control power. Fear and strength will lead to stability. That's what people want: stability. You give it to them with strict command and control."

Bolin put his arm out, interrupting Dewey.

"General Ravi, General Pervez, Colonel Ayala; you three divide up this responsibility," said Bolin. He glanced at the corpse of Garali. Bolin pointed at one of the generals. "General Lerik, you'll oversee ISI."

"Yes, Field Marshal."

Bolin nodded at Dewey.

"Finally, phase three is called transition and peace," said Dewey. "This comes after the general population becomes aware of the change in leadership, and lasts until there's stability without the need for martial law. It could be a week, a month, or a year. This is the most dangerous phase of the coup. This is about internal security across Pakistan. Bringing calm and security to the streets. This is not going to be easy. El-Khayab is popular. And he's popular with people who are crazy."

Several of the generals laughed at this remark.

"You'll need to be ruthless with Taliban and Al-Qaeda coming in from the Hindu Qu'ush. They will seek to exploit instability created by the removal of El-Khayab. Phase three requires the tight cooperation of all Pakistani military working closely with local law enforcement. It also requires a realistic assessment of internal security risks within the presidential palace and governmental agencies. Be thorough but not ruthless. Don't make the mistake of killing low-level political opponents. It's a slippery slope. A lot of people will resent you; get over it. Unless they're willing to use violence against you, control them, lock them up, whatever, but don't start killing them. Under any circumstance, there will be international outcry. My strong suggestion, when the UN calls, tell them to fuck off."

"Will we not want international support?" asked Bolin.

"They'll come around," said Dewey. "After all, you're removing a guy who just dropped a nuclear bomb on eight thousand innocent civilians. You'll be a hero. Now we have to get moving. By my count we have less than an hour and a half to remove Omar El-Khayab and get India to bring their nukes home."

"Will the U.S. help us in this phase?" asked a general in back. "Will you stay to manage things?"

"We've already helped you," answered Dewey, watching the line of generals. "We're out of Islamabad when the sun goes down."

"Tonight?" asked one of the generals, incredulous.

Dewey ignored the question. He glanced behind him, at Millar and Iverheart.

"One more thing," said Dewey, looking over the generals. "We were never here."

56

It's been over an hour, Mr. President," said Osama Khan. "You have to decide now if we are to advance the attack on India. You have my recommendation. The clock is ticking, sir. The planes stand ready to take off. The nuclear bombs are ready. The twelve targets are identified and locked in."

El-Khayab smiled, but said nothing.

The muted, steady din of the chant continued from beyond the window.

El-Khayab reached forward, pressed his hand on a button beneath his desk. In a matter of seconds, a servant entered the room.

"A cup of tea, please," said El-Khayab. "Osama, Khalid?"

"Nothing, thanks," said Khan.

"Tea would be fine, Mr. President," said el-Jaqonda. "May I also use the restroom, sir?"

"There," said Atta El-Khayab, pointing toward the corner of the room, a small wooden door that was hard to see.

El-Jaqonda stood and crossed the room.

El-Khayab sat in blank silence. His thoughts were a thousand miles away, from the room, from Khan. The dream had come again, in the night. The horrible fire at his home when he was a child. This time, El-Khayab saw his father as he carried him and Atta to the safety of the sidewalk, then ran screaming up the stairs to try and save his mother and sisters. How he'd run after him, only to be pulled back by Atta. It was the last time he would ever see his father. His last memory of his father was also his last sight before blindness came, the sight of his father's back as he ran into the flames to try and save his mother and sisters.

El-Khayab felt no pain as he thought of the vision. Rather, he felt an altogether different sensation; warmth, ecstasy, for in that moment, a moment that seemed to replay again and again in his mind, he saw the love that his father had for his mother, for his brother and sisters, and for him. It would be El-Khayab's last and final sight as a human being. If Allah was the power that had cast the flames around his family that awful morning, it was for a reason. The flames, the painful loss, the destruction; they had *created* El-Khayab. El-Khayab felt a tear on his cheek, for he knew what was next, what he had to do. He felt the stirring, awesome tension throughout his body of a higher force, guiding his thoughts now and his steps.

"You are deep in thought, Mr. President," said Khan.

El-Khayab removed his glasses. His eyes were wet. The red scar tissue surrounded the greenish, aged remains of eyeballs. Involuntarily, Khan flinched at the grotesque sight.

"It's time," said El-Khayab. "We must go ahead with your design, Osama."

"I'm glad to hear it, Mr. President. The planes stand ready."

El-Khayab stood. He walked across the room to the window. The ominous chant seemed to grow louder as he reached his left hand out from his bisht and placed it against the large window.

"But there is to be one change," said El-Khayab.

"And what is that, Mr. President?" asked Khan. "If you are going to reduce the number of bombs, I must warn you—"

"Twelve bombs are not enough. Everything Pakistan has. Everything that Allah has given us."

Khan shot a look at Atta El-Khayab, taken aback by his words. He struggled to speak.

"But . . . but, Mr. President, that is one hundred and sixty nuclear bombs." Khan coughed. "We will be committing—"

"It is only through complete destruction, Osama," interrupted El-Khayab, looking with his blind eyes to the crowd, "that true light will come."

57

AIWAN-E-SADR

The black Mercedes sedan holding Bolin pushed slowly, foot by foot, through the thick crowds of Pakistanis gathered concentrically around the iron gates of Aiwan-e-Sadr.

Trailed by half a dozen black and green Humvees, the sedan rolled up to the main entrance gates, where no less than twenty soldiers stood in a line, submachine guns aimed in front of them.

The left rear window of the sedan lowered. The guard looked inside.

"It's an honor, sir," said the soldier, recognizing Field Marshal Bolin.

Bolin returned his salute.

"Thank you, soldier. Now open the gates."

"Yes, sir."

The soldier glanced for a brief instant past Bolin, meeting Dewey's stare, then looking away.

The large iron gates moved sideways. The soldiers, standing inside the compound, trained their weapons at the teeming crowd, lest anyone try to enter the compound. The Mercedes moved forward. It was followed by the Humvees, which rumbled by the armed soldiers. The gates to the Aiwan-e-Sadr slid shut. The vehicles moved down a brick drive for several hundred yards, then went right, through a stone archway that led to an interior courtyard.

The Mercedes parked in front of a set of long granite steps that led into the presidential palace. The Humvees lined up next to the black sedan.

At the top of the steps, Colonel Martu emerged. Neat khaki uniform, medals across the chest, orange epaulets on top of the shoulders, a red beret. He descended to meet Bolin's car.

Bolin climbed out of the sedan, stepped toward the steps that led gracefully up to the presidential palace. Martu met him at the bottom step, saluting.

"Field Marshal," said Martu. "Thank God. If these walls could talk. I speak for the entire SSG leadership when I say we have been waiting for this day."

"Thank you, Colonel. What is the report?"

"El-Khayab is in his office with Osama Khan. I'll escort you."

Dewey climbed out the other side of the Mercedes. He wrapped his submachine gun across his back and kept his Colt M1911 holstered beneath his left armpit.

"Who is this?" asked Martu, looking across the front of the Mercedes.

"A friend from America," said Bolin. "His name is Andreas. Now let's move."

Dewey walked to the first Humvee, around to the rear. Rob Iverheart sat with General Lerik at the ends of the backseats, soldiers packed in behind them.

Dewey tapped his ear, looking at Iverheart, indicating to keep his COMM on.

"I'll assemble men at the top of the steps," said Lerik.

"No," said Dewey. "This looks like it's going to be painless."

Dewey turned, walked to the next vehicle, where Millar sat. Dewey glanced at his neck, where a trickle of blood was moving in a fresh path south toward a shirt that was increasingly red and wet. Millar's face looked pale and ashen.

"How you feeling?" asked Dewey.

"Fine," said Millar.

"Come on," said Dewey. "I might need you to translate."

Millar climbed out of the Humvee. Dewey and he walked up the steps, twenty feet behind Bolin and Martu.

"So this is a coup," said Millar quietly. "Do they always go this smoothly?"

"No," said Dewey.

At the top of the steps was a set of bright red doors, two stories tall, with ornate gold ornament along the frame. Two more soldiers, UZIs out, stood outside the door. They stared at Dewey and Millar as they followed Bolin and Martu inside.

Bolin glanced back at Dewey; Dewey saw a trace of nervousness in Bolin's eyes.

They walked down a long, high-ceilinged corridor with a floor of gleaming black-and-white marble. They passed door after door, all of which were shut. Ahead, to the right, was an open door. Dewey glanced inside as they moved past the door.

"Cabinet room," said Millar.

Inside, the room was half filled, government officials in suits, seated around the table, talking. At the end of the table, one of the officials turned, spied Dewey, turned away, then did a double take as Dewey passed.

"Colonel," Dewey said after walking a few more feet.

"Yes?" asked Martu.

"You need to lock down the cabinet room."

"Most of them will be supportive."

"Get some men in there and shut the door," said Dewey. "Tell them Field Marshal Bolin will be in to speak with them within the hour. Confiscate cell phones."

Bolin nodded to Martu, who took out his cell phone and spoke rapidly before hanging up.

At the end of the corridor, a stairwell led right. On the walls, large oil portraits of past Pakistani leaders. They moved past windows that overlooked Constitution Avenue, swarming with hundreds of thousands of people.

Dewey registered the huge crowd from above. It was overwhelming. The large square was packed, along with the roads leading to the square. People waved signs and flags. The crowds spread out as far as you could see, in every direction. The chant wouldn't stop.

"*Death to India! Death to India!*"

He glanced at Millar.

"That's not good," said Dewey quietly as they ascended.

"Why?"

"There are certain things that can't be controlled," whispered Dewey. "Large angry crowds are at the top of the list."

"What are you saying?"

"I'm saying we need to remove this guy then get the hell out of Dodge before things spiral out of control."

They reached the top of the stairs. Bolin and Martu were ahead, out of earshot.

"What about India?" asked Millar.

Dewey looked at his watch.

"We have fifteen minutes. Once El-Khayab is gone, India will bring home its nukes. But I wouldn't want to be a pasty-skinned American when those crazy fuckheads"—he nodded to the window—"find out their messiah is gone."

Millar stared at Dewey, a hint of concern on his face. Dewey looked away and kept walking up the stairs.

At the top step, Bolin and Martu awaited. The group moved down the corridor toward a set of doors, outside of which stood two more soldiers. They saluted Bolin and Martu as they approached.

Bolin, Martu, Millar, and Dewey stood outside the door for a brief moment.

One of the soldiers placed his hand on the large brass doorknob, then pulled the door open.

El-Khayab's office was enormous, cavernous and ornate, light-filled. Closer to the door was a large sitting space with two long bright red couches facing each other and a table between them. Along the far walls, windows ten feet high looked out on the capital district.

At the far end of the office was a long green marble table. In front of the table was a tall, middle-aged man in a tan suit, with neatly combed black hair whom Dewey recognized immediately: the father of Pakistan's nuclear program, Osama Khan.

From behind Bolin's hulking frame, Dewey's eyes flashed to the window where a tall man in an immaculate white bisht stood. He recognized him from the photographs. Omar El-Khayab.

El-Khayab's long gray beard spread down across his chest. His glasses were off and even from across the room, the hideous scars were visible.

Behind Khan another man stood, this one in a dark blue bisht. This was El-Khayab's brother, Atta.

When the door opened, Khan turned and stood.

"Field Marshal Bolin," said Khan from across the room. "Come in, join us."

Bolin crossed the room. The chants from the square seemed to grow louder as he crossed the soft, ornate carpet underfoot.

Martu stayed at his side, a foot behind him.

"Field Marshal Bolin," said El-Khayab. "Thank you for coming all this way."

Khan's eyes drifted past the approaching Bolin, past Martu, then found Dewey and Millar.

Khan moved a step to his left, as if in disbelief. His arm lifted. Khan pointed a finger at Dewey.

"Americans," said Khan. "What's going on?"

"It's over, my friend," said Bolin.

"What is this?" shouted Khan. "President El-Khayab, *Bolin is a traitor!* He is accompanied by Americans. CIA!"

Dewey said nothing.

"Pakistan is taking back its government today," said Bolin forcefully. He glanced at Khan, then addressed El-Khayab. "Omar El-Khayab, you have brought Pakistan to the brink of self-destruction."

"*America* is *stealing* our government!" yelled Khan, stepping toward Bolin.

"America is our friend. Mr. Andreas helped to save our country."

"You'll pay for this, Bolin!"

"You've endangered the lives of every man, woman, and child in Pakistan," barked Bolin, outshouting Khan.

Khan reached to a holster at his waist.

Dewey pulled his Colt from his shoulder holster in one fluid motion, then pulled the trigger. A slug tore into Khan's forehead and he was knocked backward as if kicked by a horse.

Dewey stepped forward, took aim again, and fired. The bullet cut a gumdrop-sized hole through Khan's chest.

Bolin and Martu looked at Dewey, momentarily taken aback by what he had just done.

"I do have one question for you, Field Marshal Bolin," said Omar El-Khayab calmly.

"What is it?"

The chanting outside continued.

"Death to India! Death to India!"

"When they find out I am gone," he said, his voice trembling but smooth, barely above a whisper, nodding his head toward the window, the noise of the chants pounding menacingly at the air. "When they move toward the gates. When the people at the back push and crush the ones at the front, and the ground is spilled in crimson. When the gates come crashing down. When they climb the stairs, and they find you. Tell me, what will you say to the people?"

Bolin paused.

"Well, Field Marshal, have you no answer?" asked El-Khayab, his voice trembling as he slowly moved away from the window. "It seems a simple question."

"I'll tell them the truth," said Bolin. "I will tell them their children will live to breathe another day."

58

Four members of SSG, along with Millar, escorted Omar and Atta El-Khayab to the basement of Aswan-e-Sadr. In the basement, a green Humvee awaited. A pair of soldiers helped move El-Khayab into the back of the vehicle. Iverheart and General Lerik climbed into the vehicle across from them. Atta El-Khayab sat next to his brother.

Millar sat directly across from the blind cleric, their knees almost touching, Iverheart across from Atta. El-Khayab's eyes were now hidden by dark sunglasses. He seemed to focus in on Millar.

Iverheart looked at Lerik.

"Where will we take them?"

"North," said Lerik. "To the hills."

Bolin commandeered an office down the hall from El-Khayab's office, a smaller room with several phones. Dewey followed Bolin to the office. He shut the door behind him.

As Dewey picked up one of the phone receivers, he looked at his watch: 11:49 A.M. Eleven minutes to spare.

"It's Andreas," said Dewey to an operator once he'd been patched through to the Pentagon. "Let's make the call."

Dewey listened as the phone clicked several times, then started a short beeping noise. He hit a button on the console and put the call on speaker.

"Yes," said the voice.

Dewey nodded at Bolin.

"President Ghandra. This is Field Marshal Xavier Bolin."

"Field Marshal Bolin. I've been expecting your call."

"I'm pleased to tell you that Omar El-Khayab is no longer in power," said Bolin. "He's gone. The government of Pakistan is now in the hands of the Pakistani military. I must now get through the next few hours and a smooth change of regime. After that, my immediate goal is to work with you on a rapid and peaceful resolution to the conflict in Kashmir. If you will allow me, I would also like to discuss the creation of a long-term peace between us."

"I'm happy to hear this news," said Ghandra.

"As of noontime, in about ten minutes, Pakistani Armed Forces will cease offensive war operations at the Kashmir front," said Bolin. "My field commanders have been ordered to stop all activities offensive in nature directed toward India. We will not abandon our defensive positions or any sort of right to self-protection, but we are no longer at war."

"Thank you, Field Marshal Bolin."

"Later today," said Bolin, "I suggest that you and I reconvene by phone. Obviously, I ask that you join me in this general stand-down of battle. It would be my suggestion that we declare an immediate cease-fire and begin to discuss in earnest the terms of a lasting peace for our two countries."

There was a long pause.

"India will stand down," said Ghandra. "It could take me a few minutes, but I will order an immediate stand-down."

"Thank you, President Ghandra."

"As for the larger question of peace between our countries," said Ghandra, "I will tell you that it is Pakistan who has dropped the nuclear bomb on India. How we come to terms with this I frankly do not know."

"Nor do I, Mr. President," said Bolin. "But I must tell you, I was as shocked and appalled by the dropping of this bomb as you were. I can only express my condolences, President Ghandra. I think the foundation of any future peace between our countries must be built on the recognition that there is a new and profound enemy among us. Today, he wore the clothing of a Pakistani. Tomorrow, he might speak Hindi. But make no mistake, the religious fanatic is enemy to us all."

"I agree with you, Field Marshall Bolin," said Ghandra.

At Indian Army Headquarters in New Delhi, General Vinod Promoth climbed out of the back of a black Range Rover, followed by two aides. He cast his eyes suspiciously to his left and right, then walked quickly toward the front door of the Main Administration Building.

Inside his spacious office, Promoth had gathered seven generals, including the top commander of Strategic Defense Command, the military branch charged with oversight of India's nuclear weapons. In addition, Promoth had with him several high-ranking commanders from within the Indian Army. Promoth himself was the second-highest ranking officer in the Indian Army.

"It's noon," said Promoth. "Have there been orders from the president?"

"No," said one of the generals. "All's quiet from Rashtrapati Bhavan."

"And are we all in agreement?" asked Promoth, looking into the eyes of his cadre.

"Yes," said one of the commanders. "It's time for India to fight back. The president has failed to protect the motherland."

"Should we at least ascertain the status of the coup and the progress of the American team?" asked one of the generals.

"It's too late for that," said Promoth. "Noon was the deadline. The president had his chance. It's time for the men in this room to reclaim our country and fight back against the Pakistani enemy. Ghandra is obviously not going to do that."

"I've laid out a digest of the steps necessary to ensure smooth regime change," said one of the commanders, looking at Promoth. "The first step is a general meeting of the Army and Air Force hierarchy here in New Delhi. With your permission, I will order a general session to take place this afternoon."

"So be it," said Promoth. "In the meantime, let's go through the logistics of Ghandra's removal and the process of parliamentary approval."

In a deserted field fifteen minutes' drive north of Islamabad, the black and green Humvee left the dirt road and began crossing an uninhabited landscape of stub brush, rocks, and sand.

The Humvee drove for more than a mile across the untouched, empty terrain. Finally, the Humvee came to a stop.

Omar El-Khayab grasped his brother's forearm, then cast his blind eyes in Millar's direction.

"Please spare my brother," said Omar El-Khayab in Urdu. "He's done nothing wrong."

"'The sins of the brother,'" said Millar, also in Urdu. "So tell me, did he try to stop you, Imam?"

"He did nothing," said El-Khayab, "except take care of me. He is innocent."

"Like the people of Karoo," said Millar.

El-Khayab nodded, then placed his hand on his brother's.

The soldiers removed Omar El-Khayab and his brother from the back of the Humvee. They were led away from the vehicle, a dozen feet or so. El-Khayab tripped, causing his glasses to fall from his head to the ground, where they remained. Lerik led them a few feet farther. Finally, they stopped near a low, flat boulder.

Standing behind the Humvee, Iverheart aimed the small video camera at General Lerik as Lerik removed a pistol from his waist holster. Lerik lifted the weapon and aimed it at Omar El-Khayab. El-Khayab stood, motionless. His murky eyes stared blankly into the distance. Lerik fired. The thunderclap of the shot was shocking in the quiet air. El-Khayab dropped to the ground, rolled awkwardly to the side, his face smashing against the earth. Lerik turned his weapon and aimed it at Atta, then fired.

Iverheart watched the film clip once, then uploaded it to CEN-COM. He looked at the time stamp on the upload: 12:07 P.M.

59

At 12:18 P.M., President Ghandra's motorcade pulled in through the gates of Indian Army Headquarters in New Delhi. He was accompanied by a force of two dozen of the President's Bodyguard, uniformed members of the household cavalry regiment of the Indian Army.

Ghandra climbed out of the limousine and walked to the front doors of the Main Administration Building.

"Wait here," said Ghandra to one of the officers accompanying him.

"General Dartalia ordered me to accompany you," said the officer.

"No need," said Ghandra. "Please wait for me here. I will do this alone."

Ghandra walked down the hall and stood outside a large oak door, now closed, that led to the office of General Vinod Promoth.

Ghandra knocked on the door, then turned the doorknob and stepped in to Promoth's spacious office. A group of military commanders, all of whom Ghandra knew, was gathered around the conference table in the middle of the office.

Ghandra stepped inside the office, but said nothing. He looked at General Promoth, who sat in a large, black leather chair behind his desk. Promoth appeared to be stunned, his mouth agape, speechless. The generals seated at the table were also in shock at Ghandra's surprise appearance.

"Since when do the officers of the Indian military not salute their commander in chief?" asked Ghandra, a hint of anger in his voice. He stared at Promoth, who stood up and quickly moved his right hand to his brow. One by one, the occupants of the conference table followed suit.

"May I ask the purpose of your visit, Mr. President?" said Promoth.

"No, you may not," said President Ghandra. "Where's your phone?"

Promoth glanced nervously at the conference table.

"Yes, Mr. President," stammered Promoth. "Please."

Promoth pointed to the black phone on the desk.

Ghandra picked up the phone, dialed a number, then waited several moments in silence.

"It's the president," Ghandra said. "Let's make the call."

Ghandra pressed the speakerphone. After a short time, the phone beeped.

"President Ghandra," said a voice over the speakerphone. "Thank you for calling me back so quickly."

"It is my pleasure, Field Marshal Bolin," said Ghandra, glancing around the office at the faces of the gathered military commanders. "I must tell you that you are on speakerphone, Field Marshal Bolin. I am joined by several of my top military commanders, including Field Marshal Ramaal Domki, the senior commander of Strategic Defense Command."

"Gentlemen," said Bolin over the speaker. "As I explained to President Ghandra, Omar El-Khayab has been removed from power. He is dead. The Pakistani military is in control of Pakistan and I've ordered an immediate cease-fire in Kashmir and a withdrawal of our troops back to the Line of Control. In addition, all nuclear devices have been brought back from their offensive strategic positions.

"What you should also know," continued Bolin, "is that the bombing of Karoo was a surprise to me and to most, if not all, of my fellow officers, as well as the citizens of Pakistan. In my opinion, it was a grave mistake, a crime committed by war criminals. I did not know about the attack until after it occurred, and I am deeply saddened by it. But I cannot take back what happened at Karoo. What I can do is tell you that the reason we effected a change of regime was so that we could prevent further unnecessary loss of life in both of our countries."

The room was silent.

"Thank you for your sentiments," said Ghandra, who stared icily at Promoth.

"I know that you have designs on retaliation for what occurred at Karoo," continued Bolin on speaker. "Let me be frank. I ask for your commitment—for India's commitment—that you will stand down your nuclear arsenal."

Ghandra looked into Promoth's eyes, then turned to Field Marshal Domki.

"Would you like to answer him, Field Marshal?" Ghandra asked.

Domki, the senior commander of India's Strategic Defense Command, was momentarily stunned, then gathered himself. He stepped from the conference table to the desk, next to President Ghandra. He looked briefly at Promoth, then leaned over the phone.

"You have India's commitment, Field Marshal Bolin," said Domki. "We will order the stand-down of our bombers immediately."

"Thank you," said Bolin. "I suggest we reconvene in a few hours."

"I look forward to it," said Ghandra.

Ghandra pressed the speaker button on the phone, hanging it up. He walked toward the door. At the door, he turned.

"General Promoth," said Ghandra. "I will expect your letter of resignation by one o'clock. If I do not have it by one o'clock, you will be arrested and charged with high treason."

60

Bolin stepped into the cabinet room. The room sweltered in the heat, despite the air-conditioning. El-Khayab's cabinet sat at the table. At the door, four soldiers stood, machine guns out, guarding the door.

Bolin was immediately besieged.

"What have you done with the president?" shouted one of El-Khayab's ministers.

"Who's is in charge here?" demanded another.

Shouting overtook the room.

Bolin raised his hand, but to no avail. The shouting continued.

"Where is Omar El-Khayab?" yelled another minister.

Bolin stood listening for more than a minute, waiting for the group to calm down. Finally, one of the ministers at the far end of the table succeeded in quelling the angry group.

"Let the man speak, for God's sake!" he screamed.

Bolin waited for silence to finally come to the crowded room.

"One hour ago, Omar El-Khayab was removed from office," said Bolin. "The Pakistani military, under my direction, effected this change in order to prevent what we believe would have been a full-scale nuclear attack on Pakistan by India and the destruction of our country and our people. We acted today with a heavy heart. We acted to save Pakistan. I am proud that we did so."

Bolin paused. He glanced around the room. The cabinet ministers remained quiet.

"Some of you will be asked to continue your service to Pakistan," said Bolin. "Others will not. Under no circumstance will anyone be harmed, unless, of course, you attempt to disrupt the smooth transition of power. Today's actions are about ending further unnecessary bloodshed. Right now, until we have managed down the crisis caused by Omar El-Khayab's nuclear bomb, it is imperative that we control the news coming out of Islamabad. Therefore, you will remain here. Food and drink will be brought in, and these men will accompany you to the bathroom, when necessary. Good day."

Bolin turned and left the room as the shouting started up again.

As of two hours following El-Khayab's removal from office, nobody in Islamabad, press or otherwise, knew of the takeover of government.

To the massive crowds surrounding Aiwan-e-Sadr, nothing had changed.

ISI, now under Bolin's control, succeeded in shutting off power and communications to all media outlets with bureaus in Islamabad or Rawalpindi.

But it was only a matter of time before reporters, unable to broadcast, became suspicious, then found alternative means of communication to the outside world.

One reporter, a BBC News correspondent, called BBC headquarters in London and described the power outage on a live broadcast. Soon, the office of Pakistan's foreign minister, Darius Mohan, was being pelted with calls. But Mohan was gone, and even members of his own department were clueless as to his whereabouts. This led to even further questions and confusion.

A new and broader news cycle commenced just a few minutes after the BBC report. This wave of reports was sparked by a report from Kashmir. From Srinagar, near the war front, Al Jazeera reported that the battle between India and Pakistan had moved to a state of cease-fire.

More calls flooded into the Pakistani Foreign Ministry as well as El-Khayab's office.

CNN, BBC, and Fox all picked up Al Jazeera's story from Srinagar.

Sometime in the early afternoon, Fox's New Delhi correspondent, Caitlin Montgomery, went live with a report that quickly and dramatically altered the dynamics back in Islamabad.

"According to anonymous sources inside the Indian Foreign Ministry," said Montgomery, "a temporary cease-fire has been negotiated between India and Pakistan. As reported earlier, there has been no battle activity at the Kashmir war front for several hours now. Perhaps more important, according to one source—repeat, this has not been corroborated—but according to my source within the Indian government, Omar El-Khayab, the president of Pakistan, has been removed from office in what he termed a 'coup d'état' . . ."

61

W e sent a military jet to pick you up," said Jessica. "It'll be there by six. They'll take you three to Qatar. Rob stays in Qatar. The jet will bring you and Alex back to Washington. Alex is joining Special Operations Group out of Langley. Then there's you, Mr. Andreas. There are a lot of grateful people running around here. I was hoping maybe I could have five or ten minutes of your time in between all the accolades you're going to be receiving."

Dewey stood in a large conference room down the hall from Bolin's office, staring out at Constitution Avenue. Iverheart stood next to him. Millar sat in a chair at a large conference table.

"Alex is wounded," said Dewey into the phone, glancing at Millar, whose bandage had been recently changed. "He needs a doctor."

"There's a military hospital in Qatar," said Jessica. "They can patch him up and Bethesda can handle the rest after you guys arrive. By the way, Islamabad police figured out he killed the customs agents. Hector is working with ISI to kill the warrant, but exfiltrating him to Qatar is probably a good idea."

In the distance, at the far side of the square in front of Aiwan-e-Sadr, Dewey heard a crash, then the tinkling of breaking glass. He reached to the table and picked up a set of binoculars. Across the square, perhaps a quarter mile away, he could see a group of young men hurling rocks at a storefront, whose plate glass was now broken.

"How is Bolin?" asked Jessica. "Can he do the job?"

Dewey watched through the binoculars as one of the men in the square lit something on fire. Smoke suddenly wafted up from the sidewalk. People spread away from the small fire. From the corner, a pair of soldiers ran, weapons out. Dewey heard the faint crack of automatic weapons fire. One of the men fell to the ground. The others dispersed.

"Yes, he can do the job," said Dewey, still watching the scene through the binoculars. "Without question. It was good intelligence work. He was the right choice. But you need to get us out of here. It's heating up."

"What are you talking about?" asked Jessica.

"The crowds are learning about El-Khayab's removal. It's going to heat up here and Bolin's going to need to clamp down. I've never seen more bishts in my life. I don't want to be around when they find out El-Khayab's dead."

"Is Bolin aware of this?"

"I don't know," said Dewey. "I haven't seen him in a few hours. They've restricted access to him."

"Even to you?"

"Yes."

Dewey watched as another pack of men came at the pair of soldiers at the far side of the square from behind. As a soldier was attempting to stomp out a small fire, one thug came from behind, a piece of wood raised over his head, and struck the soldier in the back of the head. He fell to the street. As two more men charged, the other soldier turned and raised a machine gun. The two men fell, shot to death, the sound of the machine gun fire coming half a second later. From the corner, four more Pakistani soldiers ran over, weapons out, and the remaining youth ran into the crowd.

Pulling the binoculars away from his eyes, Dewey could barely make out the section of the crowd, much less the specific people. How many more small conflicts like this were taking place, here, in

Islamabad? Rawalpindi? Peshawar, Karachi, Lahore? How many more fires and riots were just beginning in large towns and small, across the country?

He glanced at Millar and Iverheart. Iverheart was calm. He had moved to the conference table. In front of him, he'd disassembled his SIG P226 and was absentmindedly cleaning it. Millar looked tense. Every few minutes, he wiped sweat from his brow nervously. He kept staring blankly out the large window at the crowd.

A loud crash came from the square, the sound of glass breaking. Then, a big plume of smoke burst into the air. Dewey moved to the window, joined by Iverheart and Millar. To the right of the palace, on a block just east of Constitution Avenue, a four-story office building was engulfed in flames, which mushroomed out from a first-story window. People ran from the flames, dispersing chaotically.

Dewey's eyes met Iverheart's.

"You need to get that jet here earlier, Jess."

62

The first nervous minutes had turned into anxious hours for Khalid el-Jaqonda. He sat in the dark on the quarry tile floor of the small private bathroom off of what had been President El-Khayab's office, glancing every few minutes at the glow-in-the-dark dial on his Rolex Submariner watch. It had been more than four hours since Bolin had interrupted their meeting with SSG in tow and a large, dangerous-looking American by his side. Whoever he was, he was running the show. Whoever the mean-looking American with the quick trigger finger was, he'd changed el-Jaqonda's world forever.

He breathed deeply, as his cardiologist had instructed him to do, to try and control his anxiety, but it was of little use. He'd sat inside the dark, windowless bathroom for hours, trying to figure out how the hell he was ever going to get out of the bathroom, out of Aiwan-e-Sadr, out of Islamabad, and out of Pakistan—alive.

His roughly sketched-out escape plan was simple: wait until well after midnight, then try and slip out of Aiwan-e-Sadr. Once outside the presidential compound, he would attempt to go to his house to retrieve some belongings, then head north, above Peshawar, where he had allies inside the Taliban.

But there were major problems with the plan. First, there was the simple fact that eventually Bolin would come back to his office, and if he wanted to use the bathroom, he would just get one of his guards to unlock the door. If he found el-Jaqonda inside, he would be shot on sight.

If he made it to midnight without someone finding him, he would then have the challenge of getting out of the building without being seen. There were soldiers from SSG on every corridor, and multiple soldiers at every entrance.

If he could get outside, el-Jaqonda felt confident the rest would be manageable. The military was likely using all of its energy and power quelling popular uprising in the streets, especially the cities. No one would have the time to think about one little man, even if that little man, along with his boss, had, intentionally or not, instigated it all.

El-Jaqonda had his cell phone and every few minutes he pressed the button in order to have some light inside the small room. But the battery was running down. He'd scrolled through the numbers five or six times, thinking about whether any of his stored contacts could help him. The problem was, colleagues at the Ministry of Defense, even his assistant, Sharit, would all be worried about their own hides right now. Any one of them would turn him in. A different dynamic existed with counterparts in other countries. He considered calling Mi Jong, his closest associate in the Chinese Ministry of National Defense. But Jong would care only about future sales of Chinese planes and missiles to El-Khayab's successor. Jong would turn him in faster than you can say wonton soup.

The one person el-Jaqonda came closest to calling was his brother, who lived in Chicago and owned three dry cleaners. He thought of calling him because he wanted to talk to someone, that was all, and to say goodbye. But el-Jaqonda was scared that someone would hear his voice.

Then, it came to him, and he cursed himself for not considering it first.

You fucking idiot.

He hadn't considered calling the one person who might be able to help him because his phone number was not in his contacts list. He had memorized the number instead, at that person's insistence.

More than two thousand miles away, a phone rang. Aswan Fortuna walked to his desk and picked it up.

"What is it?"

"Aswan," he said. "It's Khalid."

"Khalid, are you okay?"

"I can't talk," said el-Jaqonda.

"What's wrong?" asked Fortuna. "I can barely hear you."

"Coup d'état," said el-Jaqonda. "There's been a coup d'état. President El-Khayab is dead."

"*What?*" said Fortuna. "This is . . . this is unbelievable, Khalid."

"I need your help," said el-Jaqonda. "I know of no other."

After a long pause, Fortuna cleared his throat.

"Where are you? Of course I will help you."

"I'm hiding in the palace. If they find me, they will kill me."

"Calm down. It's going to be fine. Who did this?"

"Field Marshal Bolin, commander of the war against India. But the Americans were behind it all, Aswan."

"The Americans?" asked Fortuna, momentarily taken aback.

"It was America. Some sort of special forces. I watched the whole thing."

"Americans," Fortuna said, barely above a whisper.

"Yes, Americans. They did the entire thing. I saw him. I heard his voice. Bolin was like a puppet to him. It was an American who shot Osama Khan."

Fortuna gasped. "This American," he said. "What did he look like?"

"Big," said el-Jaqonda. "Tall. Scary-looking. Toughest I've ever seen. He looked like he would kill you just for looking at him the wrong way."

"Go on," said Fortuna, his heart racing.

"He had brown hair," said el-Jaqonda. "He was plainclothed,

jeans, a T-shirt. A beard and mustache. Black paint beneath his eyes, but you could see that he was very tan."

Fortuna's breathing grew rapid.

"This is important, Khalid," said Fortuna. "Did you hear his name."

"They called him Andreas."

63

At 4:30 P.M., down the hallway from his temporary command center, Field Marshal Bolin walked into the media briefing room. He stepped behind a dais. Behind him, a navy blue backdrop covered the wall. Just in front of the backdrop stood an orderly, colorful line of Pakistani flags. In front of the flags, but behind Bolin, stood two men in business suits, Azra Ankiel, the leader of the Pakistani National Assembly, and Seranas el Debullah, the leader of the Pakistani Senate.

A single camera sat in front of Bolin, providing a pool feed to all news outlets. The address was being broadcast live on all stations inside of Pakistan and was carried live on news outlets across the world.

Bolin wore his military uniform.

"This morning, in order to end the violence and bloodshed that threatened to destroy our homeland, the Pakistani military acted to bring stability and peace to Kashmir, Pakistan, and our region," said Bolin, reading from prepared remarks that he had placed on the dais in front of him. "These actions were done in order to prevent further escalation of violence between Pakistan and India. I have spoken several times with Indian President Rajiv Ghandra, and our countries have agreed to stand down all offensive military activities directed against each other. The terms of this cease-fire will be made permanent over the coming hours and days. Moreover, President Ghandra and I have committed to meeting face-to-face in order to discuss what went wrong in Kashmir, and how we might create systems and measures to prevent other such terrible activities from occurring in the future."

Dewey watched Bolin's address on a television down the hallway from the briefing room.

Within minutes of the address, he could sense a change in the chemistry of the still substantial crowds gathered around Aiwan-e-Sadr and down Constitution Avenue. It was as if a lightning bolt had come down and struck the square. The crowd became more energized and violent.

The sun was going down. Darkness had begun to cast itself across the Islamabad evening.

The chant seemed to stop, then start again, several times. What had been a unified chorus turned into an unpredictable, louder, chaotic wave of shouts.

Some of the people left the square, no doubt India haters who nevertheless saw no point in remaining for what was sure to be a bloody evening.

The others, the ones who remained, became aggressive.

In several parts of the square, smoke now drifted into the sky. Fires started, too many fires for the Pakistani soldiers to extinguish.

The sound of breaking glass became common now. Rocks, bricks, hurled through storefronts and office building windows. The occasional popping sound of gunfire interrupted the noise every few minutes.

At one point, the chant alternated. "*Death to India*" became "*Death to Bolin.*"

For the first time since landing in Pakistan, despite the severe risk involved during the execution of the coup itself, Dewey felt a small, electric wave of fear spread up his back.

"There's no fucking way we're getting a Humvee through that crowd," said Iverheart.

"Chill out," said Dewey.

He glanced at the table. Millar's new bandage was crimson.

"How are you?" asked Dewey.

Millar stared at him. His eyes were glassy.

"Not good," he said quietly. "I need some painkillers."

In front of him, in the middle of the table, the MP7 machine gun lay on its side.

Dewey left the room and walked down the hallway to Bolin's temporary office. Two guards stood outside the office door. When Dewey approached, they would not move to the side, their Kalashnikovs remained trained at Dewey as he approached.

"I need to see him," said Dewey, stepping between the two soldiers, despite their raised weapons.

"We're under orders—"

"Yeah, I don't give a fuck," said Dewey. He reached the door and pushed his way in, throwing aside the two smaller men.

Bolin sat behind the desk, speaking into a phone. When he saw Dewey, he glanced behind him at the two guards disapprovingly. Two men sat in front of Bolin, one of them General Lerik, and another general he didn't recognize.

Dewey stood, waiting for Bolin to finish his call.

Bolin hung up. He glanced at the two generals seated in front of him.

"Yes, Mr. Andreas," said Bolin, a hint of anger in his voice. "It seems the job is complete, yes? Time for you and your team to disappear. What do you want from me now?"

"We need a chopper in here," said Dewey. He nodded to the window and the crowds gathered down Constitution Avenue. "There's no way we're going to make it through that. By Humvee or any other vehicle."

Bolin nodded, a slight grin on his face.

"You like to order people around, don't you?" asked Bolin. "Have you ever considered the use of the word 'please'?"

Dewey stared at Bolin, at first in disbelief, then with unvarnished anger.

"Please, . . . *Mr. President*," said Bolin, grinning at the two generals in front of him. All three started to laugh.

Dewey remained silent until the laughter stopped.

"Just get me a fucking chopper," Dewey said.

He turned and walked toward the door. At the door, he turned and looked at Bolin.

"One more thing, Field Marshal," said Dewey. "One last piece of free advice: you need more soldiers out there. Your battalion is soon going to be overrun. El-Khayab was right: in case you're not listening, they're calling for your head."

64

El-Jaqonda unlocked the bathroom door, opened it, then stepped into the cavernous, empty office of the president of Pakistan. The room was eerily silent and dark. The chanting from Constitution Avenue had stopped. He walked to the window and looked out. El-Jaqonda saw fires smoldering in buildings along the wide boulevard, and smoke in the distant sky. Hundreds of soldiers patrolled the streets.

El-Jaqonda had one opportunity to save his own skin, and it was right now.

He walked to the door of the office. He reached for the engraved brass doorknob and opened the big door. El-Jaqonda stepped into the hallway, raising his arms above his shoulders as he did so.

He was immediately besieged by three armed guards, who raised their weapons.

"Who are you?" shouted one of the soldiers, aiming his Kalashnikov at el-Jaqonda's head. "Down on the ground!"

"My name is Khalid el-Jaqonda," he said, kneeling, then lying stomach down on the marble floor. "I place myself under your arrest. I was the deputy minister of defense under President El-Khayab. I intend no harm."

"What were you doing in there?"

"I was locked in the bathroom. Please, I must speak with President Bolin."

One of the soldiers placed flex-cuffs on el-Jaqonda's wrists.

"You'll do no such thing," said one of the soldiers.

"I was in charge of the nuclear weapons program," said el-Jaqonda. "It's imperative that I speak with him. One of the nuclear weapons is loose. It's outside the control of the Pakistani military. Khan sold it. I must speak with him."

"You'll tell me—"

"I'll speak to nobody other than Bolin," said el-Jaqonda. He craned his neck from the ground and looked at the soldier, who stood now with four other soldiers, surrounding el-Jaqonda. "Tell me, soldier, do you want to explain to your superiors—when another nuclear bomb goes off—that you knew about it and could have prevented it?"

They moved el-Jaqonda to a small office a floor up. He was placed in a metal chair, his wrists and ankles cuffed. He waited in the room for twenty minutes; every minute felt like an eternity. Finally, the door opened. Bolin walked in.

"Khan's water boy," said Bolin as he walked in, two aides by his side. "I remember you. What do you want? What is this about a rogue nuclear device?"

"I'll tell you," said el-Jaqonda. "But I want to speak to you alone."

Bolin looked quizzically at el-Jaqonda. He shrugged, then turned to his aides and pointed toward the door. They left. Bolin shut the door.

"Talk," said Bolin. "I'm busy. Busy cleaning up the fucking mess you idiots made."

"There's no nuclear device," said el-Jaqonda. "This has to do with the American."

Bolin was momentarily silent, stunned by el-Jaqonda's words.

"What? You dragged me up here to talk about the American?"

"Andreas," said el-Jaqonda. "I represent someone who is willing to pay you for Andreas. It's personal. Andreas killed his son."

"Who?" asked Bolin.

"Aswan Fortuna."

Bolin was silent, and he showed no emotion.

"How much are we talking about?"

"As much as you want, Mr. President."

65

Y oussef was awakened by the ringing of his cell phone. He opened his eyes. For a moment, he had trouble remembering where he was. He glanced about the cabin of the Hawker, then sat up. On the seat next to him was the leather coat that he'd taken off the dead rancher, Talbot. The sight jolted him, and he remembered where he was.

He reached for his phone.

"Hello," he said.

"Change of plans, Youssef," said Nebuchar.

"Oh?" said Youssef. "What do you mean?"

"You're going to Pakistan. We need you to pick up a package."

As nightfall approached, the situation in Islamabad went from bad to worse.

Countless fires dotted the city. Smoke and flames were rife in the square mile surrounding Aiwan-e-Sadr, small fires started by young, angry El-Khayab supporters.

A second battalion of Pakistani Army soldiers helped to quell the vandalism. But the jihadists just spread out across the city, their anger now dispersed in neighborhoods and alleyways across Islamabad and nearby Rawalpindi.

Reports of similar violence came from Peshawar, Karachi, and Lahore.

At 5:30 P.M., Bolin declared martial law. A general curfew would begin at 6:00 P.M.

Dewey, Millar, and Iverheart waited in the office down the hall from Bolin. On a small Sony television, a replay of a Pakistani cricket match was on, volume down. Millar watched, but neither Dewey or Iverheart joined him. Instead, they stood at the large window, looking down across Constitution Avenue, and beyond, into east Islamabad.

The evening sky shimmered, a streaky orange-purple sunset, a picturesque ceiling above the smoke-filled chaos that teemed at ground level.

In more than a dozen spots, distant neighborhoods far away from the square, cloudy silos of black smoke drifted up to the sky. Inside the square, which had been mostly cleared of people, soldiers with helmets and shields moved in lines against hold-out militants, who came at the soldiers in waves, throwing rocks, bottles, and other debris. Ambulances moved across the square, picking up bodies. It was hard to tell how many people had been killed, but the muted crack of automatic weapons fire from the soldiers came in a steady if unpredictable rhythm.

"Still glad I picked you?" asked Dewey.

"Yes," said Iverheart.

"Good," said Dewey. "I was worried you wouldn't invite me to your Christmas party."

"You realize we're going to die if we don't get out of here soon," said Iverheart.

"We'll be fine," said Dewey. "I promise."

"Should we have done something different?" asked Iverheart.

"We accomplished our mission," said Dewey. "That's what matters. Our job was to remove El-Khayab. The rest of this stuff is irrelevant."

At 6:35 P.M. Dewey's cell rang.

"The jet is at Chaklala," Jessica said. "I sent in one of the VIP Gulfstreams. I'm sorry it took so long."

"That's okay," said Dewey.

"What's the situation on the ground? All the networks are still down. The CIA Karachi station chief said it's chaos."

"It's getting ugly," said Dewey. "El-Khayab had supporters. Islamabad is on fire."

"President Allaire would like to speak with you," said Jessica. "Thank you, that sort of thing. Can I patch him in real quick?"

A spectacular red flash burst at the far end of the square, an explosion that was bigger and louder than the small fires and Molotov cocktails up to that point.

"Not right now, Jess. I need to focus on getting the hell out of here."

Dewey shut his phone just as the door to the office was opening. Field Marshal Bolin entered, followed by a servant.

"Gentlemen," he said as he stepped into the room. "Your chopper is on its way. You'll forgive me, but I have had a few fires to put out, so to speak."

In the servant's right hand, he held a green bottle, in his left, a small tray with five glasses on it. He placed them on the table, then turned and left.

"I haven't thanked you yet," said Bolin. He unscrewed the cap to the bottle. "Pomegranate wine. Made in Faisalabad. I hope you like it."

Dewey smiled and picked up a glass. He glanced at Iverheart and Millar. Iverheart grabbed a glass.

"No, thank you," said Millar, who looked ashen and remained seated.

Bolin poured wine into Dewey's and Iverheart's glasses, then into his own. He put the bottle down on the table. He raised his glass and looked at Dewey.

"To the United States of America," Bolin said. "For saving my country."

Bolin moved his glass against Dewey's, then against Iverheart's. He smiled, then threw the drink back in his mouth, downing the wine in one gulp.

"Thank you," said Dewey as he drank the sweet-tasting wine.

They heard the faint rhythm of helicopter rotors, somewhere off in the distant sky.

"No, my friend, thank *you*," said Bolin smiling.

Bolin poured refills, which they drank down quickly as the chopper grew louder. Turning, Dewey looked out the window at the darkening sky. The lights of the chopper were now visible.

"Come," said Bolin. "I'll walk you there myself."

They followed Bolin down a long, cavernous hallway. At the end of the hallway, an armed soldier stood at the entrance to an open elevator. They rode the elevator up in silence. At the sixth floor, the top floor of the building, they got off. Bolin led Dewey and his team down a short hallway to a stairwell, which led to the roof.

At the edge of the helipad, the group watched the approaching chopper. From the vantage point atop Aiwan-e-Sadr, the chaos of the teeming, anger-fueled crowds was shocking. Sirens pealed from several locations. Gunfire was now steadier. Fires dotted the terrain in virtually every direction. The chant was no longer uniform, but the shouting was constant.

Thank God, Dewey thought to himself as he watched the chopper descend.

A stiff breeze had arrived, sweeping down from the hills, helping to cool the humid, muggy city.

A dark green Mil Mi-17 chopper approached from the east. It circled twice overhead, then descended in a slow, bouncy hover toward the helipad. The chopper lurched as it came closer, buffeted by the crosswinds. It settled onto the yellow triangle of LED lights at the center of the helipad.

Ever so slightly, the rotors slowed.

Millar stepped forward as the chopper's wheels touched down.

He reached out to the rear door of the chopper. As he slid the door open, the loud crack of gunfire came from inside the chopper. Millar's head abruptly kicked sideways; blood erupted from his head. He toppled backward to the helipad, dead.

Dewey reached for his shoulder holster. His hand caught the butt of his Colt just as someone grabbed his arms from behind.

"*Look out!*" Dewey screamed.

The next bullet tore into Iverheart's arm as he lunged, trying to evade it. He ducked just as another bullet struck his throat. The killer inside the chopper kept firing. A third slug ripped straight into the bridge of Iverheart's nose. The front of Iverheart's head cratered. He was pummeled backward by the force of the bullets, falling into a growing pool of blood.

Dewey was lifted off his feet and thrown to the ground, his shoulder slamming to the helipad. He tried to move, but the soldiers gripped his arms tight. One of the soldiers knelt on his back, while another gripped his ankles. He felt flex-cuffs tightening around his wrists and ankles.

He turned his head toward the chopper.

The killer climbed from the chopper. He held a Glock in his right hand. He stepped toward Dewey, training the weapon on him. The killer was young, no more than twenty-five years old. He had short, spiky black hair and a sharp nose. Dewey registered the face; it jogged a memory. Then he felt a sharp kick to the head. He looked up to see Bolin standing over him. He kicked Dewey again, this time cracking a rib. Dewey felt nothing. For several seconds, the pain somehow pushed its way to a different part of his mind as the shock and horror of what had just happened washed over him in a numbing wave.

Then, he tasted the blood in his mouth, and the pain began.

"Stop!" barked the young Arab. "You'll kill him."

"Goodbye, Mr. Andreas," said Bolin. He kicked him one last time, a blow to the stomach. Dewey groaned and coughed as blood filled his mouth, then vomit.

Bolin turned and walked toward the door to the buildings.

Four soldiers grabbed Dewey by his shackled arms and legs, hoisted him up, then carried him to the open door of the chopper. They threw him inside the chopper, feet first. He struggled to move his head. He looked across the roof to Bolin, whose back was turned as he walked away.

"Bolin," Dewey said in a clotted voice, barely above a whisper.

Bolin kept walking.

"*Bolin*," repeated Dewey, louder this time.

At the door, Bolin turned. He walked casually back to the chopper. He stood over Dewey, smiling down at him.

"What is it?" Bolin asked. "Do you need a Band-Aid?"

Blood coursed from Dewey's mouth and nose as he struggled to focus his eyes.

"You better pray," Dewey said, staring up at him.

"And what should I pray for, Mr. Andreas?" he asked, shaking his head, glancing at the faces of the soldiers who stood watching. "What should I pray for, *Dewey*?"

Dewey heard the rotors on the chopper accelerate. He felt a bounce as the first wheel lifted up from the ground.

"You better pray they kill me."

66

AIWAN-E-SADR

Bolin stepped out of the elevator and walked past a pair of soldiers, who stood in silence. He walked to his office. Opening the door, he stepped inside.

Inside, el-Jaqonda stood at the window, staring out at Constitution Avenue.

"He's on the chopper," said Bolin.

"Shall we make the call, Mr. President?" asked el-Jaqonda.

Bolin walked to the desk and sat down. On the desk was a laptop computer, which he flipped open and turned on.

El-Jaqonda sat down in a chair in front of the desk. He hit the speakerphone button, then dialed. The phone started to ring.

"Yes," said a man on the speaker.

"Good evening, Aswan," said el-Jaqonda, leaning toward the phone. "It's done. Andreas is on his way to Beirut."

"Did he see his men die?" Fortuna asked. "Did he watch them suffer?"

"Yes," said Bolin. "They died in front of him, just as you requested."

"Good. Very good, President Bolin."

Bolin started typing into the keyboard. The screen flashed to the Bank of Zurich customer portal. Bolin logged in to his account.

"Now it's your turn to act," said Bolin, leaning into the phone. "Until the money is wired into the account, the plane doesn't leave Rawalpindi."

"Are you logged in?" asked Fortuna.

"Yes," said Bolin. He glanced at el-Jaqonda, sitting in the chair in front of him, sweating and overweight.

The Funds on Deposit line of Bolin's Bank of Zurich account flashed. The number jumped in length. Bolin smiled, temporarily shocked by the amount now in his account. He knew the amount. When the man had offered the obscene amount of money for Andreas, he hadn't even negotiated. It was more than he would ever need.

Still, seeing it now before his eyes, the numbers laid out in a line, somehow it still sent a shock through him: $250,000,000.00.

Bolin sat in silence, staring at the screen.

"Well?" asked Fortuna.

"Our business is done," said Bolin, flipping the laptop closed. "Thank you, Mr. Fortuna. The plane will leave Rawalpindi when we get off the phone. Flight time to Beirut will be approximately six hours. Enjoy your new toy."

Bolin leaned forward and hit the speakerphone.

In front of him, el-Jaqonda sat back in the chair. He smiled nervously.

"Field Marshal Bolin," said el-Jaqonda. "I trust this has been a fruitful transaction."

Bolin looked at el-Jaqonda in silence, a blank look on his face.

"Would now be a good time to discuss our arrangement?" continued el-Jaqonda.

"Arrangement?" asked Bolin, grinning.

"My share of the transaction," said el-Jaqonda.

Bolin leaned back in his chair. He folded his hands together across his chest and looked at el-Jaqonda. He had never met el-Jaqonda, the deputy defense minister, though he had heard of him. A political appointee. Bolin viewed el-Jaqonda, and others like him, as detritus, leeches who traveled for free on the backs of people like him, who took the actual risks. He stared at el-Jaqonda with a wide, friendly grin on his face, a smile that masked the contempt he felt for the rotund man in front of him; Khan's deputy, who had helped drag Pakistan into the mess it was in.

"And what were you thinking?" asked Bolin.

"Since you asked, sir," said el-Jaqonda. "I believe splitting it down the middle would be a reasonable approach. After all, while you delivered the goods, I delivered the money, as it were."

El-Jaqonda smiled at Bolin.

"Fifty-fifty?" asked Bolin, contemplating the offer. "Are you sure you could survive on that much?"

"Of course I could survive, Field Marshal," said el-Jaqonda, shifting in his seat. "But, of course, perhaps less. What if we split it more like sixty-forty? Or even just one quarter? Yes, that's it. One quarter is just fine, sir."

"One quarter?" asked Bolin. "Why, I would be too worried about you, Khalid. How could any man survive on such a pittance? A fat fuck like you needs money for food. What if I give you two hundred million? That seems better for me. I would be worried about you with anything less. Or better yet, why don't you just take the entire thing?"

Bolin laughed contemptuously.

El-Jaqonda's happy demeanor slipped away. His smile disappeared. He blinked nervously and beads of perspiration appeared on his forehead.

"Field Marshal—"

"*President*," said Bolin harshly.

Bolin casually reached to his waist and removed his weapon, a Smith & Wesson .45 caliber handgun. He raised it in the air and aimed it at el-Jaqonda.

"Mr. President," said el-Jaqonda, holding his hands up. "I will go. I need none of the money. I was being greedy. I'm sorry."

Bolin fired the weapon. The gun made a loud thunderclap in the tall-ceilinged office. The slug entered el-Jaqonda's throat at the larynx. He reached his hand up to his neck in the same moment the force of the shot threw him off balance, the chair leaned sideways, and he fell backward.

Bolin stood and stared down at el-Jaqonda whose hands gripped his throat. Blood coursed over el-Jaqonda's fat fingers. Through a clotted, blood-filled throat, el-Jaqonda tried to speak from the ground.

The sound of footsteps came from the hallway, then a knock at the door.

Bolin aimed the gun at el-Jaqonda. He pulled the trigger and fired another round that ripped into el-Jaqonda's chest. He died instantly.

The door opened. A young soldier entered. Seeing el-Jaqonda on the ground, the soldier paused, then looked at Bolin.

"Call the janitorial department," said Bolin. "Then get back to your watch."

67

Fortuna placed the phone back on the receiver. He stood up. A smile creased his lips. He shook his head in disbelief.

Fortuna walked out of the room that served as his office, a small room whose walls were lined with bookshelves. He went to the kitchen. Behind an island at the center of the room, beneath a line of copper pots that hung from an iron rack, stood Candela. She was tall and stunning. Her dark hair lay halfway down her back and shimmered like black leather. She stood at the marble counter, quietly grating a piece of ginger into a silver bowl.

On the other side of the kitchen was a long harvest table. Five men sat around it, smoking cigarettes and talking.

Fortuna walked to the table.

"It's done," said Fortuna. "Andreas is in the air. The plane will land in six hours."

"Be careful what you wish for," said Nebuchar. "That is what you used to always say."

Tonight, in a matter of hours, Aswan Fortuna would finally have his quarry. He thought briefly of the many hours, dollars, and lives that had been sacrificed searching for Andreas. The payoffs to various middlemen, arms dealers, corrupt intelligence officers. The lead that sent them to Australia, then the failure there too. He grinned. He considered the fact that he could simply have taken the year off, saved his money, and done nothing. For Andreas had found *him*. Now, for a mere pittance, Andreas would be dropped off like a FedEx package on his doorstep.

"That's not the expression that comes to mind right now," said Fortuna.

"And what is, Father?" asked Nebuchar, laughing and glancing at the four men seated with him.

Fortuna walked to the large door that opened out onto the terrace. He stared at Beirut's twinkling lights in the distance.

"Vengeance is mine; I will repay, sayeth the Lord."

68

The door to the chopper opened. Two soldiers pulled Dewey from the backseat by his arms, then let his large body fall to the hard cement of the tarmac.

The two soldiers were joined by two more. The four men lifted Dewey and carried him more than a hundred feet across the dark tarmac. They carried him toward the rear of a large, dark green C-130 cargo plane.

A young Arab walked behind the soldiers, smoking a cigarette.

"Is that all you could get?" he asked, flicking the cigarette to the ground. "It's a fucking cargo plane. We need a jet. A fast jet."

The soldiers carried Dewey's 225-pound frame up the rear ramp and into the cavernous, empty cargo bay. The soldiers dropped Dewey to the hard steel at the right side of the bay.

"We follow orders," answered one of the soldiers, barely acknowledging the young terrorist. "It's a six-hour trip. I'm sure you'll survive."

The Arab looked around the spacious cargo bay as the soldiers exited through the rear of the plane. Long canvas benches were strung on each side of the plane. Above, an array of equipment, piping, and electronics spread across the walls. He looked down at his prisoner. Blood continued to ooze from the American's nose and mouth, forming a puddle in front of him. On his left shoulder, blood now coursed down from a long, wide scar that had torn along the edge.

The hydraulic buzz of the rear ramp interrupted the silence. That was joined by the sound of the big plane's four turboprops sputtering to life.

After a few minutes, the plane began to move down the runway. The roar of the propellers grew louder, then the plane began a slow, steady roll down the tarmac, accelerating, picking up speed, then lumbering into the air.

Dewey opened his eyes. In front of him, across the cargo bay, the young Arab with the spiked black hair, who killed Millar and Iverheart, sat on an orange canvas bench, smoking a cigarette, his legs crossed.

Dewey felt pain in multiple locations. It emanated like electric current from his rib cage, shoulder, and stomach. There was nausea too, from Bolin's last kick. He began throwing up on the ground. When he was finished, he struggled to move his head away from the vomit. The flex-cuffs around his ankles and wrists made it almost impossible to move.

The sound of the plane's engines drummed out all other noise. Dewey felt the nausea again, but he held the vomit down inside his throat.

"You almost killed me there on the mine road," the Arab said, flicking the cigarette across the cabin, where it landed next to Dewey. "This is where you hit me."

He removed his leather coat. He pointed to a white bandage on his arm.

"Australia?" said the terrorist. "Do you remember? My name is Youssef. Enjoy the flight. Because when you get to Beirut, Aswan Fortuna is going to make you wish you were back in Cooktown getting eaten by a shark. By the way, you killed my brother. So I'm enjoying this."

Dewey said nothing. A memory came into his mind. Why it came to him, at that very moment, he didn't know, but it did. In his head, he had a vision of a small gray tombstone.

After killing Alexander Fortuna more than a year ago, Dewey had flown to Boston, then driven to his parents' farm in Castine. He'd arrived at the cemetery at four in the afternoon. It had been a bitter cold day. He pictured it now and tried to remember what the cold felt like, the wind tearing off the ocean. He tried to remember walking down the fence line of the old cemetery.

He'd walked to the tombstone of his son, his only son, Robbie. It was the first time he had ever seen it.

Dewey understood then, at that very moment, as he thought of his own son's grave, that Aswan Fortuna would never stop. The old man had hunted him to the ends of the earth for a reason. Finding Dewey had not only been predictable, it had been inevitable. In some strange way, Dewey respected what Fortuna had at long last accomplished.

Dewey felt his body shiver. He understood, in that moment, that what awaited him in Beirut would be a death unlike any man's. It would be days, weeks perhaps, of torture, humiliation, degradation, but mostly just pain.

Dewey steeled himself. He fought through the nausea. He needed to fight now. He had to focus and he had to fight. If he was to avenge the cold-blooded murders of Alex Millar and Rob Iverheart, he needed to fight now. If he was to survive, he needed to swallow the pain. It was beyond skill now. Beyond training.

The bullet had been fired, and in that hellish moment Dewey grasped that he was trapped between the end of the gun and the target.

"Help me, God," he whispered as the nausea returned and a fresh flood of blood-streaked vomit came rushing from his mouth.

69

The phone on Jessica's desk rang. She hit the green button on the console.

"Yes," she said. She glanced at the clock on the wall: 5:34 P.M. "What is it?"

"I have CENCOM, Josh Brubaker."

"Put him through."

The phone clicked.

"Hi, Josh. Are they in Qatar yet?"

"I'm in contact with the pilot," said Brubaker. "He's still on the tarmac at Chaklala Air Force Base."

"Are you kidding me?" she asked, incredulous. "It's past midnight over there. Have you spoken with Polk?"

"Yes," said Brubaker. "They're en route back to the U.S. The operation is over. Should I have them turn around?"

"Dewey and the team should have been on the ground in Qatar by now, or, at the very least, up in the Gulfstream flying somewhere over the Arabian Peninsula, out of Pakistan."

"I'm sure there's an explanation," said Brubaker.

"Are you in the Situation Room?" she asked.

"Yeah," said Brubaker.

"I'll be right down. Keep trying to reach him."

She hung up the phone. She hit a red button in the right corner of the phone console. "Calibrisi."

"Where are you?"

"Langley," said Calibrisi. "Why? You want to celebrate? You deserve it. Let's grab a drink at the Willard."

"Hector," said Jessica. "We have a problem."

Jessica ran down the hallway and climbed on the elevator, inserting a thick black plastic card into the slot on the wall panel inside. The elevator descended two flights. She exited and walked through a security checkpoint, then into the Situation Room.

Six people were gathered in the room. All were members of the interagency group that had been assembled to monitor the coup. They were, if not relaxing, at least pausing in the aftermath of the successful takeover of the Pakistani government. Four of the large plasma screens displayed scenes from Pakistan, either live MQ-9 Reaper feeds of Islamabad, Karachi, or another city in Pakistan, or news, volume down, alternating between Fox, BBC, Al Jazeera, or CNN. On one of the screens, a replay of a Washington Redskins football game was playing.

Assembled were Josh Brubaker, an NSC staffer who was point on the Pakistan operation; Andrew Corrado, from the NSA; Tony Helm and Bo Revere, both from CIA; and John Balter, from the Pentagon, a marine serving on the staff of the secretary of defense.

Every person sat at the table, a computer screen and phone console in front of them on the table.

Helm, Brubaker, and Balter were each on the phone. When Jessica walked in, she went to the wall and stood in front of a large plasma screen.

Two of the screens displayed alternating aerial shots of Islamabad and Rawalpindi, the lights of the city glowing in the evening darkness. The sight of orange clusters, small fires, dotted the screen. There were at least a dozen fires raging across the cities.

One of the screens replayed a blurry clip of Aiwan-e-Sadr, followed by a flash of red.

"What is it?" she asked.

"It's the chopper sent in to pick up the team," said Corrado, from the NSA, without looking up. He was typing on his computer. "Circa hour and a half ago."

"Where's it going?"

"That's what I'm trying to figure out. I'm trying to do a patch of the Reaper feeds we have running."

"Meaning?"

"I'm overlaying different Reaper video sequences of that particular flight path, at that particular time, trying to build a unified narrative."

"Has anyone spoken with Bolin or someone on his staff?"

Brubaker hung up the phone.

"Yes. That was Martu, the head of Special Services Group. He said the chopper took off with them on it. He said it should have arrived at Chaklala more than an hour ago. He's going to try and reach the pilot."

"Do we actually believe him?" asked Jessica.

Balter, from the Pentagon, held up a finger. He was finishing a call. He listened for one more moment, then hung up the phone.

"That was Polk," said Balter. "They were able to get a hard location on the GPS inside their earbuds. According to Polk, all three are still at Aiwan-e-Sadr. They haven't left."

"Maybe they left the buds there?" volunteered Revere from the CIA.

Jessica looked at Brubaker. "Find Bolin. Tell him I want to speak with him right now."

Brubaker picked up the phone, directed the team back at the Pentagon to find Bolin. Within a minute, Brubaker's phone buzzed. He hit it, then held up a finger, covering the mouthpiece.

"It's Bolin," said Brubaker. "You want privacy?"

"Put it on speaker," Jessica said, stepping toward Brubaker.

"Good evening, Ms. Tanzer," said the voice, a husky, deep voice in broken English. "What can I do for you?"

"Good evening, Field Marshal Bolin," said Jessica. "We haven't heard from Dewey Andreas and his team in more than an hour and a half. Where are they, sir?"

"I ordered them a chopper," said Bolin. "It left more than an hour ago."

"We've got their communications devices traced to Aiwan-e-Sadr," said Jessica. "We can't reach any of them. Our pilot is sitting at Chaklala and hasn't heard a word from them."

"In case you haven't noticed," said Bolin, exasperation in his voice, "I've been a little busy, Ms. Tanzer. As I told President Allaire, I am grateful to you and to America for helping my country. I will look into it and get back to you."

"Thank you, Field Marshal."

The phone went dead. Jessica looked around the table. Her expression was blank. She tried to remain calm. She gripped the edge of the mahogany table and, out of view of everyone in the room, squeezed as hard as she could, trying to calm herself.

"Check out the screen," said Corrado. "It'll be choppy but I think I have it."

Corrado stood up and moved to the left side of one of the plasmas.

On one of the screens, a video began to play, the first clip beginning at Aiwan-e-Sadr. The red flash of lights moved in a line away from the palace; the four lights the only part of the chopper visible against the black of night.

"That's the chopper," said Corrado, pointing at the lights. "We're heading west now, toward Chaklala."

"What time is it?" asked Balter.

"Twelve forty local time," said Corrado. "Now here's the first transition, from the first UAV to the second."

The chopper's path on the screen shifted as a new video stream replaced the last one. This one captured the same lights, but from a higher altitude.

"Here we're getting closer to Rawalpindi," said Corrado. "The chopper starts picking up speed here."

The lights moved steadily across the black sky, the occasional sight of lights below sparking on the screen. The chopper moved across the screen.

"One more UAV patch," said Corrado, pointing at the plasma. "On three, two, one."

The view shifted once again. The screen displayed a new frame that picked up the red lights of the chopper coursing across the black sky, past an occasional cluster of lights. It moved across the screen, slowed, then stopped.

"The picture's not great," said Corrado. "But this is Chaklala. We know that because of this." He pointed to a green light on the screen. "That's our Gulfstream. According to the video, the chopper landed at Chaklala."

Jessica glanced around the table, frustrated. The phone at the center of the table buzzed.

"CENCOM, I've got President Bolin for Jessica."

"Go CENCOM," said Jessica.

The phone clicked.

"President Bolin," said Jessica.

"Ms. Tanzer, I may have something," said Bolin.

"We do too, sir," said Jessica. "In reviewing the—"

"Ms. Tanzer," interrupted Bolin. "I am sorry to report that the chopper appears to have crashed while en route to Chaklala Air Force Base."

A cold wave shot up from Jessica's spine. She looked around the room, the shocked glances of the group greeting her eyes.

"Everyone aboard was killed in the crash, including several Pakistani soldiers," said Bolin. "I'm very sorry. Andreas and his team were truly brave."

"I don't understand," said Jessica calmly. "I'm in a bit of shock."

"The chopper, I'm afraid, is still smoldering," said Bolin. "We, of course, will do everything we can to find the remains and ensure they are returned to the United States."

"Field Marshal Bolin—" Jessica said.

But before she could get her words out, the phone clicked out.

The Situation Room was silent for more than half a minute.

Jessica walked to the screen and stared at the shot of the chopper, sitting on the dim tarmac.

"Is there any way we tracked the wrong helicopter?" asked Jessica.

"That's the only chopper to or from Aiwan-e-Sadr in the past twenty-four hours," said Corrado.

Jessica stared at the screen. "What do we do?" she asked, a hint of helplessness in her voice.

"Why would he lie?" asked Helm from CIA.

Jessica stared back blankly at him.

"At the very least, we should get a team in there," said Balter. "I've got Rangers we can send in from Kabul."

Jessica's face showed a stoned, shocked look. She turned from the screen. She leaned forward and pressed the speakerphone, which started ringing.

"This is Calibrisi. What is it?"

"We have a big problem," said Jessica. "According to Bolin, the chopper crashed. Dewey, the others, they're all dead."

"My God," said Calibrisi.

"NSA tracked the chopper," said Jessica. "It didn't crash."

Corrado raised his finger. "I have something," he said.

"What?" asked Jessica.

"The same UAV. Check it."

The screen showed the chopper lights, then the screen went black.

"This is five minutes later, same aerial view."

The screen showed a line of yellow lights in the exact spot where the chopper lights had been.

"That's a plane," said Corrado. "Hercules."

On the speakerphone at the center of the table, the sound of Calibrisi clearing his throat.

"It's fairly obvious, isn't it, everybody?" asked Calibrisi.

"What's obvious?" asked Jessica.

"You've got a plane taking off?" asked Calibrisi. "Right after they're flown to Chaklala by chopper? You can track it all you want, but you're wasting your time."

"What are you talking about?" asked Corrado.

Jessica stared at the plasma screen. "Beirut," she said, finally.

"That's right," said Calibrisi on speaker. "Run the financials on Bolin. I want to know how much Fortuna paid him."

"On it," said Revere.

"The question is not, did Bolin sell Andreas," said Calibrisi. "The question is, how much did he get."

"How did Fortuna find out he was there?"

"It doesn't matter," said Calibrisi. "We need to figure out a way to divert that plane."

"I don't have the flight path," said Corrado. "We weren't tracking it. Looking at the satellite feed, there are about a dozen planes now heading toward Beirut. I don't know how we pick out our plane from the others."

"What kind of plane was it?" asked Jessica. "Can we at least determine that?"

"It's a cargo plane," said Balter. "C-130."

"How long do we have?" asked Jessica.

"The plane took off an hour ago," said Corrado. "Assuming it was a C-130, that means it will land in Beirut in approximately five hours."

"I've got something," said Revere, slapping his hand down on the table.

"What?" said Jessica.

"Holy Toledo," said Revere. "I looked at the Fortuna funds we have a track on. Half an hour ago, he transferred two hundred and fifty million to an account at the Bank of Zurich."

"Can we get into that account?" asked Brubaker.

"Not if we're going to stay within the boundaries of international law," said Corrado.

"Fuck the law," said Calibrisi. "Hack it!"

"I'm in," said Corrado. "I should rob banks for a living."

"I assume there's no name attached to it," said Calibrisi. "We'll have to petition the bank itself."

"That will take too long," said Jessica. "It's Bolin. There's no other explanation. Josh, get Bolin on the phone."

"Freeze the money while you're in there," said Calibrisi, "if you can."

"Done," said Corrado. "There was two-fifty, plus another thirty in a different account. I froze it all."

Brubaker leaned forward and pressed the speaker button. The phone clicked several times. After a minute, Bolin came on.

"You're very persistent, Ms. Tanzer," said Bolin. "What can I do for you now?"

"Stop the plane," said Jessica sharply. "Order it diverted. Right now."

"The plane? What plane?"

"The cargo plane that left Chaklala one hour ago headed for Beirut."

"You're accusing me of lying to you?" asked Bolin, indignant. "I explained to you: the chopper crashed on its way to Rawalpindi."

"We watched it from the sky. *The chopper landed* safely."

"How dare you!" barked Bolin.

Corrado held his thumb up, nodding. Jessica leaned in, pressed mute.

"What?"

"I got a link," Corrado whispered. "I found a way inside one of the bank's databases. It's his account."

Jessica pressed the mute button again.

"Field Marshal Bolin, explain why Aswan Fortuna transferred a quarter billion dollars into your bank account less than two hours ago."

Bolin was silent.

"This is an act of war," said Jessica, not making any effort to hide her rage. "You are a corrupt and vile man. These men risked their lives for your country."

Bolin was quiet.

"We expect you to order that plane diverted," said Jessica. "Right now."

"The plane went with the deal," said Bolin. "The pilots don't work for me. I have as much control over that plane as you do."

"So you admit it?"

"Grow up," said Bolin. "El-Khayab is gone. India and Pakistan have stood down their nuclear arsenals. You have your coup d'état. Isn't that what this was all about?"

The phone clicked and went silent. Jessica glanced around the table. She sat down and shut her eyes. She reached up and rubbed the bridge of her nose.

Finally, she opened her eyes and looked at Balter.

"How long until they land?"

"Five hours, tops."

"There's nothing we can do," said Jessica, looking at the phone. "They're going to land. Aswan Fortuna is waiting for them. He'll . . . he'll torture Dewey. He'll torture him, then kill him. And there's nothing we can do."

The room was silent. All eyes were on Jessica. She stared straight ahead, with a look on her face that none of them had ever seen; a pained look, innocent and broken.

Finally, Calibrisi spoke up:

"There is something," said Calibrisi. "I'm just not sure there's enough time."

"What is it?" asked Jessica. Tears were in her eyes, which she made no effort to hide.

"You'll need the president to make the call, Jess," said Calibrisi.

"Make the call to who?" asked Jessica.

"Tel Aviv," said Calibrisi. "The Israelis might be able to save him."

70

Two hours after sunset, Beirut Rafic Hariri International Airport was crowded.

One of the busiest airports in the Middle East, a pair of flights, an MEA flight from Damascus, the other a Lufthansa flight from Munich, had just landed. Hundreds of people packed the main terminal building, greeting the arriving passengers. Meanwhile, people getting ready to board the planes gathered with their families.

The main terminal at Beirut Rafic Hariri spread in a straight rectangle nearly half a mile long. Its soaring, modern white lines showed the country's effort to try and resurrect a feeling of safety, security, wealth, and beauty that had once been the hallmarks of this troubled city, especially its architecture. Some cracks, chipping paint, and, in one section of the terminal, a partial hole in the roof near the Cedar Lounge, showed the reality of present-day Beirut and its generations of conflict and war.

A few miles from the airport, a white school bus rumbled along through a busy neighborhood in Dahieh, a suburb in southern Beirut.

Inside the bus, Rueq Khalid, a commander in the Al-Muqawama Brigades, the paramilitary wing of Hezbollah, walked down the center aisle of the vehicle.

Khalid wore jeans and a short-sleeved button-down khaki shirt. A thick nylon ammunition belt was wrapped around his waist. Khalid had a thick black beard and mustache, short-cropped black hair, thick eyebrows. His eyes were blank, cold, as he walked the line of soldiers, who, like him, all wore jeans and a khaki shirt. They sat upright, staring out the window at the passing neighborhoods of southern Beirut.

In Khalid's right hand, aimed at the ceiling, a Kalashnikov, its gray steel chipped and scratched, the weapon's half-moon magazine clutched tightly in his right hand.

He walked to the back of the bus and tapped the glass of the back door with the toe of his boot, then turned and walked forward to the front of the bus.

He counted forty-two men in all, plus himself.

The bus passed the entrance gate to Beirut Rafic Hariri. At Rue Farid, the driver took a right, then a quick left onto a service road. After more than a mile, the driver took another right onto a small, unnamed service road along the south edge of the airport. The bus moved down the quiet, dark road. It passed several small office buildings, a large lot filled with parked bulldozers and forklifts, and a few warehouses. At the last building, the driver took a right and drove past a darkened corrugated steel warehouse to an empty parking lot in back. He parked at the back of the lot, the front of the bus a few feet from a chain-link fence, at the southern perimeter.

Behind the fence, the runway spread out in a gray plain in front of the bus. Wide and flat, the tarmac moved in a straight line for more than two miles, from the unlit end, where they were now parked, to the brightly lit main landing area at the far end of the runway. The lights of the main terminal building twinkled in the distance.

Khalid stepped down the bus stairs. He was followed by two similarly dressed Hezbollah soldiers; plainclothed, neatly attired. One of the soldiers carried a set of long-handled wire cutters. In near darkness, he began to cut through the links of the fence, starting at the ground and working his way up. Soon, he had cut a line six feet high. Then he cut to the right. He took the fence and pushed forward. He stepped through, dropped the wire cutters, then with both hands yanked the fence toward himself. The section of fence fell to the dirt.

Khalid stepped through the opening. He nodded at the young Palestinian who had just cut the fence.

He pulled a pack of cigarettes from his pocket, took one, then lit it.

"That will do," he said.

A few miles away, in a busy, densely populated industrial area in northern Beirut called Bourj Hammoud, Aswan Fortuna entered a plain, run-down six-story cement and glass building through the front door. Nebuchar followed behind him. It was nearly two o'clock in the morning. They swept past a pair of young Palestinians who stood guard, glancing about nervously. The guards' weapons were not visible but their leather coats bulged at the sides.

Aswan and Nebuchar stepped quickly inside the lobby of the building.

Inside the door, they were met by a stocky man in his late twenties. He was bald and olive-skinned. He had a thin mustache. His left ear was noticeable because half of it was missing, severed in a jagged line across the top, as if it had been cut by a saw. His skin was badly pockmarked with acne. He had a look, a demeanor, that could only be described as vicious. His black eyes were like pools of raw anger. He gripped a weapon, a sawed-off Beretta 12-gauge shotgun, in his right hand, aimed down at the floor.

"Hello, Muamar," said Nebuchar.

"Nebuchar, Aswan," said Muamar, nodding. "Come in. Quickly now."

He waved then inside.

Muamar nodded to one of the two men, who quickly shut the door.

"Bless Al-Muqawama," said Nebuchar. "Thank you for your help on such short notice."

"I received the call from Na'im Qasim himself," said Muamar.

"We're happy to help. But we must be quiet. Lebanese Armed Forces does not know we're here. Even the airport operation; it will be tricky."

"How tricky?" asked Nebuchar, concern in his voice.

"Don't worry," said Muamar. "It will be difficult, but we will get it done. LAF is very, very disorganized. Getting him off the plane will be easy. Getting away, that will be more difficult."

Aswan and Nebuchar followed Muamar back through the darkened lobby of what had been an office building, now empty.

At the back of the lobby was a door. Muamar stopped, glanced at Nebuchar and Aswan. He held up a finger.

"Listen," he said. "Do you hear anything?"

"Nothing," said Nebuchar. "Why?"

Muamar did not answer. He turned, went through the door, then flipped a light switch on the wall. It was a dark, musty-smelling stairwell. The three men descended two flights of stairs. They went through a doorway, into a long hallway that was lit up by a single bulb dangling from a wire in the ceiling. The floor of the hallway looked derelict; it was littered with empty bottles, soda cans, and old newspapers. It was a squalid place; abandoned, as if it hadn't had visitors, occupants, anyone for years. There was no sound, save for the footsteps of the three men walking quickly across the cracked cement.

Aswan and Nebuchar followed Muamar down the long, dim hallway. At the end of the hallway they took a left. They walked down another long, littered corridor, beneath another lightbulb that dangled from a wire. At the end of the second hallway, Muamar turned.

"Can you hear it now?"

Aswan glanced at Nebuchar, then at Muamar. He heard nothing. Then, after several seconds, he heard something. Barely above a whisper, someone's voice. Or perhaps a radio playing somewhere far away.

"A radio?" asked Aswan.

Muamar turned the knob on a large steel door. As it cracked open the silence was replaced by music, a rap song, blaring at full volume.

Muamar pushed the door completely open. The room was large

and windowless. In the middle of the room stood a long steel table. To the right was a wooden chair. Both were empty. Against the right side wall, chains hung from hooks in the ceiling and dangled down to a machine on the floor with a large steel wheel and handle. He walked to the radio and turned it off.

Aswan stared at the chains. He let out a small gasp as he registered the splatters of dried blood layered on the walls behind where the chair sat, the ground covered in red.

Nebuchar walked slowly across the room. His eyes bulged in horror.

On the ground against the left side wall, a collection of objects was arranged on the floor in a line. Saws, knives, a machete, piles of rope, several car batteries with wires coming out, red plastic gasoline canisters, a chain saw, a television, several more radios, too many hammers to count, a pile of pliers, garbage bags, a large leather whip, chains, bricks, a small pile of long branches from a tree, a staple gun, filthy towels.

"You look like you're going to be ill," said Muamar, looking at Aswan. "This is the war. This is what happens in the war, on both sides. The Jews are just as bad."

"Do not mistake my mood," snapped Aswan. "I am nauseous, yes, but this is my duty as a father. This place, this room, is precisely what we have asked you for. It could not be any more perfect."

"You have given us much, Aswan," said Muamar. "We share your thirst for revenge. This man, his name is Andreas?"

"Yes," said Nebuchar. "Dewey Andreas."

"We have all heard his name," said Muamar. "He is an enemy to us all for killing Alexander. It is an honor to help you destroy the American."

"Is the team at the airport?" asked Nebuchar.

Muamar glanced at his watch. He reached for his cell phone and pressed a button. He spoke rapidly in Arabic, listened for a few moments, spoke again, then hung up.

"They're waiting," said Muamar. "Forty-three in all. The pilot is in touch. They're two hours away."

"And their instructions are clear?"

"They are to bring Andreas directly here. They are not to harm him."

"Good," said Aswan.

Muamar smiled briefly and glanced at his watch.

"It's going to be a long wait," said Muamar. "There's a more comfortable room upstairs."

Muamar turned and walked to the door. Nebuchar followed. Aswan remained still.

"I'll wait here," said Aswan. He walked to the chair and sat down. "I would like to wait here. This is the last duty I will perform for my son."

71

Dewey awoke with a shudder. Slowly, he moved his head. For a moment, he had forgotten where he was. But it came back to him now in a wave of pain, fear, and nausea.

How long have I been passed out? He was angry at himself. *How could I drift off like that?* Then he remembered: Beirut. Fortuna. He would be waiting. Whatever it took to get Bolin to turn on him, it just showed how far Aswan would go to avenge his son. Dewey shuddered at the thought of the torture that surely awaited.

Dewey shut his eyes. He shook his head.

"No," he whispered to himself. "Not yet. I'm not ready to die."

He needed to think. To strategize.

Dewey focused his eyes. The nausea was gone now. He saw, first, the pool of blood and vomit that spilled across the corrugated steel of the cabin floor. It ran back toward the rear, the motion of the plane pushing it backward.

Dewey's legs were straight in front of him. Flex-cuffs held the ankles together tightly. His arms lay on his lap, flex-cuffs tight around his wrists.

He looked across the cabin at the young terrorist. He sat on a fold-down canvas seat, staring at Dewey, smoking a cigarette. On the ground in front of him, a small pile of butts had collected.

Dewey's eyes met the young killer's. The terrorist stared at him, refusing to look away.

"He's awake," said the terrorist. "I was afraid I lost you. Do you know that if you're dead when I deliver you to Aswan I myself will be killed?"

Dewey said nothing. Slowly, painfully, he sat upright.

"You killed my brother in Australia," said the terrorist. "You recognize me now, yes?"

Dewey leaned back against the steel rebar. His hands were between his legs. With his shoulder, he wiped blood and vomit from his beard.

"What's your name?" asked Dewey.

"Youssef."

Dewey showed no emotion, but the memory stirred. The face of the terrorist in the car, shooting at him.

"Now you remember," said Youssef. "Thought you killed me? You thought wrong."

Dewey stared in silence.

"Would you like some peanuts? We'll begin the in-flight movie in a few minutes. Today we're showing *Bambi*."

Dewey ignored him. Looking down, he saw a glint of steel at his ankle. They had neglected to remove his Gerber blade from the sheath at his ankle.

Slowly, he leaned forward, his wrists cuffed tightly together, and pulled the cuff of his pant leg down, making sure the tip of the blade was covered.

"When do we land?" asked Dewey.

The terrorist stood up.

"That's a good question," he said. "I myself would like to find that out. I have a woman in Beirut and tonight I would like to get laid. I haven't fucked anything in over a month."

"I guess you guys don't count goats, do you?" asked Dewey.

Youssef laughed. "That was good. You see, I appreciate a sense of humor. Not bad, Andreas. I would never fuck a goat, though. A cow maybe, but not a goat."

Youssef walked to the front of the cargo hold. A large steel door shut off the hold from the flight deck.

Quickly, Dewey moved his cuffed hands to his ankle.

The terrorist took a small mouthpiece from a radio near the door.

With difficulty, Dewey pulled the knife from the sheath. Working as fast as he could, his hands bound tightly together, he sliced the flex-cuffs from his ankles. He turned the knife and slowly, carefully inserted the tip of the blade between his tightly-bound wrists, then pushed.

In Arabic, Youssef spoke into the mouthpiece and then placed it back on the radio. He walked back and stood over Dewey. He took out a cigarette and lit it.

"You smell like throw up."

Dewey stared up at the terrorist as he clasped his big hands over the hilt of the Gerber, concealing it just in time.

"Where did you train, Youssef?" asked Dewey. "Jaffna? Darfur?"

"Bekaa Valley."

"Have you ever guarded someone before?" asked Dewey. "Did they teach you how to keep watch?"

The terrorist smiled. He shook his head as he looked down at Dewey.

"Stupid question," he muttered. "Of course."

"What's the first rule?" asked Dewey.

The terrorist took another puff. He exhaled, then smiled.

"The first rule is don't look away."

"What's the second rule?" asked Dewey.

"Keep your weapon with you," said the terrorist.

"Very good," said Dewey.

"What's your point?" asked the Arab. "What does it matter? You are tied up like a pig. I could fuck your mother in front of you and you couldn't do a thing."

"My point is, in the span of a minute, you broke the two most important rules," said Dewey. "You looked away and you left your weapon over there on the seat."

Dewey stared at the terrorist. Youssef took a drag on the cigarette, shaking his head. His eyes revealed a small streak of fear.

Dewey glanced from the terrorist's eyes across the hold. The killer's Glock sat on the canvas seat, the silencer pointing out. Dewey looked back up at the terrorist.

Calmly, Dewey took his wrists and held them up toward the terrorist. The blade was now tucked between his wrists. He yanked and pulled the flex-cuffs apart. They dropped like ribbons to the ground.

Youssef paused. He was momentarily confused. Then he lurched backward. But Dewey caught him with his leg, tripping the terrorist as he tried to run for his weapon. Youssef fell to the ground.

Dewey stood. He was dizzy and weak. He stepped toward Youssef, who was desperately trying to stand up. Dewey caught him in the mouth with a hard kick from his steel-toed boot, shattering his jaw. A tooth fell to the steel floor. A piercing scream rose in the hold as Youssef tumbled sideways.

In Dewey's right hand, he held the combat knife. He pounced to Youssef's chest, bringing the blade tip in a slashing motion down above the killer's heart. He plunged it halfway in, pausing as the killer looked up at him. Dewey waited for the moment of recognition. He wanted to see the panic in the black eyes of the terrorist and the final understanding that he had been beaten. Blood flamed out from his nose, ears, and mouth.

"That's why the rules are so important, Youssef," said Dewey as he stared into the terrorist's eyes for a brief second, then thrust the razor-sharp blade through his heart.

72

J essica sprinted out of the Situation Room, past a pair of Secret Service officers stationed just outside the door. She took the flights of stairs two steps at a time. At the first floor, she slowed slightly, stepped through the office of Cecily Vincent, the president's executive assistant, who looked up but did not try to stop the national security advisor, one of only two people allowed to walk into the Oval Office at any time, the other being Vincent herself.

Jessica opened the door to the Oval Office and stepped inside. Inside the Oval Office, President Allaire was seated in a wing chair. On the chesterfield sofas in front of him sat half a dozen U.S. senators, one of whom, the senate majority leader from Texas, Senator Greer Callahan, was in midsentence.

Jessica's eyes immediately met the president's.

"Excuse me, Greer," said the president, interrupting Callahan. "Ladies and gentlemen, we're going to have to reconvene."

"Jessica, should we be concerned by that look on your face?" asked one of the senators, Joe Sharp from Missouri, as he stood up to leave the Oval Office.

"I apologize," said Jessica, not answering Sharp's question directly.

Cecily Vincent shut the door as the last of the senators exited.

"What is it?" asked the president.

"Bolin," said Jessica. "He double-crossed us."

"What do you mean?" asked the president.

"Bolin sold Dewey to Aswan Fortuna. We believe Dewey's on a plane right now, bound for Beirut. The rest of the coup team is either with Dewey or already dead."

The president stared at Jessica in disbelief. Anger crossed his face, then reddened his cheeks.

"How do you know?" he asked, stepping behind his desk.

"Video, cash transfers," said Jessica. "I confronted him and he admitted to it."

"That son of a bitch," said the president. He reached for the phone on the desk. "Ungrateful motherfucking bastard."

"Right now, Mr. President, we have to forget about what Bolin just did," said Jessica. "We have at most four, maybe five, hours until that plane lands in Beirut."

"So let's intercept the goddamn plane," said President Allaire. "Scramble some F-18s."

"It's too late," said Jessica. "We weren't tracking the flight path. We don't even know if it's going to land in Beirut. We're guessing. But it's all we have. We need to meet the plane."

"How?" asked President Allaire.

"Israel," said Jessica.

"Prime Minister Shalit," said Allaire a few minutes later, clutching the phone to his ear as Jessica listened in on another handset. "I apologize for interrupting your vacation. I'm here with Jessica Tanzer."

"It's quite all right," said Shalit. "Gstaad will get along without me for a few hours."

"We need your help," said the president. "We have a situation. I don't have time to brief you fully on all of the details, but the bottom line is, there's a plane bound for Beirut. On board is one and possibly several American GIs. They were kidnapped."

"Why Beirut?"

"Aswan Fortuna," said Jessica. "He paid handsomely for one of the men. When he receives possession of him, he's going to torture and kill him. This man is very important to us. To America. To me personally. He saved our country when Alexander Fortuna attacked us."

"Benjamin, this is the team we sent in to remove Omar El-Khayab," said Allaire.

"So that was you," said Shalit. "Thank God for that. What's your soldier's name?"

"Andreas," said the president. "Dewey Andreas."

"So Aswan paid for his revenge?" asked Shalit.

"Yes," said Jessica. "The CIA's assumption is that Hezbollah will be waiting for the plane."

"I'm curious," said Shalit. "How much did Fortuna pay?"

"We believe the figure is two hundred and fifty million dollars," said Jessica.

"My God," said Shalit, momentarily taken aback. "How much time do we have?"

"Four, maybe five hours," said Jessica. "Maybe less."

"Four hours?" asked Shalit. "That's not a lot of time. Hold on the line. Let me get General Dayan."

"Menachem Dayan," said Jessica to President Allaire, "the head of IDF."

The president put his hand over the receiver.

"I know who the hell he is, Jess," said Allaire.

"Sorry. Habit."

"It's okay. I'm not senile yet." A slight grin came to his lips. "Israel."

It was all he said, but Jessica knew exactly what he meant. It was moments like this when you understood who your true allies were.

The phone clicked again.

"There we go," said Shalit. "President Allaire, Jessica, I'm joined by General Menachem Dayan."

"Good evening," said Dayan, his voice deep and gravelly, a heavy smoker, with a thick Israeli accent. "President Allaire, Ms. Tanzer. It sounds like we have a little bit of a predicament on our hands."

"Yes, General," said Jessica. "Do we have enough time?"

"It'll be tight," said Dayan. "We'll try our best."

"Thank you," said Jessica.

"What I need right now are two things," said Dayan. "First, I need to know what kind of plane the prisoners are on."

"C-130," said Jessica. "It will be tan, desert camo. The colors of the Pakistan Air Force."

"Okay, that's good," said Dayan. "Second, I need photos of the prisoners. Immediately. Can you do that, Jessica?"

"Yes," said Jessica. "Give me sixty seconds."

Jessica typed furiously away on her BlackBerry.

"Can you help us, General Dayan?" asked President Allaire.

"I have already dispatched a squad from Shayetet Thirteen," said Dayan, referring to Israel's elite team of special forces commandos, their version of the Navy SEALs. "My best commander, a kid named Kohl Meir, will be running the recon. Fortunately, Rafic Hariri is near the sea. But there's not a lot of time. We'll do our best. Get me the photo. My Shayetet team will be doing a lot of killing tonight. I don't want them to accidentally take down any of your team."

73

Dewey sheathed the knife at his ankle and walked to the front of the cabin.

A steel door led to the flight deck. He grabbed the door handle and moved it slowly down, but it was locked. The door was hermetically sealed; the edges of the door were seamless, steel on steel, no edge.

He looked at the radio next to the door. He could pretend to be the terrorist in the hope of luring one of the pilots back. But if he failed, he would only be giving whoever was waiting on the ground more time to prepare. Dewey's Arabic was nonexistent and as much as he wanted to risk it, he knew the odds were low. Right now, the element of surprise was his only asset. That, along with his trusty Gerber blade, and Youssef's Glock no doubt reloaded, sitting on the canvas bench.

Dewey stepped past the blood-soaked corpse of the terrorist. Near the rear of the plane, there was a small bathroom. He stepped inside and flipped the light switch on.

Dewey looked in the mirror. From the nostrils down, his face, mustache, and beard were covered in blood and dried yellow vomit. Blood continued to drip from his nose. At the side of his face, the skin was broken where Bolin had kicked him; his boot had left a gash near Dewey's ear that continued to bleed. The ear itself was caked in dried blood. He turned on the small faucet and splashed his face with water. The sink ran red with his washed-off blood and vomit.

Dewey looked at himself in the mirror. He had to think. Killing the young, overconfident Youssef was easy. What happened to him now, upon landing, would be beyond his control. A heavily armed team of Fortuna's men would be waiting for him at the airport. If they caught him, he knew his fate. The revenge of an angry father, a man who also happened to be one of the world's foremost terrorists. Dewey knew it would be more pain, more torture than any amount of training had ever prepared him for. There was torture designed to elicit information. That was torture he'd been trained to survive. There's an advantage when your abductor wants something—information, ransom, whatever—because they must at all times worry about keeping you alive. But what waited for him on the ground was something altogether different. It was the torture of vengeance; a father's vengeance.

He reached into his coat pocket. He felt the small white cyanide pill that he took off the terrorist in Cooktown. He removed it from his pocket. For several moments, he stared at the small white pill.

Dewey looked in the mirror. He focused his eyes, his head still clouded in concussion. He stared into his bloodshot eyes. There, he found himself. He tossed the small pill into the sink and watched it go down the drain.

If I die, it won't be at my own hands, he thought.

Dewey exited the bathroom. He searched the cargo hold for anything that might help him escape. A parachute would have been a godsend. On the right side of the hold were steel storage cabinets. Most were empty. One contained a first-aid kit. The last one held several round coils of wire.

He searched the other side of the cabin. But there was nothing of any use. He ransacked the bathroom, the space beneath the orange canvas troop benches, everywhere. He searched frantically for a parachute. But he found nothing.

Dewey had flown in so many Hercs in his life he'd lost count. During Ranger school, the interior of a C-130 became almost like a second home. This was an old one, but still, he couldn't remember ever being in one and not being able to find a parachute. Above one of the troop benches, he found the switch box that raised and lowered the rear ramp. Dewey had run down enough Herc ramps to know exactly how these worked.

The plane arced right, then began a lazy downward descent. The pilot had begun his approach into Beirut.

If you have no options left, you must create opportunities.

Dewey moved to the storage cabinet at the side of the cabin. He lifted the steel door. He reached in and removed more than a dozen heavy coils of thick steel wire. Beneath the wire, he found a toolbox. Inside the toolbox, he found a large socket wrench.

Dewey moved to the middle of the cabin. A long, rectangular steel plate was bolted in place. He took the socket wrench and placed it on the nut, then, with all of his strength, turned the wrench. The bolt loosened and he removed it. He worked his way down the edge of the steel plate, removing bolts as quickly as he could. Sweat poured from his face and chest as he loosened the bolts. He removed eighteen bolts in all. He took his knife, pried it into the edge of the steel plate, then lifted it up, getting his fingertips beneath the small seam. He lifted the heavy plate and pushed it to the side.

Beneath was a dark compartment, the opening approximately the size of a refrigerator. He reached down and felt the hard rubber of one of the Hercs big wheels.

The plane dipped and lurched to the right.

Dewey stood and ran to the small porthole window at the left side of the cabin. Through thick glass he could see the lights of buildings. They were still a few thousand feet in the air, but were descending quickly.

Dewey ran back to the rectangular opening. Next to the opening was the round coil of wire he had found in the storage locker. He unfurled the wire. At one end was a round eyelet. Dewey took the eyelet and reached down into the wheel compartment. He threaded the eyelet through a hole in the steel hubcap at the center of the wheel. He pulled the eyelet through. The thick wire was now threaded through the center of the wheel.

Dewey pulled the eyelet across the cargo hold. Protruding from the wall was a steel hook. He put the eyelet over the hook.

The plane turned again, this time to the left.

Dewey found the other end of the steel coil. He went to the other side of the cabin and wrapped it around a steel pipe along the wall until it was tight, then placed the other eyelet on a hook. The wire now ran from one side of the cabin to the other, through the hub of the wheel, taut as a guitar string. But would it hold? He'd find out soon enough.

Dewey moved to the window. Beirut was lit up like a Christmas tree.

From the canvas bench, Dewey grabbed the terrorist's handgun. He checked the magazine, then tucked it into the back of his jeans. He sat down and strapped himself into a seat near the ramp. He reached up and opened the box containing the ramp controls.

A green light flashed inside the cabin. A loud bell chimed three times.

There was a loud cacophony as the landing gear hatches opened to the air. Wind abruptly blew into the hold from the one open compartment.

Seize the opportunity.

Dewey reached up and placed his hand on the ramp switch. He flipped the switch down. The ramp at the rear of the C-130 cracked open. Slowly, like an alligator's mouth, the ramp opened wide to the Beirut sky. He felt the vacuum as his body was pulled toward the open air. But the seat belt held him to the canvas bench.

As the landing gear descended, the steel wire he'd strung through the wheel went tight. The cabin was filled with a loud grinding noise as the wheel hydraulic fought against the coil. But it held.

The C-130 struggled to maintain a steady landing course as the back of the huge plane lurched violently to the left.

Youssef's bloody corpse rolled, then bounced through the open hold.

The seat belt was strapped across Dewey's chest and he held it with both hands. It was the only thing preventing him from being blown out the back of the plane. He closed his eyes as dirt and debris blew through the furious hurricane of wind. The plane was nearly sideways, lurching nearly vertical as the pilot struggled to right the craft.

Dewey braced himself. He had either just committed suicide, or he'd created an opportunity; the opportunity he would need to avoid the clutches of Fortuna, whose men, he knew, would be waiting on the ground below.

74

MEDITERRANEAN OCEAN
OFF THE COAST OF LEBANON

A mile from Beirut's rocky coast, due east of the now empty public beach called Ramlet al-Baida, the black waters of the Mediterranean glimmered under the starlit sky.

Moving across the water's surface, four dull yellow embers of light coursed steadily toward the shore. Eight feet below the surface, four specialized delivery vehicles—SDVs—moved at a fast clip. These SDVs were bottle-shaped objects designed to deliver Israeli commandos as quietly, as invisibly, as quickly as they could to enemy shores.

The front of each SDV was lit by a pair of powerful halogen lights. At the rear of the slender, six-foot-long units, water churned in a bubbleless, frenetic eddy.

On the back of each SDV were two steel handles. Clinging to each handle was a frogman; two commandos per SDV, eight men in all. A squad from Shayetet 13—S'13—Israel's elite special forces unit, their version of the U.S. Navy SEALs.

Each frogman was as black as the ocean itself. Each man wore tactical combat wet suits, light-duty scuba packs, and carried airtight weapons caches. The commandos kicked their flippers in a steady rhythm, helping move the submersibles through the cold water toward Beirut's heavily patrolled coast.

They ranged in age from twenty-one to twenty-seven. They were young, but the men of S'13 were the most fearsome and the most fearless soldiers that Israel dispatched to the most dangerous of places. They were the cutting edge of a deadly conflict that had no end.

The commandos swept into Ramlet al-Baida. The SDVs slowed, then shut off a hundred yards from the coastline.

One of the commandos decoupled a coil of wire cable from his belt, then hooked it through the nose of his submersible. He passed the lead to the next diver. Soon, all four subs were linked by the cable. The first diver cinched the cable taut. He and another diver dove down beneath the water. They searched the murky seafloor with a small halogen flashlight for more than a minute. Finally, they found a small steel ring sticking up from the ocean floor, a red LED glimmering on its side. One of the frogmen clipped the end of the cable to the ring, then cinched down the other end until the four units were submerged and secure.

They moved along the wave break to the far west side of the resort beach where an old pier still stood on barnacle-covered, withering timbers. The S'13 team knew the beach like the back of their hands. Infiltration of Beirut's unfriendly shores was a core part of the frogman's training and ongoing activity. Each commando removed his fins, then jogged up the wet sand to a dark break beneath the overhanging pier.

Cloaked in the shadows, the eight commandos quickly removed oxygen tanks, masks, fins, weapons caches, and wet suits.

Quickly, each man pulled a pair of running shoes from backpacks and put them on. Nylon ankle sheaths were strapped on next, one for each calf; the left for an SOG double-serrated combat blade, the right for a Glock 26. Next each commando pulled on a pair of black Adidas running pants. Each man removed a Heckler & Koch MP7A1-Z customized fully automatic submachine gun, retractable stock, Zeiss RSA reflex red dot sight on top, silencers screwed into the nozzles, then strapped the weapons over their shoulders and across their chests. Each man strapped a Colt M203 combination carbine and grenade launcher across his back and fastened a nylon ammo belt around his waist. Finally, they put on matching black Adidas running jackets, which loosely covered the weapons that now covered their torsos like armor.

They did it all in silence. It took each man less than two minutes to complete the wardrobe change.

A trained soldier, looking at any of the men, would have noticed the telltale bulge of the weapons. A trained operative would also have identified the look in their eyes. It was the death-cold stare of the trained killer now mission operative.

The leader of the S'13 squad, Lieutenant Colonel Kohl Meir, was a twenty-four-year-old Israeli from Bethlehem. He gathered his team in a circle. He wrapped his arms around the men on his left and right. The others followed his lead. Soon, they all stood in a tight huddle.

They stood in silence, praying.

Meir removed his arms while the others held the huddle tight. In the center of the huddle, he flipped a small wrist light on. He pulled a sheet of paper from his waist pocket. He shone the light on the paper. It was a photograph of Dewey.

"He has a beard and long hair now," said Meir.

"What's his name?" asked a commando to Meir's left.

"Andreas," said Meir. "Dewey Andreas. He's American. He was Delta. He was on the team that killed Ayatollah Khomeini's brother."

Every commando knew exactly what Meir meant by this comment: *He's a brother.*

Meir then showed them photos of Millar and Iverheart.

"These are the other Americans who were with him and might be with him now, if they are still alive. Let's move."

75

BEIRUT RAFIC HARIRI INTERNATIONAL AIRPORT
BEIRUT

A cell phone in Khalid's chest pocket vibrated.

"Yes," said Khalid.

"The plane is on approach. Less than fifteen minutes. A C-130. Try not to damage the plane; it's ours when this is all done. A gift from Aswan."

"That's nice," said Khalid.

Khalid stood next to the white bus. He could hear the faint, rhythmic chant of some of the men on board, praying. While he believed, of course, he certainly didn't have time for such things at a time like this. Every thought, every ounce of his being, was instead focused on the mission at hand. In this case, an easy job: picking up a package, delivering the package.

"After the pilot lands, he'll taxi, turn back to face the terminal, then stop. He'll lower the rear ramp so it's out of sight line from the tower. That's when you move. The prisoner will have to be carried. He's in very bad shape. Carry him to the bus, then move him to the project building at al-Aqbar."

"What about airport security?"

"Be careful and be quiet. The police won't notice a thing. You're almost two miles away from the main terminal. They're focused on security inside the building. Grab the American and move. The plane is large enough to hide any movement should someone be observing."

"Who are we delivering?" asked Khalid.

"The man who killed Alexander Fortuna."

"Andreas?" asked Khalid, a hint of shock in his voice.

"Yes. He's bound, weaponless, and outnumbered. Keep it simple."

"Oh, I will," said Khalid angrily.

"And don't hurt him. He is to be delivered. That's it."

The phone clicked out.

Khalid tried Youssef, but there was no answer. He took a last puff on the cigarette, then dropped it to the ground. He stepped back onto the bus. The sky was almost pitch-black outside, the only light being the light of the stars, and even that was partially blocked by the fir trees whose branches hung overhead. The air was humid and fetid. The smell of the forty-two Hezbollah soldiers—and his own odor—filled the tight space in stench.

After a few minutes more, Khalid clapped his hands twice, loudly.

"It's time," he ordered.

76

The eight Israeli commandos moved inland from the deserted public beach, one at a time, at different points along the dark, empty boardwalk. They spread out over a quarter mile so that any sighting would be of only one man, alone.

The distance to Rafic Hariri Airport was just more than three miles. They would split up and move across the western edge of the city along eight separate routes. It was an indirect infiltration; the airport sat on the water on the opposite side of Beirut, but the Lebanese patrols near Rafic Hariri were virtually impenetrable. Crossing the city was the only option.

Each commando began a fast jog. Eight different routes through the coastal neighborhoods, down eight separate streets.

Each man knew the neighborhoods of Beirut well, better even than many of the city's inhabitants. Through a secretive network of informants, they knew where Lebanese Armed Forces (LAF) tended to congregate. Each man knew he had to avoid being caught. Hezbollah had friends throughout Beirut, including many in the senior leadership of LAF. Many had learned to play both sides of the conflict between Hezbollah and the Lebanese government, knowing that it was a question of when, not if, Hezbollah someday ruled the entire country.

The capture of one of the S'13 commandos this night by LAF could quickly lead to a transfer of the Israeli prisoner to Hezbollah. Then, a terrible journey would begin to one of the Al-Muqawama camps in the Bekaa Valley.

Meir ran at a six-minute pace up the street. A baseball cap was pulled down low just above his eyes. The windbreaker covered his weapons.

Meir's short-cropped brown hair was soaked with sweat that then covered his face. Beneath the windbreaker, sweat drenched his arms, back, and torso. He ran with his head down, along the sidewalk, a jogger out for a night run. Meir had taken the busiest route, along Rafic Hariri to Al Akhtal El Saghir. He jogged past storefronts, electronics stores, past throngs of Lebanese, past cafés and bars. A few noticed Meir as he ran along the tar edge of the cracked street, enough to look up, but people went about their business. At one street corner, Meir ran past two LAF regular corps soldiers, who noticed him but did nothing.

On seven other streets, the other members of the S'13 recon team moved toward Rafic Hariri, a little more than three miles from the public beach. For the most part, the quickly designed infiltration to Rafic Hariri went smoothly.

Not for Ezra Bohr.

Bohr, a twenty-two-year-old commando from East Jerusalem, ran through a poor neighborhood abutting the coastline, less busy this time of night. He ran south along a thin, winding, darkened street barely wider than an alley, toward the airport. A mile into his run, beneath a lone streetlamp two blocks ahead, Bohr saw three men loitering against the wall of an apartment building, smoking cigarettes.

As he came closer, they stepped away from the wall. They stared down the dimly lit street at the approaching runner. The young Israeli felt his heart race. The perspiration poured down.

"Jew," said one of men, pointing.

Bohr quickened his pace slightly as the men stepped toward him.

He saw an alley halfway between him and the thugs. Sprinting, he ducked right into the alley as the three men dropped their cigarettes and began a sprint toward him.

A dozen feet inside the shadow-cast alley, Bohr stopped. He listened to the footsteps of the Arabs as they ran down the street. He reached down to his left calf and grabbed the SOG combat blade from its sheath.

Dim light from the street cast diffuse shadows into the alley.

The Arabs moved quickly and entered the alley at a sprint.

Bohr pressed against a cement wall and held the blade in his right hand. He waited for the first man to pass, then lurched at the second and slashed the razor-sharp blade at the thug's throat, dropping him with barely a sound. As quickly as he stabbed him, Bohr pulled the blade out. He took a step back and waited. The third punk entered the alley and tripped on the corpse of his dead friend. He let out a yell as he tumbled forward. Bohr swung the blade viciously down, stabbing the man in the chest, a quick hole in the man's heart that killed him instantly.

The first Arab heard the yell from the second man, then turned and came at Bohr with a silver switchblade. Bohr stepped back, evaded the swinging arm of the thug, then lunged, stabbing him deeply in the gut. As the Arab tumbled to the ground next to the others, screaming, Bohr completed the kill with a quick stab into the man's carotid artery at the base of his neck.

It had taken less than a minute to kill the three attackers. Bohr watched the alley entrance for movement. Seeing none, he moved back to the street. He began his run. He glanced at his watch, then quickened his pace slightly to make up for lost time.

77

BEIRUT RAFIC HARIRI AIRPORT

Khalid pointed to the opening in the fence at the end of the runway. He nodded to the first Al-Muqawama soldier.

"Go," he barked.

The soldier ran across the dark tarmac at the end of the runway. He moved toward the dirt edge of the blacktop, running in a low crouch, Kalashnikov at his side. At the corner of the runway, he went right. He arrived at a line of low cement barriers.

Khalid surveyed the airport. He waited several seconds for signs that his first man had been discovered. Seeing none, he nodded to the next terrorist in line.

"Go," he barked.

Khalid sent half the men, twenty-one in all, in fifteen-second intervals. They moved to the edge of the runway, up along the cement barriers. After the last soldier moved out, Khalid held his hand up. He looked at the first man in the line.

"Wait here," said Khalid. "Do nothing unless there's trouble."

"Trouble?"

"Airport security. That sort of thing. We'll be back quickly."

Khalid stepped back through the fence. His men were at the cement barriers at the point in the runway where the C-130 would be turning and lowering the ramp. In the dim light, he could just make out the tops of the heads of his soldiers.

Khalid followed the others to the cement barriers. He took up his place at the end of the line of soldiers, crouching.

In the distance, he heard the loud engines of a jet preparing to take off. The plane moved down the runway. Its nose lifted up, followed by its front wheels, and soon the jet was off the tarmac, sailing loudly overhead. The Al-Muqawama soldiers watched from their positions behind the barriers.

One of the soldiers, down the line from Khalid, leaned forward, pulled a cigarette from his chest pocket, and lit it.

Seeing the spark at the end of the lighter, Khalid jumped up, ran to him, and yanked the cigarette from his mouth. He threw it to the ground and stubbed it out with his boot.

"Stupid idiot," he whispered, staring at the young terrorist. "*Stupid fucking idiot.*"

He grabbed the lighter from the man's hand and hurled it into the dirt field beyond the tarmac. Khalid moved back to his position at the end of the barrier.

A few minutes later, another plane took off. Then, the low drone of an approaching plane rumbled in the distant sky. The terrorists got up on their feet as the plane descended.

The roar of the plane's engines was what the Hezbollah soldiers heard first, then they could see its red and white lights. The silver nose of an approaching jet appeared. It came smoothly toward the runway, its wheels touching down. The jet landed and sped down the tarmac. It wasn't the plane they were waiting for. The Lufthansa jet came to a sudden halt, more than a quarter mile from the soldiers, then turned back around toward the main terminal.

Khalid leaned back against the cement barrier, relaxing slightly, along with the other soldiers.

But as the Lufthansa jet taxied back toward the terminal, there came a sudden noise from somewhere off in the dark, distant sky. It was the deep drone of another plane, accompanied by the high-pitched sound of straining metal.

Khalid looked for the lights; there, in the sky above the main terminal, he saw the silhouette of an approaching cargo plane.

The plane was tilted sideways, its wings tipped diagonally. The right wing struggled to level out. The plane crossed perilously close to the top of the control tower. The dipping right wing of the C-130 seemed to almost brush the top of the tower.

The noise grew louder. The deep pounding of the plane's four propellers combined with the high-pitched scream of the broken hydraulic.

"It's going to crash!" yelled one of the men.

The cargo plane barreled over the control tower, leveling out as it approached the tarmac.

It was at this point that Khalid registered the plane's missing landing gear.

Emergency sirens sounded at the main terminal building.

As if in slow motion, the plane lumbered to the tarmac, dropping like a wounded duck. The right wing, which had been dipping, popped up. The plane leveled, bleeding off airspeed.

Khalid stood. Sweat poured down his face as he watched the distance between the plane's bare underbelly and the black tarmac shrink, then disappear.

78

Kohl Meir came to Old Saida, on the outskirts of Lebanese University. He turned into a parking lot behind a tall cement dormitory, just east of Rafic Hariri. In the distance, he could see the airport.

Meir was the first of the commandos to arrive at the meet-up point.

Within a minute two more commandos had arrived. Within three minutes, the remaining men, including Ezra Bohr, were there, eight in all.

The team moved toward the airport. Running in pairs, they sprinted in the shadows, across the dark lawns of the Lebanese University campus.

Meir registered the loud roar of an approaching plane.

"Pick it up!" Meir commanded.

At a hard sprint, Meir led them past the walls at the western edge of the campus. They came to a service road that ran along the south perimeter of the airport. Meir led the seven commandos across the service road. At the other side of the road was a chain-link fence. Two commandos removed wire cutters from their waist belts and began to furiously cut metal.

The could see the white fuselage of the jet descending from the north.

"Hurry, hurry, hurry!" barked Meir.

After a minute of cutting, Meir reached down to the bottom of the fence and lifted it up. He held it as his commandos crabbed through.

They ran across a hundred-yard apron of gravel and dirt as the descending plane came closer, a commercial airliner, the bright yellow Lufthansa logo on its side. Its tires touched down on a runway to the north, followed by the earsplitting roar of the jet braking.

The S'13 squad stopped at the edge of the tarmac. They were halfway down the runway, cloaked in darkness. Each commando ripped off his running jacket. They unstrapped their carbines from their backs and the SMGs from their chests.

On the tarmac, the commercial airliner that had just landed quieted, the high pitch of its braking replaced by the deep barreling of an approaching plane. In the distance, above the brightly lit main terminal building, the PAF C-130 suddenly appeared out of the dark sky.

The plane's wings were sloped at a forty-five-degree angle, the right wing hanging perilously low. As the plane descended, the wing looked as if it was aimed directly at the control tower. The pilot was clearly struggling to prevent the plane from going completely sideways and tumbling over onto its back.

Meir watched, mesmerized, as the plane dropped toward the tarmac in front of him. The wing recoiled and passed just feet above the control tower, then leveled as it continued a rapid descent. Then it struck the ground. Sparks burst from the belly of the plane. Flames abruptly shot out from the fuselage. The plane slid, out of control, down the runway. The sound was horrible; metal ripping apart against the cement tarmac.

One of the Israeli commandos removed a small night vision thermal monocular. He scanned the fence line around the airport. Meir took the monocular and looked through it. He found the cut in the fence line at the end of the runway left by the terrorists. Several hundred yards in from the fence, Meir saw movement in the dim light. He adjusted the magnification. He saw the telltale red from the body heat of men at a cement barrier. He counted heads.

"They're here," said Meir, pointing calmly.

The C-130 kept sliding, gaining momentum as it moved in a fiery slalom down the runway. Sirens roared at the terminal. Flames on both sides of the fuselage plumed as the fire spread. The front of the plane began to rotate to its left and the plane began a slow, destructive spin as it slid.

Meir stared through the monocular. Straight ahead, across the tarmac, he counted yet more men, waiting for Andreas.

"I've got Hezbollah all over the place." said Meir. "At least a dozen, maybe more. We need to move *now*."

Meir looked again at the cement barriers at the end of the runway. He saw the silhouettes of men, now standing. They started moving toward the plane, anticipating where the plane would come to a stop as the flames grew brighter around the fuselage.

Meir removed a small earpiece and inserted it in his left ear.

"We're at the main tarmac," barked Meir. "Send the chopper."

The flames from the plane illuminated the south end of the runway, not brightly, but enough for the Israeli commandos to be seen. The attention of the Arabs, however, was on the sliding plane.

Meir moved the fire selector on his carbine to full auto. Three commandos took up positions to Meir's right. The other four, to his left.

One of the wings tore off, dropping with a loud crash to the tarmac. There was a sudden burst of flames as one of the fuel tanks behind the propellers exploded. Flames—black, orange, and blue— shot into the sky.

Meir began his run across the tarmac. The team of Israeli commandos sprinted into the darkness just behind him They moved in a straight line toward the Hezbollah position.

As he ran, Meir had a sudden, momentary flash of panic: the situation at Rafic Hariri was moving rapidly beyond his control.

79

IN THE AIR

$\mathbf{A}$s the plane descended, the steady, high pitch of the landing gear fighting against the cable grew louder, like fingernails on the proverbial chalkboard. Dewey stared out through the open hatch. The city of Beirut was lit up, a canopy of lights that appeared to be closing in on the descending craft. He could see automobiles, the lights of apartment buildings and offices, people walking beneath lamplights. The ground was coming, he knew.

Had he done too much damage to the plane? Could the pilot land the badly lurching aircraft? If they hit a building, a field, if they missed the smooth plain of the runway, it wouldn't matter. Death would happen before Dewey had time to realize it. He shut his eyes and clutched the Glock.

He heard a siren from somewhere on the ground. He opened his eyes. Out the open hatch, he saw the control tower as the plane barely slipped over it. Inside the tower, panic-stricken workers were running frantically around the glass-enclosed room at the top.

He gripped the weapon and braced himself in the same instant he was bounced violently back against the wall of the plane. Dewey's head slammed into the steel brace behind the bench. Then he felt the plane's fuselage hitting the tarmac. Looking back, he saw flames through the hatch and the black tar of the runway, a line of orange sparks and flames as fuel ignited on the ground.

The plane slid quickly and began to turn sideways. The sound of metal scraping against metal was deafening. The bottom of the ramp bounced violently, rubbing hard against the ground, until it broke off and tumbled to the side.

The big cargo plane slid down the tarmac, spinning counter-clockwise. It completed one three-hundred-sixty-degree turn, then another, slowing all the while.

Dewey reached up and uncoupled the seat belt. The front of the hold burst into flames and the steel braces buckled at the sides.

Instinctively, Dewey checked the magazine on the Glock. It was full. He stepped to the back of the plane and looked out the open hatch. Flames danced at the hatch's entrance. He saw nothing but darkness at the end of the runway. He heard sirens in the distance.

Dewey paused a moment, then leapt from the hatch—through the smoldering flames—and landed on the tarmac. He began a sprint down the runway, toward the dark woods at the end of it. His feet were unsteady at first, but then he forgot it all, the dizziness, the blood that now coursed from his nose and shoulder, his cracked rib; he pushed it out of his mind as he ran for his life.

Dewey was suddenly struck from the side; steel hammered into his ribs. He tumbled to the ground. He rolled, looked up, then saw his attacker. Bearded, long black hair, a submachine gun held sideways. The terrorist smashed Dewey across the rib cage again; he screamed in pain. Behind his assailant were others, too numerous to count.

As Dewey rolled, he turned the Glock up at the first assailant and fired. The bullet killed the terrorist instantly, his body dropping to the ground.

Dewey pulled the trigger as fast as he could, shooting at any-thing he could. He pumped a slug into the chest of one man, an-other struck the eye of a tall man, dropping him in a mist of brains and blood. He kept firing into the marauding crowd descending around him.

From the side, Dewey got a sharp kick to his head, while another kick to his hand sent the Glock flying. Someone slammed a boot down on top of Dewey's head, pressing his face against the black tar. Dewey smelled gasoline. He felt his wrists being forced behind his back. Dewey kicked out, striking someone. He heard a dull crack, then screaming as blood burst from a destroyed nose.

A terrorist jammed the nozzle of his Kalashnikov into Dewey's cheek as someone finally succeeded in shackling his ankles.

"*Stop!*" screamed another man, and Dewey looked to his left. A tall Arab stepped through the small circle of terrorists. He pulled the nozzle of the Kalashnikov away from Dewey's face. "Carry him. Quickly now!"

Dewey felt himself being lifted up from the ground. On the ground, he counted four bodies contorted on the tarmac, blood pooling around them.

One of the Arabs looked back at Dewey as they lifted him, a murderous stare in his dark eyes.

A moment later, the staccato thud of silenced machine guns came from up the runway. Dewey turned his head around and tried to get a view. A fast-moving line of black-clothed commandos was running at them. Automatic weapon fire pulverized the air. Dewey watched as the men carrying him fell one by one, blown away by the oncoming hail of slugs.

Then Dewey felt the hands gripping him let go; his body dropped to the ground, shackled, within a loose, bloody circle of dead Hezbollah.

80

BEIRUT RAFIC HARIRI AIRPORT
BEIRUT

Meir watched as he ran across the runway as a dark figure leapt from the rear of the burning C-130 onto the tarmac. Partially obscured by smoke, the figure began a desperate run down the tarmac, away from the terminal, in the direction of the waiting terrorists, obviously guessing wrong.

It was Andreas. It *had* to be Andreas.

The Israelis moved in unison behind Meir, a fast-moving, almost silent line of commandos running toward the American. As they came within a hundred feet, Meir watched in the dim light as Andreas was tackled to the ground by the waiting Hezbollah. There was a struggle. Andreas fired a handgun, killing one of the Arabs, then another. He kept firing.

The Israelis continued a silent run toward the scene, coming at the tumult from the dark edge of the runway. The gunfire from Andreas abruptly stopped. At least four men were now atop the American; two holding his feet down, while a third man bound his wrists and a fourth held a rifle at his head. He heard shouting in Arabic. The terrorists bound Andreas, then lifted him and began to carry him down the runway, away from the plane, toward the fence through which they'd infiltrated the airport.

The terrorists—and Andreas—were oblivious to the oncoming wave of S'13.

Meir's men awaited his go; his shots would be the first.

Meir leveled his M203 as they came within twenty feet of the scene. He fingered the steel trigger of the carbine, then fired. A spray of silenced bullets flew across the first man carrying Andreas, blowing him back onto the tarmac, then more bullets struck the one next to him, then the terrorists holding his feet. Andreas dropped to the tarmac.

"Cover three!" shouted Meir, pointing left, down the runway, ordering Bohr to take a couple of commandos and engage the terrorists to the left, at the end of the runway.

Meir reached Dewey, who now lay on the ground. From his knees, he pulled a combat blade from his ankle sheath as bullets hit the runway behind them. He sliced off Dewey's flex-cuffs.

"Israel?" asked Dewey.

"Welcome to Beirut," said Meir. "Grab a weapon."

Unmuted automatic weapons fire erupted from the cement barriers at the end of the runway as Bohr and the pair of commandos moved to face them, firing their silenced carbines at the Hezbollah positions behind the barriers, crouching to avoid bullets, aiming their weapons down the runway where at least a dozen men pulverized the air with weapons fire in their direction.

A violent firefight enveloped the southern end of the tarmac, but the Israelis were out in the open; only the darkness helped protect them, and that would not hold for long.

Bohr, down the runway now at Meir's command, glanced behind him toward the burning C-130, then to Meir, who was cutting the American loose. Bullets from Hezbollah were seemingly everywhere around them. He kept his trigger pulled back, but he started to panic amid the onslaught of bullets.

"Fall back!" screamed Bohr, crouching, realizing that he and the two other commandos were badly outnumbered, sitting ducks in the

middle of the runway. Suddenly Bohr was propelled violently back-ward as a slug hit him in the chest. He was thrown to the tarmac on his back, dead.

"*Ezra!*" screamed the Israeli to Bohr's left, who reached for Bohr, then was himself struck in the neck with a bullet, knocking him to the ground. He screamed as his hands went to the bullet hole and he attempted in vain to stem the blood flow.

Meir heard Bohr yell, then turned to see him hit, then watched as another one of his men, Ben-Shin, went down next to Bohr.

"*Fall back!*" Meir screamed over the din to the last of the three, Rabin, who was firing desperately at the terrorists from the ground, on his stomach, next to the contorted bodies of Bohr and Ben-Shin.

Beyond them, in the dim light, Meir saw a wave of Arabs pouring through the cut in the fence. At the barriers, the nozzles of weapons sparked red like fireworks.

Meir glanced to the western sky, looking for the Israeli chopper, but saw nothing except for the starry night, now clotted in smoke and fire.

Next to Meir, Dewey was on one knee, a Kalashnikov in each hand, firing at the terrorists. Four other commandos were on their stomachs, firing back at the cement barriers.

"*Josh, fall back!*" Meir screamed again at Rabin.

"We need to get beyond the plane!" Dewey yelled.

To Meir's immediate right, another Israeli, Lutanz, was suddenly knocked to the ground as a bullet struck him in the chest. Meir ran to Lutanz's side and knelt. His eyes had rolled back up into his head. Meir placed his hand beneath Lutanz's neck.

"Jon," he said. He shook his friend's head. "*Jonathan!*"

But Lutanz was gone.

Meir didn't have time to think, to register emotion, to pause, but as he watched Lutanz's eyes roll white he felt a kick of desperation as he understood he was in danger of losing his entire team.

As Meir held Lutanz's head, he was interrupted by Andreas as the American—out of ammunition—pushed his arm away from Lutanz and yanked the carbine from the dead man's hands, then turned, firing at the terrorists now surging closer.

"*Fall back!*" shouted Andreas, glancing at Meir. "*Get your men behind the plane.*"

Meir reached down and grabbed Lutanz. He lifted the dead soldier and threw him over his shoulder as Dewey kept firing down the runway, holding off the steadily encroaching swarm of Hezbollah.

Another explosion rocked the air as a second fuel tank on the C-130 ignited. Orange and black smoke-crossed flames shot up violently from the wing of the plane, less than a hundred feet from where Dewey now crouched.

Dewey moved his index finger forward and pulled the second trigger of Lutanz's M203. A grenade lofted into the air, flying toward the Hezbollah stronghold. A terrible blast ripped the ground near the back fence as the grenade burst. He heard screams. Dewey fired the grenade launcher again, the round landed behind the barriers, and again screams echoed down the tarmac from the Hezbollah positions.

Within the lull following the grenade blasts, Dewey sprinted forward, toward Bohr. He reached the bodies, where he saw that all three men were now dead, including Rabin. He threw the carbine strap over his shoulder, moved the weapon over his back, reached down and, with great effort, picked up two of the dead Israelis and hoisted them onto his shoulders. He ran for his life, with the dead commandos on his shoulders, back toward the shelter of the plane as cover fire from Meir and the others sailed over his head. He passed Meir, running to retrieve the third corpse.

As he reached the back of the plane's fuselage, Dewey found three remaining commandos, crouched, sniping terrorists as they came in through the fence cut.

"We're running out of ammo!" yelled one of the Israelis.

The staccato crackle of weapons fire again filled the air as the Arabs regrouped, along with the smell of smoke and burning fuel. The scene was chaos.

A slug struck the commando to Dewey's right, knocking him forward, screaming. Dewey crawled to him. He was on his stomach, face down. Dewey flipped him over. The young Israeli could not have been more than twenty-two or -three; he had a gaping hole at the top of his neck where the slug had hit. Dewey tore off the man's shirt. He wrapped the shirt around his badly bleeding neck, then began to perform CPR, pressing down on his heart in timed rhythm.

Dewey pushed against the Israeli's chest, trying to keep the young boy alive. He looked into the boy's eyes; brown eyes that stared out at Dewey in the light from the burning plane.

"*Hold on!*" said Dewey, trying to save the boy who was about to lose his own life saving a man he didn't even know.

Dewey had seen fierce battle before. He had watched as men he knew were killed by enemy fire. But he had never been in such a hellfire as they were in now, running out of ammunition, outnumbered and outgunned. Dewey felt no pain or fear. He felt nothing. There wasn't time.

He heard rotors cutting the distant sky. It was a chopper somewhere above. He looked up at Meir, now next to him, a shell-shocked look on his face.

The chopper moved down the runway from the main terminal building.

"What kind of chopper are we looking for?" yelled Dewey.

"Panther," said Meir, looking up, shaking his head. "That's not Israel."

The black chopper moved quickly down the runway from the terminal behind them. It honed in on the Israelis.

"LAF!" yelled Meir. "*Cover!*"

From the chopper's right side, a minigun began firing rounds on the Israeli position as they dived for the protection of the wing. Bullets rained down on the cement, riddling the tar around them. The chopper circled overhead and around the flaming C-130. It swept back in, and the sound of the minigun cut the air. The weapon pounded the steel wings just in front of the Israeli position.

From down the runway, Hezbollah moved closer, their bullets dinging the metal of the C-130.

From the ground, crouched against the fuselage, Dewey, Meir, and the remaining commandos fired blindly up at the chopper, which attempted to move into a position directly above them. One of the Israelis, three feet to Dewey's right, was struck in the head by a round from the sky. The round tore his head clean off, down to the shoulders, and he was thrown violently back from the fuselage.

The sound was deafening now. Chopper blades ripped the air. Machine-gun fire was like a drumbeat. Sirens pierced the silences in between.

Dewey counted three men alive, including him, Meir, and one other commando. The deadly circle was growing closer, Hezbollah to the south, and now LAF from the north, hemming them in by chopper, cutting them off.

Dewey made eye contact with Meir. He could not have been more than twenty-five years old. He had short brown hair and freckles. He was tan, with a sharp nose. Meir looked at him with a blank look. There was no anger there, nor fear. There was no emotion at all. And Dewey knew that in some way he was looking at himself. Both men knew time was up.

"I'm sorry," said Dewey.

Meir stared back, expressionless. "You would've done the same. America would've done the same."

Dewey had had tough moments like this before, in other battles, with other men, the moments that forged the brotherhood of soldiers. But he'd never felt as close to death. The look, both men knew. It seemed to say: We'll die this day, at this hour. But we'll do it together. We'll do it the way soldiers are supposed to, believing in something right, fighting against the forces that would destroy us all.

A loud hissing noise rose above the pandemonium of the battle theater.

Dewey's head jerked up. A white comet of movement blazed through the black, smoke-clogged sky. He traced the trajectory of where the missile had come from. In the distance, a single black object, an attack chopper that Dewey recognized immediately: Panther.

The Israeli chopper lurked like a deadly metallic vulture, moving into the air above the airport with menacing speed.

The Mistral air-to-air missile fired from the Panther emitted smoke from its tail as it accelerated through the humid Beirut air, its high-pitched whistle cutting through all other noise. It tore into the side of the LAF chopper directly overhead, bright white light mushroomed, then the detonation an instant later as the chopper and everything inside was pulverized mid-sky. Metal and body parts dropped in a fiery wash across the tarmac just behind their position.

Another piercing hissing noise as a white burst sparked from the Panther, followed by the telltale comet of the Mistral. The missile ripped across the sky in the opposite direction, toward the end of the runway. Hezbollah dispersed in every direction as the missile honed in, but it was futile, they were too late. The missile exploded near the fence in the center of the Arab position. Every terrorist within twenty feet was eviscerated by the blast. The Panther turned its nose and began firing 20mm rounds from the Giat M621 on the side of the chopper, pounding the Hezbollah positions behind the cement barriers, closer to Dewey, Meir, and the other commando.

Then the Panther turned and swept forward, moving down the tarmac. The chopper descended onto the runway, twenty feet from Dewey and the Israelis.

Dewey picked up a dead Israeli, then moved with Meir and the other commando, carrying corpses on their shoulders to the Panther.

Dewey ran, the corpse over his right shoulder, his left hand triggering the carbine down the runway at yet more Hezbollah, who were still attacking.

Up the runway, a pair of troop carriers sped down the runway from the direction of the terminal carrying LAF soldiers.

Dewey reached the Panther first. He lay the body inside the cabin, then turned toward the terminal, where LAF troops began firing from the north, moving closer to the Panther, whose rotors tore the air as Meir and the other surviving Israeli hastily loaded the corpses of their fallen comrades. Dewey swept his carbine across the line of Lebanese soldiers, killing several men, while the others dived for cover behind the troop trucks.

The Panther's nose remained targeted at the south end of the runway. As they finished loading the dead, the gunman fired 20mm rounds through the smoky, chaotic din, back at the terrorists at the southern end of the runway.

They packed in six dead Israelis.

Dewey and Meir stood side by side, Dewey gunning up the tarmac at LAF soldiers, Meir firing at Hezbollah to the south.

"*Get on!*" screamed the commando already on board. "*Kohl! Andreas!*"

Dewey and Meir stepped back toward the chopper, which was already above its weight capacity, and packed to the rafters with dead Israelis.

Meir sat in the door, feet dangling out. He grabbed a safety strap above the door frame with one hand and started firing behind the chopper, up the runway. Dewey sprinted to the other side of the chopper and knelt in the door, holding a safety strap with his left hand while he fired.

"*Go!*" screamed Meir.

The pilot lifted off, but the weighted down Panther barely got its wheels off the ground before it settled back down onto the tarmac.

Lebanese soldiers moved closer as the chopper stalled. The low hiss of a surface-to-air missile sounded. A white blur scorched through the air from behind the cargo plane, sailing just in front of the Panther. Then, a second later, Meir lurched forward as a slug from somewhere on the ground struck him in the leg, just above the knee.

"*Get rid of the fuel!*" screamed Dewey to the pilot. "*Now! Dump it!*"

Beneath the Panther, a flood of gasoline spread as the pilot emptied three of the four tanks on the chopper. The smell of gasoline was suddenly everywhere.

The pilot revved the Panther's engines and the chopper lifted slowly into the sky.

Meir, blood pouring from his leg, fired at the ground as the chopper climbed. He fired his weapon north, at the government troops who now ran in groups, weapons raised, trying to shoot the chopper from the sky. Meir picked off soldier after soldier, creating clusters of corpses in a loose line behind the smoking C-130, ignoring the pain in his leg.

Dewey, on the opposite side of the Panther, registered half a dozen Hezbollah, running up the tarmac, like ants, firing at the climbing chopper. He fired calmly from the open door, striking terrorist after terrorist, like target practice.

The chopper climbed higher. Dewey and Meir gunned from the open doors, firing their weapons as the black Panther AS565 AA climbed higher and higher above the tarmac into the smoldering, smoke-clouded sky.

Suddenly, the chopper arced hard right, the engine churned furiously, and the Israeli Panther rushed away from the battlefield into the protective sky above the black waters of the Mediterranean.

81

FOUR DAYS LATER

Jessica walked through the open gates of the cemetery. The simple, solemn burial ground sat on a windswept hill a few miles south of downtown Jerusalem. The cemetery was Israel's most solemn burial ground, more than three thousand years old. Many of Israel's greatest heroes were buried at Mount of Olives. Today, that number would grow.

Long, uneven lines of tombstones ran in every direction. Dotted throughout the cemetery were olive trees and small patches of lush green lawn. In the background, the cemetery arose in sandstone hills, uneven steppes of graves that spread to ivy-laced walls, Jerusalem's clustered mass of buildings in the distance. The sky was bright blue. The sun shone down fiercely. The temperature was in the seventies. Wind came softly from the east. It was a perfect day, a comfortable, clear, beautiful day.

A single violin player near the gates played a soft, slow, mournful sonata by Boccherini.

In straight lines, beginning at the north cemetery wall, gravestones descended in simple, serial geometry: rectangular slabs of sandstone, decorated in Hebrew letters. These were the markers of Israel's sons and daughters, her buried heroes, the pained, proud legacy of a young country whose survival was earned only with the barrel of a gun, the thrust of a blade, the blood of its children.

Jessica took her place in line at the heavily guarded gates to the cemetery. She followed an elderly couple, who walked slowly down the long, pebble stone, center aisle. When she reached the rows of seats, which were mostly filled, she looked to the front. She saw her boss, Rob Allaire, the president of the United States, seated next to Israeli Prime Minister Benjamin Shalit. Behind them, she saw Secretary of State Lindsay, Ambassador Priest, several senators and members of Congress. Toward the front, on the left, she saw Hector Calibrisi seated by himself, his eyes closed in prayer.

A uniformed Israeli soldier, standing at the front of the aisles, nodded to her, then walked to meet her.

"Ms. Tanzer," he said. "Please follow me. General Dayan has asked that you be seated next to him."

Jessica felt herself pulled, her gaze drawn, to the right away from the Israeli soldier. Her eyes moved to an empty seat in the back row. Next to the empty seat sat a lone figure. Large, muscled arms filled a navy blue blazer. He had long brown hair that was combed back. His face was covered in a beard and mustache. He was an outcast here; a rugged-looking man, with a blank, merciless look on his tanned face. He returned her glance, his eyes drawing her to him from across the crowd.

Jessica held his gaze for a long moment. She felt her heart race; the familiar feeling. She stared at him, trying to understand what he was thinking at that moment. Guilt, she guessed, at the death of the Israeli commandos, men he hadn't even known but who, Jessica knew, he wouldn't want to have died so that he could live. Responsibility, he probably felt that too, she thought to herself, for the murders of Rob Iverheart and Alex Millar in Islamabad. She looked for something, anything, but he was emotionless; the wall that she'd worked so hard to climb over was now as tall as ever, shielding memories she knew were too fresh, too painful. Jessica willed herself to avert her eyes, to look away. She followed the Israeli soldier down the pebble aisle.

Jessica stepped to her seat, just two seats from Prime Minister Shalit, next to the head of Israel Defense Forces, General Menachem Dayan. In front of her, in the front row, the mothers and fathers, brothers and sisters, of the dead Israelis, the families of the six men who died at Rafic Hariri Airport. The men who died saving the life of the American in the back row.

In front of the families, six wooden caskets lay atop a green hill. On top of each casket, the flag of Israel, white with the blue Star of David.

To the right of the caskets stood two men. One was a rabbi, dressed in a long robe, a yarmulke on his head. He had glasses on, a beard, and was elderly. The other was a young Israeli with short brown hair, a large, sharp nose, tough-looking. He stared ahead, above the caskets, above the walls of the cemetery, toward a place only he knew.

For several minutes, the soft strains of the violin were the only sounds that could be heard. Time, during those moments, seemed to fall away, to stand still and linger as if the finality of what was about to happen, the bitter memorial, the ending of it all, could somehow be prevented, delayed, or altered. But it could not.

Finally, the violin went silent.

The Israeli soldier standing at the front of the gathered crowd stepped forward and walked behind the caskets. He limped as he walked, and for the first time, Jessica saw that he held a cane. He moved slowly across the ground to a simple wooden podium.

The young Israeli officer looked out at the large crowd. He stepped to the podium and spoke into a microphone.

"My name is Kohl Meir," he said, his voice deep and soft.

For the first time, in the light of the direct sun, which now illuminated the Israeli's face, Jessica saw that the area beneath his eyes was wet with tears.

"I would like to read to you the names of my six colleagues who died at my side. All six were members of Shayetet Thirteen and served under my command. Please remember them as the heroes they were. Lieutenant Colonel David Ben-Shin, Tel Aviv, age twenty-seven. Lieutenant Joshua Rabin, Dimona, age twenty-two. Major Ezra Bohr, Hafiz, age twenty-four. Lieutenant Colonel Samuel Ivri, Beer-sheba, age twenty-five. Lieutenant Colonel Jonathan Lutanz, Uvda, age twenty-five, Major David Iza, Tel Aviv, age twenty-seven . . ."

Dewey remained seated as the last of the funeral guests left the cemetery. He was alone now. He stared down row after empty row, to the caskets.

"You okay?"

Dewey turned. He saw Jessica's legs first, thin, brown, sculpted legs that climbed to her white skirt, blue piping edged just above perfect knees, white button-down blouse, auburn hair, then her face, green eyes, sharp nose covered in freckles, so pretty.

"Yeah. I'm okay."

Jessica moved down the aisle and took the seat next to him. They sat, silently, for more than a minute. Finally, Jessica placed her hand on Dewey's thigh.

"I know you don't want to talk, but I'm here for you."

"Thank you," said Dewey. He looked at her hand on his thigh. Such a small gesture, and yet it sent a large wave of warmth through his body, warmth he needed so badly in that moment.

"We retrieved the bodies. Alex and Rob. The president and I are meeting the families at Andrews tonight."

Dewey looked at the ground, then back to her.

"I'm leaving for the United States in one hour," Jessica said. "I would like you to come with me. Would you come with me?"

"No. I can't."

"It's not your fault, Dewey. I'm the one who asked you to go to Pakistan. I'm the one who called General Dayan. I'm the one who got the Shayetet team sent in. I'm the reason the six Israelis are dead, the reason Alex and Rob are dead. If you're going to blame someone, blame me, but don't blame yourself."

"I would never blame you."

"You saved millions of lives this week," said Jessica. "Innocent lives. Children and families all over India and Pakistan. You prevented the United States from being dragged into a war that could have cost millions of American lives. Had Omar El-Khayab remained in power, it is certain that our allies, Israel first among them, would have been dragged into the conflict. You prevented what could have been war between America and China. You *alone*, Dewey. Do you understand that?"

Dewey placed his hand on top of hers, covering her hand. He held it tight, but said nothing.

"We're the front edge of a very sharp blade," she whispered. "'The tip of the spear,' isn't that what they say? And at the edge, there's death. That's the world we live in. But without the spear, our world, our freedom, would disappear before you know it."

"What happens to Bolin?" asked Dewey.

Jessica paused. She looked at the ground, then shook her head.

"The Middle East is a screwed-up place, you know that," she said. "We're only at the beginning. This conflict, this war, it's barely even begun."

"You're not ready to fight the war I was born to fight," said Dewey.

"What's that supposed to mean?"

"I'm going to kill Fortuna," he said. "Then Bolin."

Jessica stared into Dewey's blue eyes.

"There are no winners over here, Dewey," she said, turning her hand up and interlocking her fingers in his. "Let's get out of here—you and me—before something bad happens. You promised you'd come home alive. Let's go home. Let's put it all aside for a while." She paused, then squeezed his hand. "Let's try and build something," she whispered.

"They killed my men in cold blood. They died in front of me. Alex Millar was twenty-four years old. I can't just walk away. I can't let them get away with it."

Jessica forced a smile across her face, but it held back deep sorrow that brought tears to her eyes. She had to bite her lip. "I didn't want to talk about this," she whispered finally. "I wanted to tell you that I miss you. Save Fortuna for another day. Please let's leave before . . ."

Her voice trailed off. Dewey said nothing, his eyes looked away from Jessica, up at the caskets at the front of the cemetery.

"Okay," she said in resignation. Slowly she stood up.

She looked at Dewey, placing her right hand on his shoulder, then brushing it across his cheek. He looked at it, thin, long, elegant fingers, short, unadorned fingernails, a simple, shining emerald ring on her finger. He looked up at her beautiful face.

"Can I ask you something?" she asked, looking into Dewey's eyes. "Did you . . ."

"What?"

"Well, did you . . . find someone else while you were in Australia?"

Jessica stared, then looked away, afraid of what the answer might be. She waited, looking at the white chair in front of him, but he said nothing. After several moments of pregnant silence, she turned, closing her eyes as she did so. She walked away from Dewey, down the pebble stones, to the aisle.

"Jess," he said.

She turned as Dewey stood. He walked down the pebble path. He didn't stop until his chest was pressed against her white blouse, the neat, perfect crown of her auburn hair just beneath his chin. He leaned toward her; their lips nearly touching. Jessica's red lips were close enough to feel the gentle wind from her breathing.

"Promise me something," he said.

"What?"

"You'll be there when I come home," Dewey said.

She looked into his eyes without expression, then a smile appeared on her lips. A breeze blew through her hair, fanning it across her shoulders. She leaned forward on her tiptoes and their lips touched, and they kissed, and for a moment they escaped together, escaped it all.

"Promise," she whispered.

82

The bar at the Ritz Tel Aviv was nearly empty. A couple from Spain sat at one end, the woman laughing every few minutes, slightly inebriated. Two older women, visiting from England, sat near the middle of the bar, chatting with the bartender.

It was one thirty in the morning. Dewey sat at the bar, his fifth Jack Daniel's in a glass on the obsidian marble bar top in front of him. After a few minutes, the Spanish couple stood up, holding hands, leaving to go upstairs to their room.

Dewey swigged the last of the whiskey, then nodded at the bartender and ordered another.

"Certainly," the bartender said. "I must tell you, we close at two."

Dewey said nothing.

A woman walked quietly into the bar, taking the seat immediately to Dewey's right. She caught the bartender's eye, he did a double take in fact, as most men did when they saw her for the first time.

"Bordeaux," she said, barely above a whisper, a soft French accent. "Petrus."

"I'm sorry," said the bartender. "We don't sell Petrus by the glass."

"Then give me a bottle," she said.

She turned to Dewey. He looked at her blankly. Her long black hair, behind her ears, shimmered, so straight, down past her shoulders. Dark skin, the color of soft leather. Blazing eyes of smoldering blue. She was perfect; a dazzling, exotic-looking beauty. Saudi, Dewey guessed. He glanced at her, then looked away without saying anything.

The bartender opened the bottle of wine. She tasted a small amount, then nodded to the bartender, who poured her a full glass. She took a sip.

"He said you were quiet," the woman remarked after several moments.

Dewey sipped his whiskey without looking at her.

"He didn't tell me you were such a, how do you say, 'tall drink of water.' "

She turned and looked appreciatively at Dewey's face, now clean-shaven, his blue eyes, then down at his blue, short-sleeved shirt, arms tanned and ripped, then back to his eyes.

"Who sent you?" Dewey asked coldly.

"Hector Calibrisi."

Dewey turned, his bloodshot eyes becoming slightly more alert.

"My name is Candela," she said. "You are to come with me."

"Where?" Dewey asked.

"A house in Broumana," she said. " 'I always live up to my end of the bargain.' Hector told me to tell you that."

Dewey looked at her. He bolted down the last of his whiskey as the first smile in a long time appeared on his face.

83

Dawn arrived at six o'clock sharp. The horizon brightened by incremental shades, black to gray, gray to peach, peach falling away to dust-filled, ageless yellow.

The villa, made of ornate, interweaving sandstone, spread out in a rambling line atop Patula Hill. The early sun caught the villa's terracotta roof, heating the clay. Shimmering tendrils of steam drifted almost invisibly up to the sky.

Inside, the house was so silent you could have heard the proverbial pin drop. A mistle thrush, sitting on a distant tree branch, sang a song, repetitively, the high, staccato tune barely audible, and yet the only sound that could be heard inside the large house.

The sound of footsteps came from down the hallway.

Aswan Fortuna walked into the kitchen. He was naked, his body tanned and wrinkled, yet still retained a healthy tone despite its seventy-five years. He walked slowly to the counter, filled a teapot with water, then placed it on one of the burners on the large stove and ignited the gas. He coughed several times, working himself into a lather, then spat into the sink.

He walked around the marble island, toward the wall of glass that looked out on the swimming pool. He looked above the pool to the distant, dark waters of the Mediterranean, shimmering in the early morning light.

Fortuna's head jerked back as his eyes focused for a second time on the slate deck surrounding the gunite pool. On the ground, in various states of contortion, lying in pools of blood, four armed guards lay dead.

He reached his hand toward the door handle.

"Don't."

Fortuna turned to the table. Sitting at the head of the table was a man. He had a face Fortuna immediately recognized. Brown hair, cut short now. Penetrating, vicious eyes of stone blue. Older than the photograph, meaner. Adrenaline shot through Fortuna. In a strange way, he had found the quarry that for so long had eluded him. The man who had killed his son. But then, he realized, it was the quarry who had found the hunter, and that he would soon be like dust in a hurricane, wiped from the face of the earth forever.

In the man's hand, a weapon was trained casually upon him. Fortuna didn't have to guess the make of the weapon. He already knew: Colt M1911 semiautomatic .45 caliber handgun. Screwed into the nozzle, Fortuna noticed, a long, black silencer, whose cap end hole was aimed directly at his skull.

"Ever have one of those days you just wished you'd stayed in bed?" the man asked.

Fortuna shut his eyes and shook his head.

"Andreas," he whispered.

Dewey stood up from the chair. He stepped calmly around the back of the table. He wore an old blue T-shirt, a large orange Puma logo on the front. Jeans. His boots made a loud tapping noise on the slate floor as he walked toward Fortuna, weapon trained at all times on the terrorist.

Fortuna stepped away from the window. He faced Dewey, waiting for him as he walked toward him.

"May I at least get a towel?" asked Fortuna, remaining still. "To cover myself?"

Dewey walked around the long pine harvest table not answering.

"Candela?" Fortuna asked.

Still Dewey said nothing. He moved closer to Fortuna, keeping the silenced M1911 aimed at his skull.

"I always suspected," Fortuna said nervously. "Nebbie said, 'Why would such a stunning girl as her be interested in someone as old as you?' but I thought, perhaps, at first, it was about the money."

Dewey pulled the trigger. A mechanical thud sounded as a silenced .45 caliber slug tore into Fortuna's left shoulder. Blood and flesh splattered across the glass behind him in the same moment the cartridge passed through the shoulder, shattering the glass door. Large pieces of glass rained loudly to the slate ground below. As if kicked in the chest by a horse, Fortuna was knocked backwards. He tumbled sideways onto the floor. An instant later, he screamed and reached his right hand reflexively up to grab at the wound. His hand returned, covered in blood. The side of his face and neck were dotted in crimson, splashed up from the shoulder.

Dewey took another step forward. Fortuna turned from staring at his destroyed shoulder and looked up at him, a grimace of unspeakable pain on his sweat-covered face. Sweat covered his face. His breathing grew rapid.

"There will be more," Fortuna coughed.

"That's what your son said," said Dewey. "Bring 'em on. I'm starting to like this."

Dewey aimed the handgun at Fortuna's right foot and fired. A silenced bullet ripped into the front part of the foot, shattering the bones. Blood washed across his legs and torso from the shot. Fortuna screamed horrendously, tried to reach for the ruined foot, but could barely move because of the wound to his shoulder.

"Nebuchar will hunt you down," said Fortuna, struggling. "He's the one. Alexander always had the poetic side, his mother's side. But Nebuchar is pure stone. He'll find you. He will—"

Dewey pumped yet another slug. This one ripped into Fortuna's right chest, silencing him. His head slammed back on the hard slate. His eyes shot back into his head as the pain went from acute to a level only people about to die know. Finally, he opened his eyes and looked up helplessly at Dewey.

"If you had left me alone, you'd be sitting by the pool, drinking your chamomile tea right now," said Dewey. "If Nebuchar minds his business, he has no reason to worry."

Dewey stepped closer, then trained the weapon at Fortuna's head. He waited, one moment, then another. He watched as Fortuna's eyes opened and shut, then opened again.

"But if Nebuchar fucks with me he'll die the same way as you and your precious Alexander: from a bullet stamped 'Made in the U.S.A.'"

Dewey flexed his finger on the steel trigger. A slug ripped out and tore a crisp, dime-sized black hole in the middle of Fortuna's forehead.

Dewey stared for a moment longer, turned, and stepped toward the door. He heard the teakettle beginning to whistle.

As he crossed the kitchen, a thought came into his head, a memory, out of place, out of context, but there it was: a rain-soaked afternoon during Delta training so many years ago, running with a hundred-pound pack on his back through the North Carolina woods, torrential downpours, rain storms the likes of which Fort Bragg hadn't seen in a generation; the water drenching his team in blinding sheets of warm, cleansing rainwater. The kind of afternoon no Delta likes, and yet, that was the memory he had at that moment. Like the rain that day, Dewey let the memory wash over him then, cleansing him as he walked the first steps that would take him away from the villa, from Broumana, from Lebanon, from the Middle East; the steps that would deliver him away from the war he knew had only just begun.

84

The black Mercedes limousine moved slowly out of the basement-level parking lot beneath Aiwan-e-Sadr. Two dark green PAF Humvees moved in front of the limousine. Behind the limousine, two more Humvees trailed.

Inside the bulletproof Mercedes, President Xavier Bolin sat alone in the backseat, staring out the window.

Constitution Avenue was quiet and empty. The protests that followed the removal of Omar El-Khayab had lasted for a week, but eventually the overwhelming force of the Pakistani Army, deployed in cities across Pakistan, had snuffed out the popular uprising before it spiraled out of control. Martial law, a general curfew, and an almost complete blackout of the media had succeeded in calming the country down. The fear of being locked up or shot had driven El-Khayab's supporters back to their apartment buildings, back to their villages, back to their mosques, back to their caves. Most people assumed that hundreds had died in the aftermath of the regime change, but no one knew for sure except Bolin and his advisors. As of that morning, following yet another nighttime riot in the Taliban hotbed of Peshawar, the body count stood at more than two thousand dead Pakistani citizens, not including casualties of the war with India.

Bolin reached for a small black button on the center armrest and pressed it. A thick sheet of black glass slid up behind the driver, sealing off and soundproofing the rear compartment. Bolin picked up the phone tucked into the armrest and dialed. He waited for the phone to ring.

Bolin's chest felt tight. He could feel his heart beating wildly.

Bolin had accomplished many things in his career. He had risen to a rank in the military he never would have dreamed of when he first enlisted, the son of a factory worker. Bolin was proud of his accomplishments. But try as he might, his presidency was marred by what he had done to the Americans. He'd let his greed get the best of him.

It had all been so chaotic. First, there was the war itself, days on end without sleep, the pressure of managing the rapidly escalating war with India. Then there came the unexpected, even bizarre use of the nuclear device by El-Khayab, a man Bolin already despised, and yet the leader of the country. Then there followed the constant fear that India would counterstrike at any moment with nukes of their own.

And like a lightning strike, the most shocking event of all, the infiltration by the Americans.

All of it, Bolin knew, had made him act irrationally. He wasn't thinking correctly. Surely, no human being could be expected to act perfectly under such pressure. Yet, as much as Bolin sought to rationalize his horrid behavior, nothing could remove the stain of what he had done. Bolin was ashamed of what he had done. He hated himself for doing it. But there was nothing he could do now except move on, put it behind him, forget about it.

Bolin had already squirreled away nearly $30 million in a Swiss bank account by the time Aswan Fortuna offered him the staggering amount of money for Andreas. Like so many other military leaders in Pakistan, Bolin had figured out a clever way of skimming money from his own government. There were no victims. Everyone did it. Why, he asked himself as he listened to the phone begin to ring, why did he need more than the $30 million nest egg he'd already built for himself? The $30 million would have been more than enough. Now there was nothing. Not even one rupee. America had sucked the money out of his Swiss accounts within hours of the deal with Fortuna. So much for the vaunted secrecy and security of the Swiss banking system. America's CIA hackers had found a crack in the Swiss armor quickly and easily. They'd sucked his thirty million out of Zurich faster than a vacuum cleaner sucking up a lint ball.

Now Bolin had nothing.

"White House," said the female voice.

"Jessica Tanzer," said Bolin.

It was a call he did not want to make. He knew he had made her his eternal enemy by what he had done. Still, he also knew that he had to make the call. He braced himself. He could not show weakness, even though he felt truly weak.

"Office of the national security advisor," said a male voice.

"May I speak with Jessica Tanzer?"

"Who's calling?" asked the receptionist.

"This is President Xavier Bolin."

"Hold, please."

Bolin stared out the window as the motorcade crossed train tracks and headed into the Margalla Hills, north of Islamabad.

There's a way to do this, he thought to himself. *Be strong and fearless.*

The phone clicked.

"Jessica Tanzer's office," said a female voice.

"Jessica Tanzer, please," said Bolin.

"And this is President Bolin?"

"Yes."

"May I tell her what this is regarding?" asked the woman.

"You can tell her that the president of the sixth-largest country in the world would like to speak with her," said Bolin, a hint of impatience in his voice.

Nice, he thought to himself.

"Hold, please."

A few moments, then two beeps.

"This is Jessica Tanzer."

"And this is Xavier Bolin," said Bolin.

"What do you want?" asked Jessica.

"Ms. Tanzer, thank you for accepting my call," said Bolin. "As angry as you might be at me, we both know that there is no benefit to either of us if our two countries are enemies. Therefore, I am apologizing to you. What I did was wrong. It was extremely wrong and it was reprehensible. I don't blame you for being mad. All I can say is that it was the by-product of a week's worth of no sleep, the stress of managing a war, and, I'm ashamed to say, my own greed. I can't take back what I did. But I can say that I am sincerely sorry."

A long silence settled over the phone. Finally, Jessica cleared her throat.

"Your apology means nothing to me," said Jessica. "You killed two American soldiers who had just risked their lives for your country. You did it for money. You sold the leader of the team to a known terrorist. If it wasn't for Israel, that terrorist would have tortured Dewey Andreas to death. You even kicked him in the head as he lay helpless on the ground. You are a vile creature, Bolin. If there is an afterlife, you will spend it in hell."

"I have gone on the record as saying that I am sorry," said Bolin. "But now we need to find a way to work together."

"I agree that the United States and Pakistan must cooperate in the struggle to maintain stability in the region," said Jessica. "But you and I will never work together."

Bolin shook his head.

"There's something else I'd like to talk about," said Bolin.

"And what is that?" asked Jessica.

"I want my money back," said Bolin.

"*Your* money?"

"The money that America stole from my bank account," said Bolin.

"Unbelievable," said Jessica, bitter laughter echoing over the phone.

"I'm not referring to Aswan Fortuna's money," said Bolin. "You can keep that. As I said, I should not have done what I did. But when your CIA hackers were in there taking those funds, they swiped everything, including money that was mine, thirty million dollars."

"The money you stole from your own government," said Jessica.

"It's irrelevant how I earned that money," snapped Bolin. "The point is, I want it back."

Jessica listened to Bolin's deep voice booming over the phone, sensing his anger. It made her happy, the angrier he became.

Jessica was seated in a windowless room four stories below ground at CIA Headquarters in Langley, Virginia. The room looked like the cockpit of a spaceship.

In front of her, seated in a large, tan leather captain's chair, his back turned, was a UAV pilot. In front of him, a pair of thirty-inch plasma screens displayed black-and-white video, from the sky, of a road. He grasped a pair of joysticks which he maneuvered; they controlled a MQ-9 Reaper armed with Hellfire missiles, which was now flying quietly in the air above Islamabad.

Holding the phone against her ear, Jessica covered the mouthpiece with her left hand.

"Have we got it yet?" she asked.

Hector Calibrisi stood against the wall, holding the phone to his ear, listening.

"Not there yet," said the pilot. As he maneuvered the two hand controls, the images became focused, the road coming into sharp relief.

"How much longer?" she whispered.

"I almost got it," said the pilot. "Give me a sec."

Jessica removed her hand from the mouthpiece of the phone.

"Tell me," said Jessica, speaking to Bolin. "I'm just curious. Why do you need the money?"

"It's none of your business," answered Bolin.

Jessica stared over the shoulder of the Reaper pilot, watching as the screen suddenly found a line of cars on the road, like small toys.

"It might be none of my business," said Jessica, staring at the plasma screen, "but I'm the one with the money. I'd like to know how you intend to spend it."

"I won't be president of Pakistan forever," said Bolin. "Someday, I will retire. Perhaps soon. When I do, I will need resources, just like any ex–head of state."

The cars grew larger on the screen. The long black limousine became defined, the image crisp and precise; a Mercedes, its distinctive, round hood ornament visible as the Reaper honed in on its target.

"Why don't you just steal some more?" asked Jessica. "You're president now. Just steal a few hundred million."

Jessica smiled at Calibrisi, who shook his head.

"Troublemaker," he whispered, his hand over the phone.

"You think this is funny?" said Bolin, surprised, then exasperated at Jessica's needling. "You steal my money and you sit there in your office in Washington laughing about it? I'm not asking for the thirty million. I am *demanding* it."

The Reaper pilot pressed a red button on the right-hand control and a green rectangular digital box appeared on the lower of the two screens, surrounding Bolin's limousine. The pilot pressed another button on the control and, within the rectangular box, bold green target lines appeared. At the center of the lines, a round circle locked in on the limousine.

The Reaper pilot turned to Jessica. He smiled at her and nodded, indicating that the ten-million-dollar UAV, with its quartet of $75,000 Hellfire missiles, was ready.

"Thirty million dollars is a lot of money," said Jessica. She smiled and glanced at Calibrisi. "I don't think you're going to need that much."

"What are you talking about?" Bolin asked, his frustration turning to anger. "What business is it of yours how much I need?"

Jessica walked to the pilot. He flipped open a metal cap on top of the joystick. Beneath the cap was a red button. The pilot turned to Jessica.

"It just seems like a waste," said Jessica, moving her left middle finger to the red button atop the joystick. "To give a dead man thirty million dollars."

"*Goddamn you!*" Bolin screamed, so loud that both Jessica and Calibrisi had to move the phones away from their ears. "How dare you threaten—"

"Look up in the sky," said Jessica. "That's America flying over your head. I'll see to it that the money goes to the families of the two soldiers you murdered. Goodbye, Mr. Bolin. Good riddance."

Jessica pressed the red button. She watched on the plasma as, a moment later, a silent burst of smoke and flames exploded out from the road where the limousine had been driving, smoldering from the wreckage.

"Nice shot," said Calibrisi. "You're a natural."

She stared at Calibrisi for a moment, saying nothing.

"He deserved it," said Calibrisi.

"Is Itrikan Parmir in place?" she asked.

"He's all set," said Calibrisi. "Lerik, the military, and the Pakistani parliament are all supportive. General Parmir will be sworn in within the hour."

Jessica patted the UAV pilot on the back, then reached for her Louis Vuitton briefcase, picked it up, and stepped toward the door.

"You want to grab a drink?" asked Calibrisi, picking up his beat-up leather briefcase. "It's Friday. Been a long week. I could certainly use a beer or three right now."

"I'd love to, but I can't. I'm picking someone up at the airport."

"Oh?" asked Calibrisi, following her through the door, past two armed guards, down the corridor. "Anyone I know?"

Jessica smiled, but said nothing. At the end of the hallway, they walked past another armed guard and climbed aboard an elevator. The doors shut and the elevator began to move up.

Calibrisi flipped the buckles on his briefcase. Lifting it open, he took out a bottle of Jack Daniel's with a red, white, and blue ribbon tied around the neck.

"Well, if it's who I think it is," said Calibrisi, smiling and handing Jessica the bottle, "you tell him I said thank you."

Epilogue

A Saturday afternoon in May and the streets of Brooklyn were busy. Even in this small Jewish residential neighborhood known as Borough Park, the sidewalks were filled with people.

The weather was picture-perfect, a warm day, temperatures in the seventies, one of the first warm days of the year. Everyone in the neighborhood of brownstone apartment buildings was out, sitting on stoops, talking with neighbors, walking young children, enjoying life.

At the corner, a yellow taxicab pulled over to the sidewalk. A young man climbed out of the back of the cab. His brown hair was slightly long. His face was tan. He wore khakis, a blue button-down shirt. He was big and athletic. He shut the door to the cab, then reached into the front window and handed the driver some money.

The man walked with a slight limp down the sidewalk. It didn't slow him down, but it was noticeable. His face had a hint of sadness to it. His brown eyes, however, belied that sadness. His eyes told a different story. Their deep, blank pools of brown surveyed the street with trained suspicion. It was the suspicion that is part of you when you are born into a world of conflict, bloodshed, and death; the suspicion that alone is that of the Israeli.

But here, in Borough Park, he was not alone. He was among family. He was greeted by smiles from strangers, who recognized somehow, from the way his face looked, his bloodline, his heritage. He returned the smiles with blank stares. He was here for a reason.

He had visited them all now, except for one, the families of the members of S'13 who had died that day at Rafic Hariri Airport. He had visited the families to describe to them, in detail, what had happened. He wasn't required to do so, but it was his way. It was the way he chose to lead. Only twenty-five, and already he had been made commander of all of S'13. There are some men who are born to lead. It is untrained and people follow these men, from a young age, and he was one of them. Part of the way he chose to lead was to do what he was doing today. To fly half a world away in order to sit down with a dead comrade's parents and explain to them that their son died fighting for something important, something he had believed in.

He walked up the steep, wide steps of a pretty redbrick apartment building. He nodded to a pair of teenage girls who sat on the steps, both of whom blushed, then giggled back at him.

Next to the door was a strip of doorbells. He read the names. He reached out and pressed the button of the bottom name: BOHR.

After a few seconds, the intercom clicked.

"Yes," said a woman over the intercom.

"Hello, Mrs. Bohr, it's Kohl Meir."

At precisely the same moment, less than ten miles away, on the fifteenth floor of a nondescript office building on Third Avenue near the United Nations, a red, white, and green flag with a strange emblem in the center stood near a mahogany door. Next to the door, the words were simple, engraved in a shiny gold plaque:

Permanent Mission of the Islamic Republic of Iran to the United Nations

Behind the door, past a reception area filled with people, down a long corridor, in a windowless, locked, highly secure room near the kitchen of the mission, two men stared at a large, flat plasma screen.

One of the men wore a black three-piece suit, a tan shirt, a gold-and-green-striped tie. His black hair was slicked back. He had a bushy mustache, dark skin, a thin, gaunt face. The other man had on a short-sleeve denim button-down and khakis. He was stocky, his hair curly and unkempt. A beard and mustache covered his face. He sat in the chair, behind the desk, typing every few seconds into a keyboard in front of him. The man in the suit leaned over the desk, a cigarette in his hand. Both men studied the screen intently.

"It's him?" asked the suited one. "You're sure?"

"Yes, yes," said the stocky Iranian. "Crystal fucking sure."

On the screen, in fuzzy black-and-white, they watched as Kohl Meir climbed out of the taxicab, then walked down the sidewalk.

"And it's all ready?"

"Yes, it's ready, Naji. It could not be any more precisely arranged."

On the plasma screen, Meir walked, limping slightly, down the crowded sidewalk. Halfway down the block, he started to climb the steps of a brownstone. He moved past two girls on the steps, then put his hand out to ring a doorbell.

"Just think," said the stocky man. "The great-grandson of Golda Meir herself. We could not inflict any more damage on the Jews if we dropped a nuclear bomb on downtown Tel Aviv."

On the screen, the door to the brownstone opened, and Kohl Meir stepped through. Then, he disappeared from the screen.

"Imagine," whispered Naji, "when we do both."

A small wooden sign next to a country road read CASTINE GOLF CLUB in neat, hand-painted black letters.

It was a bare-bones nine-hole golf course, long flat fairways that ran in pretty lines along the rocky ledges abutting Penobscot Bay below, like a links course in Scotland. At the opposite side of the narrow fairways, fields of olive-colored hay grass spread as far as the eye could see.

On the course's fourth hole, between the small, oval-shaped green and the tee area of the fifth hole, Margaret Hill began. Half old and cracked tar and half dirt, with a small strip of stubby green grass growing up the middle, the one-lane road wasn't on most maps of Maine or even Castine, but the townspeople knew it. Margaret Hill ran for a quiet, crooked, birch-lined mile to a farm. The farm didn't have a sign, but everyone knew the farm by the name it had been given by the man who built it more than a century ago, Theodore Andreas, for his wife, Margaret.

Atop Margaret Hill sat a pretty white farmhouse, with black shutters and a cedar-shake roof. The farmhouse was a rambling, two-story cape, built in 1891, added onto multiple times, maintained impeccably throughout its life. A cedar-shingled barn sat down a sloping, grassy hill from the farmhouse. Stables stood farther down the hill. Fields surrounded the farm. From most windows in the farmhouse, to the east, south, and west, the dark waters of the sea could be seen in the distance.

It was past midnight, on this calm June night. The farm was dark and silent. The sound of crickets chirping in the fields, the low baritone of the far-off ocean, these were the only sounds. Overhead, a canopy of stars looked vibrant, the spray of white dots made the sky undulate. At some point trees began to rustle in the wind. In a matter of less than five minutes, the stars disappeared; black storm clouds encroached in a rapid flight from the ocean.

Then the black sky lit up in a violent, fiery blaze. Electric white exploded across the summer night in tentacles; lightning bolts spread as if some god had lashed the sky with a whip, interrupting the darkness in astonishing force. The lightning was joined a second later by a tremendous thunderclap that roared like cannon fire across the peninsula.

The farmhouse suddenly shook. Dewey's eyes opened. He didn't move. *Where am I?* he thought, and for a few seconds his mind was as blank as stone.

A few moments passed, then raindrops pinged the roof. Dewey looked out the open window. And then he remembered.

"You're home," he whispered to himself.

The raindrops intensified, they became like a drumbeat as the clouds unleashed themselves on the roof, on the land, the fields, on the meadows of tall grass, corn, and tomatoes, the acres of pine that ran north to the rocky coast, on the tin roof of the barn, the stables, drenching it all, washing it, feeding the land, the farm, everything, with clean, pure water from the Maine sky.

Dewey smelled the fresh rain through the open window. For several minutes he did nothing but listen. In his bedroom, the refuge of his youth, in his bed, beneath the roof that had been the place of his upbringing, protecting him, the place that made him the man he was, he lay in silence and listened to the hard rain. He thought of other rainstorms as a child, with his brother down the hall. He thought of the time before he left Castine, before he knew the outside world, when the most powerful weapon he knew of was a barrel filled with crab apples ready to throw at his brother, or a jackknife; before Delta taught him what killing was, how to kill, what it meant to kill, what it felt like to do it with a silenced .45 caliber weapon, or a combat blade, or with his bare hands. Before he knew that outside this small, pristine, innocent peninsula there lurked people who would gladly give their lives to kill him just because he was from this place. From Castine. From Maine. From *America*.

Yet, as he lay beneath the cotton sheets, beneath the eave that smelled of cedar and salt water, listening to the rain overhead, thinking about his childhood, he knew that he could never go back, that the memories were the only things that would ever be innocent or safe for him again.

The rain pounded the roof above, the din like a cacophony, noisy and yet calming, as only a summer rainstorm can be.

Dewey glanced to his right, at an old windup alarm clock. It read 2:00 A.M.

I know what will happen next, he thought.

Anticipation mounted in his chest. He waited for it. Suddenly, in the east wing of the farmhouse, beyond the kitchen, the sound of footsteps. Someone stepping down the creaky stairwell.

Dewey smiled to himself.

He heard a squeak from a screen door spring as it opened, then the slap of the closing door a second later, steps on the porch, footsteps down the pebbles of the driveway. The iron latch of the stable door made a distant metal creak. Then he listened as his father did what he had always done in such storms; step inside the stables to calm the horses he loved so much.

Dewey pushed aside the thin, homemade summer quilt, then stood. He stepped into the alcove beneath the dormer. He looked out the open window. The rain was a deluge. A light spray of droplets, swept by the warm wind, dampened his face, his bare, muscled chest. The only light was a small, hazy dome of blue light from a bulb at the side of the barn. The cascade of rain across the farm created a misty blur.

Then, with a suddenness that startled even Dewey, another lash of lightning burst across the ceiling of black. A memory, still fresh, stirred. Perhaps it was the chaos at that very moment, the unbridled floodwaters, the lack of control he felt as yet another furious smash of lightning pounded Margaret Hill.

Dewey stared out the window and it was as if he were back in Beirut.

For several moments, it was as if the tiny alcove of his bedroom window was the open cargo hatch to the C-130.

Dewey had tried to delete it all from his mind. But he couldn't forget it. Not that night.

He stared out the window, at the rain, but all he saw was the lights of Beirut. A canopy of city streets, spread out behind the open hatch of the big cargo plane as it descended, nearly out of control, into the airport. Strapped inside the cargo hatch, holding on for dear life as the wind tried to pull him out the open hatch.

Below, he knew, they awaited his arrival.

He remembered the awful thought. Either the big cargo plane would not be able to straighten itself out and he would crash and die.

Or the pilot would find some way to land it, in which case he would have to deal with Aswan Fortuna and whatever mercenaries he'd sent to retrieve him.

Dying in a plane crash was how he'd wanted to go; quickly, the only pain being the moments just before it happened. *Now, right now*, he remembered thinking as the plane went almost vertical and came perilously close to flipping in midair.

Then, the plane had somehow straightened. Bounced upon the hard tarmac below, landing, sliding, into a three-sixty. It was then that the third option revealed itself. The one he never could have guessed: Israel.

Israel had come to save him that night. Kohl Meir had come to save him that night.

Dewey closed his eyes. He'd been trying for four months now to push Beirut out of his mind. He was haunted by the thought that even one man would die to save his life. It was a trade he would not have made. That night, six Israelis had died in the battle at Rafic Hariri Airport. Six young men who'd given their lives so that he could live. He kept trying to push the memory away. But the harder he pushed, the closer it stayed.

Lightning smacked down across the Maine sky, this time the bolt struck a tree at the near horizon, then the night lit up. Then a crack of thunder echoed across the black sky.

Suddenly, Dewey felt a hand, then two hands, wrap around him. For a moment, he was startled. Then he felt warmth against his moist chest. Soft fingers moved from his chest to his waist from behind, wrapped themselves across his muscled torso. He felt the imprints of breasts against his back, as she moved behind him, her naked body pressing against his, her hands enveloping him from behind.

"Whatcha doin'?" whispered Jessica softly. He felt her lips kiss his right shoulder.

"Thunderstorm."

Jessica's hands rubbed his chest, moving across the hard muscles of his chest, then down, across his hard stomach. Her right hand moved lower. He was naked, too, and her hand moved down, below his waist, to his front, touching him.

"I love thunderstorms," Jessica said.

She pressed her body tighter into his back.

Then, as quickly as it had come, the storm tapered off, then ceased altogether. The clouds moved on, the moon was revealed in white. The wet roof of the barn shimmered in the light.

Dewey turned. He tilted his head down. He looked into Jessica's big green eyes that stared up into his. He moved his lips to hers. He kissed Jessica for several minutes as she pressed her body against his. Dewey reached down and placed his hands on the back of her thighs. He gently lifted her light frame. She wrapped her long thin legs around his back. She wrapped her arms around his neck. She put her hands in his tousled brown hair. He carried her to the bed as she leaned down and kissed his ear.

"My, what strong hands you have, Mr. Wolf," Jessica whispered as he carried her naked body to the bed. He threw her down playfully on top of the summer quilt. He climbed onto the bed as Jessica laughed softly and the warm wind came in through the window and brought with it the scent of the violent storm that had just passed.